Wings of the

Aurora:

Northern Stars

By

M Dixie Watson

Acknowledgements

I fell in love with Alaska when my son was posted to Fort Wainwright, Alaska, in the early to mid-2000s. I'd done the traditional Alaska cruise ship routine, but had never been past Anchorage – which some wags, I've been told, joke is as close to being in Alaska as you can be without actually being in Alaska.

Multiple visits to Fairbanks at all times of the year during the time my son was there helped me fall in love with the scenery, the weather, the people, and the independent spirit I saw. Spending time later researching the various settings I talk about in the book has stamped an indelible, positive – and even mystical – impression on my heart.

And, I got to see Denali without cloud cover in 2016 – an unforgettable experience.

Another interest I've pursued for over twenty-seven years has been Critical Incident Stress Management – the emotional and psychological protection of emergency services first responders in the field, hospital personnel, and the military exposed to traumatic events that change lives, personalities, families, and their futures. Because of very real, very tragic events in law enforcement, the fire service, and the air medical community, crisis management and crisis interventions play a big role in my book.

So, two years after I thought I could write a novel in six months, it is with a great deal of humility that I would like to thank a lot of people who've helped me along the journey.

First and foremost, Lara Martin, for patiently – and expertly – editing, advising, and suggesting at the very start that having a coherent plotline with a conflict would be an advantage if I were wanting to write an interesting book that people would actually want to read;

Sgt. John Martin for introducing me to the incredible Golden Heart of Alaska;

Michael and Vicki Moore for taking the unbelievable photo of the Aurora Borealis on the cover;

Kelly Leveroni, trauma RN, Wendell Alderson, flight RN, and Suzanne Anderson Wilke (¡Que Bueno!) for reading, listening, and critiquing; Clark Mildenhall, RN, for consenting to become a trooper SERT team member who is wounded in the line of duty; and Jean de Lange for bringing joy to Chad after he crawls back to her asking for forgiveness;

My contacts at the Alaska State Trooper Post on Peger Road in Fairbanks, Alaska, for advice and suggestions;

My very helpful Alaska contacts at the Fort Wainwright, Fairbanks, Ester, and North Pole Fire Departments;

Helicopter pilots Pius Kamber and DJ Jones for flight insights and lots of laughs;

My workmates at Fort Sutter Surgery Center (Hunni, Caren, Melanie, and Jean – to name only a few) for their patience and encouragement.

Warm thanks to North Pole resident, Jeanne Fischer, for meeting with me and reading multiple chapters, and for sharing her real in-the-field knowledge about life in the beautiful Golden Heart of Alaska.

Others who have encouraged and taught me include Jacque Rose Farley, flight RN, and Dr. Tania Glenn, a crisis management trainer, teacher, writer, practitioner, Clinical Director, trauma expert, and role model from Austen, Texas.

Many thanks to Dr. Jeffrey Mitchell and Dr. George Everly, Jr. of the International Critical Incident Stress Foundation for their gracious good wishes and permission to use general information about Critical Incident Stress Management.

A special shout-out to Vilborg Björnsdóttir and her husband, Sigurður Flosason, for allowing me to use their names as our visitors from Iceland. I will never forget the "stinky shark."

I have researched places and names, fictionalized some and used others as they are. I've eaten in the restaurants I name, have run along the Chena River, and worked out at the Alaska Club. If there are errors in this book, they lay at the feet of this new author. They're no one's fault but mine.

Lastly, thanks to Hal Leonard LLC for allowing me to use the lyrics of this beautiful song:

Bless the Broken Road

Dedication

This book is dedicated to the thousands of courageous men and women who climb into a helicopter or a fixed wing aircraft to heed the frantic call of first responders at the scene of a horrific freeway crash, or the desperate voice of a doctor at a rural hospital with a high-risk mom who needs immediate transport to a skilled facility in order to save her baby's life – and perhaps her own.

These brave flight nurses, flight paramedics, and flight physicians put their lives on the line every time they fasten their restraints, pull on their helmets and cinch them tight. CJay says it best: "Being a flying caregiver is one of the most exciting and satisfying roles in medicine. And one of the most dangerous. But, I can't believe they pay me to do this job."

To all who have flown, there is no higher calling.

Prologue

15 October - four years earlier

When Clare worked day shift in Columbia Memorial's emergency department in Astoria, Oregon, Alex found pleasure in having a warm meal ready for her when she got home. Tonight, he'd made his famous tuna-noodle casserole with frozen green peas and potato chip topping – a meal she swore to him she'd learned to love over the five years of their marriage. He made it frequently, and she appreciated the effort he put into the casserole and the care he showed for her by preparing it.

This evening, while they were finishing up the dishes after dinner and anticipating some downtime chilling and watching Netflix, his cell phone rang. Alex dried his hands on a dishtowel before pulling the cell from the pocket of his Coast Guard sweatpants to check the caller ID.

"Oh no," Clare muttered under her breath as she stacked another plate into the dishwasher.

"Oh yes," he replied before he swiped the screen to answer the call and put the phone to his ear. "Val here." After a brief conversation with his supervisor, he slipped the phone back into his pocket and turned to face his wife. Even annoyed, she was pretty – and made his heart beat faster.

"I'm sorry, sweetheart. Josh's wife decided to have their baby today and they need me to finish off his shift."

Clare folded her arms across her chest and leaned back against the counter. "You'd think after the fortune we spent on the bouncy door hangy swing thing for the baby shower that little twerp would have the decency to wait until her Daddy had a day off."

"At least we didn't spring for the stroller."

"We'd still be making payments." They both laughed, but then she made a pouty face and let out a disappointed, resigned sigh. "Can't be helped, Coastie. Duty calls." She made a miniature raspberry with her lips.

Alex left the kitchen and headed for the master bedroom of their two-bedroom apartment. He heard her following him down the hall and after he'd stuffed his flight suit and boots into his "Bug Out" bag he turned around to find her jeans on the floor and his wife just stepping out of her panties.

"Make love to me before you go. I want you." She pulled off her t-shirt revealing her red lace bra over full breasts.

Alex felt his body respond immediately to the sight of her nakedness, but before she could take off her bra, he told her, "Let me do that." He finished pulling off his own sweatpants, then he reached around her and with the warm familiarity born of five years of marriage and three of courtship, he unsnapped her bra quickly and pulled her close to him.

"I'll need more than that, 'Val.' Get horizontal." She shoved at him until he fell backwards onto their queen bed, where she joined him, wrapping her arms around her lean, muscular U.S

Coast Guard swimmer husband. He returned her embrace, then rolled her over and entered her, luxuriating in her heat and moisture.

"Oh, so delicious, Alex," she moaned, as her strong orgasmic waves almost instantly pulsated around him. "I love you with every ounce of my being," she whispered against the side of his face.

He was greatly aroused by the smell of their sex, her breasts, her expression, and her response to his lovemaking. He felt the pinpointing of his own orgasm, and as he burst inside of her, the only thing he could think to say was what he'd told her the first time they'd made love when she was only nineteen years old and he was her brother's best friend. "I'm lost in you, Clare. I'm so totally lost in you. I will always love you."

"And that was the best forty-seven seconds I've ever spent," she told him, breathing heavily between kisses as they held one another for a few more moments.

Her husband laughed. "And you're the best thing that's ever happened to me, Clare, but now I *really* have to go. Dammit. I'll see you in the morning. Sleep well, sweetheart." As he rolled over and off the bed, she stretched and he watched those beautiful breasts tighten up. Once again, he counted his lucky stars – the stars that had made this woman the center of his life.

She watched him as he pulled on fresh boxers and jeans and sat on the bed to lace his running shoes. When he stood up again to shrug on his coat, she still watched him from the bed.

"You're my hero, you know, Alex. Don't ever leave me. I shall be forced to hunt you down and personally kill you."

He laughed again. She always seemed to make him laugh. "And then can we have make-up sex?"

"I'd insist upon it." She sat, then stood beside him, 5'10" to his six feet of height. She blew out a hard breath between her lips. "Fly safe, Coastie. Come back to me."

"I always will."

He kissed her once more, and when she heard the front door shut, she took a shower, put on her flannel pajama bottoms and a t-shirt, set the alarm, and read a book until sleep overcame her.

* * * * * *

"Clare?"

Inside her dream, she turned towards the sound of his voice and saw Alex, in his Coast Guard flight suit and heavy jacket standing next to their bed.

"Alex, sweetie. What are you doing back so soon? Did I miss my alarm?" She glanced over and saw the illuminated numbers on their bedside clock read 0200.

He sat on the bed. His hair was wet. So was his jacket.

"Why's your hair wet?" Then she saw he was dripping onto their carpet. "Did you take another shower? Why's your coat wet?" She reached up to smooth down his little cowlick which always stuck up after a shower.

"I just wanted to see you again. I wanted to tell you again what you mean to me."

Clare felt anxiety creep tiny tendrils around her. "What are you saying?"

"Clare, I'll always love you. For as long as you need me, I'll always take care of you and watch over you." He sat on the bed. In her dream, she was sitting up now and felt his arms around her, pulling her close to him. He kissed her warmly, intimately, as a lover should. She responded to his touch and his kiss.

"I'll always love you too, Alex. You're my hero and my lover and my husband and my best friend and...and...everything I need. And you're dripping wet...." She shook her head in her sleep.

"I need to get back now. I just wanted to say good-bye."

"Well, okay, then, I guess. Good-bye. Fly safe, Alex."

"I always shall, Clare. I will watch over you."

His image seemed to wisp away, and Clare returned to deep sleep. But when her alarm sounded at 0500, she awoke troubled.

There was a damp spot on the carpet. What in the world? she thought.

* * * * * *

She made coffee in the single serving French press and sat down to eat a breakfast sandwich before getting ready for work. It was absolutely natural to hear people coming and going from their little apartment complex in the morning because there were a number of Coast Guard families living near them, plus at least three of her nursing colleagues rented there, too. But it was an unfamiliar door slam that brought her out of the newspaper she was paging through. She went to the front window and parted the slats on the shade.

14

An official Coast Guard vehicle was sitting parked aslant below their apartment, and two men in uniform were coming up the steps to their landing. She saw Alex's Sector Commander, himself a helicopter pilot, and the Coast Guard Station's Chaplain walking together towards the apartment.

"No," she said aloud. She turned her back to the door and pressed her body against it, as if doing so would keep anyone – or anything – from coming inside. She closed her eyes. "No, God. Please, no, God," she breathed. By the time the knock came, she was on the floor, still whispering, "No, God. Please, no, God.

The Chaplain had to find the apartment complex manager to get the key to open the door before they were able to tell her that Alex was gone. But then, she already knew.

She'd known since 0200.

Chapter One: 22 March, current year

"So, what are you doing for your anniversary, Mark? This is a big deal you know," Sergeant Susan Grandin asked her trooper, riding beside her in the blue and gold Alaska State Trooper AS350 B-3 helicopter she was piloting.

"Don't I know it." Mark Sokolov, a five-year veteran of the AST's rural Wildlife division and a new transfer to the troopers in Fairbanks, chuckled, then smiled. "Dinner at the Bistro, flowers, a little dancing, a little romancing…."

"Get that in as much as possible. When's the baby due?"

"August. We're pretty excited."

"Well, you've got every right to be. Did you think a year ago you'd be a daddy?"

He laughed again. "No. But it's not like we're kids ourselves. We've been married eight years. I'm truly happy, Sergeant. I see rainbows and unicorns everywhere I look." Even here, he thought as he gazed out at the landscape 80 miles northwest of Fairbanks, frozen under leaden skies.

Susan smiled, her eyes crinkling at the corners as she looked ahead to the landing zone in Mantishka.

She and Mark were tasked to mediate a dispute between two women in the little village over the sale of a kitchen table and chairs. Evidently threats of firearms had been involved in their post-sale discussions. Mantishka, located on a frozen lake, was inaccessible during the winter except by snow machine or aircraft.

The Sergeant set the helicopter gently down at the far end of the simple runway, near the aviation shack, the fuel truck, and a lone Piper Super Cub, the ubiquitous workhorse of Alaska bush pilots. Mark and Susan walked the rest of the way into Mantishka, a quick ten-minute hoof. If necessary, they could bring back one, if not both of the women who were involved in the argument. But Susan was pretty sure she could mediate their disagreement, as she had done on multiple similar occasions before. After all, this was not her first rodeo.

She, too, was looking forward to dinner tonight with her husband and children. He was fixing his succulent moose ribs and she didn't want to be late.

After their invigorating hike into town on the icy road, the two troopers knocked on the door of the small house with a tiny porch, blue siding, and blue tin roof. "Mrs. Paul, this is Sergeant Grandin and Trooper Sokolov with the Alaska State Troopers. We're here to talk to you about the problem with Elva Dishnak. Can you open the door? We won't be long."

They heard footsteps coming across the floor towards them and the door opened far enough that Susan could see a hunting rifle on the coffee table over the head of the short, round faced woman in front of her. Not unusual, she thought. Everyone has shotguns and rifles. But then she smelled alcohol and knew they needed to get inside the home. Guns are one thing, but guns and alcohol together could spell disaster.

"We're coming in, Mrs. Paul," she barked authoritatively, shoving her way in and motioning Mark to follow her. Mark caught the brunt of the shotgun blast in his face, neck, and chest. Susan, hit with stray buckshot, thought "Shit shit shit," drew her duty weapon and fired six times through the wall next to the doorway where she'd seen the shadow of the shooter – and was astonished to realize she'd missed him. *Who is this guy?* She glanced down at Mark and knew he was gone. *Oh fuck. Mark. I'm sorry.* The Alaska State Trooper pilot looked up in time to see the shotgun pointed from around the kitchen opening at her now, and felt the second shot hit her belly and thighs.

The force of the blow her pushed back through the door and out onto the porch where she fell on her side. The dying trooper reached for the railing to help herself stand and could see the man holding the shotgun walk to where she lay. "Oh, Matt. I'm going to miss dinner," she thought. As darkness overtook her, she saw several village teens recording her reaching for the rail on their cell phones.

The video had 250,000 hits that day on YouTube before it was taken down as being inappropriate.

Chapter Two

The impact of the murders of Sergeant Susan Grandin and Trooper Mark Sokolov was felt throughout the closely connected Alaska Department of Public Safety and the rest of Alaska's law enforcement communities. Within moments of receiving a frantic phone call from the Mantishka Village Public Safety Officer's wife, troopers with the Special Emergency Reaction Team – the SERT team – located in Fairbanks, mobilized and were on their way to Mantishka to deal with the deaths of their colleagues and apprehend the killer.

Creaght Air's chartered Cessna Grand Caravan landed and came to a stop not far from where the A-Star helicopter Susan had flown was parked. The Piper Super Cub was gone, but it took only minutes conferring with the village chief to learn that the killer had flown out on the aircraft and to learn who he was. Authorities in Fairbanks, Anchorage, and Nenana were alerted to be on the lookout for him and his Super Cub.

Dealing with Susan and Mark was difficult. Darla Bustikoff, the chief's wife and other elders of the village had kept the curious away from the bodies and covered them respectfully from view. Maintaining that privacy was difficult for the troopers assigned to catalogue and record the scene. Pictures had to be taken of both the house and the bodies, and every SERT member had worked closely with Susan and then Mark in Fairbanks. There was no way to make this terrible circumstance not extremely personal and unforgivably horrifying to all of them. The final step was placing their two friends and colleagues in the black body bags and zipping the bags closed over their faces. Mark was unrecognizable, but Susan looked like she was napping.

Mina Paul denied knowing the shooter. She couldn't – or wouldn't – explain why he was in her house. But Elva Dishnak did know him, and readily told the troopers investigating the homicides his name and his business – bringing illegal alcohol and drugs to the village and selling it to Mina Paul's husband who sold it to others. As for the dispute about the kitchen table and chairs? Elva and Mina had settled that earlier today. Elva had no idea why this white guy had shot the troopers. She wished they'd come to her house instead. She would have told them everything was all right, and then they could have flown away in their little helicopter.

An official memorial service for the two officers was planned for three weeks following the incident. Frank Bridow, the Mantishka killer, had been apprehended at his house in Nenana and was currently in the Fairbanks Correctional Center, waiting transfer to Anchorage. There was satisfaction in knowing that Susan's and Mark's murderer had been captured, but that provided little closure to those most closely involved with the two victims.

For Sergeant Jeffrey Cameron Douglas, working out of the Peger Road trooper post, it provided no consolation at all. He'd been the one to send the two troopers to Mantishka to clear up a simple dispute over a kitchen table and chairs. His fatal dispatch of a favorite FTO (Field Training Officer) co-worker and her trainee to Mantishka haunted his days and his dreams. He found little solace in his log home in Ester. He confided in few. His dog, Trygve, kept to the Sergeant's side, knowing his master held a painful loss close.

* * * * * *

"Flight nurse, Pilot. Get on out to the pad. We're lifting off in fifteen minutes for the Wainwright flight line."

CJay Valenzuela shut down the dispatch computer and gathered up her wool hat, gloves, and parka. She knew Gus Coffee, her paramedic crew partner, was in the maintenance shack on the helipad and would be helping Charlie and the mechanic push the aircraft out in preparation for walk around and take off. She said goodbye to Jeanne, their dispatcher, and walked swiftly through the Emergency Department, out the ambulance bay doors (saying "Thanks, guys" to staff who wished them well on this particular flight), and back down the sidewalk to the helipad behind the ED.

Charlie was already spooling up the blades and Gus was buckled up on the inside starboard, or right, crew seat. CJay crawled up and buckled herself across from Gus, facing him in the port, or left, crew seat. A gurney loaded with a trauma and an

21

airway bag, warm blankets, and a small O2 cylinder buckled securely to it was facing at an angle front to back between them. If there'd been a patient on that gurney, his head would be to CJay's (and the pilot's) left and the rest of his body to Gus's left.

CJay pulled on her helmet and fastened it tightly, adjusting the small microphone "kissing" distance from her lips so she could speak to the other two. She heard Charlie say in her helmet headset, "Dispatch, Aurora One is off the pad to the flight line at Fort Wainwright. ETA seven minutes. Four hours of fuel. Three souls on board."

"Copy that, Aurora," she heard Jeanne say. "Off to Fort Wainwright. ETA seven minutes. Four hours of fuel. Three souls on board. Fly safe."

Charlie pulled pitch, tilting the rotors so they caught the air, and Aurora One lifted from the helipad and turned east to face into the wind for their trip to the U.S. Army post at Fort Wainwright, Fairbanks, Alaska.

CJay leaned her head back against the Aurora's port side and closed her eyes, taking in a deep, slow breath. Normally, lift off was exciting because she and her paramedic partner, this time Gus, were going to the scene of a vehicle crash or some other horrific incident where local providers had deemed it necessary to call for outside assistance to help them with a serious victim or multiple serious victims, many times close to death and needing the expanded scope of practice skills that the flight crews provided. This time, though, they were going to be part of a memorial service for two Alaska State Troopers who'd

22

been killed in the line of duty three weeks prior in the tiny village of Mantishka.

Aurora was going to be part of the "Missing Man" formation that flew over the massed Troopers and law enforcement agency members from all over Alaska and the Lower 48 who'd gathered in Fairbanks the last two days to participate in the ceremony. The ceremony itself would take place inside one of the massive aircraft hangers on post and at the conclusion, Aurora One, the AST helicopters from Anchorage and Fairbanks (the ship Sergeant Grandin had been piloting), and two Blackhawks from Wainwright would fly over the people assembled on the ground below in tribute to the Fairbanks crew that had been lost. As they flew, the Fairbanks AST helo would peel off, symbolizing the lost crew – the missing man. The Troopers had not lost their aircraft, but they had lost one of their lead pilots in Susan Grandin. And they'd lost Mark Sokolov, a fellow trooper.

On the way to the flightline, Charlie called Fairbanks International Airport (FAI) to let them know they were in the air, then contacted air traffic control at Fort Wainwright to make them aware Aurora was approaching. Wainwright ATC acknowledged them and gave Aurora permission to cross the runway and land at the flightline located near Fire Station #1. CJay opened the port slider, blowing arctic air over them, and cleared the tail as Charlie settled them down at the end of the row of four other rotorcraft already sitting there with waiting crews.

"Aurora Dispatch, Aurora One. On the ground at Fort Wainwright."

"Aurora One on the ground at 1254," CJay heard Jeanne confirm. Gus and CJay waited until Charlie had shut down the engine and brought the blades to a stop before they unbuckled their seat belts, took off their helmets, and began the wait for the ceremony to end.

Out of the corner of her eye, CJay saw a tall Alaska State Trooper step from the fire station apparatus room around an enormous Wainwright Fire Department crash rig. The man walked towards Aurora with an easy gait. Even wearing a heavy jacket and a navy watch cap, he appeared broad shouldered and slim hipped. Shoulder to hip ratio, she thought immediately. Beautiful. Lean. As he came nearer, she saw his high cheekbones and straight nose. His square jaw and symmetrical face. She also saw Charlie climb out and warmly embrace this man. There was only the hint of a smile on either one's face, but Charlie motioned for the crew to get out and greet him, too.

"Sergeant Douglas, Jeff, this is our crew today. Gus, this is Jeff Douglas." Gus shook the Trooper's hand and CJay was surprised to hear the tall man say, "Hi, Gus. It's good to see you again."

"Sergeant, it is good to see you also. But I am sorry it is for such a sad occasion."

"Thank you."

"Sergeant, this is CJay Valenzuela, our flight nurse." CJay extended her hand and he took it in a warm handshake.

"Nice to meet you, CJay."

"I'm so sorry you all are having to go through this, Sergeant." She released his hand and then looked up into his eyes. He was tall. Six two, perhaps. She was tall for a woman – five feet ten, and his cool hazel eyes were looking into hers. CJay felt a frisson of electricity flow through her body and she was suddenly almost speechless.

"I'm so sorry," she repeated – lamely, she felt, "for this terrible loss."

He looked at her for a long moment, then nodded and told her "Thank you," turning back to Charlie. "Thanks for putting this together, Charlie. I really appreciate it."

"Anything for you, Jeff. You know that."

"You two both know him?" CJay asked Gus and her pilot when the trooper turned away to walk towards the Anchorage AST helicopter.

"When I worked the street ambulance before Aurora, I met him several times on calls. Before he was a Sergeant. He has a K-9 now, too. He is a very good man and a good trooper."

"How do you know him, Charlie?"

Charlie grimaced a smile. "Met him in Baghdad when I was flying dust-offs with the Army. He was a Marine sergeant. Funny we should meet again in Alaska, but he's from here. I was stationed in Mosul with the Fort Wainwright contingent, and we got stoplossed to Baghdad and that's where we met. Camp Taji. Crap hell hole." Charlie shrugged.

"I did notice he is not wearing a ring on his left hand, CJay," Gus told her softly.

CJay looked at Gus out of the corner of her eye. And slowly shook her head. It doesn't matter, she thought. And it's inappropriate right now, Gus. He doesn't need my complications.

25

But she'd noticed, too, and was angry at herself. It doesn't matter, she repeated silently.

Chapter Three

The young bull moose took one last bite from the alder tree off the Dalton Highway in the predawn light, then strolled out of the trees and up the slope of the road. His big ears heard the roar of a mighty beast and he came to a stop in the middle of the pavement. Slowly turning his head, he saw two brilliant lights almost upon him. If the moose could talk, he would have said, in wonderment, "Huh...?"

Roger, heading south in his crew cab short bed F250 4X4 pickup equipped with a brand new stainless-steel grille guard, saw the animal move onto the road and stop forty-five feet in front of him. Fuck, he thought. *I'm screwed*. He could not avoid hitting probably five-hundred pounds of moose – there was little wiggle room here on the road between the trees.

There used to be two schools of thought with moose: (1) Hit them as hard as you can; or (2) slow down as much as possible before you hit the animal because every increment by which you reduce your speed will reduce the impact energy by the square of that increment.

Unfortunately, Roger had not seen the "Mythbuster's Alaska Special" about moose collisions and stepped on the gas. The only way to survive this collision, he reasoned, was to hit the animal hard enough to catapult him up and over the cab of his truck. Coming through the windshield into Roger's lap with hooves and antlers awhirl was *not* a viable option.

It was only as his vehicle struck the moose, Roger remembered that he hadn't buckled his seatbelt, despite his wife's loving entreaty to "Fasten your fucking seatbelt!" as he pulled out of the driveway.

Astonishingly, the five-hundred-pound animal executed a drunken somersault over the cab and landed in the truck's bed, but as the truck slewed to the right at impact, the vehicle caught air at the slope of the road, hit the trees at about eight feet off the ground, and came to an abrupt stop. Roger was thrown from the cab out the driver's side door, which wrenched open, and into the ditch. The F250 dropped to the earth, struts snapping on impact. The moose hung partially out of the bed, not far from where Roger lay. Their brown eyes met.

Sorry, buddy, Roger thought as he lost consciousness.

Quiet descended, once again, on the Dalton Highway.

* * * * * *

Alaska State Trooper Sergeant Jeffrey Cameron Douglas and his partner travelled north on the Dalton Highway in his AST-issued Ford Expedition, keeping a routine eye out for poachers, lost travelers from the Lower 48, and disoriented gold miners. The digital clock read 0630, and Sgt. Douglas could see the sun starting to peek above the birches and alders lining the road. Beautiful. The scenery and the French Roast in his travel mug worked together to wake him up.

His eye caught a brief glint of light to his left, reflecting off the rear window of a pickup truck in the trees. A young, very dead moose draped the short bed.

The trooper activated his overhead flashers and pulled his vehicle as far off the side of the road as he could. Moose, crashed truck – where's the driver?

"Anybody here?" He crunched down the side of the ditch and saw a body lying in the leaves and branches of several trees broken off by the truck's flight. Looking for signs of life, he saw movement and knew the guy was still alive.

"I'm a State Trooper," he told the driver, as he knelt by his side. "Can you hear me, buddy?"

"Moose," the man moaned. "Big moose. I think my leg's broken."

Judging by the angle of the victim's right leg, and the blood seeping through the olive-green material of his cargo pants, Jeff was inclined to agree. "I'm going to go call for help," he said. "Stay right here."

"If you insist," the man croaked. "I won't leave. I promise."

"Be right back," the trooper chuckled as he climbed back up to his vehicle and notified AST dispatch of the crash. He requested that both local emergency medical services and the air evac helicopter from North Star Medical Center respond to his coordinates. Grabbing the first responder equipment from the back of his Expedition, he slipped back down the slope to the side of the injured man. As he knelt on the damp earth and pulled the cervical collar from the kit, he asked, "How ya doin', buddy?"

"Name's Roger," the man replied, his voice tight with pain. "You're gonna to need to remember that...'cuz my wife's gonna make them change it to 'He who never fucking listens' on my headstone."

"I've been called worse," Jeff said, honestly. As he placed the cervical collar around the driver's neck to prevent further injury, he noted that the man's cheeks were cold and clammy, his lips pale, and his teeth were beginning to chatter. "I'm going to give you some extra oxygen now," the trooper said, pulling out the mask attached to the cylinder in the responder pack.

"You still with me, Roger?"

"C-c-c-cold," the man stammered.

"We'll do something about that," Jeff assured him. Covering the victim with an insulated emergency blanket to retain warmth, he waited for the volunteer fire department to arrive.

Within ten minutes, the big trooper heard the sirens of the fire engine, accompanied by the lighter shrill of the ambulance with the volunteer EMS workers. Knowing the fire rig would stage in the parking lot at the trailhead a quarter of a mile back up the road to wet down a landing zone for the helicopter, he waited for the ambulance crew to arrive on scene. They worked with the trooper to get the driver onto the EMS backboard and up out of the ditch to the road.

"Moose," Roger advised each new face. "Big moose."

"Seatbelt," one of them solemnly replied. "No seatbelt."

They loaded Roger into their ambulance and Jeff followed them to the LZ in his own vehicle. Once parked along the road, the trooper let his K-9 out to pee while they waited for the helicopter, the Expedition's emergency flashers still on.

* * * * * *

The handheld radio squawked from the calf pocket on the right leg of CJay's navy blue flight suit. "Aurora Flight I, motor vehicle crash, auto v moose. State Patrol on the scene. Driver with probable femur fracture. Saddle up!"

CJay walked swiftly from Bay I of the North Star Medical Center's Emergency Department, telling the charge nurse the helicopter had a request for a scene flight. She continued out the ambulance bay doors and around the building to the parking lot to where the AS350 B3 helicopter, painted in swirling patterns of blue, red, yellow, purple, and green – the colors of the northern lights – sat on the helipad. The pilot was already in his seat, performing his flight check and spooling up the turbine engine. The blades slowly began to turn in preparation for take-off. Her paramedic, Gus, came around the front of the rotorcraft and climbed into the open door on the left side. She joined him and they both put on their helmets and strapped in. CJay keyed her mike.

"Ready, Charlie," she told the pilot "Auto v moose, huh? Gus has his ulu out," referring to the curve bladed knife frequently used by native hunters to skin their kill.

Both men laughed. Gus keyed his mike. "I wish we could bring the moose back. It would be much easier than tracking him," he said. CJay grinned. She knew that Gus didn't really mind the hours – sometimes days – of effort he put into providing meat for his family. As well, she knew that he appreciated the unfortunate moose at the scene would be dispensed by the local food bank to those in need.

She heard Charlie communicate with Big Mike in Dispatch through her helmet's speakers. "Dispatch – Aurora I off the deck to Dalton Highway. Four hours of fuel remaining. Three souls on board. ETA twelve minutes."

"Aurora I off the deck at 0700. Three souls on board. Four hours of fuel. Fly safe," the dispatcher responded. Aurora I would check in with Big Mike every 10 minutes and again when the ship was on short final to the destination.

Charlie pulled pitch and the sleek helicopter lifted into the morning sun, rising steadily off the deck under the pilot's experienced hand. Charlie had flown Black Hawk dust-offs in the Middle East during three deployments with the Army, picking up wounded soldiers under harrowing conditions. She and her crewmates trusted him – like they trusted all of their pilots – with their lives.

This part of a mission was always the most exciting for CJay: The thrill of the powerful helicopter herself, rising on the pressure of the air generated from the swirl of the three big blades as Charlie pulled pitch; the first view of Fairbanks out the window – today, highlighted by the rays of the rising sun; and then visualizing in her head what they were going to find thirty-five miles out.

Moose are enormous and powerful creatures. This driver could have trauma from the sudden stop. He might have swerved off the road into trees. He might have been unfortunate enough to have the animal come through his windshield –sharp hooves first, acting like a furry Cuisinart. The animal's body could have landed in the front seat, frequently killing both the driver and the front seat passenger instantaneously. Bloody intubations or massive crush injuries were not much fun for patients, ambulance crews, or flight crews.

CJay and Gus had done their own flight checks when they'd come on this morning. The LOX (liquid oxygen) was full, their drugs were accounted for, their emergency equipment and tools were in the proper places, and all equipment batteries were charged.

Quickly, the two ran through various scenarios in the ten minutes they had left before the unlucky pick-up truck driver was under their care. This morning, CJay was lead crew. Gus was the one who would intubate the patient if necessary, apply a Segar splint if there was a femur fracture, help load him onto their gurney, and provide the main care during the flight back. CJay would get the story from the State Trooper, oversee packaging of the injured victim, provide report to the ED on the patient as they returned home in the air, and write the paperwork. When necessary, both team members participated equally in care at the scene and in the air.

She hoped that there would be additional personnel at the scene to help with possible extrication

The intercom crackled and a man's authoritative voice came through their headsets. "Aurora Flight, I see you three klicks out. The landing zone is the trailhead parking lot west of the scene.

The fire department has wet down the area. It's unobstructed. No wires."

"Thanks, Trooper," Charlie responded to the officer on the ground. "We'll circle the LZ a couple times, then aim for the wet spot."

The flight crew could see that a single engine from the nearby volunteer fire company was on scene, as was an ambulance. There was a collective sigh of relief – they wouldn't need to wrangle a gurney alone.

Gus tapped the window and frowned. "The Sergeant's K-9 is out," he reported.

"Sergeant," Charlie radioed. "Can you get the dog back?"

"Roger that, Aurora."

They watched as the trooper pointed to his vehicle. Without hesitation, the dog raced to the trooper's Expedition and levitating through the open door, tucked itself safely inside.

Smart dog, CJay thought.

The agile helicopter circled the accident scene as the pilot checked placement of the emergency responders on the ground and scanned for obstructions that may have missed the trooper's eye. He then centered over the LZ and settled down, raising a stinging cloud of mud and debris. Charlie kept the rotors turning until CJay and Gus had unlocked and lifted out the gurney and cleared the blades before he braked them.

The driver had been incredibly lucky in one sense. The moose had not gone through his windshield but had instead crushed the front grill guard of the big 4X4, flown over the cab, and landed in the bed.

The unseatbelted driver, thrown from the cab when the truck hit the trees by the side of the road, was covered with abrasions and lacerations. He complained of leg pain and Gus pulled the Segar splint out of its plastic zipper case. The man's right femur was definitely broken. Gus did a "killer search" – simultaneously checking mental status by asking questions while palpating the chest and abdomen for pain or rigidity. He asked one of the volunteer responders to cut open the bloody pants leg, and help him place the Segar, which would temporarily pull the broken femur into position, alleviating a great deal of pain for the duration of the flight.

"His belly is rigid, CJay," the paramedic reported. "We need to move quickly." He gave her Roger's vital signs.

"Thanks, Gus," she replied and turned to address the trooper who'd called in the crash. Without looking up from the vital signs she was scratching on the two-inch silk tapes plastered on the blue thighs of her flight suit, she asked, "So, whatcha got for us?"

"Well, I came up on the scene a few minutes after it happened. He was ejected and landed about ten feet from the cab. Put on the C-collar, gave him oxygen. He was pretty shocky so I grabbed the emergency blanket to keep his temp up."

"Good job," CJay commented as she made notes on the silk tapes. A rigid belly meant the possibility of internal bleeding and, obviously, he needed to be transported immediately. She was already planning the flight back.

"Sorry about the dog," the trooper said.

"The what?" CJay's stomach clenched and she looked up from her leg. "There was a dog involved?"

Children and animals, dogs more so than any other creature, were her weak spot. If there was a dead or injured family pet on the scene, she was going to have to compartmentalize fast. *I'm glad I didn't see that poor moose,* she thought. *And now there's a fucking dog, too?*

"Yes." The man looked confused at her response but then seemed to recognize the concern in her voice. "My dog. The one that was trying to guide you guys into the LZ?"

Relief flooded her limbs with warmth and, for the first time since arriving on the scene, CJay registered the man inside the Alaska State Trooper's uniform. Tall. Lean. Broad shouldered. Straight nose. Cheekbones. Gray eyes shadowed by the brim of his official Stetson, faint laugh lines at their edge. *Wainwright flightline.* The warmth spread to her cheeks. "Oh, *your* dog."

"He was only trying to help," the trooper added, seriously, though she thought she could see a smile in his eyes.

The trooper was not unaware of her blush, she realized. *You're the trooper I met before we flew in the Missing Man formation for your two officers killed in Mantishka.* She also remembered how she'd responded to him so viscerally that day when she'd taken his hand, looked into his grieving eyes, and offered condolences.

"I'm sure he was," CJay said now, frowning. "We were just concerned he'd get hurt around the rotors. We've had horses try to walk right into our blades when we land in their fields. Well, maybe not so much up...horses, that is...." She shrugged, trying for nonchalant.

"I understand," the man replied. "I appreciate your concern." He took one step back. "And I apologize for the inconvenience." He touched the brim of his hat.

Hurriedly, CJay tried to allay the impression that she thought his dog wasn't very clever. "He's obviously a smart dog. Probably far too smart to get his head cut off by a rotor." *Well, that was a gruesome image to conjure up. What the hell is wrong with me?* She knew her face was close to crimson.

"Yes, he is," the trooper replied, definitely smiling now. He hesitated then, as though searching for the right words. "Listen, I was...um...I was wondering if you'd mind if I called you for..."

She lifted one hand to cut him off, taking in a sharp breath to second the gesture with words but he continued speaking despite her signals. *No. Don't even think of asking for a date.*

"...an update on the driver. He's a local. I know him and his family and I'd like to follow up."

"Yes, of course," CJay said, continuing her hand up to her hair as though its intention all along had been to push a limp strand out of her face. "Sure. Give me your name and contact number and I'll get back to you as soon as I can."

As he handed her his business card, CJay took a moment to look him full in the face. "Thank you for your assistance today," she said. *Your eyes are hazel.* "You did a good job getting that guy ready for transport," she said. *Your cheekbones are beautiful.* "You probably saved his life and made ours a little safer." *You're still as attractive as that day at Fort Wainwright. Your mouth…. No wedding ring…. No, Clare. No.*

"I gotta get back to work," she said brusquely, indicating the Aurora with a tilt of her head. "Thanks again." *What the hell is the matter with me?* She turned abruptly away from him and picked up one corner of the gurney to help Gus and the medics take Roger over to the ship.

Once the patient and crew were locked and loaded, Charlie spooled up the blades, notified dispatch of liftoff with four souls on board, and within 60 seconds they were airborne and headed back to North Star Medical Center, the region's Level II trauma hospital. CJay called report to the emergency department's Mobile Intensive Care Nurse (MICN) so the docs would know what to prepare for. From her experience, CJay knew this guy was going to be in the OR moments after arrival. His belly was swollen and hard. Maybe smashed liver? Spleen? That femur might be the least of his worries at the moment.

Landing, CJay, Gus, and a trauma tech from the ED rolled the patient to the main trauma resuscitation room where their jobs ended. Now, it was helo clean-up, replacing equipment they'd used, retrieving the Segar splint, and forty-five minutes of paperwork.

"It was good to see the Sergeant again," Gus remarked, off-handedly, as they restocked the ship back on the helipad.

CJay stood at the left slider door of the helicopter and stared at Gus inside. "Hmm." She paused. "He's good looking," she told him softly.

"And he is a very good man," Gus replied

Their first flight of the day, and it was only 0730. They might have three more flights, or ten more. CJay put aside her thoughts of the trooper. They had a full enough day ahead of them without her wasting time thinking about him.

Chapter Four

Clarice Joan Herndon Valenzuela, RN, CFN (Certified Flight Nurse) – CJay, to her co-workers and acquaintances, because she wanted to avoid the Hannibal Lecter references – hit "Save," sat back and closed the computer. Done and done, she thought. Now Moose Man is in the hands of their skilled trauma surgeons. That was another one of the reasons she loved this job. Love 'em and leave 'em (for someone else to finish up).

When CJay told people what she did for a living, she frequently heard, "You must see some Really Awful Things on your flights!"

Well, yes. And some funny things, sad things, avoidable things, emotional things, and some exciting things – and absolutely incredible scenery, not to mention incredible colleagues. Take your pick. Best job in the world, she'd always tell those who asked.

"I can't imagine doing anything else. I can't believe they pay me to do this job."

And, she couldn't. She'd always wanted to be a nurse. Her dad, Mark, was a firefighter – had worked his way up the ranks and retired eight years ago as a Battalion Chief from the Eugene Fire Department in her hometown in Oregon. Her mom, Patty, was a Pediatric Nurse Practitioner and spent her days taking care of kids and their families at Eugene's PeaceHealth Sacred Heart Medical Center.

Two of CJay's brothers (Jack and Steve) – six and eight years older – were firefighters, like their dad. But the third brother, David – only eighteen months older than she and the one with whom she had the closest relationship – was a deputy with the Lane County Sheriff's Department. She was proud of him. He was her best friend – most of the time. He'd encouraged her when she told him she wanted to go to nursing school at the University of Portland after high school.

"It's a good profession, Clare. Pays well, lots of variety." he told her. "You'll always have a job someplace. You'd be a super nurse. Heck, you could even be one of those nurses flying around in a helicopter, Punk. You've got common sense, you're smart, and you're not afraid to take risks. Seriously, you come from a family of providers – it's in the Herndon DNA. You'd be a natural."

She took his words to heart and spent four challenging years studying for her BSN, and chose to extern her senior year in the Portland Memorial Hospital's Surgical Intensive Care Unit. After graduation, she was welcomed as a colleague in that same SICU where she'd made a good impression on the more experienced staff.

A year later, she moved to Astoria, Oregon, and took a job in the Emergency Department of Columbia Memorial Hospital. That same year, her young dreams came true. Six months after moving to Columbia to be near him, she married Alexander Valenzuela, David's best friend and CJay's steady boyfriend since her junior year in college. Alex was a rescue swimmer (Aviation Survival Technician) with the US Coast Guard at Air Station Astoria, and flew in one of their three MH60 Jayhawks – saving lives and property in the Pacific Northwest.

"You are the light of my life," she'd told him during their wedding vows. She was twenty-three. "I will always love you."

Chapter Five

Aurora Flight is a relative newcomer in the competitive field of air ambulances in Alaska. There are already several well-established companies (based out of Anchorage, Juneau, and Soldotna, flying locally, and also serving far flung villages with no other types of access) transporting high risk moms, neonates, severe trauma, and the critically ill. Frequently, those longer flights occur in a fixed wing aircraft. Aurora Flight has a King Air (Aurora 2) for transports such as these.

For shorter hops and for "scene flights" to local acute trauma incidents like Roger's moose crash, motor vehicle accidents, industrial trauma, shootings and stabbings, for example – twenty to one-hundred miles – Aurora Flight uses an AS350 B3, which is a single engine, powerful, agile, and versatile helicopter. It takes to high altitudes like an eagle, and is a workhorse airframe for many programs which fly in the mountains in Alaska and the 'Lower 48.'

All Aurora pilots have at least 5,000 hours flying time. The majority of them are military trained. All are VFR (visual) and IFR (instrument) flight rated, so they can fly in a variety of weather conditions, if needed. The crews also are fitted with their own NVGs (night vision goggles) for increased safety during low light flights.

Aurora Flight has been an active air ambulance program for more than fifteen years, started by local doctors who partnered with city leaders and the community in order to better serve the North Star Borough's (Fairbanks' "county") medical and trauma needs.

The program is CAMTS-certified, a coveted air medical certification that indicates that the service adheres to national safety and crew expertise standards. Transporting patients in either a rotorcraft or a fixed wing is dangerous work. The industry nationally has a high fatality record for crews, patients, and airframes. The highest safety standards are essential, especially when things can go wrong in the air so quickly.

Making a mistake frequently means a crew dies.

Because of the dangers of air medical work, the city leaders of Fairbanks, Fairbanks' faith communities, and the local Native community held a blessing ceremony before the program officially launched, calling upon higher powers to bless this fledgling project – to protect these "guardian angels" of the skies from harm.

Aurora flight personnel are generally drawn from North Star Medical Center or local fire department ranks. The crew teams are comprised of a nurse and paramedic, a fairly common configuration in the industry. Though the paramedics frequently are part-time from the Fairbanks Fire Department, several, like Gus, are full-time crewmembers with Aurora.

Because fixed wing flights may take several hours (and sometimes overnight stays if the weather turns foul), all crewmembers must be extremely comfortable with ventilators to breathe for their patients, vasopressive drips (for those in shock needing blood pressure support), high risk pregnancies, delivering babies, caring for premature babies (and their isolettes and respirators), and dealing with generally well-armed, distraught, and sometimes impaired family members from rural villages.

Both the helicopter and fixed wing crews operate under extensive Standing Orders which give them quite a bit of freedom to choose the care they need at a particular time without having to contact Medical Control for advice. Because...well...sometimes because there is no way to contact Medical Control.

Being a flying caregiver is one of the most challenging, exciting, and rewarding jobs in the medical world. And, it is one of the most dangerous jobs in an emergency medical world where circumstances can change in an instant.

Chapter Six

"Hello, Trooper Douglas. This is CJay calling from Aurora Flight. Your patient is in the OR right now. Don't know what his condition is at the present time, but feel free to call back in a day or so for an update. Truly appreciate all of your assistance. Your landing zone was perfect. Thanks. It's good to work with people who know what they're doing. You did a great job stabilizing the driver and you made our part a lot easier. It was a pleasure to work with you. Perhaps we'll see you at another scene soon. Take care. Be safe."

Jeff played the message again. "'Take care. Be safe.' I like that." He looked at his partner. "Do you think I should call her?"

Trygve thumped his tail and let his tongue loll.

"You're no help," Jeff admonished. "Let me play it just one more time."

And, he did.

For the fifth time.

* * * * * *

The Sergeant called Aurora Flight dispatch the next day.

"Aurora Flight, this is Gus. How may I help you?"

"Hi, Gus." Jeff cleared his throat before he could continue. He'd been half-hoping, half-dreading that the woman herself

46

might answer his call. "This is Sergeant Douglas. It was good to see you on scene day before yesterday. How're you doing? It's been awhile since we've worked together. How's Norma?"

"Sergeant," the paramedic answered, "It was also good to see you. Norma is well. How have you been?"

"Pretty good, thank you. I'm just calling to see, uh, to see how the patient you transported is doing. Is CJay available?"

"Sorry, Sergeant. She is off duty today. May I give her a message?"

"Uh, no. No, that's okay. How's the guy doing?"

"Not bad, considering. They pinned the femur but he had a liver laceration. He got a lot of blood products, lots of fluids. But docs say his prognosis is pretty good. His folks flew in from Idaho this morning. His wife is here, too, along with their kids."

"Thanks, Gus. Appreciate the follow-up. You guys are great. I always know when I hear your bird, things are going to be all right. Here comes the cavalry." He laughed self-consciously, knowing how hokey his comment probably sounded to the paramedic.

"Yes, Sergeant. That is us. The cavalry. But we could not do it without you in the field." After a brief pause, the paramedic asked, "Are you certain you do not want me to give a message to CJay?"

"No, no. No. That's okay," the Sergeant said, quickly. "I don't want to bother her. But...yeah...well...um, just tell her I called. Thanks, Gus." He said goodbye, then hung up and leaned back in his creaky office chair.

Ten years he'd been on duty with the Alaska State Troopers. Now as a Sergeant, he was one of those in charge at the Fairbanks Post, with many far flung and isolated settlements, and others as close as North Pole and Delta Junction, as part of his detachment and jurisdiction. It was a daunting responsibility, especially since the Troopers had only fifty commissioned officers (and here in Fairbanks three aircraft: Two helicopters – an AS350 B3 helicopter and a tiny Robinson R44; and a small fixed wing – a Piper Super Cub) to cover almost 7500 square miles.

Four years ago, he'd been given the opportunity to take over the K-9 responsibilities, and had trained with his current dog – the beautiful Belgian Malinois puppy, Trygve – who'd grown into an eighty-pound lion-hearted animal and a loyal and valuable team member. The canine also made a wonderful and sometimes quite conversational companion when he drove home to his property in Ester at night.

Jeff put his feet on his desk, and sipped his dark roast, while he considered the flight nurse who would not leave his thoughts. Although they'd exchanged names and she'd expressed her condolences at the Wainwright flyover, they'd never talked. She was polite, and appeared skilled and professional. Always just plain pretty. And at the moose v. truck incident – he'd visualized pulling her close and kissing her right then and there, even if she was frowning slightly.

He'd been impressed by the way she took his report on the injured driver seriously. She didn't rush him, didn't interrupt him as if her time were more important than his time. She'd even called him back like she'd said she would. Tall. Nice eyes. Nice mouth. Her dark blonde ponytail looked like "helmet head" after wearing the requisite flight helmet, but that was an occupational hazard. I bet she cleans up nice, he told himself, imagining her cleaning up. In his shower…naked...warm…wet….

He shook the image from his head and put his boots on the ground. "Back to work, Trygve," he told the dog.

Chapter Seven

CJay unlocked the front door and stepped inside her home – her refuge. Though it was only Tuesday, she had the next two days off, so this was virtual Friday.

TGIVF!

She tossed her flight clothes into the washing machine in the tiny laundry room off the kitchen and changed out of her civvies into fleece pants and an Oregon Ducks heavy sweatshirt. Thick socks replaced her boots.

It was starting to get dark early, and before too long they'd be experiencing sunrise at 1100 and sunset at 1440 – just short of 3PM. She'd thought that the dark days of winter would get to her – Seasonal Affective Disorder – but was surprised when they hadn't. Even having a little sunlight during the day made it bearable. In fact, she found that having it light for so long during the summer was frequently more disorienting than the opposite. How can you go to bed when it's complete daytime outside? The answer was pretty universal in Alaska: Blackout curtains on every window. But, it was also fun to run the Midnight Sun 10K race at summer solstice. She'd found a home and perhaps a new life, finally, in Fairbanks.

CJay pulled a red enamel-clad cast iron Dutch oven out of the cupboard and placed it to heat on the gas stove. Gus had given her two one-pound packs of ground moose, and she set about making crumbled moose with red tomato sauce with one of the packages. She poured herself a small glass of pinot noir, then chopped garlic, fresh Italian parsley, and basil to add to the meat. Canned San Marzano tomatoes would seal the deal. And, Pappardelle pasta. Big fat wide noodles.

She finally felt resigned contentment following the end of her relationship with firefighter/paramedic Chad Fischer seven months ago. She'd done her best to keep their relationship from becoming serious by maintaining the illusion that they were just good "friends" with fun times and pleasurable benefits, strong, warm arms, sweet lips, and the release of sexual tension. But he'd fallen in love with her anyway.

CJay sliced an apple and sat down at her little kitchen table, sipping her wine while she leafed through Tuesday's edition of the *News-Miner*, the Fairbanks daily newspaper. Drugs, alcohol, traffic accidents, moose loose in a neighborhood. She put her feet up on the chair next to her, listened to the meat sizzle, and shook away the memories.

* * * * * *

CJay ran along the downtown portion of the Chena River early the next morning. She enjoyed watching Fairbanks come alive as she passed the various tourist shops and restaurants. She ran past "The Suites on the Chena River" – an upscale hotel for visitors, the famous statue of the "Unknown First Family" in the Golden Heart Plaza, and the Chena River Eskimo Statue. By the time she got to the Alaska Club gym, she was warmed up and the sun was beginning to lighten the sky.

Because flight personnel need to be both physically and emotionally fit to do their demanding work, CJay ran at least five days out of the week. That and her strength training helped her be both mentally and physically "tough." Haha. Tough.

She looked forward to the day because tonight Gus and Norma were feeding her dinner. She showered and went shopping at Fred Meyers.

That evening, breathing in the cold air, CJay started up her Subaru Outback to make the trip over to Gus and Norma's house. The flowers she'd bought at the store were in a mayonnaise jar tied with a festive red ribbon next to her in the front seat.

She loved Gus. They'd hired on together and had learned to fly together. He was honest, plain spoken, and an excellent paramedic. Norma was a school teacher and pregnant with their first child. Both were ecstatic about this. And Norma was a terrific cook who prepared the food Gus brought home from the hunt.

Gus opened the door when she knocked, followed closely by Norma, who was wiping her hands on a towel. "The flowers are so pretty! Thank you so much, CJay," she exclaimed, giving the flight nurse a quick hug and taking the 'vase' back into the dining nook where she placed it on the table. CJay could smell the fragrance of roasted meat coming from the kitchen.

"Norma looks beautiful tonight," she whispered to Gus. "Her eyes are sparkling!"

"We have good news," he said, also lowering his voice. "But I want Norma to tell you. We are very excited."

"I can hardly wait," CJay told him. When Norma stepped out of the nook, the flight nurse stepped forward to take both of the woman's hands into her own.

"You look radiant tonight," CJay said.

Norma beamed. "This is a day of great celebration for us, and we're so happy you are here to share it with us." The Inuit's brown eyes sparkled with tears of joy. "We have wonderful news, CJay! We went to the doctor for an ultrasound and he heard two heartbeats. There are two babies. Two! Can you believe it? We are so blessed!" She squeezed the other woman's hands in joy.

"We have tried for so long to get pregnant," Gus said, his voice deepening with emotion. "We thought it would never happen. And now, we have two babies. It is a true miracle."

CJay hugged Norma and then Gus. "You both deserve this happiness. I'm so excited for you." She felt deep joy for her friends.

Dinner was moose stew and root vegetables, with rhubarb tarts and coffee for dessert. The three talked about Aurora, discussed Norma's classes, and laughed for a couple of hours. CJay knew Norma was the youngest of four children of a tribal leader from Kasigluk, Alaska. After graduating from high school, she attended community college in Fairbanks and then graduated from the University with an elementary school teaching degree.

She'd met Gus when she was a sophomore at the community college. He was working as a medical assistant at North Star Medical Center and was in the college's paramedic program. She thought he was the most handsome man she'd ever seen and had fallen in love with him at first sight. She patted his hand when she shared this with CJay.

"She is my whole world," Gus said, looking at his wife. "And a good cook." The love between her two friends was evident.

"CJay," Norma interrupted the flight nurse's thoughts.

"Norma?"

"If I may be so forward, I saw Chad Fischer at Sam's Club last weekend."

CJay stopped sipping her coffee and murmured, "And...?"

"I am wondering how you are doing. It is none of my business, but I was sorry when you and Chad ended your relationship. I thought... well it does not matter what I thought."

You're right, Norma. But I appreciate the concern. CJay looked down at the cup of dark coffee Norma had given her. "May I tell you the truth?"

"Yes, of course you can, CJay. Gus and I are your friends. We do not share things that are told to us in confidence."

"I hurt Chad. I wasn't honest with him." She turned the coffee cup around in her hands and finally put it down on the table. "I've had to make a decision about my own self. I need to step back and learn to be by myself for a while. Be content with having a good job, helping others, teaching the classes I teach for the hospital – just taking it easy." She shrugged. "No more entanglements."

But CJay knew she'd decided more than that. She'd decided no more relationships. Very few of her friends knew the whole story – and if she had her way, none would.

54

When she slipped into her jacket to leave, Gus pulled her aside. "The Trooper called for you today. You know, the Sergeant."

CJay narrowed her eyes and produced a loud sigh for his benefit.

"He was very disappointed that you were not on duty," Gus continued, with feigned innocence. "He asked me to let you know that he called."

CJay took a deep breath and sighed again before responding. "Gus, my favorite paramedic, I appreciate your and Norma's concern, but I need to take care of myself now. I hurt Chad and he didn't deserve it. But please, Gus, please. Don't try to get me involved with anyone. They don't deserve my complications."

"I understand, my friend." He cleared his throat and suppressed a chuckle. "I will be sure to tell him that if he calls again."

CJay shook her head, a half smile on her face. "You've always got my six, I know." She turned to Norma who was coming back out from the kitchen. "And Norma, I'm so happy for you both. You two deserve this good news – these two babies."

"You also deserve happiness, CJay," the woman replied softly.

CJay nodded but did not trust herself to speak. For the moment, she was content to be alone.... Indefinitely.

On the way home, she thought about the days after Chad broke up with her. She'd felt so rotten she finally made an appointment with a Licensed Marriage and Family Therapist through the hospital's Employee Assistance Program ("Six free sessions!").

It didn't take her long to connect the dots, did it? I'm still grieving over Alex. No one can take his place in my mind. And what did she tell me I was doing? Serial relationships. Leaving disruption and heartache in my wake. Trying to find solace and a salve for my scars. And, fucking failing.

She and I talked about grief and loss. About guilt. How there are ebbs and flows – especially around certain times of the year – the holidays, Valentine's Day, Alex's birthday...our anniversary. What I was experiencing was normal – painful, but normal – especially for such an unexpected, traumatic, and tragic loss.

But, what I was doing to others was not helpful to them or to me. I took the brochures and pamphlets she gave me, and read the books she recommended, too. It brought me some comfort. Accept and...well... I guess be grateful for what Alex and I had, even if it was for such a short time. But that's when I said, "No more." I won't ever allow my heart to be broken like that again. And, I will not break anyone else's heart either, just to soothe my own pain.

The heck with the Sergeant, and the horse he rode in on.
And his little dog, too.

Chapter Eight

Sergeant Jeffrey Douglas stepped from his Ford Expedition in front of the Fairbanks State Trooper post on Peger Road and opened the side door to let his partner out. Trygve jump gracefully to the ground, raced to his favorite birch, lifted his leg, and generously watered the tree.

The Sergeant's administrative assistant's car was already in the lot so he knew the brew would be fresh in the expensive European coffee maker he'd purchased for his unit last year.

"Sergeant," Ruby said, the moment he came in the door, handing him a yellow 'While You Were Out' note. "Trooper Whistler at Nenana called. He and the Village Public Safety Officer have a suspected meth lab operation over there and want you to provide ADEA coverage with them when they go in for an interdiction. I told him you'd be here any minute and would give him a ring."

"Sure, Ruby. I'll call him." The tall trooper grabbed a cup of coffee before heading into his office and dialed the phone as soon as he sat down in the creaky chair. "Craig," he said, when the other trooper answered. "What's up?"

"Hey, Sergeant. Thanks for calling back so soon. Some lowlifes have set up a meth lab over here. You know the scenario – single wide trailer, fifty-five-gallon barrels. Just got 'wind,' literally, of it a couple of days ago and started nosing around. It's the real thing. But we've only got the two of us here and we need back-up. Can you bring some other troopers so we can roust 'em?"

"Okay, I'll grab Clark Mildenhall and Grant Wilson and call you back. Give me an hour, okay?

"One hour – okay." Craig said. "Bring the dog."

The Sergeant smiled. "I don't go anywhere without him."

After hanging up with Craig, Jeff called Clark and Grant to request SERT assistance. Clark and Grant were intuitively fine troopers who volunteered for SERT – the Special Emergency Reaction Team. The presence of the SERT helped make a Fairbanks posting one of the most sought after in the state. Jeff was proud of that.

When the two officers arrived, outfitted in military camo, vests, helmets and wireless communication devices, they loaded up the Expedition with tech shotguns, three AR-15 long guns, extra ammo, and Trygve. They covered the fifty-five miles to Nenana in forty-five minutes, driving "Code 3" with lights as needed, but going under the radar outside of the small town. Craig and his VPSO met them at the tiny trooper substation to go over the plans. Unlike the majority of VPSOs, the Nenana VPSO was one of the first in the state to be trained at the Alaska Public Safety Academy in Sitka to carry a weapon.

The suspected operation was located in a wooded area of birch and alders about five miles out of town with the trailer well hidden from any roads. Law enforcement had received a tip from local kids hunting rabbits, Craig told them.

There were two ways into the area where the trailer was located. One was upwind of the trailer itself, to the east, and the other was to the north, on a rise overlooking the site. Craig planned that he and his VPSO would approach from the east; Jeff, Clark, and Grant would keep an overview from the north, and intervene when the bad guys were rousted from the trailer by Craig. Trygve would be integral in the arrests by providing backup in the form of sheer intimidation and sniffing out the alleged evidence, to be used later in a court of law.

"Harley," he indicated his VPSO, "and I'll go in and announce ourselves." Craig said, during the briefing at the substation. "You three and Trygve cover the backside. We'll do a pincer movement to corral their asses. I'm suspect they're well-armed, so be careful. I've dealt with a couple of them before on traffic stops." He looked at Jeff for follow-up.

Jeff nodded, indicating he felt all right with Craig's plan. "Okay. We'll get into position. You guys start and we'll follow up."

Jeff pulled onto the highway, following Craig who was in an AST Explorer, and they made the trip to the location situated in trees in twenty-five minutes. Craig showed him where to position his trooper vehicle, and then Craig and his VPSO worked their way slowly in his vehicle to the area east of the site, careful to not stir up telltale dust.

Craig and the VPSO approached the front end of the mobile home from out of the trees and announced their presence. Jeff, Clark, Grant, and Trygve – working their way down through the vegetation and trees to the back end – heard both the front and rear doors crash open and the sounds of AK-47s firing. Jeff, looking around the back of the trailer and trying to avoid getting shot by friendly fire, saw Craig go down, shot by one of the AK-

47s. The VPSO took cover, but managed to seriously wound one of the meth dealers. The other two rabbitted through the trees, splitting of in two directions before the three troopers could intercept them.

"Fuck," Jeff muttered under his breath. He immediately contacted dispatch, asking for Aurora to be put on standby for an officer down. He quickly gave coordinates.

Clark, crouching beside Grant, hissed, "Fuck it. We'll get the moron who went west," and took off running.

"Trygve," Jeff said, "that leaves us the idiot who went south. Let's go." Automatic gunfire rounds rang out, and Jeff was fairly sure that Clark and Grant were encountering fireworks in their direction. Jeff ran down the slope, following the cook with Trygve leading the way. Movement in the trees pinpointed the location of his target.

"Alaska State Troopers," he called out. "Come out with your hands up or we'll send in the dog!"

"Fuck you," screamed the escapee, and fired off some rounds in Jeff's direction. "Send in that dog and it's fuckin' dead!"

Jeff's heart pounded and sweat ran down the back of his shirt under the body armor. *Let's get this over with.* He was worried about Craig.

The Trooper lay on his stomach next to Trygve, the dog's eyes laser focused on the trees and his body quivering with excitement. The Trooper knew the animal looked forward to the chase but would go nowhere until Jeff gave the signal.

"Hey, buddy," the big man whispered to the K-9, putting his arm around his partner. He hugged him tight. Trygve's black ear flicked towards his master, waiting for instructions. Jeff was aware that just like his .45 sidearm, his canine was a weapon, doing what military dogs have been bred for from the beginning. When released, he would fly into a hail of gunfire to do his duty. Even as the bullets took him down, his goal would be to get the 'bad guy' – to protect his master.

I love you. He hugged him again then commanded his partner, "Fass!" Go get 'im.

Trygve exploded from his crouch. It took him 3.5 seconds to reach the gunman with Jeff following, ducking down at a run, expecting to hear automatic weapon fire and his dog screaming in pain. He knew that if his dog died, he'd be mightily tempted to shoot the creep and work out the consequences later.

What did happen was that the gunman stood up with Trygve attached to his right arm, screaming, "Get him off me! Get him off me! I give up!!" while beating on the K-9's head with the butt of his AK-47.

Jeff pointed his AR-15 at the gunman, ordered him to drop his weapon, then ordered Trygve to "Aus!" The dog opened his mouth and the trooper put the screaming meth cook down on his stomach and, with his knee pressed hard in his back, handcuffed him.

"Good dog, Trygve. Good dog. Sitz. Bleib!" Trygve stopped running around the restrained gunman on the ground, nipping at his shoes. He sat and stayed as requested.

With Trygve dancing around him, the trooper dragged the skinny, bleeding suspect with the missing teeth back to Craig's car and threw him in the back seat in the prisoner cage. He checked out the first meth maker they'd encountered. He was dead. Jeff zip tied him anyway. *Good shot, Harley.*

Craig, nearby, moaned and coughed painfully. "Shit, Jeff. That fucker caught me in the vest. I can hardly breathe. I think I may need some help." He tried to get up on his hands and knees, got halfway, collapsed. Hacked up blood.

Jeff helped him to a semi-sitting position of comfort, and punching in speed dial on his cell phone, called for Aurora Flight to be on a 'go' for an officer down.

He heard thrashing in the wooded brush and turned, his weapon drawn, to see Clark and Grant with the third meth cook handcuffed and being dragged between them. He was bleeding from a large gash on his head, rivulets of blood coursing over his filthy sweat shirt.

"He fell," Clark explained.

"Bummer" Grant added.

Jeff had Grant clear the trailer then made preparations for Aurora's LZ on the access road. He loaded Craig up into his Expedition, signaled Trygve into the front passenger's seat, then bumped as gently as he could over the terrain to the road. He waited for the helicopter with his overhead lights flashing.

Chapter Nine

"Aurora Flight, we've got a request to standby for an officer down out of Nenana, approximately 55 miles."

Gus and CJay looked at each other with raised eyebrows. "Officer down" calls are always disturbing, because air medical crews, firefighters, and law enforcement are all considered emergency services 'family.' The two gathered their coats and headed for the helicopter on the back helipad. Charlie was already there, pre-flight checking the ship, and figuring out their course and distance. The two crew members climbed in, belted up, put on their helmets and waited for the call to lift off.

In three minutes they heard, "Aurora Flight, you're a 'go' for an officer down. Alaska State Patrol requesting."

Charlie contacted their ground control about ten minutes out, and the crew heard a high-pitched voice resonating with stress vectoring them in. The voice updated their patient's condition: "Took several rounds in the vest. Chest pain, some difficulty breathing, coughing up blood. No loss of consciousness. Scene is secure. All the bad guys are accounted for. I'm on the road. You should be able to see the overheads. I can see you – you're at my 12 o'clock. Keep coming straight. You're headed right for me. No obstructions. Just put it down on the road."

As they circled the scene, CJay recognized the K-9 Expedition. Not that damn Sergeant again. Come on, Clare. Get a grip. It was only as they were landing, raising a cloud of debris two-hundred feet from the vehicle, that she realized the slender trooper in camouflage who was attempting to be helpful by showing with his hands just how far they were from touching the ground, wasn't the Sergeant. Who's hurt? She felt the hair on the back of her neck stand straight up, her heart beat faster, and her hands start to shake – an unexpected adrenaline surge.

What the hell?

CJay and Gus unlocked the gurney and headed towards the officer who pointed them to the back of the K-9 Expedition. CJay could see the injured victim with his Kevlar vest unstrapped half sitting on the back seat in the shadows, with another individual kneeling by his side. There was a non-rebreather hi-flow oxygen mask on their patient's face with O2 flowing from a small cylinder.

Up the road, another state vehicle moved slowly towards them. CJay heard sirens of the volunteer ambulance coming from Nenana behind them.

As CJay climbed into the backseat to assess the patient, she felt a wave of profound relief, followed by an intense sense of his physical closeness. It was the Sergeant at the injured trooper's side. *Damn. It's him.*

"I thought you'd been shot," came out of her mouth before she could stop it. She shook her head and attempted to look like a stern pre-hospital professional.

As he turned to make room, the flight nurse saw a look of relief – perhaps similar to the one she'd felt – come over the big man's face. "Not this time. But I'm glad it's you. We were rousting out some drug cooks and Craig here took it in the vest. He's hacking up blood. I put him in here and got him half-sitting with some O2 so he can protect his airway. I'm really worried about his lungs. These guys weren't kiddin' around with us." He continued giving her report.

"Trooper," CJay barked sharply, deliberately. "Please speak to Gus. I'm going to be busy now." *That should keep him away for a while.*

"Uh...sorry," the Trooper said, withdrawing out the other side of the vehicle, an embarrassed expression on his face. Gus reached out to him once he was standing outside.

"Talk to me, Sergeant. She's doing her size up. Tell me what happened."

"Thanks, Gus." The Sergeant repeated what he'd told CJay, adding that there were two more bad guys injured and one deceased. Local EMS and his ASTs would take care of them, he added to the paramedic.

"She didn't mean to yell at you, Sergeant. I'm lead and she's crew this time. She has to be able to do her killer search."

"Yeah, sure. I certainly wouldn't want to interrupt her 'killer search.'" He shrugged.

"It's okay, my friend."

CJay, in the vehicle, verified that there'd been no loss of consciousness on the injured trooper's side. When she unbuttoned the shirt under his open Kevlar vest she saw extensive bruising on his chest but no puncture wounds. He winced and coughed painfully when she palpated his ribs. Blood spattered his lips and the inside of the non-rebreather mask the

Sergeant had put on. Pulmonary contusions, possible cardiac contusions. Fuck.

"It hurts when I breathe," he said. She helped him sit up a bit more.

"Do you feel you're getting enough air, Trooper?"

"Yeah, I think. The Sergeant put on the mask. It helped."

"Good. We're gonna get you outta here, bud. Think you can help us get you on the gurney?"

"I'll try." He coughed again, spattering more blood.

"Gus!" CJay called, "Help me get him outta here onto the gurney." CJay backed out of the Expedition and waited for Gus to come to her side. Together they – and the Sergeant – eased Craig onto the Aurora gurney in a Semi-Fowler's position to help his work of breathing, and with the assistance of an arriving ambulance EMT carried him to the aircraft and loaded him up.

"Thanks for the oxygen, Trooper," CJay shouted at the Sergeant over the roar of the blades as she climbed into the helicopter.

"You're welcome," he bellowed back.

"See you at Med Center," Gus yelled before he put on his own helmet and prepared to shut the portside slider.

Jeff leaned in before Gus could secure the side door and shouted something that CJay couldn't hear over the AS350's turbine engine and her helmet. She frowned and glared at the trooper – frikkin' show off hero in a uniform – while hooking up their patient to the Propaq heart monitor, anxious to be away from him. Gus listened intently to the Sergeant, nodded, then pulled the slider shut. Through the plexiglass window, CJay saw the Trooper do a casual salute with his right hand, then turn away, carefully ducking under the blades.

As Charlie pulled pitch and the helicopter rose from the LZ, she started two large bore IVs then keyed her mike and nonchalantly asked, "What did he say to you?"

"He said he really hoped I would call him with an update. He said he would be by the hospital to check on Craig. And perhaps he would see me then."

Her frown deepened with confusion. "You?"

Gus nodded, his expression blank. "I think he likes me."

She narrowed her eyes and pressed down the corners of her mouth that threatened to lift. "You need to tell him that you're married. With children."

"But he's so handsome."

"Gus," she warned.

"Did you see his cheekbones?"

"Stop it," she said firmly. "Just stop it."

* * * * * *

I've never seen a prettier backside crawling out of my truck than I just saw. And such a hard-nose. Efficient. Professional. "I'm going to be BUSY now!" Guess she told me! Wonder what Gus would say…? God, she intrigues me.

She smelled good, too.

* * * * * *

They unloaded the injured trooper on the helipad and transported him to the main trauma room. Gus stayed behind to give report to the nurses and the trauma surgeon at the bedside while CJay wheeled the gurney back to the helicopter. After wiping the stretcher down, she loaded it into Aurora and locked it in place. She restocked the trauma bags and checked on the liquid oxygen. Because they didn't want to mask symptoms before he was seen by the trauma docs, no drugs had been given. Although he'd been coughing up blood and experiencing pain with respirations, his O2 sats were good, and his Propaq EKG regular. She hoped he'd have no cardiac muscle damage or major pulmonary bruising.

Sirens wailed in the parking lot and she turned to see the Nenana volunteer medic ambulance pulling into the ambulance bay of the ED. The paramedics unloaded a filthy handcuffed man with a pressure dressing wrapped around his head, accompanied by a scowling officer in SERT gear.

A trooper vehicle pulled behind the ambulance and two uniforms extracted another filthy, limping, handcuffed man with a bulky dressing on his right arm from the prisoner cage. He did not look happy.

Before she could turn her attention back to the helicopter, a third vehicle pulled in and parked at a sharp slant. Sergeant Jeffrey Douglas, accompanied by his K-9, exited the familiar Expedition.

Oh no, she thought, ducking her head but not averting her gaze.

Crap. He's going to see the helo and look over for me. He's going to want to talk to me and I just can't deal with that right now. He's got no idea what he'd be getting himself involved in. And, seriously, despite his 'professional demeanor,' he's probably working his way through every female emergency worker on the Last Frontier, anyhow, and now has me *in his sights.*

Without a glance in her direction, the heavily armored trooper and his partner strode through the sliding doors of the emergency room and vanished from sight.

CJay blinked in surprise – and confusion. Seriously? Well, good.

"That is good," she said, turning to lean her forehead against the ship's cool cowling. "We don't need the turmoil, do we, darlin'? No more." No more screw-ups.

She tugged the lines of her well-fitting flight suit into place before giving Aurora a gentle pat. She could feel the pounding of her own pulse between her palm and the ship's smooth flank.

"Adrenaline," she chuckled self-consciously, by way of explanation to no one in particular. "From the flight."

* * * * * *

"CJay – you still at the ship?" Gus queried on her handheld radio.

"Yes. Hey Gus, I need more blankets for the warmer in the shed. Can you bring some out to me? I forgot to grab them."

"Be there in a minute. Don't leave."

"Okay."

She could hear Gus's voice as he walked around the back end of the helipad. CJay wondered who he was talking to until she looked up and saw Trooper Sergeant Jeff Douglas walking with Gus, carrying blankets, with Trygve at his side. *Gus, you conniving little son of a….*

"Look who I put to work," Gus said, cheerfully smiling at her. "He was telling me about the drug bust. The K-9 was a star."

CJay frowned briefly at her favorite paramedic, but she could feel butterflies. *More damned adrenaline. Dammit.*

"Thanks for calling us. We're always glad to help law enforcement," CJay said, shaking the K-9 officer's hand after he gave Gus the blankets. She lowered her eyebrows, glaring peripherally at Gus, who whistled as he walked to the shed to put the extra blankets in their warmer.

"Thanks," the trooper answered. "I was very concerned about Craig – didn't want to have to drive him Code 3 to Med Center in the back of my truck. Really glad you were available."

CJay looked right at him. Still those hazel eyes, symmetrical face, high cheekbones, straight nose, nice lips – and then those lips smiled, and CJay realized with horror that he had been watching her watching him. She reddened and turned away, embarrassed that she'd been caught so openly appraising him.

"CJay, I need to get started on the chart. The Trooper said he'd like to see the inside of the helicopter. Can you give him our 'dog-and-pony' show?"

Gus headed back toward dispatch, leaving CJay and the trooper standing alone, with both Trygve and CJay on guard.

"I like your K-9," she said, slightly at a loss for words in the overlarge presence of this man dressed in camouflage combat clothing. "He's very good looking." *And, God help me, so are you.* She shook her head.

"His name's Trygve. He was the hero, really. He caught the third drug dealer. I...uh...," the Trooper stopped, cleared his throat and looked away.

CJay caught his abrupt change of tone. "What happened? Was he hurt?"

The big man pursed his lips, cleared his throat, then said huskily, "There was a moment when I thought I was going to lose him. I sent him into the brush to catch that crackhead, and I was afraid he was going to get...um...hurt."

CJay could see true concern in the man's eyes. Without thinking, the flight nurse reached out and touched his forearm, feeling the firmness of toned muscles under the dark jacket. She withdrew her hand abruptly as if her fingers were on fire.

"Well, I'm glad he wasn't. I'm glad none of you were hurt seriously," she added, hastily, coolly.

He smiled slightly. "Me too. Thank you."

She showed him the inside of their A-Star, and he oohed and aahed at appropriate times. He mentioned that their main helicopter at the post was also an AS350 B3, plus a little Robinson R44, and they also had a fixed wing aircraft – a PA-18 Super Cub bush plane, since they did quite a lot of highway safety work, search and rescue, and surveillance of hunters and poachers when working with the Alaska State Trooper Division of Wildlife.

"If you ever want to come see them, let me know," he offered. "And, I make pretty good coffee, too."

Trygve whined. CJay looked down at the animal and smiled.

"Trygve, are you being ignored? May I touch him?" she asked the big trooper. *I'd rather pet your dog than look at you with your damned hazel eyes.* In the very few romance novels that CJay read in moments of abject boredom and desire for distracting mental Pablum, the fictional heroine's stomach is always filled with butterflies in the presence of a lover and a touch sends electrical shocks throughout her body. *It's just the adrenaline from this flight, dammit!*

"Absolutely, you may touch him," the man told her. "Trygve, sitz." Trygve sat.

She squatted down to the dog's level. He held up his paw for a handshake and CJay shook it. Trygve gave her fingers two warm licks.

"Trygve's a pretty name. Aren't K-9s usually named 'Bravo' or 'Ninja' or 'Odin?'"

The trooper chuckled. "Sometimes, but I was given the honor of naming him as a puppy. I chose 'Trygve' because it's Norwegian for 'trustworthy.' And, he is just that."

"But he's a Belgian Malinois."

"You know your dogs." He acknowledged her animal breeds expertise and her correct pronunciation of 'Malinois' with a nod. "But I'm part Norwegian. He and I are..." he shrugged, "...family."

She looked up at him from where she was squatting, then looked away, shaking her head. *It doesn't matter if you have a beautiful dog, or you're part Norwegian or even part Klingon, or*

72

even if you make my heart beat faster and make my skin tingle. It's simply not going to happen, trooper. And, ya gotta trust me when I say it's for your own good – and mine.

"Good boy, Trygve," she whispered. "Good boy." She scratched him under his black chin and then ruffled his ears. The dog licked her hand and then reached forward and kissed her cheek. CJay couldn't help it. She laughed with pleasure.

"My dog likes you, CJay. And...um...thank you for the tour," the trooper said as CJay stood back up, a smile still on her face. "I know you're busy and I need to get back to my office and start paperwork for this bust. You guys are terrific. We troopers are glad we have you here to help us. Maybe we...you and I, I mean...can get together socially, sometime?" He looked her directly in the eyes.

Those damn hazel eyes. "Well, ...no." She paused. "No," she repeated with more certainty. She smiled faintly, then turned away.

What was there about this man standing in front of her that was so unsettling – that took her breath away?

But it will never, ever happen.

* * * * * *

Sgt. Jeffrey Douglas was disappointed the flight nurse turned down his bumbling attempt to see if she was available for a 'date.' He'd liked it when she reached out to his arm. *Thought I had a chance, but I'm losing my touch. Nope. Lost my touch a while back.*

With Trygve at his left heel, he continued across the helipad, through the gate, and down the walkway to the ED where he would check on Clark again. Looking back at the woman in the navy-blue flight suit, he saw her pretty backside bending over, as she washed mud off the helicopter floor.

* * * * * *

The Sergeant checked in with Ruby an hour later, and proceeded to the office and the creaky chair. Pouring a cup of coffee and booting up the computer, he pulled up the forms needed to document the Alaska State Patrol's role in the drug interdiction and arrest of the bad guys. He was still bothered by the incident with Trygve, fearing he was going to lose his dog to the drug dealer because of his own command. It seemed all too familiar. Too close. But, he also knew that what he was experiencing – the looping of this incident in his head – was also normal given the complexity of the event and the high level of adrenaline flowing through his system at the time.

Jeff flashed back to another moment – the first time he'd been impacted by the emotions of a situation – in Afghanistan, when he'd been forced to shoot a girl that he suspected was going to either detonate herself or be detonated near his squad on the ground below his rooftop position. It had taken a while for him to get over seeing her die instantaneously in front of his eyes, because of his own bullets. He guessed she'd been about the age of his own sister.

He'd spent two days seeing the scene over and over, dreaming about the incident every night after he'd spent hours, sweaty and sleepless, tossing and turning on the cot in his barracks. But then his gunnery sergeant noticed his distress and said one thing.

"Go see the Chaplain, now."

"What the hell for, Gunny?" the young man had snarled. "Do I need my soul saved?"

"No. You need your mind saved. I've already contacted him. Do it, Lance Corporal. Now!"

And, he'd gone grudgingly, knowing that the Padre would have nothing to say to him that would be helpful.

But he'd been wrong.

"First off, I'm not a psychologist, Lance Corporal," the middle-aged Chaplain began, "so none of this goes into your military file. This is strictly between you and me. But what I can offer is some training that I've had which can help put this incident into perspective, and perhaps take some the edge off of it. Have you ever killed anyone before this?"

What a fucking stupid question. We're in Afghanistan, dude. I mean, Padre. The Marine managed to not put that into words.

But those other times was different. The people he'd shot were trained combatants attempting to kill him and his Marine brothers. What he kept seeing was her bewildered face and her innocence. And the dog....

* * * * * *

In my peripheral vision, I see a local male forcefully goading a maybe fourteen- or fifteen-year-old female (hard to tell with the garb they wear) ahead of him, pointing towards my guys and hissing into her ear. He's not very smiley, either. She looks scared and I think I see tears in her eyes. I'm only twenty feet above him and think – Hey, asshole. Don't you see me up here?

It's not our mission to arbitrarily shoot locals on a hunch, so I'm gonna hafta wait and see what's going on – and hope I'm not too late when I figure it out. But, the male makes my decision for me when I see him hustling backwards frantically poking at his mobile phone as his sister or next-door neighbor's daughter or whoever the hell she is, stumbles towards my crew. God fuckin' dammit. I know he's not calling his maiden aunt in Kandahar.

Who do I shoot first? What if she has a switch in her hand? Multi-tasking, I see her little bare hands clasped in front of her – nothing there. But she's within damage distance from the squad, and she needs to go down first. I shoot her. I blow her head off. She goes down like a stone, but I'm not watching. I'm blowing off the male's head. He hasn't made it to the protection of the building yet. All hell breaks loose then, but at least my guys are safe. Blood and the contents of her skull are everywhere.

War is a messy business.

I'm busy puking on the roof. Not because of the blood or gore. Not even because of having to shoot a girl suicide bomber. But because I knew she was not a willing participant. She was innocent, and I had to shoot her anyway.

Then, I tell the Padre about the skinny brown street dog with the black nose and black ears. Dogs are considered filth in that

country, and she's got a little brood of pups hanging out around
another building corner. We've been leaving out food scraps for
her. She's slinking towards the female's body, licking and eating
gore as fast as she can. I pick up my weapon and aim it in front
of her – I want to scare her away, not hurt her. But I'm sweating
profusely and I feel my stomach about to erupt again, and I
fucking miss and hit the dog anyway – in the chest. She yelps in
agony and falls and flails, crying for her babies, until she just lays
still. I can't bear it. I have to push this down deep. I'm so sorry, I
tell her. I didn't mean to hurt you. I'm so sorry.

I am blinded with tears.

I hear one of my guys pounding up the stairs behind me and
he finds me doubled over, puking and pitiful. "You okay?" he
shouts, thinking I've been hit. I tell him I'm fine. He's clapping me
on the back and trying to give me high fives because I saved their
bacon down below. And I'm crying about the dog and her babies
who are left alone. I'm thinking what a miserable piece of crap
place this is. That's when I know I'm really fucked up.

* * * * * *

His stomach spasmed and he wretched bile into the
Chaplain's little trash can by his desk.

The Chaplain nodded, paused, then said quietly, "What I can
tell you, is that you're not alone, nor are you crazy. What you've
experienced is called a 'traumatic event' – it's something truly out
of the ordinary, even for you. You've been trained to protect and
survive," he went on. "That's your job as a Marine in this place.

77

But you've not been trained to kill those you might think of as innocent. This is what makes this "out of the ordinary" for you. That's the first problem. This was out of the ordinary.

"Secondly, this was completely unexpected. When you woke up that morning, did you expect to kill a young girl? Were you prepared ahead of time?"

"Fucking hell, no," Jeff answered. "Padre, I'm sorry to swear," he added, ducking his head.

"Lance Corporal, no need to apologize. You use the words you need to tell your story to me."

"She was close to my sister's age," Jeff finally went on slowly. "I saw Shannon's face. It was all I could do to carry out what I know is my duty to my marines. But, I took real pleasure in killing her brother. He deserved it." Jeff closed his eyes. A wave of nausea passed over him again and he added a second layer of bile to the little trash can.

"The third thing you need to remember, Lance Corporal," the Padre continued when the Marine lifted his head up again from the can, "is what you just told me about seeing your sister's face. That is what makes this so up close and personal for you. You said you saw your sister's face, but you had to shoot her anyway. And I sense that the little street dog you didn't mean to shoot is the shit frosting on top of this turd cake for you."

The Chaplain saw the Marine nod.

"Three components that changed you two days ago: This was *unexpected*; you had no time to prepare. It was *out of your ordinary*, even for Afghanistan; and – it was *highly emotional to you personally*. If it's any consolation right now, Lance Corporal, I would be much more worried if this event *hadn't* made an impact on you.

"What you are experiencing – and remember this – is an absolutely normal response of you – a well-trained Marine – to a terribly abnormal situation, even in combat. It's not unusual at all to be going through what you are facing right now. Can you understand that?"

Jeff nodded. Yes, he could understand what the Padre had said. *Now what? Are you going to offer to pray for me, too? Please don't. Prayer won't help me now.*

The Chaplain did not offer to pray for him. Instead, he asked Lance Corporal Douglas what the worst part of this situation was for him. What was he having the most difficulty with?

"Her face. And, her blood. I see her face when I close my eyes. I see the blood that's not on the wall behind her coming out of what's left of her head and pooling on the ground. There were brains…." The Marine stopped talking, clamping his lips shut.

"Go on, Lance Corporal," the Chaplain finally said softly.

"And shooting the dog. My mistake! My fault!" Jeff covered his eyes with his left hand, as if doing so would block the images he was seeing. "I…I…." He stopped. He could feel hot tears welling up in his eyes.

The Padre sat silent for a few moments, letting him handle this wave of emotion. Then the Chaplain reached out his fist and softly touched the young Marine on his shoulder. He waited until Jeff looked up into his eyes, ready to continue.

Choked words. "I killed two innocents. I didn't want to. I didn't mean to." He bent down and started to cry, great racking sobs that lasted for several moments.

The Marine Chaplain reached out his hand this time and placed it warmly on the Marine's shoulder. He kept it there until Jeff regained composure and looked up again.

"You told me you enjoyed killing the male because you felt he was going to detonate the girl's suicide vest and harm your men. That's not an issue with you."

This time, the Marine gave jerky head shake. No. Not an issue.

"But killing the female – who was perhaps being forced into being a suicide bomber – is more problematic, because she had no malice for your men."

"I don't think she was even mentally capable enough to know what was happening."

"And the dog?"

"Was just being a fucking, skinny mama dog. But I wanted to stop her from eating...that...that girl's...." Jeff took in several slow breaths, letting each out in a great whoosh of air. "The only thing I can say in my defense is that the girl didn't feel any pain." He felt the tears coming back.

"Fairly gnarly shit."

Jeff laughed grimly at the Chaplain's incredible understatement. "Yeah, Padre – 'fairly gnarly shit.'" The young Marine wiped his eyes with the back of his hand.

The Chaplain waited until Jeff straightened up and looked at him again. "You will probably continue to see this quite vividly for a few more days, Lance Corporal. Your brain took these high definition snapshots – this DVD – while you were in a highly agitated state – your heart pounding, your mind attempting to make decisions at lightning speed. This replay is a pretty normal survival tool for your brain. It wants to keep reminding you of what happened – to keep you safe. On total high alert. It's pretty uncomfortable, isn't it?"

The young Marine nodded and the Chaplain went on. "I can't overemphasize that this is a normal response to a truly awful event with a whole hell of a lot of emotional dynamics involved."

"Yeah, no kidding. 'Fairly gnarly shit,'" the young Marine repeated, then grunted. "How long am I going to feel like this, Padre?" he asked. "I haven't been sleeping. I'm concerned I'm not much good at the moment, and I need to be able to do my job."

"I get it. From my experience, most people can come to terms with an event like this when they talk about it to someone like me. It generally becomes less toxic as time goes on. Talking can take the edge off, help process your thinking more quickly. You'll never forget what happened three days ago – ever. But it will become part of who you are. It can help make you a more understanding person. A better, stronger, and wiser person."

The older man paused. "One other thing, Lance Corporal. Frame by frame…if you'd have known you would accidentally hit the dog at that moment, would you have pulled the trigger?"

"No," the Marine said softly. "I would not. I'dve puked, then tried to scare her away."

"And, as hard as it is for you right now, that is what you will need to remember. It was not your intention to hurt her. Your body betrayed you at precisely the wrong time."

The Chaplain reached over to a nearby table and grabbed some paperwork which he gave to the Marine. "Remember what I've told you, and as you probably can guess, I do have stuff for you to read when you want to. It's about posttraumatic stress. Not posttraumatic stress disorder – PTSD. You don't have that. You're having a not untypical response to one single truly horrible incident. Understanding the impact of that response as being a very normal response of a normal person to an abnormal situation takes it out of the realm of being terminal.

"Remember: *You. Are. Normal.* You will get through this. And I can talk again, anytime you need to talk. Often just telling your story again can make it less hot and up front in your head. It can decrease the impact. Put it into some sort of coherent perspective."

When Jeff walked out of the Chaplain's tent, he hoped this 'talk' had helped. And, as the Padre had said, within a week Jeff was able to make his killing of the young Afghan woman and that poor dog a memory – a painful and regretful memory – but one he could live with and accept as part of who he would, one day, become.

Chapter Ten

Trooper Sgt. Douglas flew down to Anchorage that following week to deal with what was supposed to be a routine AST investigation into the drug bust in Nenana. However, Jeff was reminded by the Alaska Bureau of Investigation (the AST's ABI) that what they did in the smaller village was just the tip of the iceberg in the North Star Borough. Jeff served as the Sergeant for the AST's Alaska Drug Enforcement unit in Fairbanks. His Fairbanks DEU would be tasked to work with the statewide DEU in an aggressive action against drug and alcohol traffickers – much sooner rather than later.

"Sergeant Douglas, we've got wind of some big-time stuff coming in from the Lower 48, but also being manufactured in your borough," the head of the SDEU told him. "Personally, I'm glad you guys shook 'em up with your raid last week.

The Sergeant nodded. He'd like nothing better than to get the drugs and alcohol out of the villages. Almost every serious incident the AST investigated in the isolated, outlying communities grew out of the misuse of alcohol – whether commercial or homemade – and drugs. Unfortunately, the two trooper murders in Mantishka were prime examples.

Jeff flew out later that afternoon from Anchorage to Sitka and spent the next day teaching a section on emotional and psychological trauma to the new recruit class at the Alaska State Trooper Academy in Sitka. He felt strongly that trooper newbies should have pre-incident education about what to expect on The Job, and on how to care for themselves, their fellow troopers, and their own families, not just physically, but mentally. His incident in Afghanistan, and subsequent events with the ASTs, had taught him that such knowledge and support is emotionally crucial.

In Sitka, he included a segment on the State Trooper Peer Support and Crisis Management Team, how they could be contacted, and why they should be accessed following an officer involved shooting, death or suicide of a coworker, a multi-casualty incident, or pediatric trauma or death. He knew that emotional injuries can be as damaging as physical injuries, often removing promising individuals from productive careers in law enforcement. Just as critical is the impact on families – the "ripple effect" of trauma when Mom or Dad brings home posttraumatic stress. He felt it was his duty to also "protect and serve" in this particular, very personal, arena of policing.

Before flying down, he'd called Aurora dispatch, and speaking with Jeanne, the dispatcher, left a message for CJay: "Please call or text me. Would you like to grab some pizza when I get back from the Sitka academy on Saturday night?"

He left his cell phone number. He wondered if she still had his business card.

* * * * * *

84

CJay did not call or text back after Jeanne gave her the message with a wink, because she was, quite frankly, adamant about not becoming involved. The man was powerfully good looking in his SERT combat uniform, apparently respected, and evidently quite capable as a cop. She couldn't dismiss that in a multitude of ways, he was a lot like her brother, David. Capable, respected, attractive – a 'good man,' Gus had said.

And a lot like Alex.

He seemed to like her – after all, he was pursuing her with this phone message. That felt good, she admitted. *No,* she chastised herself. *It doesn't feel good. It feels like a trap. For him. And more confusion, pain, and guilt for me. Fuck it. Leave me alone!*

"Gus," she said on Friday morning as they pre-flighted the AStar together after morning shift change.

"CJay," Gus answered.

"I have a problem."

Gus smiled. "What is your problem, CJay?"

"The trooper left a message at dispatch for me Tuesday."

"And...? This is Friday. You have not replied to him yet?"

"No."

"What did the trooper want?"

CJay sighed deeply and zipped up the Thomas trauma bag.

"He wanted to ask me out for pizza for tomorrow night. He asked if we could see 'one another socially' when you made me give him that..." she thought the word 'fucking' but didn't say it "...'dog-and-pony show' last week. I told him 'No.'"

Gus, kneeling over the gurney, sat back on his haunches, against the door.

"Because – just exactly why? I do not understand."

CJay smiled wanly. "It doesn't matter, Gus. Just *'No,'* okay?"

"All right, CJay. But can't you think of it as free food and drink? A moment of diversion? He certainly is what many women would call attractive, although I am a man and do not look at other men like that."

"So, *you* think I should go eat with him?" Disappointed, she shook her head at him.

"You have to make your own decisions, of course. When I was on the ambulance, I worked with him several times over those years. I have never heard negative gossip about him. He was a Marine and then a Trooper. He is very capable in the field. You deserve someone who will take you out for pizza. You deserve a pleasant evening. I would say 'Yes,' you should accept his 'pizza deal.' You can then decide whether there will be, perhaps, a 'hot wings deal.'"

The flight nurse sighed. *It's not that simple.*

"Why do you look so sad, CJay? What is bothering you so much?" They both put down the equipment they were handling.

"Gus, I am a like a..." she struggled for a descriptive word for herself, then chose something simple and easily understood. "...an Alaska mosquito."

The flight nurse saw her paramedic make a face, trying to visualize her analogy. "You mean you are capable of carrying off a tourist from 'Below?'"

She had to smile at that image. "Not quite, but I do inflict pain. I suck the life out and leave an empty husk." She took a deep breath and slowly blew it out her mouth, closing her eyes, resting her hand on the floor beside her.

Gus waited, then he spoke. "That is quite dramatic, CJay. You leave an empty husk? What does that mean to you?"

"I hurt Chad really bad. Our breakup wasn't his fault." She could see questions in Gus's eyes. "You know I was married before?"

"Yes. But you have not talked much about it and it is not my business to ask you questions. You do not need to speak of this if you do not wish to."

"I think I need to straighten some things out in my own mind, Gus. My husband died in the line of duty. I thought I would die, too – from the pain of losing him. We were married five years."

"I am truly sorry, CJay."

"I left Astoria and came back home to my parents. It was all I could do to get through the days without him."

"That must have been a very hard time for you and your family."

"The worst. But you know what's even worse?"

"No, CJay, I do not."

"I'm a user. I used Chad to try to forget. Some people use drugs or alcohol. But I use people – Chad. I hurt him." She looked down at the trauma bag, then back up at Gus. "Do you know why I came to Fairbanks?

"No, CJay, I do not."

"Because I hurt someone else in Eugene – a police officer who was a high school friend and then a companion after I came back home." She threw her hands up in the air. "The same story, Gus. Kept him at arm's length, used him to deal with my pain, but wouldn't let him in."

"Did he leave you, too?"

"Yes," she said simply.

"Well, you do not seem like a life sucking mosquito to me. I am not a wise one, but it sounds like you are inflicting pain on yourself by deliberately isolating your heart from any further love or joy. You do not try to suck anyone on purpose, do you?"

CJay smiled slightly at that image. *Gus, even now you make me laugh.* "No...but I know I still grieve over my husband."

"I think I see what you are saying."

"My husband speaks with me." She glanced abruptly at Gus, then looked quickly away. "Is that weird?"

"No. Does he sit in a chair at your table?"

She smiled again, the smile not reaching her eyes. "No. In my dreams."

Gus cocked his head – yes, go on.

"That's all. I've said enough already."

This time Gus took the deep breath. "You are my friend. I trust working with you. I will not tell you what to do, but your husband is gone now for several years. If I were to die in this helicopter today, I would not want Norma to be alone without joy. Perhaps you should talk with your husband the next time you dream and ask him what he wants for you. I feel, if he is as good a man as you believe, he will want you to love again. To find the joy that you had with him. I think that would be a fitting tribute to the union you two created."

"So, should I tell the Trooper I'll do pizza?"

"It is up to you. But free food is always nice."

This time, CJay softly laughed out loud. "Gus, you sell yourself short. You're very wise. I'm glad you're my partner, but I'm going to turn him down. I will not hurt another person...or *be* hurt... again."

"I know, CJay. You have told me." Gus bent his head over the gurney and frowned.

* * * * * *

Ping. Trooper Douglas looked at his cell phone. A text.

> Hello. I am very sorry, but I cannot accept your invitation for pizza. Thank you very much for thinking of me. Be safe.

He sat back in his creaky chair. *I thought she was going to ignore me, but she didn't. Nope, she turned me down. At least I have her cell phone number now. Well, nothing ventured; nothing gained.*

He texted back.

> *OK. I'll call you next week. Fly safe.*

* * * * * *

"CJay – phone." One week later, Jeanne held out the dispatch landline phone to the flight nurse as CJay sat at the computer, writing the chart for Kelly's and her last flight for an auto-pedestrian accident in Delta Junction.

"This is CJay," she said into the phone, holding it between her cheek and shoulder.

"Hello, CJay." She knew it was him as soon as she heard his voice. "This is Jeff Douglas from the State Troopers. How are you?"

Crap. She sat up and took the phone into her hand.

"Sergeant, I'm just super. And how are you doing?" She deliberately attempted to put a I'm-really-busy-right-now-so-make-it-snappy-and-I'm-looking-at-my-watch-even-as-we-speak spin on her words.

"Never better, CJay. But I'll be even better if you will have dinner with me this week – are you available Saturday, or perhaps Sunday night for a quick bite at Vito's? I'd enjoy treating you to a little conversation and relaxation."

CJay just sat there. *What is up with this dude? Just leave me alone. Let me be.*

"Sergeant, I thank you for your invitation. But may I be brutally honest?"

"Please be, CJay. And please call me Jeff."

"Sergeant," she repeated pointedly, "I applaud your persistence. But I have promised myself that I will be *celibate* for the rest of my life." She emphasized 'celibate' and heard Jeanne snort over at the dispatch console. She hoped the trooper hadn't heard it, too.

"That was *definitely* brutal, CJay. Celibate for as long as you live? Is this a non-negotiable, binding commitment? Should I take your decision personally? Is it my hat? My career?"

CJay smiled. Then sighed loudly and impatiently into the phone, hoping he could hear her.

"No, Sergeant, your choice of career is quite admirable and brave, and your Stetson is just adorable, although it looks as if it'd be a handicap in a high wind."

She heard him chuckle.

"That's what we all think, CJay. I could wear a ball cap, if it would make a difference to you." He paused, then asked seriously, "Does this mean you're shooting me down again?"

"Yes, Sergeant, that is what it means. But, I hope you have a good day and stay safe. Goodbye." She hung up on him.

"'Celibate?' Seriously, if you keep flirting like that, you'll never get rid of him," she heard from behind her at the dispatch console where Jeanne was sitting.

"I *told* him I wouldn't ever go out with him," CJay protested.

"'Your Stetson's is *'juuust adorable'*,'" Jeanne mimicked, laughing.

* * * * * *

"CJay – Dispatch." The flight nurse heard Big Mike in dispatch on her handheld in the calf pocket of her flight suit.

"Dispatch – flight nurse," she answered, after fumbling the radio out of her pants leg.

"CJay, some trooper called dispatch a minute ago and left a message for you with his phone number. I told him you were at the helipad cleaning up the ship."

Ah, geez. She should've left a note for the dispatchers:

DO NOT PUT THROUGH ANY CALLS OR GIVE ANY INFORMATION TO STATE TROOPER SGT. DOUGLAS.

"I'm not calling him back, Big Mike. I wish you wouldn't have told him where I was."

"I'm sorry, CJay. Do you want me to get security out there to the pad?"

"No. I don't think he's going to do anything except annoy the crap out of me."

"Okay, I'll keep an eye on the security camera. Give me a heads-up on the handheld if you need assistance."

"Thanks, Big Mike."

"Gus, it's that trooper again," she said, turning to her partner. "I wish he'd leave me alone."

Gus smiled at her.

From inside the helicopter, she saw the trooper K-9 Expedition pull up outside the helipad.

"Your trooper is here, CJay."

"Gus, he is NOT my trooper!"

"He is trying to be."

She saw the big man open the driver's door and step out. He was wearing torn, paint stained, denim mechanic's overalls, a filthy camouflage jacket, and a flat brim ball cap with *Sam's Club* printed on it pulled down to his eyes. He stood at the fence watching them.

"Go see what he wants, Gus. He's scary looking."

"He wants you, CJay. YOU must go see what he wants." Gus hid his smile.

Sighing deeply, she climbed out of the ship and walked over near the fence, stopping fifteen feet away from the perimeter.

"I've changed careers and I wear a ball cap now." He poked the ball cap with his finger. "I got a new job stocking the warehouse at Sam's Club. At night."

She motioned towards the trooper SUV. She heard his dog woof from inside.

"What about that?"

He looked back to see what she was pointing at. "Oh, that. I stole it. The dog, too. I'll be in Fairbanks Correctional Center as soon as my Lieutenant notices they're both gone."

He paused. CJay stared at him, incredulous.

"Now will you go out with me?" He looked so serious. He vigorously scratched his flank.

She started to laugh. She couldn't help it. She turned away and it took her several moments to compose herself.

"You're pretty used to getting what you want, aren't you?" she asked, turning back to face him. He still looked serious. So did she, but it was difficult to compress her lips that tightly to keep from smiling.

He shrugged. "Only if you say I can take you to Vito's on Saturday night." The trooper pulled a dirty handkerchief out of his overalls chest pocket and wiped his nose.

She closed her eyes and shook her head sadly. Paused for a very long moment.

"No, Sergeant. No. I…I won't. This *is* non-negotiable. I'm sorry. You seem like a really nice guy, but I can't." *I won't do to you what I've done...to the others.*

She turned away from him, walked to the helicopter and climbed inside without a backward glance and sat down again next to Gus.

"You said no?" her paramedic asked her. He was glancing out the cockpit windscreen. "The trooper is still standing there. He looks sad with that cap on."

"Geez, Gus. You, too?" She sighed loudly at him. "Just let me know when he leaves."

She heard a truck door slam.

"He is leaving."

"Good."

"Is this because of what we spoke about last week?"

"Yes. And no, Gus. I…I… There are just some things I don't want to have to go through again."

Gus nodded. "I'm going inside to get my snack now, CJay. May I buy you a latté?"

She nodded and followed him out of the helicopter to the hospital cafeteria.

94

Chapter Eleven

Why is it so hard to not just say yes and go out with this guy one time? Why am I saying "no" to Super Duper Trooper – who is incredibly attractive on so many levels? Because I just can't. I can't risk it. It hurts too much. No more. Not again. I can't harden my heart another time. I can't have my heart broken again by someone I love.

And I can't knowingly hurt another person.

* * * * * *

The second time Alex came to her in a dream, she heard him say, "Hey, my beautiful Clare."

She'd smiled and turned her face to him from where she lay on her bed. He was dressed in his Coast Guard flight suit and heavy coat, getting ready to leave the house. "I just wanted to tell you good-bye and 'I love you' before I left."

"I love you too," she dreamed.

Then, Alex was naked and on the bed. "My gorgeous husband," she dreamed and spread her legs when he ran his hand up the inside of her thigh. He pressed himself inside her, kissing her forehead, her cheeks, the corners of her mouth. She opened her mouth for his kiss and his tongue, and in her sleep moved her hips to his rhythm until finally the pulsations of her own orgasm woke her. She cried then, and vowed not to wake up next time, but to keep him there, inside of her, longer.

The next time, she made herself stay asleep, and Alex held her. He told her he would always watch out for her, he would be there for as long as she needed him, and he and Alexa Clare wanted her to be happy.

* * * * * *

Aurora Flight 1 had only three scene requests on Sunday (including another pick-up vs moose on the Dalton Highway. The crew did not see the Sergeant this time.), and CJay was able to spend a lot of time in the ED, helping the staff. In those familiar surroundings, her mind would occasionally flash back to the day the job openings for two flight personnel – a nurse and a medic – were posted on the employee "Positions Available" board.

"CJay," Melanie called to her. "Did you see this?" She knuckle-tapped the employee board. "Aurora Flight – nurse position. You should apply."

CJay moved in closer to see the notice. "NALS, ACLS, PALS certifications… I've got those. Five years' experience in ICU and/or ED. Got that." CJay's previous jobs had required Neonatal Advanced Life Support, Pediatric Advanced Life Support, and Advanced Cardiac Life Support certifications, so she was definitely prepared in that respect. Her Portland job had included both ICU and ED, ED at Columbia, plus PeaceHealth ED, plus her time in the Emergency Department here at the Med Center.

She remembered David telling her (was it already fifteen years ago?) she could even be a flight nurse. How swiftly time goes by.

"Absolutely, Melanie. Absolutely," she said instantaneously. "Yes." *Why the hell not? It's time. I've got nothing to lose anymore. Maybe I'll find out what brought Alex so much joy before...before....*

Her initial interview process put her before a board of hospital physicians, the Chief Flight Nurse, the Chief Flight Medic, the Program Director, the Medical Director, and the Chief Pilot of Aurora Flight. It was somewhat intimidating, but she came across, she felt, as composed and capable. Two more interviews and she had the position. She was excited. She knew she was prepared. *Alex, watch the heck over me. You promised, sweetheart.*

Her fellow ED nurse friends, Hunni, Caren, and Melanie took her out to the Pump House for a celebration dinner later that month. They made her promise "You won't forget us now that you're a flight nurse in the fancy blue suit." She promised, and meant it.

Her new firefighter/paramedic friend, Chad, had been excited for her. "My girl is a flight nurse. I'm so proud of you."

Chapter Twelve

CJay called her brother's cell phone during a lull on Tuesday's shift. Gus was talking quietly with his wife on the dispatch telephone while monitoring traffic over the Fairbanks emergency dispatch frequency. They might get activated for a flight anytime, but at least they could spend a few minutes talking with family. Jeanne, the dispatcher, was working the previous Sunday's *New York Time's* Crossword puzzle. In ink.

"Hey, Clare," her brother said when he picked up.

"Hey, David. How are you?"

They exchanged small talk for a few minutes, but then David stopped and said, "This isn't why you called. What's up? I'm working second shift today, so gotta get outta here pretty quick."

CJay felt her throat tighten up and knew tears would be next. She coughed and willed the tears to stay put.

"I just needed to hear your voice, David. I've been thinking about Alex. Some trooper has asked me out and I told him 'no' several times, pretty much in no uncertain terms. Just wanted to talk to you." She stopped. Breathed. She could hear David clear his throat.

"I hear you, Clare. It'll be four years in a couple months, isn't it? I was looking at some pics last night – remember when Dad and Mom took us all to Yosemite when I was fourteen and I got

98

scared going up that cable trail on Half Dome and Alex had to practically carry me back down?"

"And I waved at you and laughed as you went by and I finished the trail to the top? How can I possibly forget that?" She laughed out loud again at the memory. Scaredy cat David. Four years later, when he and Alex were 18, they and two other friends made the trip up and back down Half Dome just to prove he wasn't afraid any more. Took pictures at the very top, looking out over the valley far below to prove it. Enlarged and framed those pictures as a tribute to himself. Those same photographs hung in his 'man cave' to this day. She loved looking at Alex in those photos. Happy times. Her beautiful husband. A future stretching ahead for the two of them….

"Talking to you always makes me feel better. You're pretty good at that."

"Why don't you say 'yes' to Dudley Do-Right?"

"That's Canadian Mounties, David. This is Alaska State Troopers."

"The question remains the same, little sister. Besides, those guys all work together up there in the frozen north and their Class A dress uniforms look alike."

"I can't risk it. No more loss…"

"…sez the woman who flies around in a helicopter?" They sobered at that obvious irony.

"Clare, let me be frank…"

"…and I'll be Earnest." This time they did laugh, still the same two siblings who entertained one another for years as they were growing up with the same stale jokes. But David went on, undaunted.

"Damn it, Clare. Just go out with the poor schlemiel. You and I both know Alex would want you to be happy. Life is short and brutish. Alex died on the job. I could be killed on the job tomorrow. YOU could die in *that fucking helicopter*. There are no guarantees. Don't spend your time avoiding pleasure. Go out with Dudley. Saying 'no' because you're afraid you might lose him? Cla-a-a-are – say YES to the Stetson," he finished. CJay sensed he was checking his watch for time.

"Go to work, buddy. I'll think about it. You stay safe, okay?"

"Do my best, sis, and back atcha. Love ya much."

"Love you, too, David."

She pressed the round red 'disconnect' button and leaned back in the dispatch chair. She'd think about it. *But, I doubt he's going to call me again. Three fat turndowns? I'm pretty sure there are a lot of other females who'll yank off their panties for Sergeant Super Dooper Trooper without all the drama.*

Ping! Text. From David:

> *Forgot to mention. Coming up to Anchorage for a class in October for 3 days. See you after class is done?*
> Of course! That's great! Text me the dates & I'll work around them.
> *Will do. Fly safe.*
> Be safe. I love you.

David was coming up to Fairbanks. She could hardly wait.

Ping! Text. From David:

Go out with the poor schlemiel. You got nothing to lose.

Last word. He *always* had to have the last word. CJay smiled once again and felt better.

Chapter Thirteen

The goal of a helicopter, or rotorcraft, is to retrieve a victim in a timely fashion and get him or her back to definitive care as quickly as possible. 'The Golden Hour' is a term credited to former military surgeon, R Adams Crowley, MD, when he was head of the University of Maryland Shock Trauma Center in Baltimore. This Golden Hour describes those sixty minutes between the time an individual is injured and the moment he or she can be in definitive surgical care. Sixty minutes can be a lifesaving time frame.

The crews who fly in the helicopter must be able to assess injuries almost instantly (like Gus' 'Killer Search'), identify what care needs to be given, and then do it quickly and efficiently either at the scene or, preferably, while flying one hundred-fifty miles an hour, fifteen-hundred feet off the ground, in a variety of weather conditions. When a patient's status worsens, the crews must be able to recognize it fast and fix it even more quickly.

It is a fairly steep learning curve to become a truly competent flight crew member. There is ground school for learning to do expanded scope of practice skills that in the hospital setting are done only by nurse practitioners, trauma docs, certified nurse anesthetists, or anesthesiologists. These include intubating a patient; placing large intravenous lines; inserting a chest tube in between the ribs to re-expand a collapsed lung; or using an ultrasound machine in the aircraft to assess the abdomen. These expanded skills can keep a trauma patient alive long enough for a surgical team to get them to the operating theater.

In addition, flight crews must also learn personal survival skills. It isn't enough to fly in a machine. Crews must know how to survive in that machine, in case that machine fails – especially in such an unforgiving terrain as the subarctic in Alaska. The chances of surviving a crash in either a fixed wing or a helicopter increase if the crews know how to prepare for such an event.

The majority of the pilots fly armed with a large caliber service weapon. The helicopter and fixed wing aircraft are also equipped with long guns powerful enough to defend against bears or provide game to eat in the case the crews become stranded in the wild, whether due to unforeseen meteorological conditions – or a crash.

All Aurora crew members carry survival packs on their bodies (waterproof matches, fire starter kit, first aid supplies, fishing line and hooks, water purifiers, aluminum thermal blankets, and large folding field knives for both protection and utility.). Additionally, the aircraft carries its usual medical supplies, but also water and food items that can become the things that save the lives of crews in case the worst does happen.

And, when the pilot calls over the intercom and states, "Bend over and grab your ankles," (although in less anxious times, crews change that to the dark humored, sardonic "Bend over and kiss your ass goodbye."), he or she is not kidding. That can be the difference between a broken back and the ability to get yourself (or your partner) out of the aircraft after a hard landing or a crash – and, potentially, the resultant devastating fire.

* * * * * *

Both a flight nurse and a flight paramedic position were open when CJay applied for the nurse slot. Paramedic Augustus Coffee joined CJay the first morning they showed up for ground school. It was obvious he was as nervous as she was, but he'd already been a practicing field medic for eight years, so was comfortable with many of the advanced life support skills that CJay would need to learn as part of her training.

The two spent four weeks in ground school, learning the expanded scope of practice skills of intubation; correctly inserting chest tubes; starting large subclavian and femoral vein lines for rapid fluid infusions; and placing arterial lines for continuous monitoring of patient blood pressures invasively. She learned to use an ultrasound on abdomens, looking for blood, air, or fluid that should not be present, and to accurately assess the findings.

They learned to place airways when it wasn't always possible to put a breathing tube into the mouth and down into the lungs. The nasal intubation through the nose can work at specific times, for example when the patient's jaw is broken. Or, the patient is conscious and will cooperate.

RSI, or Rapid Sequence Induction, is also an option if the patient is anoxic and fighting your help. Give the patient a powerful IV sedative for comfort and a paralytic agent to briefly relax the muscles, and tube her while she is flaccid.

And, the cric - the cricothyrotomy. Generally last resort, but effective, especially if the patient's face is crushed or the flight crew can't place an airway for breathing any other way.

Stretch your neck back, and feel for your "Adam's Apple." Slide your finger down below the Adam's Apple, until you find a slight depression where your finger fits naturally. This is the cricoid space – an opening below the larynx where the flight nurse or medic can take a #11 scalpel, cut through the skin of the neck, then slice through the membrane of the cricoid space (without cutting any major vessels on either side of the larynx causing rapid exsanguination – excessive, uncontrolled bleeding and death), and subsequently introduce a Shiley tracheostomy tube (a short breathing tube). Inflate the trach tube's balloon to allow for effective ventilation, secure the tube around the patient's neck using cric or twill tie, and proceed to ventilate with an ambu-bag and your oxygen delivery system.

If it is not possible to place a tracheotomy tube, or the patient is a pediatric patient for whom there are no tiny tubes, the flight crew may forego the scalpel, but, after locating the cricoid process insert a special curved silastic tube with a needle stylet into the breathing space, securing it well. Ideally, when using a needle cric set-up, the flight crew then uses a jet insufflation device, which powerfully forces air through the tiny tube, allowing fresh oxygen to reach the child's lungs.

CJay and 'Gus,' as he asked to be called, learned how to program a flight ventilator, a small breathing machine designed specifically for transports. During prolonged or extremely busy flights when it's not always easy to breathe manually for your patient, this ventilator is another pair of hands for a busy crew.

Then, Gus and CJay refreshed their skills about pediatrics from the flight nurse manager of the fixed wing transport team, Jacque Rose. Though CJay and Gus both already knew a great deal from their prior training and experience, Jacque reminded them frequently that children are not just little adults. Everything about them is different, besides their sizes. And, subsequently, care for them is different. When a child's heart stops, almost always it is because there is a respiratory issue – 'the kid ain't breathin.' *Airway airway airway*is the mantra. Jacque reinforced their knowledge about how to keep kids alive during long, frantic flights.

The two new hires received flight safety training – essential for survival – from Tommy Denham, the program's Safety Officer. No, they weren't taught how to fly the helicopter in case the pilot has a heart attack. They were taught how to clear the tail when landing at a scene so the ship wouldn't hit power lines, trees, frightened horses, someone's fence or – worse yet – their outhouse.

Gus and CJay were taught to scan the skies for UFOs – generally other aircraft, birds, or, increasingly frequently, drones, and report these occurrences to the pilot. "Aircraft high at 8 o'clock" meant there was a plane coming from behind and to the left side towards Aurora Flight higher than they were. "Got it," the pilot would say and either change course or continue to fly, keeping an eye on the bigger aircraft for safety.

"There is Just. So. Much. To. Learn," she told David during one of the many calls they shared during her training. "Some days I feel like I'm on top of it, and other days – Hell! I'm ready to quit!"

David would laugh and continue to reassure her that she would do 'just fine,' and *'Just hang in there'* soon became her personal mantra.

At the end of their initial training, CJay and Gus received two navy blue flight suits, tailored for them with their names and the "Aurora Flight" insignia embroidered on the chest, and their own helmets. The first time she put her new flight suit on, she stood in front of the mirror and felt two emotions: Pride: "I've done it. I'm a flight nurse." *Alex, watch over me.*

Then: Abject terror. "What in the hell have I gotten myself into? I've got no clue what I'm doing." *Alex, watch over me!*

Kelly Peters, CJay's first preceptor when she was finally allowed to fly as a crew member, rather than as a ride-along observer told her: "The first three months doing this job you'll wonder why the hell you signed up for it. At six months, you will think, 'Okay. Maybe I can do it.' At one year, you'll know you can do it, because you have the physical skills and the critical thinking abilities. And, most importantly, you're not alone. You're part of a team."

Kelly turned out to be right.

At six months, CJay and Gus received their flight wings. They were official.

* * * * * *

107

"Hey, my beautiful Clare," CJay heard in her dream. She turned her face to Alex, dressed in his Coast Guard flight suit and his heavy jacket.

"Hey, my handsome husband," she smiled. Then he was naked and in her bed, with his hand running along the inside of her thigh. She spread her legs and he pushed himself inside of her, moving hungrily. She matched his motions with her hips, feeling his lips on her forehead, her ear, her checks, both sides of her mouth. She opened her mouth for his kiss, his tongue, feeling the pinpointing of her orgasm, then the rolling pulsations. She moaned aloud, pulling her dream around her.

Later, she remembered that he told her he loved her, he would always watch over her, and he wanted her to find joy. And love. Again.

I will always love you, she said to herself when she woke up. *But about that joy thing….* She shook her head sadly.

Chapter Fourteen

September went by quickly for CJay. It was getting cold, and there'd been some snow, but in subarctic Fairbanks, it doesn't really snow *that* much. Not so much snow as ice. Lots of ice during the winter. She remembered sailing through a few intersections in her car as if on skates before she quite mastered the art of stopping for traffic lights during the winter. After a while, she learned about the magic of tires with the three-peak mountain snowflake logo (3PMSf) from a Fairbanks cop passing through her emergency department.

She also learned that in Fairbanks, one says *'artic'* not *'arctic'*. "You're not from around here, are ya?" She knew she was still a 'Cheechako' – an Alaska newcomer – and would be for a long time.

CJay flew three or four shifts a week, sometimes doubling back for a 24-hour shift if staffing was tight or another nurse was ill. She swapped with a fellow crewmember for a shift on the fixed wing, and flew to Kotzebue to pick up a high risk pregnant mom with pre-eclampsia – high blood pressure caused by her pregnancy, which could conceivably cause the mom to have a stroke and lose the baby.

Those fixed wing flights could be harrowing, especially if the patient was in extremis – very sick and perhaps dying. Then, the flight nurse and paramedic were all he or she had. It was frightening, no matter how long one had been a flying caregiver.

Of course, weather can also be an issue. It is a little easier to fly in weather in a fixed wing than a helicopter, but that didn't make it any less "white knuckle" for the crew. But things had turned out well, both weather-wise and patient-wise. Mom, nervous to be in a plane, kissed her Inupiat husband good-bye, smiled bravely, and said, "When I come back, you will have a son. This is good."

And, she kept her promise, producing a healthy baby boy the next day. Her high blood pressure resolved immediately.

"I hope I never have to deliver a baby in the helicopter!" she told Gus later. "Shoot me!" They both laughed.

"You'll do fine," Gus said. "Between the two of us, we rock."

"Yes, we do. We surely do. But I *still* hope we don't have to deliver a baby in the helicopter!"

* * * * * *

CJay saw the trooper again on Sunday, October 1st in the NSMC triage office, flirting with her friend, Hunni, the triage nurse. He was sitting his fine butt casually on the edge of a gurney, laughing at something Hunni was telling him, his Stetson in his hand, his beautifully sculpted skull turned slightly towards her. His K-9 was on the floor. The dog looked up at the flight nurse, woofed and then wagged his damn tail.

110

Damn dog. The flight nurse felt her heart start to pound, and her skin tingle. Hunni was married with three daughters – no danger there, but CJay was surprised to find she was...jealous(?) – of all things. Then, Hunni caught her eye and waved her in to triage. *No!* The flight nurse turned to flee, but the triage nurse called her name and came to the door.

"Get back here, CJay! We were just talking about Aurora. I want you to meet Jeff."

Reluctantly, CJay turned around.

"We've actually met before, Hunni," the trooper said as he politely stood up to face CJay. "On a couple of responses for the AST... and once at the helipad." He smiled at her. "It's nice to see you again, CJay. How're you doing?"

I'm tongue tied looking at you. Then she realized she was looking at his shiny boots. She lifted her eyes, traveled up his dark blue pants *(Don't look at his groin!)*, past his lighter blue shirt with the AST patch on the arm and his Kevlar with his name embroidered on the front, and then up into his face. His slight smile. His hazel eyes on her. He extended his hand and she took it, like she had on the helipad the day of the 'dog and pony' show. His hand was warm. She could feel calluses.

Reluctantly, she let it go. "I...I'm fine, thank you, Sergeant. How are you? It's nice to see you again, too." *'Life is short and brutish.' I can't let my fear keep me from saying something.*

"Great talking to you, Hunni," the trooper said. "I need to get back on the road. Say 'hi' to Emmett for me. Tell him we need to take the boat out and catch a fish pretty quick before things ice up." He and CJay's friend hugged. The flight nurse knew her jaw

111

was hanging open and clapped it shut before the trooper could see her tonsils.

"I meant it when I said it was good to see you, CJay," he said as they walked down the hallway towards Dispatch, with his dog (Trygve, she remembered) at his left side.

"I see you're not in prison yet," she commented, looking up at him out of the side of her eyes.

"They haven't noticed that I'm not coming to work anymore," he said casually, seriously. Shrugging.

She suppressed a smile, but could feel her heart continuing to pound and knew her face was red. *Am I sweating, too?* She felt his warm presence by her side as he matched her steps. *I want to push you against that wall and put my legs around your waist. No, wait. I want YOU to push ME against that wall so I can put my legs around your waist…. What the fuck is the matter with me?*

Had she said that out loud?

Now she *knew* beyond the shadow of a doubt that she was blushing and sweating. Did he see it? Could he hear her breathing increase?

"You all right, CJay?" They'd reached the door to the Dispatch center and he spoke when they paused.

"I'm good, Sergeant. I just have some things on my mind, that's all." *David said to say 'yes' to you. If you ask me, Sergeant, I will say yes.* She turned to him expectantly. Hopefully.

"Well, this is where you were going I suppose, so I'll see you another time, perhaps," he said, saluting her casually with his right hand. "Fly safe." Then he turned and walked away, the dog

112

keeping pace. The good news was that she got to watch him leave with that easy gait, slim waist, and beautiful ass. The bad news was that – she had to watch him walk away. CJay was dismayed to find herself profoundly disappointed.

She heard the secondary line ringing as she walked in to dispatch. Big Mike was busy on the main line, so CJay picked up for him.

"CJay! Get back here," she heard Hunni whisper loudly on the other end.

"What?"

"Just come back to Triage."

Big Mike was looking at her, so CJay mouthed 'Be right back."

Hunni had a wide-eyed expression on her face and was almost vibrating at her desk with excitement (as she sometimes did) when the flight nurse arrived. CJay chuckled.

"What's up?"

"Okay. Jeff and I were talking…"

"…you know him?" CJay interrupted.

"Oh, yes! Known him for years. He and Emmett are friends from high school – in Wasilla. On the rugby team together."

Once again, CJay was speechless. *Does everyone know and love this man?*

"And…?"

"He was asking about Aurora, the crews, Gus – he knew Gus before he joined Aurora. And… *you*."

CJay stared at her. "Me."

Hunni laughed. "You, silly. Yes. He said he was really impressed by your 'demeanor and expertise' at the scene calls you ran together. He wanted to know if you're involved with anyone. I told him you'd been going with a firefighter, but broke up in February." Hunni suddenly looked frightened. "Did I say the wrong thing?"

"Is he a nice guy? A good guy?"

Hunni reached out with her left hand to get CJay's attention and made the hand sign with her right of two fingers in a V pointing from the flight nurse's eyes to her eyes. *Pay attention to me.*

"CJay, he's absolutely the very best."

Chapter Fifteen

"Aurora Dispatch, Fire Dispatch. We're requesting you for a motor vehicle crash on Steese Highway, auto versus Wainwright Stryker with serious injury and extrication in progress."

I hear Fire's request and hit "Save," shut down the computer, stand and grab my heavy coat. I see Gus on the surveillance camera already on the helipad helping Charlie and the mechanic button down the aft port cowling in preparation for the flight.

It's Thursday, 1430 – 2:30PM – and already dusky outside and definitely cold. It's not change of shift for several hours, but there's no telling how long this flight will take – or how much extrication will be involved.

I like extrication on the scene. I enjoy watching the firefighters figure out the logistics of how to stabilize the vehicles so no personnel are injured, how to cut away car doors, roofs, and other vehicles, especially if it's a "grinder" – high speed with the metal of each car becoming one with the other car. It's a real science. We practice this kind of thing on a semi-yearly basis with the local fire departments using wrecked cars and trucks for training purposes.

My partners and I climb inside vehicles at crash scenes to start IVs and maintain patient safety. Frequently, the firefighters put protective blankets over all of us, especially when there is glass breaking, sparks flying, or sharp pieces of steel threatening either us or the victims. I've intubated upside down, started IVs left handed and backwards. It's challenging and rewarding. On occasion, it can be a lot of fun.

It's always a learning experience.

While Charlie circles the scene before he puts Aurora in an open area near the site of the accident, Gus and I both check out the activity below. There are multiple emergency vehicles and several ambulances. The fire department's light plant (a truck with lights that turn the night to day) makes it easy to see the little black pick-up truck with its front end smashed clear back into the driver's compartment and I know this isn't going to be much fun. The heavily armored military Stryker vehicle from Fort Wainwright probably felt no more than a slight hiccup when the two of them front-ended.

Gus is lead, so he climbs out first and I follow, both of us pulling out the gurney, ducking under the blades and heading towards a fence where a firefighter has cut some barbed wire so we don't have to crawl through and rip our pants. I thank him on the way past.

The fire captain is one we've both worked with before and he directs us to the passenger truck.

"Watch your step, guys. It's really icy here. I think that's why she lost control – veered into the oncoming lane and nailed the Stryker. We're trying to get her truck pulled away enough to release her. The engine block's in her lap. She's awake and cooperative. One of our medic's got a line in her left arm, but you *need to get in there and take care of the rest. We need all hands on deck out here."*

He points me to the right-hand passenger door – or where the door used to be. The firefighters have removed it with the Jaws, cut the A and B front posts and pulled back the truck's roof to allow better access to the driver. I see it's a girl. Maybe sixteen or seventeen. Her face is bloody and I can clearly see that the truck's dash and firewall is up to her chest with the engine block not far behind. All I can think is "Fuck a duck."

Gus is already on the driver's side as I climb into the passenger seat and take over holding C-spine from a firefighter who scrambles out to get back to extricating her.

"I'm going to start another line, CJay. You will need to intubate her before they pull her out. She will need airway support immediately." He looks down at what we can see of her hips and I understand what he means. The dash, firewall, and engine block have crushed her legs and more than likely her pelvis. At this moment, the only thing keeping her from bleeding to death before our eyes is the fact that all that mass has acted as a hideous 400-pound metal and plastic airbag and is tamponading her lower body – keeping her from exsanguinating on the spot. When it is pulled away from her, she's going to decompensate, go into shock, lose consciousness, and we'll be lucky to get her back to the hospital alive.

She is going to die. We won't be able to save her. All we can do is not hurt her any more than she's already been hurt. I feel sorrow for her. I see her watching me. I put on my game face.

"Get us some long leg air splints," Gus shouts over the sounds of the generator and the hydraulic tools to the nearest paramedic. She hustles off to her rig to comply with his request.

I get close to her right ear. "Hi, sweetie," I ask. "What's your name?" I saw those eyes watch me when I climbed in beside her so I know she's conscious. I ask her name to check out just how alert she is. While she's answering, I place a C-Collar around her neck to hold it straight because I'm going to need both my hands in a moment.

"Rachel," she says as I move on to attempt to palpate as much of her chest as I can access for crepitus, cracked ribs, flail chest. Her chest seems to be more or less intact.

"Does this hurt when I press here?"

"No. But I can't feel my legs."

"We're going to get them unstuck here in a minute, Rachel. I'm going to…"

"Am I going to die?" she interrupts me. I can't look in her eyes and lie to her, but I don't have to. Gus puts his face close to her other ear and says clearly, "Not on our watch, Rachel. We're going to take care of you." He nods sharply at me. Get her intubated.Now. I understand his urgency.

"Please tell my Mom and Dad I love them." I tell her I will.

"Rachel, I'm going to help you breathe. I'm going to put a little tube down your nose into your lungs so I can take care of your breathing for you and you won't have to worry about it." I see her eyes go wide with fear. "It won't hurt, but it will feel weird and there will be some pressure. I need you to keep breathing

118

normally and when I say take a deep breath in, you need to do that for me. Don't fight me. Do you understand?"

She nods. I put two squirts of Afrin in each nostril to help reduce bloody trauma in the girl's nose during the procedure, then insert a #7 French intubation tube liberally slathered with a water based lubricant to help the tube pass through her nose into her pharynx and then into her lungs through the vocal cords. It's a quick slick process, especially when the person has good respirations to assist and a stable face – which she has.

"Breathe deep," I order, and she does. The ET tube slides into place and I fill the tube's cuff with air from the 20cc syringe hanging from the thin inflation line. Gus places the CO_2 detector cap on the end of our ambu-bag (which is hooked up to our O2 cylinder from the gurney) then onto her tube and gives her puffs of pure oxygen. The detector turns a friendly shade of yellow-tan, indicating proper placement in the lungs. Then I breathe for her with the bag and Gus auscultates lung sounds with his stethoscope on what he can reach of her chest, making a circle with his left thumb and forefinger and, nodding grimly, indicates both lungs are ventilating well. He secures the tube with twill tie and we wait for the firefighters to let us know when we can move her.

The car jolts and lurches as they pull the engine block away from the front. There's no wiggle room behind the driver's seat – no crew cab, no extended cab. I can't imagine a vehicle that could be worse for extrication than this medieval piece of crap truck. I can't hear her scream because the tube is preventing her from making any noise. But her hand grabs my arm, she looks at me, her frightened eyes locking onto mine, her brow grimacing with pain, and then I see the light begin to fade as she loses consciousness. I know that my face is the last face she will ever see. I'm so sorry, sweetheart, I tell her.

I will not cry.

"We're ready to get her out. You kids set?" the fire captain asks. We kids are. Gus has already asked for blankets to pad the fire department's backboard – to soak up blood, but also to provide warmth. It's freezing cold. The driver's seat is covered with blood. I crawl over it helping to get her transferred to the backboard. I feel the warm wet on my knees and shins through my wool leggings and flight suit pants that instantly becomes the icy wet in the outside air.

In a coordinated effort, we get her on the backboard, put on the air splints to provide some stability to her crushed legs and perhaps stanch some of the bleeding. One more lift and she's on our gurney and secured. We take her back through the barbed wire fence, one firefighter at each corner of the gurney with me bagging at the head. Gus climbs into the ship to help lock her in place.

Charlie's ready for us, and as soon as the tail is clear and we know we won't behead any ground personnel or an errant moose, we're in the air with four souls on board and a six-minute ETA. I know she's comfortable now. Her heart is still beating according to our Propaq monitor. We're running warm fluids into her. Her soul is still here.

Two minutes into the flight, I feel an icy finger touch my neck and run down my back under my flight suit. I'm so startled I *almost drop the ambu-bag I'm using to breathe for Rachel. My eyes slide past the Propaq monitor where I see a fast cardiac rhythm on the screen and then they latch onto Gus's eyes which are looking at me. He dives for a femoral pulse and I look for a carotid pulse under the C-collar. Nothing. Gus shakes his head, points to himself and pantomimes CPR – one-two thrusts of his hands. He unbuckles his seatbelt and positions his shoulders over her chest. I know he's singing* 'Staying Alive,' *in his head – the song that supposedly corresponds to the beat that saves lives.*

I know I'm *singing it.*

"Hot mike," I tell Charlie. I hold respirations for a moment and spike another bag of normal saline. Gus continues CPR. Rachel's heart is bravely beating, but it's empty. Her blood is no longer inside the cardiovascular system. We all know the statistics for success with traumatic CPR with Pulseless Electrical Activity – PEA. It's like…zip. But I breathe for her and Gus does CPR anyway, because we told Rachel we wouldn't let her die on our watch.

Since Charlie has called ahead for 'hot offload,' the trauma tech and two security guards are waiting at the helipad gate. With the blades still turning, Gus, the tech, and I pull Rachel's gurney out and put it on the ED's rolling gurney and I climb on board this time, straddling Rachel's hips, ducking to avoid the blades, and continuing our useless CPR. Out of the corner of my eye, I see photographers from the local TV station and also the News-Miner. Super, *I think. This is what Rachel's family needs now. At the ED, the tech takes over CPR and I jump down. My shoulders ache and I'm gasping for air. I'm crying.*

But, I can't think about it. I need to wash the fucking blood out of my pants and long underwear.

And off my boots. I pull off my gloves and throw them on the linoleum floor like some newbie intern. I have blood inside, on my hands….

The trauma team 'pronounces' Rachel within four minutes of her arrival in the main resuscitation room.

Yeah. Technically, we kept this sweet girl alive in our ship. We're good like that.

* * * * * *

Rachel's parents (Her blood covered driver's license was found in her pants pocket.) sat devastated and weeping in the ED Quiet Room. The Social Worker and hospital Chaplain were with them.

The mother immediately stood when Gus and CJay entered. The teen's father rose solemnly to shake their hands, and CJay was jolted to see he was wearing army BDUs, or fatigues, with a colonel's eagle velcroed on his chest.

CJay and Gus offered their support, telling the parents that the fire department had worked very hard to help get Rachel out of the car as quickly as possible so Aurora Flight could bring her back to Med Center for help.

"She wasn't awake when we transported her. We made her as comfortable as we could in the car. She was talking to us

122

then." CJay paused. "We are so sorry for this loss. She wanted you to know she loved you."

Her mother wept once more, then finally composing herself, said "Can we see her?" CJay glanced at Gus, who looked at the Social Worker, who nodded. They knew that except for the endotracheal tube in Rachel's nose, her face was relatively unmarked. Staff would wipe off the blood.

"Of course, you can see her," the Social Worker told them. "Are you ready for this?" She went on to tell them what to expect, how Rachel would look, what kinds of IVs and equipment they might see in the trauma room. She didn't want anything to be a surprise to these grieving parents.

"Can you pray with us?" the mother asked the Chaplain. And the six of them joined hands while the Chaplain asked for the grace of God to accompany them and to be with Rachel's spirit.

"What the heck, Gus. His kid was hit by his own post's Stryker vehicle. What a fucking mess. No mom deserves to lose her baby," CJay muttered when they finally finished restocking and cleaning the blood out of their ship. She'd changed into the clean spare flight suit she kept in her locker after taking a quick shower. The two spent the rest of the shift writing reports and not speaking.

CJay anticipated she'd sleep poorly that night. What a sad situation. Just not fair. The only thing that made her feel better was that she'd see David in four days. They'd have fun together.

Now, she just needed to put that fucking flight completely out of her mind.

Chapter Sixteen

Hunni caught CJay just after the flight nurse had changed uniforms and stepped into the chapel, slumping down on the last pew facing the plain altar with the fake stained glass window feature behind it. Hunni sat down next to her friend and put her arm around her. At that simple gesture, CJay released a sob and let the tears flow. Hunni pulled her close.

"This was a rough one, wasn't it? I think it hit us all pretty hard in the resusc room, too."

CJay wiped her eyes on her flight suit sleeve and straightened, snuffling up her runny nose. "The mom and dad – it just sucks. Nobody should ever have to see their child die."

Hunni nodded and handed her friend a crumpled Kleenex from her pocket. She had three daughters. "My middle girl...she's Rachel's age. Yeah. I can't even begin to imagine...." Her voice trailed off. "Listen, CJay. Melanie, Caron, and I are going out to the Pump House after shift. Why don't I stop by your place and pick you up? You don't have to be alone tonight. I'll be your designated driver and you can have some wine and food and be with your friends. How 'bout it?"

CJay looked at her. Then slowly nodded her head. "Yeah. I'd like that. I'd like it a lot. Thanks, Hunni."

Aurora flight nurses work 12-hour shifts with no guaranteed lunch period. Their shifts start at 0630 and 1830 and end (barring change of shift flights) 12 hours later. Passover report takes 15 minutes and the majority of the time off-going nurses are driving out of the parking structure at the 50-minute mark. Tonight was no different. CJay made it home and was waiting in her civilian clothes for Hunni when the ED nurse arrived at 7:30PM.

CJay reassured her that she was 'fine,' and looking forward to some food and laughter with her friends. And some music – because the Pump House had a live band venue, and CJay knew from reading the *News-Miner* that "The Eclectics," a band from Delta Junction, was headlining the entire week.

The restaurant was jammed and CJay and her three friends waited in the noisy bar until their reserved table was ready in the other room which was away from the music and quieter for talking. The flight nurse treated her friends to a round of drinks as they shouted to one another over the band. Hunni excused herself to use the ladies' room.

"CJay," Hunni hissed to her friend when she returned to the bar.

"Hunni," the flight nurse hissed back.

"Guess who's in the next room?"

CJay wrinkled her nose and shrugged her shoulders. *Not a clue, Hunni.* "I dunno. Super Heroes?"

"No. but pretty doggone close!" She giggled. "Jeff is there with some of his trooper buddies. I let him know to watch out for some wild women comin' his way!"

You've got to be kidding. And now he knows I'm going to be there too.

It was even worse than she anticipated. Their table was two away from the Trooper and his five friends and by the time she got to her seat, she had direct line of sight contact with him. He saw her and dipped his head in acknowledgement. CJay held her head high and indicated with a chin lift that she'd seen him. His eyes lingered on hers before he looked away, and the flight nurse felt the color rise in her face. *You are very fine and I am miserable tonight.*

The women ordered. CJay opted for Chicken Caesar salad and another glass of chardonnay. She was hungry and the second generous glass of wine, coupled with the scant Romaine lettuce, garlic croutons, chicken bits and parmesan cheese mixture hit her hard. She knew she was starting to relax, but didn't worry. *Hunni's my DD. She'll get me home tonight.*

Several times, she looked up and saw him glance away. His group was interacting, but he had time to look at her. Finally, as she finished up the last of the lettuce, she made up her mind. She stood.

"I'm going to ask the Trooper to dance," she whispered to Hunni. Hunni glanced up quickly. Uh, okay, she indicated, with arched eyebrows – and a questioning, lopsided smile.

CJay saw the Trooper look at her as soon as she stood and watched his eyes follow hers as she strode to his table. "Can a flight nurse ask a trooper to dance?" she asked when she reached his chair.

Chapter Seventeen

He watched her stand and march his way. *I don't know what she's about to do, but she looks determined.* Several other of his troopers and the lone female at his table followed his eyes and sat back as the woman approached them.

"Can a flight nurse ask a trooper to dance?" He could see the smiles on the faces of his team, and knew the ball was now in his court. He felt himself blush like a high-schooler. He cleared his throat.

"Of course," he said pushing back his chair and standing. A chorus of hoots followed as his AST Peer Support Team board members cheered him on. *I will personally kill all of you tomorrow.* He glared at them. They smiled back. The team's female Mental Health coordinator winked and did a tiny fist bump his way. *You're all off the team.*

CJay put her hand in the crook of his arm and led him into the other room where the band, "The Eclectics," was playing. He saw the drummer look up and raise a drumstick his way, and the bass player add an extra riff to his part.

"You know them?" she asked and turned to face him at the edge of the dance floor.

"I've arrested the bass player and the drummer twice for possession with intent. They still like me." He saw her laugh and pulled her close. The song was a slow dance, but ended immediately, and segued into a Texas two-step.

"You ready for this, Trooper?"

"Born ready," he said, and took her loosely into a two-step embrace. He saw her surprise and then her pleasure as she realized he knew how to dance. *I'm not just a dumb cop, flight nurse.*

His felons then shifted into old school with "The Tennessee Waltz."

"This is why they're called 'The Eclectics,'" he told her when she shook her head at the rapid change of musical pace. He put his arm around her and propelled her into a three step. He saw her stifle a laugh.

"Where did you learn to dance?"

"I wanted to go to the Senior Prom. Knew I needed to learn. My grandmother taught me."

"Your *Grandmother?*" This time she did laugh out loud. "She must be an excellent instructor. You're good."

"She has many talents," he acknowledged.

The sergeant glanced up and caught the eye of the drummer who nodded his way, and immediately, the music slowed as the band pulled out a romantic dance "for all the lovers at the Pump House." *I've trained them well....*

He felt her soften. He tried not to pull her close, but he wanted to feel her body against his. He wanted to feel her breasts against his chest and her pelvis close to his. Face it. *I*

129

want her naked and in my arms. He deliberately held back and kept her at a respectful distance. But she pulled his left hand close to her breasts and pushed as close as she could into his body. *Oh, crap. Don't do this to me, CJay.*

Too soon the slow song ended and the band busted out with the "Electric Slide." He could see her watching his feet, an amused expression on her face. He saw her eyes slide up his pants, lingering a moment on his groin before glancing up at his face. He caught her eye – and winked. And he saw her laugh out loud.

"I like your smile," he mouthed at her over the music.

"Thank you," she replied back, her eyes half lidded in what he perceived to be her version of a sexy gaze. Whatever it was, it worked on him. He was aroused, making it somewhat difficult to be the Texas Ranger of the dance floor here at the Pump House.

Once again, the music slowed, but when he took her in his arms this time, there was no pretense. He pulled her close and she wrapped her arm around him, and held his big warm hand tightly to her body, between them.

At that moment, Hunni tapped her hesitantly on her shoulder. "Uh, CJay," he heard her say. "We're leaving…." She left the unspoken question up in the air.

What is the flight nurse going to say? He felt her loosen her grip on him. He glanced down at her, relaxing his arms...and raised his eyebrows at her hesitation. Then, he spoke.

"Hunni, if it's okay with CJay, I can see her home. She'll be safe with me."

He saw a moment of concern pass over Hunni's face before she said, "Okay Jeff. CJay – you all right with that?"

"I am, Hunni. And thank you for inviting me out tonight." CJay released her grip on the Trooper long enough to quickly embrace her friend. "Seriously, thank you. I'll see you day after tomorrow at work."

She accepted his offer of a drink and he held her hand as they found two places at the bar. He ordered a Bud Light, and she asked for another chardonnay. "I need to settle my bill, CJay. Can you wait for a minute?" She nodded.

When he returned, he saw her head bent over the drinks. It looked like she was massaging her temples. "Are you having a sacred moment with our beverages?" He put his hand on her shoulder as he took the seat next to her.

"I was just thinking you're a good dancer. I enjoyed being out there on the floor with you."

He smiled. "Had I but known that dancing would be the thing that got us out together, I'dve asked sooner."

"Well, thank you for dancing with me tonight."

I could dance with you all night long, CJay. "Likewise, flight nurse. You look considerably happier now than you did when you first got here."

He could almost see the wheels turning in her head, trying to think of what to say to him.

"It was a bad day, Trooper. The girls asked me to go out with them for dinner."

"Why didn't you leave with them? I'm glad you stayed, but..."

She smiled.

131

"You're smiling. Is that a good thing?"

"I wanted to be with you tonight. It's a woman's prerogative to change her mind. Is that too forward for you, Trooper?"

He smiled back and raised his Bud Light to toast her. Then they both drank and chatted with their heads close together because of the loud music. When her drink was finished, the Trooper helped the flight nurse on with her coat and guided her out to the edge of the parking lot where his Subaru Forester was parked under the street light.

She told him where she lived and when he parked at the curb in front, he held the car door as she got out, then walked with her up the slippery steps to her door.

"Come in for some coffee, Sergeant. I'm making some for myself anyway."

Watch it, Sergeant. Easy boy. He hesitated, took a breath, considered some more, then said, "Thank you, CJay. I'd like that." She took his jacket when they were inside and hung it on a coat rack inside the front door, then went into the kitchen. The Trooper waited in the living room.

Her living room was mostly uncluttered – some modern furniture, some lamps, Alaskan art and photography. But there were bookcases and books everywhere. He spotted family pictures on a crowded bookshelf and inspected several, including one with CJay in a simple, long white wedding dress in a park, casually dangling a sheaf of wild flowers while a good-looking young man dressed in Coast Guard Class As, including a sword, kissed her cheek. Her face had a luminous glow, detectable even in the black and white photo.

132

Husband? Where is he now? If she still displays that picture….

What's going on, he wondered. It was obvious she was flirting with him now, despite turning him down three times. She could not have pressed herself closer to him when they were dancing if she'd wanted to. *She was actually smelling me!* He also knew her body was both soft and firm in the right places and his hormonal self wanted her naked in his arms in her soft bed. Thrashing about...and very sweaty.

The sergeant shook his head then passed through her small dining area, past a cozy table for six people and more bookcases, and into her kitchen. Small, with nice appliances. He could tell she liked to cook. He saw heavy enamel clad pots, wooden and metal utensils hanging from a rack, and – unexpectedly – an herb garden in her kitchen window. And a grow light. He checked the pots. That really *was* oregano.

She handed him a coffee grinder filled with beans to him to grind. Then, she pulled out a French press coffee maker from the cupboard. Two coffee cups. A tea kettle was already heating on a gas flame.

Finally, she turned to him. "How do you like your coffee?"

"Black," he said.

She nodded. "Me, too. Like my heart."

Really?

The tea kettle boiled, and she took the beans he'd ground, measured them into the French press, and poured water over them. Then she turned to him, suddenly shy.

"I...uh...this was a bad day. I enjoyed dancing with you. It made me feel good." She flushed red.

"Well...um...and here we are with coffee. I enjoyed dancing with you, too." He paused, then added, "I think you already know that I find you attractive."

She nodded. After a long pause she finally said quickly, "Sergeant, I don't want to be alone tonight."

His situational awareness alerted and he changed the subject. "I saw you on the 6 o'clock news, CJay – doing CPR on that girl."

She poured their coffee into two mugs and went back into the living room. He followed and sat where she indicated – the left side of the sofa. CJay sat on the other half of the sofa.

"Rodeo CPR," she said. "Always looks dramatic, doesn't it? Doesn't feel that way, and her parents don't need to see it, either. I know it will be on the front page of the paper in the morning. Above the fold."

"Probably," he acknowledged.

"I don't want to be alone tonight," she repeated.

He was silent for several long moments until he finally asked her, quietly, "What does that mean to you, CJay?"

Unexpectedly, she turned towards him and ended up on her knees next to him – facing him, her left thigh tight against his left thigh. "I don't want to be alone tonight. Do I need to say it slower? I...don't...want...to... be...alone tonight."

He coughed, cleared his throat. Her left arm wandered over to his right shoulder and then cupped his neck. "Do you mean you want me to stay here tonight?" he asked, aware of her closeness.

She nodded. And pulled him towards her.

"On your sofa? What about that vow of celibacy for the rest of your life?"

She hesitated. "This...I.... God." She turned back around and sat down on the sofa, not touching him. "I'm sorry." He could see her face redden. "You've got to think I'm nuts. You want me to be honest?"

"Oh, yes, please." He turned as much as he could to look at her directly, and saw tears in her eyes. He reached for her and she allowed him to put his arms around her and pull her close. "I'm sorry you had a bad flight."

"She was seventeen years old. She shouldn't have died. She didn't deserve that."

Tell me about it. "What can I do to help right now?"

She kissed the side of his lips, and then she kissed his lips, fully on. The Trooper's body responded as it generally does in red-blooded males, and it took all of his integrity and professionalism not to lay her down and take off her pants.

I can do pity sex, he realized.

He pulled back. "CJay, I can't do this." *Please don't think I don't want to.* "This is taking advantage, and I don't want to do that to you."

"You don't want to? You don't *want* to?"

He saw embarrassment? anger? on her face, and she pulled away and stood up. He knew she was saying "Fuck You" in her head, but not out loud.

"Look at the time," she said, holding out her wrist with the watch on it. "You must be exhausted and surely you have to work tomorrow. Let me get your coat." She grabbed his jacket off the hook by the door and threw it at him. "You know your way out. 'Bye now. Be safe. Thanks for the dancing."

She turned away, walked through the tiny dining room area, through the kitchen, and he heard a door open, then shut in the back somewhere.

I have been summarily dismissed. Be gone, knave. Well, I think not. He put his untasted cup of coffee down, shrugged on his jacket and took hers off the hook next to where his had been, and went through the kitchen to the outside door off her laundry room. Through the window he saw her sitting on a tiny side porch, hugging her arms around herself in the bitter cold. He opened the door, stepped outside and stood there. He distinctly heard her say, "Please go the flaming fuck away."

"Not 'til I've had a chance to clarify things, CJay." He draped her coat over her shoulders and was gratified when she put it completely on. He helped her with it. Then he sat down next to her.

"Why don't you just go away?"

"You know I like you, right?" he asked, ignoring her 'Why don't you just go away' question, repeated for a third time.

"I guess."

You guess? "I've asked you out three times and you've said 'no' each time. Doesn't that qualify as maybe I like you?"

"It definitely means you're persistent."

He smiled and nodded, but ignored the comment. "And tonight you ask me to dance, and then ask me to come have coffee in your home, and then try to get me in the sack."

"Yeah. I can't deny that."

He saw her hand come up to her face and rub her eyes. "There are two things I no longer do," he told her.

"You've become a monk?"

He laughed out loud. "Not yet. Not by a long shot. But I don't take advantage and I don't do hook-ups. I don't want a hook-up with you, CJay."

"What *do* you think you want from me?" She glanced sideways at him. He could see her frowning in the light from the street lamp at the front of her house.

"You scare me, CJay."

She snorted in disbelief.

He chuckled. "I want dinner with you. I want talk from you. I just want to get to know you better. That's it."

"It made me happy to dance with you, Sergeant."

"Good. Perhaps we can do that again, sometime."

"Perhaps."

"May I be honest with you?"

She sighed deeply and rolled her eyes. "Of course. Oh, *puhleeze* be *honest* with me." He could almost see the sarcasm drip from her pretty lips.

"CJay," he said finally. "We don't even know one another. You can't even say my name. Please don't take this wrong, but you won't go out to pizza with me, and yet you want me in your bed?" *Trust me, I'd love that, too, but….*

He saw her face turn even more crimson...again – with embarrassment, anger, shame? "You're right. Like I said, it's just been a crap day. Forget it." She pressed her lips tight, then snapped, "Just *forget* it."

"Let me finish. The very last thing I want is a one-night hook-up with you. I'd like a relationship that means something – not just a temporary antidote."

"I'm sorry I said anything to you. I was way outta line and stupid, too. Not your fault, Sergeant. You're a swell guy. But just go away. Go home to your...*dog*."

That went well. "I'm sorry your shift was rough, CJay, but I don't want to be your short term emotional 'Mr. Fix-it' for what you had to deal with today. I'm looking for more than that. Personally, I'd like to see you again sometime when your day *hasn't* sucked. When we can just go have fun together."

"Good *night,* Sergeant." She kept her face turned away from him, but he could see her embarrassment.

Yes, that went very well indeed. He started to laugh – at himself and at the total weirdness of the evening as he stood up, went back through the kitchen and out the front door.

The porch light snapped off before he even reached the driveway.

* * * * * *

Dear Lord, CJay. If this were ten years ago, I'd be 'with you' on the sofa, the dining room table, then in your bed, then maybe again at 2AM, and most definitely at 0600 before I go to work. But

138

I'm not 25 anymore, and I have a career to protect. I don't want tomorrow morning to be filled with regrets and your accusations and my losing my job. You are so beautiful to me, and I'd love to take your clothes off and fuck you until you beg for sweet mercy. But not this way….

* * * * * *

CJay shut off the lights in the front of the house, and walked back to her bedroom, leaving the bedside lamp off. She sat on the bed and put her head in her hands.

Stupid, stupid, stupid, Clare. Next time just be cool. Keep your emotions to yourself. Tough it out. Bury it. Deny it. Suck it up. She smacked her forehead with her right hand. *Idiot. I just made a fool of myself with the Trooper. I humiliated myself. He probably thinks I'm a freak simpleton who uses sex as a survival skill – a coping mechanism. And has no boundaries, either. Maybe he's right. On both counts.*

She shook her head sadly as a tear rolled down her cheek. *No. More.*

Chapter Eighteen

CJay spent the next few days on high alert – looking for the Sergeant so she could avoid him. Hunni caught her in the dispatch hallway two days after the abortive tryst and asked how the rest of her evening had gone with "Jeff." Just ducky, CJay replied. We had coffee and then he left. I'm glad you asked him to dance, Hunni shared. He's a respectable guy.

And I'm a humiliated, mixed-up slut, Hunni. I can't even begin to tell you. And you can bet I won't!

* * * * * *

"Hey! CJay! Wait up, girl."

CJay slowed and turned around when she heard Kelly Peters' voice behind her. They both went into dispatch, ready to start their Sunday day shift.

Kelly was an experienced flight paramedic and had helped mentor CJay in those first few weeks of the new flight nurse's training. Kelly'd flown for a few years with one of the nation's premier flight programs, CareLift, out of Seattle, but met a firefighter/paramedic in the North Star ED during a long distance interfacility transport from Fairbanks back to Spokane. After that flight, Kelly and the firefighter kept up their texting and skyping. She was in love. And, so was he. Now what?

North Star was thrilled to receive her application and flew her up for the interview. Because of her knowledge, experience, and teaching skills, she was hired on the spot. Kelly and Kevin, her Fairbanks Fire husband of eight years, married immediately. CJay and Chad had even double dated with them several times over the year that Chad and she were together.

"Wahoo, girl! Everyone's talking about you and your trooper! I'm so happy for you! It's about time," she finally exploded after the two greeted Big Mike, their day shift dispatcher, and set down their backpacks.

"Trooper?"

Kelly guffawed and put her arm around her friend.

"I don't *have* a trooper, Kelly," CJay repeated, shame and embarrassment making her face flush.

"EMS in Fairbanks is a small world, CJay. I've told you that. Everybody saw you two dirty dancing at the Pump House and knows he took you home that night." Kelly raised an eyebrow at her colleague and did a little pelvic thrust.

CJay's face colored a dark pink. "We didn't do anything. We had coffee, that's all. Then he went away."

"'Coffee?' Is that what they're calling it these days? Wish I had a little 'coffee' like that – puhleeze." She heh-heh-heh'd lasciviously. "Have I told you that I like my 'coffee' like I like my Death Stars?" Smirking, she went on "'Big, dark, and powerful enough to destroy a planet.'"

Anger bubbled up hot inside CJay. "Kelly! Nothing happened. Stop it," she hissed. She could feel her throat tightening and her tear ducts constricting. She coughed and turned away from her friend. "Nothing happened, goddammit. *Nothing*." She emphasized the final 'Nothing.'

Kelly was silent, then she spoke softly. "You want to talk about it?"

The flight nurse said nothing.

"You okay? CJay – what did he *do* to you?" There was genuine angry concern for her friend in the paramedic's voice.

"Nothing! And I've never been better, Kelly." She didn't add the 'freakin'' she wanted to add because Mike was talking on the AST frequency and the last thing she needed was for listening ears to hear her yapping about her abortive evening with the Sergeant.

"Okay, then. You wanna hear about Chad?" Kelly asked next.

"Kelly, you know I love you, right?" Kelly nodded. "Why the f..." CJay mouthed the f-word "...would I want to hear about Chad?" Her heart twisted. More pain. Damn.

"He's disappeared. Evidently, he jumped into that F250 of his and drove off yesterday. No one knows where he is."

"Just why are you telling me this?"

"He hasn't been the same since you two broke up, CJay."

"He broke up with me, Kelly. And, besides, what he does is *not* my business and I'm truly sorry if he's 'not the same,' but he's been covering it up pretty well with all the gossip about him and his red-headed nurse girlfriend from South Africa – per the Fairbanks EMS telegraph you keep talking about. And I'm sorry." CJay was angry. "You wanna know something, Kelly? I haven't been the same since…." she stopped. "Never mind. It's not your fault."

"What, CJay?"

Chad's not the same? Well, whoop-de-do and booyah. Kelly, I haven't been the same since Alex died. And I never will be. CJay took a slow deep breath and then blew it out quietly. "I'm sorry, Kelly. It's not your fault. Shit happens and I'm sorry for Chad. I hope he shows up safe." She put her hand on Kelly's arm. "Let's just pre-flight and we can talk later. By the way, I don't have a Trooper. This one you just gotta trust me on."

He's running like the wind and he should. I'm obviously a crazy woman.

CJay and Kelly pre-flighted the aircraft on the helipad, making sure the ship was prepared for the day. They talked about Kelly and Kevin's daughter – now five and going to kindergarten – as they worked, and about CJay's brother, the deputy from Oregon. CJay mentioned David's class coming up – a peer support crisis training or something for emergency services personnel following bad stuff. Kelly said she'd heard of that, knew the Troopers had a crisis program of some sort, and kinda wished the fire department could get on board. Bad things can mess up the home life, she added, softly.

* * * * * *

Aurora I was requested shortly after that. It was a quick out and back for another moose versus truck. Glancing blow, but smashed truck and shaken driver. Animal control was contacted,

143

and the moose's carcass was retrieved so the meat could be donated. The animal had come only partially through the windshield, but the hind hooves had slashed the driver's face and right shoulder. Had there been a right front seat passenger, there would have been major fatal crush injuries to that individual. But, there were only lacerations which needed treatment, and no loss of consciousness to the driver.

"Am I going to die?" he'd asked CJay, with fear and pain.

"Not on our watch," she said, thinking of Gus with Rachel. *Not on our watch. We do CPR until we get to the ED and then…then you get to die.* CJay closed her eyes. *I'm so sorry, Rachel. And Chad – I'm so sorry.*

At 1030, Big Mike checked the security camera at the dispatch door and opened it for a flower delivery - a single red rose with greenery and some baby's breath in a simple white ceramic cylinder.

"CJay, Dispatch. Flowers for you."

"Yeah, you don't have a trooper, CJay," Kelly snorted.

"Fuck you, Kelly,"

Her paramedic laughed out loud.

"I enjoyed dancing with you. Perhaps we can do that again. Jeff." She tore up the note in dispatch – her face flaming with shame – and gave the flowers to the girls in ED Registration.

Chapter Nineteen

Gus and CJay came back on shift the next morning, relieving Tommy, the pilot, Judy – his flight paramedic wife, and Jacque Rose, who'd swapped a fixed wing shift with another nurse for a helo night shift. They all chatted for a bit, and then Gus and CJay did their morning pre-flight.

"You look like you have had a rough night," Gus observed, watching CJay as she checked through the Thomas trauma bag. "You are okay?"

"Just a lot on my mind, Gus."

"Do you want to talk about it?" Gus asked. "What is going on now?"

"I'm not quite sure, Gus. A couple of things in the past few days. You know – Rachel. Don't need to talk about it. I'm fine."

Gus nodded. "I can listen, CJay. We are here together all day today. But, are you all right? We need to be 100% for our shift."

"I understand. And, I will be. Sorry." She patted his hand and smiled. "It's all good. I'm good."

"Well, I am glad we are all good." He strapped down the EKG monitor, and turned to get out of the helicopter. "I am going to get some breakfast. Do you want something from downstairs?"

"No, Gus. Thank you. I'll see you in dispatch. Not really hungry." She smiled again, hoping it looked genuine.

"That smiley thing you are doing with your face does not look genuine," he told her before he continued on to the helipad gate.

Gus knew her way too well.

CJay was not used to being emotional. As a nurse, she was used to doing what needed to be done, unemotionally, and with expertise. Perfect storm of events right now. Starting with the crash on Steese Highway, the upcoming anniversary of Alex's death. Her stupid stupid *stupid* humiliating actions with that trooper. The rose. Her face flamed in embarrassment and shame.

And then the news that Chad had disappeared. She was sorry for what he was going through – knew it was her *fault,* but also knew she hadn't done it deliberately.

But the Sergeant. He was just a man, yet everything about him stirred her to the tips of her steel-toed boots. His physical attractiveness, his face, the shape of his head and those beautiful hazel eyes. His shoulders. His gentle hands. His mouth. His easy stride. His sense of humor. His sense of honor. His kindness. His common sense. Even the way his ears lay against his head. His warm skin. His strength and courage. His willingness to put himself in harm's way to make life safer for others. He was a walking embodiment of the word *Hero.* She had responded this way only once before – with Alex.

God. Why did life have to be so complicated and full of potential pain. And death. He did not deserve her sadness and memories.

* * * * * *

David called five days later before CJay was awake – at 0730 – an unheard of sleep-in for her, but she hadn't really dropped off until 0430. She swam to the surface when her cell played her brother's ring tone – *'Da Dum'* - the signature notes from a long-running TV series about New York City cops and lawyers.

"Hey, sleepy head," he replied cheerily when she croaked "hello" into the phone.

"David, hi. Sorry. Didn't sleep good last night." Dreams of Rachel, Alex, death, bloody gloves, humiliation, and irreconcilable loss had kept her restless and tearful in her sheets.

"I won't keep you long, Clare. Just wanted to confirm you're picking me up at the airport after class."

God. That's today. She willed herself to wake up. "Of course, David. Of course."

"Cool. Clare, I can't tell you how great these first two days have been. It's just unbelievable."

"Well, you're going to have to tell me all about it when we get together tonight." She sat up in bed, forcing herself now to sound enthusiastic. "Now, explain again exactly kind of a class it is? You sound pretty pumped for someone who usually hates conferences and big crowds."

147

"I do – but it's that peer support and group crisis training thing. The Sheriff's department wants to get a support group started in the department, so they volunteered me to take this class along with two chaplains, one mental health person, and three more deputies. Like I mentioned before, it's for helping after line of duty deaths, multiple casualty calls, kid calls, close to home calls, stuff like that. We usually call those teams 'cry baby squads" or 'Tissue Teams,' and the last thing I wanted to do was waste three days sitting on my ass listening to some jerk-off shrink pontificate about 'sharing your feelings.'"

"And yet, there you are. I'm still marveling that they chose you to start some sort of 'Tissue Team.'" CJay was definitely waking up now.

David laughed. "Yeah, me too. If I wouldn't have had visiting you to look forward to, I'da for sure dug in my heels and suggested they put their invitation where the sun don't shine. It's your fault I'm here."

Great. Another thing I'm to blame for. "I can think of worse reasons for you to come up. Glad I could help."

"Uh, one other thing?" He paused. "The co-instructor lives up there – he's just an absolutely extraordinary trainer – law enforcement – a trooper. There was a lot of teaching, and a boatload of role playing – which I loathe with a passion – but what a great way to learn! My group and I took him out for pizza last night and picked his brain about starting the support team. He gave us a lot of suggestions, resources, and even his team's protocols. When I grow up, I wanna to be just like him – professionally and as a human."

"And, David? Your point…?" She yawned, trying to stifle it so David wouldn't hear.

"Uh, well I kinda invited him to dinner tomorrow night." There was a long pause. "Is that okay?" CJay pictured David with his "He followed me home – can I keep him?" look on his face, and grinned, honestly.

She laughed out loud. "You're so cute. Of course. Bring your new best friend to dinner, David. I'll just make more red sauce."

CJay climbed out of bed. Her conversation with her brother lifted her spirits and she knew a run would make her feel even better – more energetic – and would also distract her. If Rachel came up, she immediately thought of something else. If the trooper came up, she pushed those thoughts down. When Alex came up, she said a prayer of blessing. *I will always love you. Now, what shall I buy to eat for tonight and the weekend? Steak, ribs, chicken Italian something?*

She planned the grocery list in her head, making sure to remember beer and wine, two baguettes for garlic bread, cheese, vegetables, a couple of yams, and ice cream. She smiled at people she met on her run. She breathed deeply of the cold air. She whispered "Be safe, Chad" as she ran by Fairbanks Fire Station 1 on Cushman. *I do hope someone finds his body….*

She tidied the house and put the dishwasher through its paces. The guest bed had clean sheets and there was even a tiny space in the packed closet for David to hang a shirt.

She marinated the ribeye steaks she'd decided to buy in chopped garlic and olive oil with generous ground pepper, and wrapped up the chicken breasts that would become Chicken

149

Parmesan after she pounded them flat the next day. She drank some tea, then picked her brother up at 1900 at FAI – Fairbanks International Airport. He met her at the curb, embracing her, after breaking away from conversation with hugs and handshakes in the terminal with several people she could see through the windows of baggage claim.

"Look at you, David," she said once she was back on the road. "Looking gregarious and making friends in Fairbanks already? Who were those people you were talking to in there?"

"They were students in the class from this area – a couple firefighters, one Fairbanks PD, chaplains, three state troopers, and that co-instructor from my class! What a great group!"

"Did you enjoy yourself?"

"I can't begin to tell you how happy I am that I got to take this course!"

"Excellent. Let's go home, drink beer, and put steaks on the grill. I'm all ears."

* * * * * *

They sat down to steaks at 8:30PM after a couple of beers and some unwinding time catching up on family news. Patty, their mom, had been "blue" per David for the past couple of weeks, like CJay had been.

"I learned about that in class, Clare. It's pretty common for people to start feeling down on the anniversary – maybe not even know why. And holidays – well, Thanksgiving, Christmas – and even Valentine's – all are colored by what happened. I know I've felt that." He reached over and patted CJay's arm.

"Hmmm," CJay replied. "Yeah. No kidding." *That's what the MFT counselor told me.* "Tell me more. Anything *besides* death, carnage, pain, despair, tragedy, grief and sorrow?"

"Survival and resilience." CJay raised an eyebrow. "We can get burned out doing what we do – taking care of others, protecting, seeing people die, risking our own lives. What this support training does is help us to help each other – our coworkers – stay on the job healthy and mentally intact. Decreases tension in the home, reduces stress at work, helps us deal with the drama and tragedy we see on an everyday basis. Also, makes us stronger – encourages bounce back – learning from our mistakes, but also learning from good things that happen – making us wiser, more empathetic, stronger, kinder. Saner."

CJay sat back in the chair and looked at him. "All this in three days? Sounds like you *really* drank the Kool-Aid," she muttered, trying not to sound too skeptical. *Rachel kept me up last night. When the light left her eyes…. And Alex, too.... And my own humiliation….*

CJay shook her head – David was still yakking.

"…you should take the class, too! Listen, the trooper instructor, Jeff, taught about traumatic stress, 'Flight or Fight' – 'cuz the animal brain is wired to run from danger before it will fight, critical events, and helped proctor the role-playing scenarios. He shared about his own 'critical incident' in Afghanistan that changed his perspective. He said crisis support

151

kept him from doing something stupid or tragic. He also talked about how important these peer and group discussion skills became for him and the AST after the deaths of two of his troopers who were killed in Mantishka this past Spring. I've learned a lot this week. About myself, I mean, and The Job. I'm actually kinda excited about us going back to Lane County and getting a similar peer support program rolling in the department. Seriously, we all need it."

Goody for you, David Dumbhead.

David was quiet for a moment, then said abruptly, "He's got tattoos."

She looked at him. "Who the hell are you talking about now? Who has tattoos?"

"Jeff. He shared in one of the class portions he taught that everyone has different ways of coping with the things they experience on The Job. One of his ways is memorializing events or people he cares about with a tattoo." David held up his left arm and ran his hand along the tender inside part of his upper arm.

"And?"

"He tattooed the names of six of his marine buddies on his inner arm after they were killed."

"Why'd he do that?"

"Well, for one thing, he's a Marine. But, they were all supposed to go on patrol together, and Jeff got sick. Food poisoning. So, he didn't go on patrol. Their armored vehicle hit an IED. Two were killed instantly and when the other four scrambled out of it, they were ambushed. Shot."

"God, David. That's a terrible story."

152

"He knew about traumatic stress by then, but was tormented by the fact that he hadn't been there with them."

"But he would have been killed, too."

"Survivor's guilt, Clare. It's pretty powerful. He knows that too, but it didn't make it any easier, because *we* always think that if only we'da been there, it might have been different. *And,* why did *I* survive and *they* didn't? Why did *I* get sick and not one of them instead? He said he has a picture of them by his desk at home so that he can see them every day and say a prayer. He has his dog tags there, near them."

"And the tattoo inside his arm?"

"Tattoos." Dave corrected. He stopped, swallowed, cleared his throat, paused, then went on, his voice hoarse. "He says he hopes the pain he endured having their names inked there 'can somehow take away a bit of the pain and fear they went through when they were killed.'" He made a face, then bent his head and rubbed his eyes.

She reached over and grabbed David's hand, then released it. She could feel her tear ducts spasming. *There is something so very wrong with me.*

"Jeff's a good man," David finally said.

"Wow. That's pretty incredible," she replied, breathing out carefully.

"You okay?"

"This Trooper Jeff, huh? What's he look like?" *No no no no no God no…. Simply* not *possible.*

David smiled and winked at her. "Uh, let me just say that every female in the class would have loved to've gone out to pizza with us last night. During breaks, he was surrounded at all times by questioning students with fluttering eyelashes."

"What does he look like, David?" CJay repeated precisely through clenched teeth. Her brother looked at her quizzically.

"Six-two, shaved head, lean. I heard several women say..." he lilted his voice, mimicking swooning females "'...Oh, his shoulders are to *die* for.' He was a hit. No ring, either. A number of girls were discussing that."

"Jeepers, David. What's. His. Name?" Her voice was getting higher and thinner.

"Jeff."

"Jeff WHAT?" CJay wanted to scream at him, her eyes wide.

"Jeff Douglas. He's a sergeant up here in Fairbanks. Has a K-9."

"Oh...my...God." *I can't escape this guy.* She moaned and put her head down in her plate. Then she raised it and wiped meat juice off her nose. "You have invited *him* to *my* house tomorrow night to have dinner with us?"

"Um...uh...yeah. Why? Have I stepped in it?"

"This is the guy I talked to you about – the one who's been asking me out and I keep saying no and you said to say yes and then the last time I saw him I was going to say yes..." *(well, almost the last time I saw him)* "...and then he didn't ask me out again. I felt stupid. I was left standing there with my metaphorical pants down around my ankles watching his fine ass walk away. Jeepers, David."

She paused, embarrassed. *And this is the guy I tried to seduce at my house, and he turned me down. I've never been so humiliated or shamed in my whole life.* She saw David looking at her, a questioning expression on his face, but there was no way she could, or would, elaborate. No way she could admit to her own indiscretion and stupidity.

"What can I say, Clare? Had I known, I'da still invited him, 'cuz he's a nice guy and deserves a home cooked meal."

"Did you talk about me?" *Would the Sergeant tell David about that night?*

"I talked about Mom and Dad, Steve and Jack." He got very quiet. "And I talked about losing Alex. How his death affected all of us. He understood."

"Did he say anything about me?"

David looked puzzled. "We talked about you a bit. He wondered who I was flying up to see. I said you – Clare – a flight nurse with Aurora. He didn't know a Clare Herndon. I said your married name's Valenzuela. That's all. He talked a bit about his family, his deployments with the Marines overseas, the troopers, his dog, his first marriage – he was twenty at the time. He said he thought he'd met you through work – asked if you were also called CJay. I said yes. He said he thought you were very professional. He also said he thought you were pretty."

"Did he say anything else about me?"

"Uh, no. Are you disappointed?" David still had that quizzical look on his face.

"Not at all. Not one little tiny bit. No." *Thank you, Sergeant, for being kind – for not kissing and not telling, too. For saving my face.*

"Glad to hear that. Did you say you had ice cream?"

155

"Yes. Listen, butt breath, I can't believe you've done this to me." *I am so screwed. How can I face him?*

"It'll be okay. It'll be fun. Trust me."

The look she gave him would have melted the skin from his face while simultaneously blinding him, but he wasn't looking at her. He was picking up dirty plates.

Chapter Twenty

Well, isn't this an unexpected turn of events?

She shoots me down three times in a row, then tries to get me in the sack, and then her brother invites me directly into her lair for a 'home cooked meal.' Wonder if she's as uncomfortable as I am right now? Wonder if she'll glare at me over the entrée until my glass of wine turns to vinegar? I told Dave I thought she was 'professional,' but I didn't tell him that the curve of her cheek turns me on and that her fine little backside looked delicious when she stooped down to care for that guy on Dalton Highway. And when she crawled out of my truck in Nenana….

Didn't tell him that I wondered how she looked when cleaned up. In my shower.

Didn't tell him that I dreamed about pulling down the zipper on her flight suit, one tooth at a time…with my teeth.

Didn't mention that I was tempted to ask one more time outside the door to her dispatch – but thought better of it.

Didn't tell him I righteously wanted to strip her naked and take her to bed that night at her place – but not under those circumstances….

Didn't tell him about the day I first saw her – on the Fort Wainwright flightline….

Should I bring flowers? A bottle of wine…? Wear my vest?

* * * * * *

CJay made marinara sauce early the next morning for the Chicken Parmesan dinner with David and the Trooper. Her mind was racing with thoughts: Rachel's mother grieving; Alex – gone four years; Lexie; David – enthused over that crisis crap.

And the Sergeant (I can't call him by his first name.). He won't understand why I didn't want to go out with him and then tried to take him to bed. He won't understand why I'm so turned around – confused – sad – bursting into tears half the time. He won't understand why I didn't want to be alone that night….

I can't believe this is happening. I can't believe he's going to be here, in my own house, looking at me over the table. Probably smirking inside. Laughing at me. Fooled you! *I'm* here in your house *and your* BROTHER *likes me a lot! Hahaha!*

And, Hunni likes him too.

She imagined him sticking his thumbs in his ears and waggling his fingers at her, chanting "Nyah, nyah, nyah!" She smiled and imagined putting her own thumb on her nose, shouting "neener, neener," and waggling her own fingers back at him. Then she laughed, imagining the look on her brother's face at the two of them insulting one another with grade school finger waggles.

Maybe it'll be okay. I'll be polite, civil. I will thank him when he compliments my absolutely delectable Chicken Parmesan and garlic bread. I'll look him in the eyes – his warm hazel eyes – and

158

not be daunted by them. I will NOT respond physically to his shoulders. Or his hands. Or eyes. Or voice. Or waist. Or that beautiful butt.

She shut her eyes and gritted her teeth. *I will deny deny deny all my embarrassment, pain, grief, guilt, mourning…and desire.*

* * * * * *

David did his part with dusting CJay's book shelves and keeping the bathroom clean. He even vacuumed. They took a run together downtown where she showed him highlights, including Chad's fire station. They ended up at the Alaska Club for weight training. After working out, David wanted to get gifts for Cindy, his wife, and their two kids, so CJay took him to a local gift shop for authentic Alaska gifts – made by local artists. His twelve-year-old daughter wanted an Eskimo doll. He bought a reproduction of a traditional Inuit mask with a wry face for his ten-year-old boy. Cindy would love the female face pendant made from sterling silver, ebony, dendritic quartz, beryl, and 'ethically sourced fossilized ivory,' CJay knew.

"You have good taste, David," CJay remarked as they ate their sandwiches at The Fudge Pot not far from the Chena River. "You didn't buy the traditional tourist Ulu," referring to the curved blade all-purpose knife used by Inuit and Aleut cooks and hunters – and purchased by folks from the Lower 48 who promptly put them in drawers at home and never used them.

"Cindy informed me she'd skin me with it, if I did. Besides, she has so many high-end knives, she doesn't need one more. She *did* say if I bought her an ulu, it had to be authentic and of museum quality so she could display it. I saw plenty of beautiful ulus, but I think the pendant will get more use – and was less expensive."

"You're smart too. But, I already knew that…" she paused "...except for inviting the Trooper to dinner."

"You'll find that wasn't a mistake. He's a nice guy. Just be polite."

"I'll do my best to not chop him up like garlic." *I respond to him viscerally, David. I don't want to chop him. I want to… be held tight by him. And I can't let that happen. I can't, I can't, I can't.* She twisted about in her seat.

"I'd appreciate that, Clare." He looked at her closely and then asked quietly, "Are you afraid of him?" He emphasized the word "afraid."

She snorted derisively. "Why the hell would I be afraid of him? He's just another frikkin' 'hero' in a damned uniform."

"No reason. Just be civil. I'll carry the conversation and you can just sit there and pass the salad and keep our glasses filled. Like a good girl." He made a Cheshire cat grin and CJay glared at him. He flinched appropriately.

"I'm not afraid of him, not afraid to talk, and you two children can keep your own glasses filled, buster."

He laughed. "Yes, ma'am. Duly noted." And winked at her.

Chapter Twenty-one

The Trooper could feel the anxiety dance in his stomach as he got ready for his dinner visit, but knew it was normal, given his attraction to David's sister and the fact that, apparently, she wanted nothing to do with him at one moment and then wanted to go to bed with him at another. *Just how confusing is that to a guy?* He'd had a bit of experience, but this was more or less a new twist on borderline personality for him. But then, he wasn't a psychologist.

He liked David a great deal – they'd hit it off quickly at the conference because they were both law enforcement, close to the same age, with nearly the same experience in the civilian street. David asked intelligent questions and *listened* to the answers. He appeared to have the authority and street creds to be able to help put together a peer support program in his agency with the help of the other four men and one female who accompanied him. Jeff looked forward to spending more time with him.

I'm nervous about seeing CJay – Clare. 'Whatevah, yo.' Yet I'm also interested in how she lives. Maybe after spending tonight

*with her and watching her interact with her brother – and me – I'll
be less inclined to fantasize about her body. Or care who she
is… and how – or if – she might fit into my life. Or me in hers….*

*I really, really wanted to…um…get her between the sheets
that night….*

He pulled on new jeans, a new collared shirt, his favorite
oatmeal wool sweater, and leather hiking boots. Carrying a
bouquet of brightly colored mixed flowers from Fred Meyers and
an expensive California red wine, he got into his Subaru Forester
and drove the twenty-five minutes to CJay's house, arriving ten
minutes before 7PM. He sat in the front seat scrolling through the
Trooper Dispatches website on his phone for eight minutes
before unfolding himself from the vehicle. In his peripheral vision,
he saw the shades move and someone peek out at him. Standing
tall, he walked up the driveway, climbed the six stairs to her front
porch, took a deep, slow breath, held it for a four count, blew it
out slowly, then knocked on the screen.

* * * * * *

David answered the door, holding it open for the Trooper to
come into CJay's 'lair.' Jeff smelled Italian spices coming from
the kitchen and felt the butterflies fighting with his growing
appetite.

"Doggone, Dave, that smells great. I'm hungry."

"Chicken Parm – Clare's recipe. She's not a bad cook. Can I
get you a beer? Glass of wine? Let me take the flowers and she
can put them in some water."

162

I'll have a beer and your sister too, thanks. He smiled broadly. "A beer would be terrific, Dave, thanks. Let me give these to CJay…um…Clare?"

"Sure. She's in the kitchen."

Jeff followed the younger man into the kitchen, but it was empty. David called. "Clare? Where are you? She was here a minute ago. I'll find her."

David followed an icy breeze into the laundry room where he found his sister standing in the open side doorway with frigid air coming inside. She was taking slow breaths and blowing them out.

"You okay?"

"Just havin' a coupla tokes. And some fresh air."

"You don't toke."

"Okay. Then just some fresh air."

"You need to come back inside. Jeff brought flowers and a bottle of wine. You need to thank him and be pleasant."

CJay looked at him from under lowered eyelids. And snarled softly, "Fuck you."

"No, thank you. Southern Oregon boys do not roll that way. Come on, I'll help you. Cowboy up." He put his arm around her shoulder, turned her towards the kitchen and, starting to shiver, shut the side door.

Jeff stood in the middle of the kitchen feeling like a fool with flowers in one hand and wine in the other, listening to their hushed conversation out on her back porch. He was halfway tempted to turn around and walk out, tossing the flowers into the sink and taking the wine with him except he wanted to spend some time with Dave and the two were already coming back into the kitchen and he couldn't make an exit without looking like a jerk.

And I want to see her again. He laughed to himself. *I'm like Roger – just put "Glutton for Punishment" on my tombstone instead of my name.*

"Jeff, this is my sister, Clare. She was just grabbing a breath of fresh air outside."

Jeff put the wine down on her sink counter and held out his hand yet another time to the tall, pretty, dark blonde woman who'd tried to seduce him last week and now wanted to avoid him while wearing blue jeans and a silky blue, long-sleeved V-necked tee shirt which accentuated the color of her eyes and the softness of her breasts. Jeff felt himself become aroused. *What the fuck.*

"It's good to see you again, Clare...uh...CJay. Your kitchen smells wonderful. I'm pretty hungry." He saw her straighten her back, then take his hand firmly, give a perfunctory shake and release it again. He started to hand her the flowers.

"It's nice that you could come. David's said many nice things about the Anchorage class and your teaching skills." She looked into his eyes. He wanted to tell her she had beautiful blue eyes and her skin this close up was so pretty and her lips (*I want to kiss them even though they're still frowning at me*) looked shiny. *And soft like they did that night on your couch.... Damn it. Thinking with my dick again.*

"The wine is for you. If you have a vase or jar, I'll put these flowers in some water. I've already cut off the ends," he *did* say,

164

instead of all those other things. He had an urge to belch loudly too, so she wouldn't think he was a single bit slapped silly by her presence.

"These are very pretty, Sergeant. Thank you for bringing them. That's a nice gesture."

Nice gesture? Nice gesture! Shucks, ma'am, just doin' my job. Barrrrrrappt! He held his lips down to keep the ends from smiling. *This is a no-win situation.*

CJay turned, and reaching into a high cupboard, pulled down a simple clear glass cylinder which she handed to him. He thanked her and filled the cylinder with water from the faucet, stirring in the little packet of unknown chemical particles (that keep flowers fresh for millennia) with a wooden spoon he found in the sink. He arranged the flowers so they looked pretty to him, then put them on the counter.

"Would you like a beer or a glass of wine?" she asked.

"Thank you, yes ma'am, I'd like a beer."

"Pale Ale, Bud Light, or something darker? I've got an amber ale and a Stout."

"Bud Light sounds good."

She opened the fridge, took out two Bud Lights and handed one to the Trooper and the other to David. Then she smiled slightly and motioned at her brother. "David thinks you're the cat's pajamas. He's very excited about being able to talk shop with you."

"I'm glad I could come."

"Jeff, come into the living room while Clare's finishing up and we can shoot the breeze for a while," David interrupted from the dining room door. "I think there's a football game on, too."

"Sure, Dave. In a minute." The Trooper saw several cloves of garlic on her cutting board, soft butter and a long baguette close by. "May I chop your garlic for you? I'm a whiz at chopping. And my sister thinks I make the best garlic bread in town."

She turned to look at him. "Sure. Of course. That'd be nice."

"Do you have some more parmesan cheese?"

"Yes, but you'll have to grate it. I only use fresh cheese."

"That's fine. I can chop AND grate. Dual talents." He smiled at her. *God. For my next act, I'll do a little soft shoe for you! My name is Fred Astaire!* He felt his toes tingling.

She smiled back slightly and handed him the grater and a triangle of fresh Pecorino Romano cheese from the refrigerator. His fingers touched hers as they exchanged the grater. He saw her look up at him sharply and her cheeks pinked up. *Perhaps we can try that again, sometime, CJay. And I will always want to grate your cheese and chop your garlic. And want to kiss you, dammit.*

He washed his hands, then smashed the garlic with her Chinese chef's knife and peeled off the paper. He minced the aromatic cloves and mixed them with the butter. The tall man dressed in the oatmeal sweater with a navy collared shirt peeping out the top then grated the cheese and fine chopped some flat-leafed parsley she handed him next. He folded both into the garlic butter. Then he turned back to her. She was standing in

166

front of the stove looking at him. He couldn't interpret her expression, but it definitely wasn't happiness.

"Awkward?" he guessed out loud.

"Sergeant, you have no freakin' idea," she finally said, looking down at his feet and shaking her head.

"CJay, you don't need to feel awkward. You really don't." *I wanted to take you to bed the other night, but I couldn't. I wouldn't have felt right about it. And it was a risk I couldn't take.* He reached out his left hand and put his palm on her right cheek. She leaned into it, then looked up at him.

"I'm so humiliated by the way I acted. I'm so sorry. I can hardly even look you in the face."

He smiled. "CJay, if anything's going to happen like that, ever, I would want both of us to be stone cold sober and know what we're doing. Does that make sense?"

"Of course it does." she put her hand on his hand on her face, and he turned his fingers and squeezed hers gently, then released them.

"And here I am in your kitchen again. You're going to have to blame your brother for that. You want to know the truth?"

"I'm not sure," she answered, looking up at him again.

"I'm glad Dave invited me here." He paused, considered, then changed the subject. "Shall I cut the baguette and butter it now?" She nodded at him and he deftly sliced the Italian bread with her bread knife and slathered the halves thickly with the garlic mixture.

"Baking sheet?" He watched her backside appreciatively as she bent over to retrieve one from the storage drawer under the oven.

"How was your view?" she asked, smiling slightly as she turned around to give him the baking sheet.

"The view?" *Damn. Are you flirting with me now?* He felt his own face redden this time."With all sincerity, it was quite pleasant, CJay. I will not lie."

He arranged the two bread halves on the pan and knew he'd better quit before he got into trouble. Besides, David was back in the doorway to the dining room motioning for him to come sit down and talk, apparently oblivious to any underlying dynamics.

"If there's anything else *we* can help you do, just let *us* know," he told her as he grabbed his Bud Light and retreated to the other room. He also wanted to grab her face and kiss those pretty lips, but that would go poorly. Maybe…. He was beginning to have a little hope.

Jeff inspected CJay's jammed book shelves again as Dave chatted. The television was on, but they weren't watching. The Trooper wasn't a football fan – he'd played soccer, ice hockey, and rugby in high school. With no professional team up here in the Last Frontier, the interest wasn't there. Jeff secretly thought it was a wimp sport (too much padding and protection and way too many timeouts – not to mention those pesky traumatic brain injuries), but seldom voiced that opinion: The troopers had a lot of Fantasy Football fans.

CJay had hospital nurse textbooks, flight and transport nurse training manuals, espionage and legal fiction. No superficial bodice ripping romance novels or erotica that he could see. But perhaps women didn't keep those kinds of books in the living room. He noted non-fiction political and historical works. He saw some of the same authors he liked to read when he had the chance – Conroy, Grisham, Malcolm Gladwell, Nelson de Mille, Connelly, James Rollins – and sci-fi – Hugh Howey. He saw Scandinavian, Icelandic, and Alaskan authors. He enjoyed some of Dana Stabenow's stuff and books written by retired troopers, himself. Very eclectic and action oriented reading list, he noted appreciatively.

She had authentic local art and photography. Those pictures of Dave and her, a photo of her family when CJay was about twelve. He recognized Dave. Two parents and two other older boys – twenty and twenty-two? Must be Dave's firefighter brothers that he'd mentioned. He saw her graduation from nursing school. She was pretty then, too, but looked very serious. *Like she does now.* He looked at that wedding picture again, more closely – Clare and her groom – in Coast Guard Class A's. He noted simple joy in her face and pride in the young man's.

"Clare's the smartest one of us all, Jeff," Dave said when he saw the Trooper looking at Clare's books and photos. "Mom and Clare. The rest of us just "Serve and Protect.""

"That takes brains, too, Dave. Not to mention courage and nerve."

"Clare's got nerve. She's always held her own with us three brothers. She can't outshoot me, but she outshoots both Steve and Jack. I'm really proud of her. I think she's special."

I want to find that out, Dave. "It's nice when a brother says that about his sister. I feel the same about my little sister, too. She's up here in Fairbanks – at Wainwright. Her husband Jordan's a stand-up guy – Military Police."

The Trooper paused, indicating the wedding picture on CJay's shelf. "And you liked her husband?"

David nodded, paused, then spoke thoughtfully. "Yeah. We were best friends for years in school. Then he got into the Coast Guard academy in Connecticut and on breaks Clare'd hang out with us. After he graduated, they started dating, but didn't get married until Clare graduated from her nursing program. He was at Air Station Astoria. She worked in Astoria at the local hospital. Got married in our church in Eugene when Clare was twenty-two or twenty-three."

"Refresh my memory about what happened, Dave"

David grimaced. Shook his head, then spoke slowly.

"Tail rotor failure on a routine pick-up off a cruise ship at sea. Hit the ship, into the drink. Those fucking Jayhawks – top heavy, of course, turned over, went to the bottom. The corpsman survived. They recovered Alex's body. One pilot's body was pulled out by a fishing boat days later. Never found the airframe or the other pilot." He paused. "Alex's service was at our church, too." He ducked his head, then smiled sadly at the Trooper. "Fuckin' tough time."

The Trooper felt a rush of adrenaline course through his body. If he'd had hair on the nape of his neck, it would have stood straight up in a primordial display of alarm. *God damn it. I remember that crash. I was in a class at the academy at the time*

– those Sitka Air Station Coasties were devastated. That was CJay's husband. I'm so very sorry, CJay.

CJay came into the room while David was talking about Alex. She leaned against the door frame and took a slow breath before she finally said, "If someone can come toss the salad, I'll put the chicken and garlic bread on the table."

"I'll help you, CJay," Jeff offered, following her back into the kitchen. He took the wooden bear paw salad servers she offered him and poured some blue cheese vinaigrette over the greens and fresh vegetables sitting in her carved birch bowl. The chicken parmesan looked delicious as she passed by him with the pan held securely in oven mitts. For some reason, those oven mitts softened her. She wasn't the stern, official flight nurse-couch seductress with your fate in her hands. She was a cook with your dinner in her mitts. She was a woman whose husband had died at sea on The Job. He almost said "I'm so sorry," and took her in his arms still holding the bear paws to comfort her, but stopped himself, because that baking pan looked pretty damned hot and her jaw looked shockingly tight.

Chapter Twenty-two

They sat down to dinner with CJay at the head of her compact table for six, putting Jeff on the flight nurse's right. The Trooper held her chair so she could sit. She served the main dish and the men passed the salad and crusty browned Italian bread. It smelled delicious and tasted even better. He *did* say that to her.

"Thank you, Sergeant. It's our mom's recipe. She's half Italian – Northern Italian, though. She taught us how to make white sauce – Béchamel. David and I have perfected Southern Italian, haven't we?" David nodded, his mouth full of chicken stringy with hot mozzarella cheese and a moist slice of garlic bread in his hand.

They sat and ate, small talking and sharing about the Anchorage class for thirty minutes. Then CJay spoke quietly during a lull in the conversation.

"Sergeant..." CJay began. Jeff looked at her. She paused, then went on. "I heard you talking about your sister? She's at Wainwright?" The Trooper nodded and waited for the flight nurse to go on. She didn't. The silence grew long.

Finally, the Trooper spoke. "Are you still thinking about the crash last week?" She nodded.

172

"My sister knows the family," he said. "They go to the same church on post. Rachel's mother and Shannon were active in the MWR – the Morale, Welfare, and Education program – at Wainwright together for a couple of years." He finally said, "I'm sorry, CJay. That was pretty bad for you." He didn't phrase it as a question. Nor did he mention the abortive visit to her sofa the day the crash happened.

Pretty bad. I should have pushed it down. I'm fucking going to cry. Oh God. That's one of the reasons why I was so strung out with you....

CJay ducked her head and put down her fork. She coughed, cleared her throat. Took a sip of the Meiomi Pinot Noir that Jeff had brought. It was incredibly delicious. A burst of raspberries in her mouth. So, she inhaled a second big swallow, then looked up at him and knew he could see her eyes glistening with tears. She took a third swallow, self-medicating she knew. *Here goes.*

"Pretty bad doesn't even begin to describe it, Sergeant. It goes beyond pretty bad to the saddest, worst thing I've ever seen – and I've seen some stuff. We *all* have. I'm not talking about anything that you two haven't already experienced." She could see the Trooper and her brother look at one another. CJay paused, swallowed, pressed her lips together then said, "She died on the ship. Gus and I both felt her soul leave." A tear gathered at the corner of her right eye and slid down her cheek.

"Do you want to talk about it?" the Trooper asked her. She looked at him. *Fuck no I don't want to talk about it. I don't need you to see me even more screwed up than you've already seen me lately.*

173

"No. I don't want to interrupt dinner. I don't need to talk about it. I can deal. I'd prefer NOT to talk about it, really. Sorry I mentioned it."

"I understand."

"Are you sure you don't want to talk about it?" her brother asked.

CJay glared at him, then said impatiently, "I do not want to talk about it, I said. I do not want to ruin dinner. I'll deal with it. It was just so gnarly and sad. Her parents – I feel so sorry for them." She ducked her head and cleared her throat. "There wasn't anything we could do to help her. She was awake and talking to me, and when they pulled the engine block away to get her out, I saw the light go out of her eyes. She was looking at me, grabbing my arm...and then she just wasn't there anymore."

And, so much for not talking about it you freakin' moron dummy idiot.

CJay stood up abruptly from the table, mumbling "Excuse me, please" almost knocking over her chair, and disappearing around the corner to the hallway going to the back of the house. The two men heard a door close rather loudly.

"Bedroom door?" Jeff asked.

"Yeah. Now what?"

"Well, you've had the training. Why don't you go talk to her? Take her a glass of water or a cup of tea and just have her tell you her story. Just like we practiced in Anchorage. You were a good student. You know what to do. You know what to say to her."

"But, you're better," David said. "You've got experience."

174

"Yes, that's true. However, I think it'd be better if *you* talked with her. She doesn't know me very well and I'm actually quite positive she's not comfortable with me. Or even trusts me. She trusts you. You can do this. I'll make the tea. If you can bring CJay out here, I'll cover your six if you need it. But, seriously, Dave, I doubt you will."

Jeff got up from the table and filled a glass with ice and cold water from the refrigerator door and handed it to David, motioning for him to go down the hall. Then he put the tea kettle on to heat.

* * * * * *

CJay heard the knocking on her bedroom door. *Please don't be Sergeant Wonderful coming to do his fucking crisis thing with me…. God. Can this night get any worse?*

"Clare, can I come in?" *David. Not Sergeant Wonderful. I don't need to hash and rehash this. It just makes it more painful. And becoming so emotionally stupid twice in front of the trooper doesn't make it any better.*

"David, I'm okay. Really. I'll be out in a bit. Just washing my face." She put the cold, wet washcloth over her eyes to dry her tears and soothe the puffiness. "I'm fine. Just let me be."

"I've got a nice glass of water for you."

CJay started to laugh. "Super, David. That's very thoughtful. Now go away."

"Let me come in."

"You are just as annoying as you used to be, you know that?"

175

"I do. Now let me come in."

She sighed. "Come in, then." She could never win with David. He was a persistent pest. And bullheaded. She could hear the teakettle whistling in the kitchen. Evidently Sergeant Pepper Wonderful Super Duper was making a hot drink, too. She'd managed to make herself into a weak baby needing two cops to take care of her. What an image. She grabbed the glass of water out of David's hand and took several sips to make her brother feel better about it.

"Mmmm. That tasted fabulous. Now go away."

Her brother laughed. "Talk to me."

"I'm not a baby. I can take care of myself. Just leave me the hell alone." She put the glass on her night stand.

"How come you couldn't sleep the other night?"

Oh, let me count the ways, brother dear. CJay looked at him and knew he was trying to get her to talk so he could practice his brand-new peer support skills. *I don't want to be your guinea pig, David. Go talk to someone who needs help.*

"You think I'm trying to get you to talk so I can do peer support, don't you?"

CJay wiped her nose and nodded.

"I'm not trying to do that, Clare. I do know that talking about an incident helps us put it into perspective. Helps us reframe and reorganize our understanding of the event and its impact on us. Helps us put an incident into its proper place in our minds and our memories. Takes off the sharp edges. You couldn't sleep? Talking about this can help you sleep better. Get back to kinda normal faster. Remember that resilience and bounce back I

176

talked about? Talking about this can make you a stronger, better flight nurse." He paused for a long moment, then started to speak again...

"You've got the whole spiel memorized, I see," CJay interrupted. "Is this what Sergeant Pepper does out there?"

"Sergeant Pepper?" David laughed. "You mean Jeff?" CJay nodded. "Yes, it's what he does, besides maintaining law and order in the tundra and taking his K-9 out to pee. And, he's good at it. Do you want to talk to him?"

"Absolutely not. I..." She paused, shook her head, then made a decision. "...I'll talk to you."

"Okay. Jeff's making some tea. Let's go out and sit at the table and we can talk and have some tea. It won't take very long – maybe ten or fifteen minutes, but I know you'll 'feel' better and maybe even sleep better tonight."

CJay pressed the cool cloth against her eyes for a moment, then reluctantly followed David. When they got out to the dinner table, CJay found that the Trooper had put the tableware in the dishwasher, packed away the food, and had three cups of hot Rooibos tea waiting for them. *Well, he's monumentally efficient if nothing else. Is this night ever going to freakin' end?*

CJay told her story starting at their first dispatch to the scene, the extrication process, her intubating the cooperative teenager, the pulling away of the engine block, the girl's loss of consciousness and the life leaving her eyes. And that infinitesimal feeling of cold dread in the helicopter when Rachel went into PEA and they knew she was truly gone. The hair on the nape of CJay's neck and on her arms stood erect when she mentioned that last...when Rachel's soul had passed on.

She talked about the family at the Med Center. Finally, she talked about when Rachel's mom and dad said their goodbyes in the trauma resusc room at their daughter's side. Rachel's mom had held her child's hand and sung the old hymn *May choirs of angels lead you into Paradise* in her strong contralto voice. Every person in the room had wept from the grief expressed in her prayer.

"No mother should ever have to say goodbye to her baby," she whispered.

CJay cried then, quiet gulping sobs. David handed her some tissues and then both men waited patiently until she blew her nose and could continue. Finally, the Trooper asked if she could tell them what the worst part of this whole event was for her.

"Two things," the flight nurse said, after a moment. Both men waited for her to go on.

"In the helicopter when she was no longer there, Gus and I knew she was gone. She had unsurvivable injuries. But we kept her as comfortable as we could. She'd asked me to tell her mom and dad that she loved them. I almost lost it then, but knew I couldn't. I had to stay focused and care for her – and we ended up doing CPR in route. I felt as if all the air had been sucked out of the ship."

"The second thing?" David asked quietly.

"The blood…. I was covered in blood from the knees down. My boots were covered in it. I know that dad saw it, too. He's been over there." She glanced at the Trooper. "Dad knows blood.

I was covered with his daughter's blood. I still smell it. I washed my flight suit and leggings three times and I still see it and smell it. It's still in the seams of my boots and I scrubbed those freakin' things with Ajax."

CJay glanced at her watch. It was getting late and she knew that both David and Sergeant Pepper were tired from three days of non-stop class.

"One other thing. Sergeant, I heard David talking about my husband when I was in the kitchen. Talking about Alex. It's been a little over four years..." She glanced at a large yearly planner calendar that she had tacked to the wall between two bookcases "...almost to the day that my husband was killed. When they found his...his...him, they gave me his personal effects – and his boots. Boots are very personal, you know," she said, looking up at the Trooper. "Even if they're big and heavy, they conform to the feet. I slept with his boots for a month – to comfort me. They were almost all I had left."

CJay wiped her eyes and took a sip of lukewarm tea. "My *fucking hero* in a uniform," she whispered softly. David took her fingers in his and squeezed them. She nodded at him. Then she looked into the hazel eyes of the Trooper across from her and felt a rush of warmth, some of it still humiliation and embarrassment, but also a sense of – how could she define it – *You know who I am.*

But that, Sergeant Pepper, is why I can never become involved with another emergency services cop or firefighter or medic or military-uniform-wearing-hero again for as long as I live.

I don't want to lose someone else I love with all my soul. And I don't want to abandon my husband's memory.

* * * * * *

The Trooper took his leave soon after that, man-hugging David and saying how much he enjoyed meeting him in Anchorage and meeting his sister in a more informal setting this evening. He didn't add *"…and I appreciate that she didn't try to take my clothes off this time."*

Jeff wished him luck with starting the peer support crisis team in Lane County and offered his services and resources whenever David wanted to email or call him. David was grateful.

CJay also came to the door to say good-bye, but then she turned to her brother.

"I'm going to walk the Sergeant to his car, David. I'll be right back in." She followed the Trooper down the driveway and stood at the curb while he unlocked his driver's door and then turned back to her.

"I need to apologize to you. And...I guess I really want to thank you too."

"What for?"

"For everything. I tried to seduce you. Thank you for not telling David about that. I've been rude to you. You didn't deserve it. I'm sorry. This thing with Rachel, her death, and Alex's death – this month – it's been really hard for me. I'm pretty sure you can understand that. But I'm not trying to make excuses for myself. I have no excuses for the way I've acted towards you."

180

"I understand, CJay. And, I understand even more now."

"I'm so very sorry about that night at the Pump House."

"Why? I enjoyed dancing with you a lot. I was looking forward to drinking coffee at your place."

"I was unstrung. I didn't want to be alone. I'm humiliated that I acted...hell...came onto you like I did. I'm ashamed of my actions. I hope you can forgive me."

"The only reason you 'came onto me,' CJay, was because you were 'unstrung?'"

She smiled shyly and looked up at him. "No. I liked dancing with you too. You have good moves." The flight nurse paused. "You can call me Clare, if you want."

"Only if you stop calling me Sergeant and call me Jeff." *Does she want me to ask her out again? Dunno, but I* will *leave her an opening.* "If you ever want to grab another cup of coffee or shoot those guns of yours, give me a call."

He sat inside the car and closed the door, rolling down the window in case she wanted to add anything. He started to give her his business card.

She squatted down next to his Forester and smiled quietly at him, looking directly across into his eyes. Then she put her hand on his jacketed arm which was resting on the window frame and squeezed her fingers.

"I still have your card, Jeff. Thank you. Thank you for being...I don't know. Not mad?" She squeezed her fingers again on his arm, then stood.

"Never, Clare. Fly safe, flight nurse."

"Be safe, Trooper."

181

Chapter Twenty-three

"My beautiful Clare." She turned her eyes to him in her dream and saw him sitting next to her on the bed in his t-shirt and boxers, propped up against the headboard with a pillow. She smiled at him.

"My handsome husband. But aren't you supposed to be going to work?"

"I have all the time in the world for you. Do we need to talk?"

CJay sighed and sat up in bed next to him. "I have a dilemma."

"I'm very accomplished at dilemmas, Sweetheart. How may I help you?"

"It's about you."

"Ah. The old 'What do I do with Alex now that I think I have found someone who might be able to fill his fucking boots' dilemma?"

In her dream, she smiled. "You know I love you with all of my heart."

He nodded. "And you always shall. Just as I shall always love you."

"But what do I…"

"Stop. What did your very wise medic, Gus, tell you?"

"He would want his wife Norma to find happiness again if anything were to happen to him in the helicopter."

"And...?"

"He said you would want the same thing for me."

Alex put his warm, strong arm around his wife's shoulders and pulled her close. "You know that song, something about a 'broken road'...?"

"Are you a 'broken road', Alex?"

"I am most definitely *not* a 'broken road,' Clare. What you and I had was the real thing that got cut short. What I am is your very own guiding star, Clare. I am guiding you to a new adventure – a new joy. My Inca warrior forebearers built 25,000 miles of sophisticated roads and I'm a hell of a good guide. Do you trust me?"

"With my life, Alex." She turned to him, embraced him with both of her arms and kissed him.

"Good. Trust your instincts with this one, Clare, and despite your major fluff up with him on the sofa, I give you kudos for trying at least."

"But..."

"Hunh uh, Clare. No 'buts.' Why do you think it's so difficult for you to move on now?"

"Because I love you."

"But that won't make me come back. I've moved to another level."

She was silent in her dream.

"You think about it, Clare – why you're holding back from moving on in your life. I could tell you, but I think it would make more sense if you figured it out for yourself. Remember that I love you and I always will."

The alert on his phone that was now suddenly hanging from his boxer's waistband went off. "Darn. I have to go. Some roughneck on an oil rig off the coast had an acute appendicitis attack and we gotta go pick him up."

She watched him morph into his flight suit and heavy jacket and appear at the bedroom door.

"Fly safe, Alex."

"I always shall, Clare. I always shall."

CJay rolled back into sleep, but before she totally succumbed, she finally understood what Alex was trying to tell her.

Fear – that if she found someone new it meant that Alex had been just a glitch in her life – only a waypoint. And, guilt. Guilt that Alex would think she had not loved him if he could be so easily replaced.

But Alex had told her to trust him – and to trust her own instincts….

Chapter Twenty-four

"Aurora Flight I, request from AST for a motor vehicle crash, St Nicholas Drive, North Pole, at the Santa Claus House. T-bone, pick-up versus car, four serious injuries, pregnant female, possible abdominal injuries. They're requesting 'Expedite.'"

The helo was in the air within three minutes, shortly before 1300 – 1PM – heading southeast towards the MVC scene near Richardson Highway. They could see the overhead lights of the emergency vehicles in the distance, and circling the scene, were directed by the LZ contact to set down in the secondary parking lot, near the giant fiberglass Santa statue, no wires or obstructions. CJay opened the A-Star's side door and leaning out, told Charlie the tail was clear. They wouldn't kill old St. Nick today. CJay was lead and Gus was crew this time, but they quickly realized that this was going to be a team effort for the two of them.

Two young school-aged children were already secured on gurneys and being loaded into ambulance rigs in preparation for the trip to NSMC's ED. The driver of the pick-up truck was handcuffed and in the back of a state trooper Interceptor with a paramedic attending to slight facial lacerations.

The North Pole fire captain headed over to the flight crew, who were picking their way on the ice with their gurney towards the scene, and updated them.

"The pregnant woman is your patient. The car driver was pulling out of the Santa Claus House, turning left on St Nicholas Drive, and this A-hole just plowed into them. They didn't have a chance. The right front passenger's about eight months pregnant and she caught the brunt of the impact on the front of her space. We got her out fast, but she's really complaining of abdominal pain and her water's broken – may be in labor. You need to get her outta here fast."

* * * * * *

I learn that the woman's name is Shannon and I kneel down next to her to assess her level of consciousness – her LOC. I ask her name and palpate her chest at the same time. She answers appropriately and exhibits no pain on palpation. Ribs stable. Her right leg and ankle are bleeding, but the paramedics have applied pressure dressings, and there are no apparent broken bones.

I palpate her abdomen and she cries out. "Oooooh – I think I'm in labor. Take care of this baby. Please help me." Honest to God, I see terror in her eyes. Never, ever, discount what a traumatized patient tells you, whether it's with words, or their eyes.

Well, fuck me.

"We gotta get her on her side, guys – so tilt up this backboard up with blankets so baby's not on her aorta. Let's get her secured in the left lateral recumbent position." LLRP is almost always protocol for pregnant trauma.

I think of Rachel in the cold. I tell Gus to get as many warm blankets as he can. Shannon has warm winter outerwear on, but she'll need more protection from the icy conditions. I slit the sleeve of her expensive coat and stick a #14 gauge IV in her right arm with warm fluids infusing.

(Your mother always tells you to wear your nice panties when you go out, because you never know if you're going to be in an accident, and you don't want the paramedics finding rips and skidmarks in your undergarments. Well, she's wrong. Wear the crappiest clothes you've got, because when we get our hands on you, we're gonna cut it all off and you don't want your Victoria's Secret silk knickers hitting the floor in pieces. Or your expensive winter coat, either, for that matter. So, actually, it's a crap shoot. I frequently dress like a hobo when I have to go to Fred's – just in case. But, seriously, folks, why is it that the cotton crotch always blows out first? What's up with that?)

However, I digress.

Gus sees that Mom is secured on both the backboard and our gurney and that the IV is infusing and secure, and says, "Let us rock and roll," he tells me. I try not to laugh.

I love Gus.

Charlie has kept the blades turning and Gus, two firefighters, and I duck under them and load the woman onto the ship, locking her in place. The two of us both climb in. Because she's on her left side, I end up facing her. She's grimacing.

Charlie pulls pitch and notifies dispatch that we're lifting off from Santa Claus house with "Four souls on board." I see the woman trying to say something. I key the mike and ask Gus, "What's she saying?"

Gus gets down close to her face, and lifting up her mask tries to hear what she's telling him through his helmet. "She is saying the baby is coming," he informs me through our mikes. His eyes are as big as pies and I have absolutely no doubt that mine are exactly the same. My worst nightmare is about to happen.

I've birthed a baby before. I know Gus has also. Well, between the two of us (and the video I watched once – har-de-har-har) we should be able to do this if necessary.

"Ask if baby has turned around yet," I suggest. He does, and I know the answer Shannon has given him is "No." Baby is still butt down – breech. Now, I see that she's having another active contraction.

I tell Charlie, "Hot mike and pull out all the hamsters." If my nursing license and the integrity of this helicopter program weren't hanging in the balance, this would be funny. Hot mike so Gus and I can talk without keying our microphones. "Pull out all the hamsters" – pedal to the metal. I see Charlie smile and lean forward, imitating speeding up. This typical pilot maneuver is always hilariously funny. I have to smile at him – well, at least briefly.

She's on her left side facing me, so I check between her legs, cutting her stretch pregnancy jeans in order to see better. I see a foot in her underpants. Oh, Sweet Holy Baby Tiny Infant Jesus and Talladega Nights.

I tell Gus we have a footling breech birth. Baby is not only not turned, but its little foot is sticking out, making a normal birth of any type extremely difficult. In the hospital, this wouldn't be a deal. C Section! STAT!

In our helicopter? We could be well and truly fucked. I ask Gus (Why do these things pop into my mind?), "Do you happen to have any opera length surgical gloves?" My heart is pounding out of my flight suit. I know my hand is shaking.

"Aitaaq," he replies in Inuit. "'I am so sorry.' I left them in my tuxedo." I smile. We are so fucked.

I smile despite the fact that I am kissing my nursing license goodbye (and maybe even Gus's) and possibly going to jail. And, if I am wrong, very possibly mommy and baby will die inside Aurora. No. I smile because there is no fucking *way this woman is going to lose her baby.* No fucking way! None! *I won't fucking allow it. No mother should fucking have to say goodbye to her baby.*

I tell Gus, "Please support me in this." When I took NALS (Neonatal Advanced Life Support) in Portland, my instructor talked about a footling breech she did at a home birth. I tell Gus we need to get mom on her hands and knees right now. I see the question in his eyes. I have no doubt it matches the fear in mine.

Charlie is still leaning forward in his pilot's seat. I hear the sound of multiple teensy hamster paws running in an armada of squeaking wheels…. Faster, fellas.

I strip off my gloves and grab the sterile surgical gloves from the trauma kit. Gus yells at mom to get on her hands and knees. He loosens the gurney straps and uses his strong arms to get her up on all fours. There is a good chance we will all lose our jobs and go to jail. Or hell.

Oh, wait! Have I already mentioned that?

"Get her legs open wide, Gus," I say while I pull down those fucking stretch pants further, cutting underwear and anything else I can reach with my trauma shears. She is ignominiously mooning us and sopping wet with dark amniotic fluid. I see her legs trembling.

"I'm going to put my hand up her vagina," I say to Gus on hot mike, "and try to get that other leg down." I see Gus attempting to tell the terrified woman what's going to happen. Twenty-five minutes ago, she's buying Christmas decorations and putting funny, furry, big eared animal hats on her daughter's head and taking cute pictures with her cell phone to send to the family on Facebook and now she's fighting for the life of her baby. And her own, too.

I see that protruding foot dangling between her legs turn purple and know she's having another contraction. I wait until it becomes light puce.

"Gus, tell her not to push – only short panty-pants for now." Gus nods and yells into mom's ear. By the time this trip ends, she'll be deaf from our shouting at her and the roar of the rotors.

No one will ever believe this. I put my fingers and hand up this poor woman's vagina and stretch her cervix gently, feeling around, until I find the other slimy little leg. I can't believe it myself. I manipulate this little sucker down and out of the uterus. What the fuck! "Blanket, Gus," I yell. I see Gus wince from my *shouting into his headset. Maybe we'll ALL be deaf by the time this flight is over.*

I feel another contraction and am suddenly, overwhelmingly grateful that this is going to happen down and dirty fast.

Baby's little butt comes out.

Posterior. Whatever.

"Posterior, Gus." *Fucking scary. Breech and posterior. And mom is unbelted. If anything happens to this helicopter, mom becomes a one-hundred-and-seventy-pound SCUD missile with a fucking baby attached. I am so screwed. And, Gus is unbelted. Thank Gawd it's not snowing outside on top of everything else!*

Hello! There's meconium, too, indicating stress and possible meconium aspiration into baby's lungs. I say 'Doggone it.' No, I say fuck fuck fuck!

Wendell is one of our best flight paramedics – like Gus, and he's a delight to crew with. He once noted that during difficult flights the inside of the helo sounds like a free-range chicken farm with the crew simultaneously muttering/shouting "Fuck! FUCK fuck-FUCK!" I smile, knowing that when he visits me in prison, I will be able to share this story.

Well, we're doing our best.

I attempt to turn baby as gently as possible in order to get this potential rugrat through the birth canal. Then he stops.

Gus, my man, I say, I believe baby's arms are stretched over his head and his shoulders are stuck. I have one option, barring trying…I don't know what. We're over the Rubicon at this point. I reach up again into the birth canal, groping until I have a little arm. I slither it down. Maybe it will be enough for baby boy (I can

191

tell these things! Nah, I jest. I see his little winkie.) *to slip through. I hear mom cry out.* Sorry, lady.

God is with all of us. Mom contracts and baby squirts out into my arms. "CJay – cord!" *Gus shouts in my face and bangs his helmet into mine reaching over to untangle the slimy umbilical cord from the kid's neck, preventing strangulation. We are the freakin' Keystone Kops of baby birthing. An icy hand of pain washes over my heart, but this time I can shake it off. I quickly suction baby's mouth and nose with the blue suction bulb from our OB kit.*

Clamps, Gus? I hold out my gloved hand which is trembling almost as much as mom's legs.

"Tunngahugit," *Gus utters gutturally, welcoming the newborn to our very cold and scary world, I later learn. He hands me the warm blanket I requested six hours ago, and I wrap up infant "Baby Boy Aurora." Gus clamps the cord in two places and clips it. I put the baby in the butt-in-the-air position and stimulate his back by rubbing it. I hear him hiccup, then squall.*

I have never heard a more welcome sound in my entire life. Fuck me, I think.

I can't say the word 'fart,' but I truly love the word 'fuck.' In case you hadn't noticed.

I tell Gus to get mom down on the backboard and for heaven's sakes to buckle himself up.

Placenta is born next, baby is on mom's adoring breast, and everyone is strapped in.

Text book, Gus. You rock, CJay, he tells me. No, Gus. WE rock.

I tell Charlie to request 'hot offload' at the helipad, and he tells us "Aheada ya, darlin'. Trauma, L&D (Labor and Delivery) and Neonate will be there to greet us."

Gus opens the helo door at landing and gets out, motioning the teams to come in under the spinning blades. He guides them safely to the ship and unloads mom's gurney onto the hospital's wheeled gurney. The neonatal team takes the tiny infant and whisks him away for assessment in a warmer, more suitable environment.

Tell them about the meconium I yell, but the rotor wash blows my words away. I lean back with my helmet against the bulkhead. I trust Gus to take care of the ED report. Then reality hits me. Eight days ago, we'd watched a young girl die in this ship. This afternoon – we'd brought a life into the world. We saved a life.

I start to cry. What a fucking week. What a fucking day. What a fucking world.

I love my job.

Chapter Twenty-five

Jeff stood at the gate to the helipad and waited until Charlie slowly braked the blades. When the pilot waved him onto the pad, the State Trooper walked toward the door of the helicopter. He could see Clare inside, resting her helmeted head against the wall, her eyes closed. CJay took off her helmet then and opened her eyes. Jeff was standing in the helicopter's doorway.

"Thank you for my new nephew," he said. He saw her hair matted to her head with moist tendrils around her face and the nape of her neck. Although it was 15 degrees outside, she was sweating. Her eyes – puffy and red. She'd been crying. He thought she was beautiful.

CJay did not understand his words at first, but then she did. She crawled out of the helicopter and into his arms. He held her tightly.

"She's your sister?" she said against the side of his face.

"Yes. Thank you. You guys are amazing."

Jeff smelled her sweat and kissed her ear. He tasted her saltiness and found himself becoming aroused. *Dammit. Clare, I want you so much.*

"The luck of the draw, Trooper. Charlie, Gus and I are a team. We did the best we could and it worked out just right."

"Gus said you pulled off a miracle. He was impressed."

Jeff wanted to say more. He wanted to tell her he loved her even though he'd never even been on a real date with her. He wanted to tell her that he wanted to spend the rest of his life with her, but he didn't even know who she was. Out of his peripheral vision, he could see Charlie watch them with a smile on his face and then climb out of the cockpit.

The pilot did a post-flight walk around the ship to make sure everything was buttoned up, then stood a respectful distance from the two until Jeff pulled away from CJay, letting his hand linger on her shoulder, then her arm.

"Sergeant, yer not trying to poach my flight nurse, are ya?"

"No, Sir. Just thanking her for delivering my sister's baby upside down and backwards. I'da hugged Gus, too, but he was otherwise occupied. Can I hug you?"

Charlie laughed and backed away four feet. "Maybe later, Jeff. But, you gotta watch this one. She's got balls of steel."

"So I'm discovering, Chief."

Charlie held out his hand. "How the hell are ya, bud?"

"Doing well, Charlie," the trooper said, taking the pilot's hand and shaking it. "Thank you. It's good to see you again."

Charlie winked at CJay. CJay discreetly gave him the finger, making her pilot laugh.

"I need to check in with Gus..." she told Jeff as they walked toward the helipad gate "...and I want to see your sister and the new baby. And you know Charlie from Afghanistan, right?"

195

"From Iraq – Baghdad. And he put together the "Missing Man" flyover after the memorial service for our two troopers who died in Mantishka."

Clare turned to look at him, then nodded. "I flew that day – in the formation. I'm so sorry. That was awful."

"Yes, it was. I remember you being there."

"You remember me?"

"Yes." *Who can forget you, flight nurse? But I was still reeling from the crash, Helen's decision – and the loss of the life I'd envisioned with her.* "Let's go see Shann, Clare. And if I haven't already said 'thank you,' then 'Thank You'. For the job you guys do, you need steel balls."

She stopped and looked him directly in the eyes.

"You're okay with that?" It didn't come across as a challenge.

"Yeah. I am." *And I think I love you for it.*

"Well, Trooper, your sister did a heckuva good job too."

She turned to walk off the helipad and Jeff followed her. Though he wanted to walk with his arm around this woman, he held back. When they entered the ED sliding glass doors they were walking side by side, but CJay had a pink glow which was noticed by several who saw them together.

Jeff dutifully packed warm blankets, IV fluids and towels back to the helicopter while CJay pushed the gurney. He could have put them on the gurney, but he held them instead – to keep his arms from going around her. Then, after Aurora I was ready for her next flight, they went back in to see his sister.

Shannon was in Bay Ten, wrapped in warm blankets. The Labor and Delivery team was preparing to take her upstairs to her post-delivery, or postpartum, room. She looked exhausted, but perked up when she saw her brother and CJay, the flight nurse who "delivered my son and saved both our lives."

"That's very kind of you to say, but you did most of the work," CJay said modestly. "I'm just glad your baby is okay – and you are, too."

"How's Clarice?" Shannon asked Jeff.

"She's good, Shann. She's over in the pediatric ED. She got shaken up, but at the moment, she's playing with a new stuffed puffin she got. The Social Worker is with her and your friend's daughter. This has been kinda fun for them…well, except for the actual trauma part."

CJay lowered her head and grinned. Then, she looked up at Jeff. "Your niece's name is Clarice?" she asked.

"Yeah, it is. For our grandmother. She helped raise us and Shannon wanted to honor her that way."

Shannon grabbed her brother's hand and squeezed it, looking serious. "Does Jordan know about the accident? I need him back here."

"I've contacted the post commander, Shann, and he's writing up orders for Jordan to be pulled back to Wainwright. I don't know what's going to happen, but we're trying to get this going ASAP. Have you seen the baby yet?"

Shannon chuckled, then replied, "Only for a moment when this angel here wrapped him up, held him up, spanked him and that boy cried like a champ!"

"Uh, just stimulated him," CJay amended.

Shannon laughed out loud. "I know, but his cry was the best sound I've ever heard. I can never thank you enough. I've almost forgotten how much it hurt and how scared I was to be in that helicopter on my hands and knees with my bare butt hanging out. But, as far as I'm concerned, you're a total rock star. Thank you."

"I think she's a rock star too,' Jeff said, and this time he did put his arm around her and pull her close. He could feel her melt against him and he held her closer. She placed her hand on his arm and squeezed, like she had on that night after chicken parmesan and crisis intervention at her house.

Shannon's eyes opened wide, questioningly.

"This is my… uh… friend, Clare," Jeff told her. "David – sheriff deputy from Oregon – from my class in Anchorage. Uh, his sister. She lives in Fairbanks…flies for Aurora…um, obviously…." He listened to himself stutter, trying to figure out what their relationship might now be that he'd put his arms around her twice and felt her conform to his embrace.

Shannon smiled, then grimaced. Blew air out. "It's nice to meet you formally, Clare. Thank you."

"I'm going to see how your baby is doing, Shannon. My crewmate's writing up the chart, and I need to be there, but I want to make sure your baby's fine."

"What's your partner's name?" Shannon asked.

"Gus. Augustus," the flight nurse answered.

"Augustus. That's a wonderful name," Jeff's sister said. "I like it."

* * * * * *

CJay reluctantly pulled away from Jeff's arm, and stepped out to the pediatric trauma resuscitation room where Baby Boy Footling Breech was being cared for by the neonatal team. When she saw him, he was pink and squirming, warmed by the resusc lamps and looking well.

"You delivered him?" the OB-GYN doc asked. When CJay nodded, the doc said, "Incredible job. I'm more than impressed. It's a very fortunate thing he was only about thirty-four weeks or you could have had a real situation. We'd had to've done a crash C-Section right here in the ED, and he and mom still may not have made it. He's very strong and looks pretty good. Impressive. In case you ever want to come back inside the hospital and work with us…?"

CJay thanked him, but no. Inside again? Perhaps some time, but not for a while. She'd found her wings and her heart inside Aurora.

Chapter Twenty-six

Gus and CJay had one more quick flight, but when Tommy, Judy, and Wendell arrived for night shift, CJay's charting was done and pass over report was uneventful – except it was kudos all around for CJay and Gus – not the first birth in the helicopter, but the only footling breech, and a "Get outta town!" exclamation from Wendell, giving CJay an enormous hug. She was exhausted, but still buzzing from the excitement of the afternoon. She told Wendell about the flying free-range chicken ranch and they laughed – and she wasn't even in prison.

Her little house was cold when she finally unlocked the door to let herself in, but she put some wood in the cast iron stove in the front room, and soon her nest began to warm. CJay poured a small glass of Black Box red blend from her refrigerator and, taking off her flight suit, took a quick shower, washing away the various fluids of the day. She pulled on sweats, microwaved honey barbeque chicken wings, and sat down to decompress. Turning on Netflix, she chose an episode of Alaska State Troopers to watch for a little while.

"I might have my own Trooper," she mused, a little unbelieving. She visualized taking the Sergeant's clothes off, and pulling him into her bed, touching him everywhere, kissing him, having him on top of her, being kissed everywhere by him, having him inside of her.... *Oh Alex. My sweetheart. My guiding star.*

Her phone interrupted her daydream – a text from the Trooper:

> *Working tomorrow? May I take you out to dinner tomorrow night to celebrate Augustus's birth?*
> *His name means 'venerable.' I think it fits. I'd really like to see you again.*

CJay typed back:

> Not working tomorrow. Would like dinner. 5PM?
> *I look forward to it.*
> 1700 hours, Trooper.
> *As you wish, Rock Star.*

CJay smiled. She took a sip of wine, relaxed into her sofa with her feet on the coffee table, and watched the Alaska State Troopers save the day in the Mat-Su Valley and Fairbanks and Nome on NatGeo TV.

* * * * * *

The flight nurse went to the Alaska Club the next morning and worked out, raising up a cleansing sweat. She shopped for groceries, bought a bottle of good red wine, ran the vacuum cleaner, swabbed the toilet, mopped the kitchen floor. She admitted to herself that she was nervous. *Do I serve the wine? Will he think I'm putting moves on him again?*

Alex, I'm trusting my instincts. Like you said to do, my darling.

* * * * * *

CJay wore new black jeans and a soft, thick rust flannel shirt and black Western style boots embroidered with green and blue leaves coiling around wildly colored flowers that she'd purchased at a tourist gift shop in Skagway following a fixed wing transport. She coordinated with a wool scarf the color of the boots' dark red flowers, and planned to top it all off with her brick colored snow jacket from Big Ray's.

Tonight, she put on eye makeup and perfume. And earrings. She curled her hair. Then put it in a ponytail. Then, took it down and curled it again. Then, twisted it up and put in a platinum-colored hair claw with sparkles and 'pearls' low on the back of her head. She checked her outfit in the mirror. Four times. She fidgeted.

She was ready at 4:45PM. Anxious, her heart beating fast. Butterflies in her stomach. I am ready, she thought.

At 4:55PM, she heard the Forester pull up in front and the door slam. A moment later, the doorbell rang. And she opened it.

Jeff stood there, in freshly pressed Levi's, clean hiking boots, a dark red ski jacket, white shirt, oatmeal crew sweater and red roses. She could smell his Old Spice.

202

"It seemed like flowers were called for tonight, for the angel of the sky. The rock star," he said somewhat formally, handing them to her. They were beautiful – three red roses, baby's breath, ferny greenery, some curly sticks, in a graceful clear vase.

"Red roses signify gratitude...affection. I hope you like them." He appeared a little nervous. *Good.*

"Please come in, Jeff." *Do you feel as anxious as I am right now, Trooper?*

"Thank you. You look very nice tonight."

He stopped, looked at her, shrugged, then said simply, "I think you look beautiful."

"Thank you, Jeff." *You're very handsome to me.* She took a deep breath in. "You smell good." *God, now I look like his dog, Trygve, making a new friend. Don't turn your butt to me.* "Make yourself comfortable on the sofa. I've got some wine – um…" pausing. *In for a penny, in for a pound, Dad always said.* "Would you care for a glass of wine?"

"I would enjoy that, Clare."

Clare turned to go into the kitchen and Jeff took a moment to look around once again. He saw the photo of her and Alex getting married. Such pure joy on her young face. Then he followed her.

"I can't hang out in there while you're in here," he said simply, standing outside her personal space as she got glasses out of the cupboard. "Let me pour the wine for you." He picked up the bottle that had been airing on the counter, and poured four ounces into each of the glasses she held out to him. "Thank you for going to dinner with me tonight."

203

"Thank you for asking me. I haven't made it easy for you. I've really tested your patience and understanding."

"No, you haven't." He held his glass up for a toast and she clinked her against his. "To a nice evening with a friend."

"With a friend," she repeated. *I want to put my arms around you, friend. I want to pull you close and put my head on your shoulder. I want to kiss your neck and feel your body. I want to pull that sweater off of you and pull your shirt out of your pants and put my hands on your warm skin and smell you, touch you all over...friend.* She shut her eyes and turned away before her tingling fingers betrayed her and unzipped his jeans.

"Come sit with me for a few minutes," she told him. "Then we can go to dinner."

"I need to thank you, Trooper," she said as soon as they were seated in the living room – CJay on one end of the sofa and Jeff on the other.

"Why?"

"Well, I haven't been nice to you. I've acted irresponsibly, and I ruined our dinner the other night.'

Jeff didn't roll his eyes, but he did shake his head. "You're already apologized twice. And, no, you didn't ruin our dinner. Why would you even say that?"

"I got emotional about that girl we brought in. And I let my past intrude on your conversation with David. Suddenly it was all about me, and I generally don't operate like that. Grabbing the spotlight. And I tried to...seduce you."

He chuckled. "To be honest, I can't think of a single, unmarried hetero male who would object to having a good-looking woman attempt to seduce him. Seriously. But that night with your brother, you said what you needed to say. We need to be able to talk about the things that hurt us. Otherwise, we get eaten up inside. As for your past, we all have things that hurt bad – that will always be with us. May I ask you one question and then we don't need to talk about this again too soon?"

She nodded.

"Did you sleep better that night?"

She paused, thought, then said, "Yeah, sort of I did. And...for a couple of reasons. Something David told me made a big difference right off." She looked at him and he nodded for her to go on. "He said I was having a normal response of a normal, strong person with incredible coping skills to an absolutely unfair, awful, brutish situation that should never have happened – but did happen. And I couldn't fix it. All I could do was watch her die in front of me. Twice. I was powerless. Helpless to save her. For us, that's one of the worst things that can happen to us – not being able to 'fix it.' And neither could the surgeons and all our fancy fucking equipment at the Med Center. Or is it fucking fancy equipment? I can never keep it straight."

She stopped and put both her hands on her face, then looked back at him through her fingers. "I'm sorry. I have a mouth like a sailor."

"Or a longshoreman." He smiled. "But, if it's any consolation, a wise man once told me that I could use any words I needed to tell my story to him. I think that fits this situation."

"But I talk like that all the time."

"All the time? Even if I introduced you, to…say…my mother?" His eyebrows flew up.

CJay laughed. "Okay. I've got a pretty good filter when necessary. But, being raised with only brothers – and working in an industry where 'life' happens on a regular basis… I'll be honest, Jeff. Sometimes there *isn't* time for niceties. It's just blurt it out and get the fu….uh, get the freakin' job done."

"Well, for what it's worth, I understand what you're talking about. But you said there were a couple of reasons you slept better. What was the second reason?"

She could feel her face redden. *You can see me blush, can't you?* "I got to see you as a person. A nice guy. David wants to be like you when he grows up."

Jeff smiled gently. "For what it's worth, he's right up there on my big list of good guys. And he thinks you're pretty special, too. I'm inclined to trust his judgment. Flight nurse." He paused and looked at her. "I'm not intending to dwell on your flight with Rachel, but I'd like you to also consider that Rachel *was* in that unwinnable situation. Even if she didn't know it, you and Gus did. You two were there to protect her and comfort her. Her last human contact as she passed from this world was *you*: Someone who cared about her, grieves for her and her family today, and will never forget her. You were there in her time of need."

Tears filled Clare's eyes. She reached for a tissue and wiped her eyes, trying not to smear her mascara, but she knew it was totally gone. *Thanks, trooper. Do I look beautiful now?* She thought about what he had just said, and knew he was right. She and Gus knew their role was to help Rachel be comfortable….

And help her say good-bye.

She cried again for a few moments, picturing Rachel, picturing that she and Gus had, perhaps, made her last moments easier, more peaceful.

The Trooper did not touch her, but sat quietly until she regained her sense of composure and looked up at him.

"Thank you. I hadn't looked at it like that. Just...just...thank you."

He helped the flight nurse with her coat and then took her to Wolf Run restaurant, set back in the trees. The hostess seated them by a window where they could see strategically placed lights illuminating the alders, birch, and spruce around the restaurant. The warmth from the fireplace behind them felt comforting to her. She and Jeff sat across from one another, both still a little nervous and formal.

The Special was rack of lamb with rice, which CJay ordered, rare. Jeff chose a ribeye steak, rare. They were into their salads before either of them really started to talk.

"So, tell me how Shannon is doing and the baby – and your niece, Clarice."

He told her. Shannon is going home in the morning. Baby Gus will stay for at least two to three weeks to make sure the trauma, breech footling birth, meconium, and his early birth status remain resolved. The neonate docs feel he's doing well, but are being cautious. Reese is fine. Jordan, his brother-in-law, is on his way home from Afghanistan. His unit comes home in two months – hopes are high that the new baby's dad won't have to go back to join them.

The meth head?

In the FCC – Fairbanks Correctional Center. History of drug abuse, DUIs, several warrants out for him. Won't be coming out anytime soon. Might have local connections…. He became quiet after that last.

CJay said she was glad to hear such good news.

"My mother came up this morning to stay with Shannon and Reese for a few days. Would you want to meet her? She said she'd like to meet the nurse who saved her grandson's life." He hesitated, perhaps sensing her concern. "This isn't meeting anybody's parent. It's letting my mother thank you for…doing what you and Gus did."

"Well, in that case, yes. That would be nice. She can see the helicopter. Just call or text – I'd like that."

Their entrées arrived then, and they concerned themselves with savoring the rare lamb and steak for a bit.

"Jeff, you know quite a bit about me, but I don't know much about you, except what you told David at the conference. Tell me about you."

He looked up at her with a forkful of rare rib eye, put it in his mouth, chewed slowly, drank some wine and put down his utensil. Then he proceeded to talk.

"I started out bullheaded and stubborn. I've gotten a lot better…but, honestly…I'm still bullheaded and sometimes stubborn, too. Just thought you'd like to know that up front. I wouldn't be a good cop if I didn't have some common sense and confidence. I love my job and helping people. I love my dog. I love my house and property. I want to settle down now and raise a family. In Alaska. I can't guarantee it will always be Fairbanks, because we get moved around from time to time. I started out in King Salmon in a little crappy studio apartment – I was the AST for the whole area. But it taught me a lot about the people, the sense of community, and policing."

CJay indicated she was listening, and he continued after a sip of water. He talked about high school, being the son of a University of Alaska Anchorage tenured and published Professor of North American History with a focus on Arctic Indigenous Peoples and a lot of expectations for her children. His dad? Chief prosecuting attorney for the Anchorage Borough. With a lot of expectations for his children.

Sounds tough, CJay commented. The Trooper shrugged. Smiled.

Jeff'd toyed with becoming an attorney, like his dad had been, but not right after graduating from high school. So, he joined the Marines, figuring on using the GI Bill after the required amount time in the military. Figured the discipline would do him good.

"Is your dad still alive?"

Jeff shook his head. No. "My dad died when I was twelve. I watched him die on a hospital bed in the family room for six months while our mom and hospice nurses took care of him."

"I'm so sorry. That must have been just awful for you two kids." She paused. "Did you tell me that your grandmother raised you and your sister?"

"Pretty much. My grandparents came to live with us from Ketchikan after Dad died. Granddad was a retired Lutheran pastor there, and our house was big enough for both of them. I loved him. But, my granddad died when I was twelve, and from then on, the house was ruled by women. Don't get me wrong. I love my mother and my grandma, but they are two formidable Tlingit women and Tlingit women run the ranch."

"Your Grandmother is Tlingit?"

He smiled. "Full blooded. And my Granddad was full blooded Norwegian. Second generation Alaskan and spoke fluent Tlingit. One of the reasons Grandmother's family accepted him."

"Wow," CJay said. "Was your dad Norwegian?"

"Scots. I'm kind of a mutt."

Mutts make the best combos, Trooper. "I don't think you're a mutt. But, if you don't mind my being nosy, you joined the Marines to get your education benefits?"

He shook his head again. "I joined the Marines for two reasons. One – I'm repeating myself – to get out of a house where I was the only male, and two – how can I put this? To find an atmosphere where there was some kind of structure, rules, protocols...to work within. After my dad died, I was lost. I missed him a lot. I wanted to show him I could be a man – a Marine. A hero. A good guy like he was. A son he could be proud of."

She looked at his face – his hazel eyes with green glints, she saw. The smile lines. *You are a good man.*

"So, tell me about your marriage," she asked, casually.

Jeff smiled. "Dave spilled the beans on me, huh?"

"Perhaps. He told me a lot about the class."

"Are you sure you want to listen to old history lessons?"

"Yes. Absolutely."

She could see him watching her closely.

"Well, we got married when we were twenty-one. Too young. But we'd been together since high school in Wasilla and I cared for her. Her parents and mine had been longtime friends. It just seemed natural and normal to the two of us kids that we'd be together. Clare, are you certain you want to hear all this?"

Yes. I want to know who you are. "Yes," she said aloud.

"Well, like I said, I joined the peacetime Marines at eighteen. No one could anticipate 9/11 and the fact that we'd be at war. I was with the First Expeditionary Marines who went into Baghdad. I was twenty years old. I killed my first person before my twenty-first birthday."

"Wow," CJay whispered.

He paused. "I'm not proud of this. I said I was bullheaded and stubborn and sometimes when I get an idea in my head... well, I push until I get what I want."

I can see that, Sergeant. She smiled up at him. "I believe you."

"I came back from the sandbox and told her we needed to get married. I wanted to protect her if anything happened to me. I was home for a year, and then got deployed again, this time to Kabul. While I was there, Monica got lonely, moved back to Wasilla from down below to stay with her parents, and started hanging out with a good friend of mine who'd been on the rugby team with me. Got pregnant. Sent me a 'Dear John' letter in a big manila envelope with divorce papers for me to sign. I signed them, then volunteered for the next six months for any patrol that meant I could kick in doors, yell, wave around a big gun, and be a tough guy. I'm pretty sure my twenty-two-year-old self wanted to die."

He sat back and took a sip of water, swallowed, then drew in a breath and blew it out sharply between puffed cheeks.

"Clare, I was so very angry then and so hurt. But, you know, it was the absolutely best thing that could have happened to me. I was released from a decision that a hard-headed boy had made and I was allowed to grow up. I was free to become what I know now my life was intended to be. It also taught me a little bit about being less bullheaded and self-centered."

"Well, that's a good attitude to have."

"Yeah, I guess, but I didn't have that good of an attitude back then. It took a while. I learned a hell of a lot in the Marines. I learned about resilience and bounce back. Learning from the stuff that happens to you – and even your own dumb mistakes – is one of the most important things I took away from that time. I am so grateful for what I've gone through."

He sat back and smiled at her.

"And you know what? Monica and Brody are very happy. He's a really nice guy and a hard-working auto mechanic making a gazillion dollars with his own high-tech shop for fancy cars, and she's a stay-at-home mom with five kids, including a toddler. Happier than pigs in slop. Still live in Wasilla."

I like your smile, Trooper. And I really like your attitude.

The trooper looked at his watch. "You're on duty tomorrow, and it's getting a little late. Do we have time for dessert or coffee before you have to get back home?"

CJay snapped back to reality and frowned. *I don't want this night to end. I want to know everything about you, Jeff. I want more time.*

She sighed. "Coffee. I'm not done talking to you."

"Okay. Box for your leftovers?"

"Yes. And coffee – black and bitter – like my heart."

He laughed softly at her comment. "Your heart may be many things, but I sincerely doubt it's black. Bitter, perhaps," he looked askance at her, "but hardly evil."

They lingered for another forty-five minutes, talking quietly. CJay shared how she and Alex had met. She did not try to hide from this man the fact that she'd loved her husband from the very bottom of her heart and soul, and had anticipated growing old with him. Her heart had died that day – broken – but there was nothing she could bring out of her husband's death that would make that loss better or instructional in any way.

"I figured we'd just go off into that incredibly beautiful Oregon sunset, watching our children and grandchildren grow up and watching the waves slowly fade to shadows."

The trooper hesitated for a long moment, then asked, softly, "If I may be so bold, Clare, why haven't you remarried?"

CJay smiled sadly. "Yes, you are bold," she told him. "I could ask you the same thing, couldn't I? I kinda talked about it during dinner with you and David. But, it sounds to me like the subject for another time."

He helped her with her coat and drove her home in the frigid Fairbanks night. *Will he want to kiss me?* When they reached her door, CJay opened the screen, unlocked the door, reached in to turn off the porch light, then turned back to him. *Here I am, Trooper.*

"Thank you for going out with me, Clare." He tentatively held his arms open and she slipped into them, pulling him close to her. He bent to smell her hair – apple something. He held her warmth close and closed his eyes, slowly rocking from side to side, savoring her nearness and the fact that because she was so tall her face was near to his own.

"Thank you for bearing with me, Trooper. Text me when you want to bring your mother around to dispatch tomorrow." She stepped away, hesitating, turning slightly towards the door of her home. He put his left hand on her shoulder to prevent her from turning completely away from him, and his right hand softly on her jaw and said, "Don't go yet."

She closed her eyes and lifted her face to his. He kissed her forehead, her ear, her cheeks, the right side of her lips, and then the left side of her lips. She opened her mouth to his kiss and his tongue. And he kissed her fully. She groaned with pleasure – and desire.

She could feel her knees give way and his arms close around her, holding her up. She gripped him tightly. *Oh. I'm so gone. I want you so badly. Oh, Alex. Watch over me. I will always love you.*

* * * * * *

What the.... Jeff felt pressure against his chest and looked down to see Clare's hand on his sternum pushing him away.

214

"I...I can't," he heard her say. "No. Not yet."

"Okay. That's all right. I'm not ever going to pressure you."

"You're not, Jeff. I just can't. You don't understand."

You're right about that, Clare. "It's okay, Clare. Really it is. I...I just need to know I can see you again."

She looked up at him, her lips still wet from his kisses, slightly parted, her eyes on his. "I want to see you," she finally said. "I...want to be with you," she said softly, so low he wasn't sure that's what he heard.

"That's all I need to know, Clare. I just want to know I can see you again."

Chapter Twenty-seven

Gus and CJay flew to Delta Junction to pick up a teen who'd been hit by the school bus when he slipped on the ice and the bus ran over one of his legs, crushing his tib-fibs – the two bones in the lower leg.

"Ouch," CJay remarked, as the two packaged him up with an air splint.

"Indeed," Gus answered.

Out and back. Scoop and grab. Neither of them minded this kind of flight any more – not since Rachel or the breech birth of the Sergeant's nephew. It was nice to have 'margarita flights' occasionally that actually followed their training and protocols.

"CJay, if you do not mind my asking, are you and the trooper 'seeing' one another?" Gus asked his partner as she sat at the computer writing up their bus-pedestrian flight.

CJay looked at him, surprised. She loved Gus. He'd learned English as a second language in school, and his grammar was perfect.

"Gus, do you know how much I love you?"

"No, CJay. I do not."

"A lot. To answer your question, no, maybe." She shrugged. "I don't know. I believe the Trooper and I are interested in one

216

another. But, Gus, to be truthful – I'm just taking it one day at a time."

"Your smile does look genuine today. I am very happy for you. I think he is a good man. Norma was asking about you. I will be able to tell her this good news."

CJay nodded. Not a problem.

Chime. Her text alerted.

Are you available for me to bring my mother over?

Absolutely, Trooper.

20 minutes, flight nurse?

Yes. Can you come to dispatch?

Anywhere you want me to go.

Just come to dispatch, Trooper

As you wish.

She turned to Gus. "The Sergeant wants his mother to see the helicopter. They're going to be here in about twenty minutes. You guys stay because I want her to see our team."

Jeanne looked around the dispatch console. "I wouldn't miss it." She'd heard through the grapevine about the trooper giving CJay a hug in the ED after the baby was born in the ship.

When Jeff knocked in twenty minutes, Jeanne deactivated the door's lock. The trooper held the door open then followed his mother into dispatch. CJay could see her dispatcher giving the tall man a thorough once over.

Jeff's mother was beautiful. Tall and regal. Wearing a Helly Hansen dark burnt orange knee length winter coat, black slacks, and slender black knee-high boots. Mocha skin, straight nose, high cheekbones. Black hair streaked with silver, pulled back into a chignon, low on the nape of her neck. CJay could have pegged her for Jeff's mom out of a line up because of her cheekbones and straight nose. The flight nurse took a deep breath and stepped forward. Gus and Jeanne both stood.

"Dr. Douglas. I'm CJay…Clare. I'm so happy to meet you." CJay extended her hand.

The other woman took it in both of hers and said, "I am happy to meet you, also, Clare. But, please, call me Hannah. You are the angel from the sky who saved the lives of my daughter and my grandson. Thank you."

"I'm only one of the team here, Hannah. Gus and Jeanne – this is Shannon and Jeff's mother."

Gus came forward and Jeanne stepped out from behind the dispatcher console. Jeff's mother greeted each of them with hand clasps and thanks.

"We were the team, Dr. Douglas, but CJay delivered your grandson," Gus said.

"That is true. But my grandson has your name. Augustus."

"Absolutely, Dr. Douglas," CJay said. She looked at Jeff. She could see what she thought was pride in his face.

"May we go out to the helipad? I'd like to show my mother where you all did your magic."

"Yes, certainly," CJay said.

Jeanne told them to go ahead. If they were requested for a flight, she'd let the crew know. Gus indicated he'd stay in dispatch and finish up some chart audits.

CJay grabbed her radio and outer gear, then led Jeff and his mom out to the helipad, unlocking the gate and shutting it behind them. Jeff put his arm around her shoulder and gave her a quick hug.

"We're on camera, you know, Jeff," CJay whispered to him.

"Seriously, do you think I care?"

CJay laughed. No, she didn't. And, she could imagine Jeanne in there, lapping it up. But 'Mom?' Perhaps not so much.

But, his mother was thrilled when CJay pulled open the portside slider and showed her where Shannon had been when baby Gus was pushed out.

"Augustus was afraid," Jeff's mom said, her hands on the helo's gurney. Her eyes were closed. "He knew he was not ready. He knew this was not his time. Everything happened so fast. He was shaken, distressed and fearful."

CJay looked at Jeff, a question in her eyes. The trooper shrugged slightly.

"He was coming out backwards and his hips hurt and he knew that was wrong. He felt like he was suffocating – something around his throat. Then, it was so cold. His mouth and his nose were full. You suctioned him, didn't you?" She turned to CJay.

"Um…yes, of course. And Gus unwrapped his cord. You're right. It was around his neck."

"Then he felt he could breathe. He wasn't afraid any more. He knew it was all right. He took his first gasp and looked for his mother. He knew her sound and her smell."

Hannah turned back to look at CJay, a spasm of pain crossing her face as she gazed into the flight nurse's eyes for

219

several long moments. "I am so very sorry, Clare," she finally whispered.

CJay did not change her expression, but she felt the hair stand up on her arms and a frisson of adrenaline made her shiver. *What the flaming flying…?*

"Clare, you saved my grandson," Hannah finally continued. "He would have died without you and Gus and your helicopter. He would have died at that fiberglass Santa Claus in North Pole without you. There are not enough words to thank you."

The older woman took CJay into her arms. Clare returned the embrace. She had no words either. She could still feel the surge from earlier.

They walked back to dispatch, stopping in the hospital chapel to sit and talk for a while. Jeff stepped out to get them tea from the vending machine in the hallway.

"My son is enamored of you, you know," Dr. Douglas shared, leaning over to CJay.

The flight nurse looked at her. His mother nodded.

"I find him a good man. A strong man."

His mother nodded again. "Oh, he *is* a good man. He is also a different man this morning than he was yesterday afternoon at Shannon's house. I know how much Helen hurt him so it does my mother's heart good to see him perhaps find joy again. Nothing could bring me more pleasure than that."

No pressure there, CJay thought. *But, who the heck is Helen?*

Jeff returned bearing cardboard cups of tea, giving them to the flight nurse and his mother. They thanked him.

"Mom," he said, looking at his watch after a few more minutes of tea and chatting, "We need to get back to Shannon's."

"Yes, yes, you are right." She rose, embraced CJay, then looked at her son. "You two take care of one another. Clare, thank you for the tour and thank you again for what you did for Augustus and Shannon. I'm going to stand out in the hallway for a moment." She turned away from them and stepped out of the chapel.

The Trooper put both hands on her cheeks and kissed her, told her he hoped they could see one another soon. Then he kissed her a second time.

I love your mouth, she thought. *Please kiss me forever.*

Chapter Twenty-eight

CJay texted Jeff two days later from dispatch.

Would you like to go shooting at the range?

After all, he'd told her that if she ever wanted to go 'shoot those guns of yours' he'd be glad to take her. The flight nurse knew he liked her. Knew he wanted her physically. She knew she liked what she saw about him. She wanted to take it slow – not get sexually entangled immediately – although at their age – why wait? But that's what she'd been doing since Alex died – using other people to salve her own pain. It's not just for fun.

But it is for fun and...because you care for the other person. But, there has to be accountability. Damn, it's complicated.

He didn't respond immediately. CJay fretted a moment. Is he having second thoughts? When they talked on the phone last night, he told her he was looking forward to seeing her soon. He had some 'time sensitive investigative work' they were doing outside of Fairbanks, couldn't really plan 'a whole heck of a lot ahead' at the moment. Things would 'probably slow down in a week or so'. But he was glad they could talk on the phone.

He finally called her two hours later.

"I'm sorry, Clare. I was tied up – couldn't talk."

"Or text?"

"Or text."

"Tomorrow?"

A pause. "No. Um…how 'bout breakfast day after tomorrow? I'm supposed to be off – at least that's the plan now."

"Okay. Day after tomorrow. Breakfast. Shooting after?"

"I like it. But can I see you tonight after we get off work? Meet you at Little John's for wings? I want to see you…and feed you."

CJay's heart did a little flip. "I'd like that, Jeff." She could feel that thrill of anticipation – that pleasurable sense. That tenderness…between her legs….

"Text me, Clare, when you're leaving the hospital. I'll be at the bar waiting for you."

"Okay, Trooper. See you soon."

* * * * * *

Little John's dirt and gravel parking lot was full and she could hear music pumping out the door as it opened and closed while she walked from where she'd parked her Outback. She saw Jeff in the dark corner at the end of the bar – and noted he was watching her in the big mirror behind the lineup of colorful liquor bottles.

"I couldn't sneak up on you if I tried, Trooper," she said when he stood up to greet her.

"That's kinda the point." He helped her with her jacket, hanging it up on a nearby coat rack over the top of his. She scooted up on the bar stool just as Little John approached.

223

"John, this is Clare," Jeff said, introducing her to the six-foot 5-inch bartender/owner of the popular burgers and wings brew pub, himself retired career military.

Little John grabbed CJay's hand in his own big hand and shook it warmly. "Jeff, I do believe I've seen your friend Clare and her girlfriends in here before – doing what nurses do best – talk shop, dance, laugh, and drink. Good to meet you officially, Clare. Jeff says you delivered his sister's baby in the Aurora. Impressive! Now, what can I get for you? And, it's on the house tonight, 'cuz you made the Sergeant a happy uncle."

Smiling in gracious acceptance of his kindness, she ordered a draft amber ale and they sat up on the bar stools in their dark, more private corner, listening to the music, close but not touching. *I'm not near enough to you.* She got off her stool and pushed it closer to his, then got back up. She put her hand on his knee which was now pressing on hers and squeezed her fingers. She heard him blow out a breath at her touch.

"You do know you're a witch, right?" he breathed.

She smiled at him. *I hope so.* "Did you like that?" He nodded and put his hand over hers.

CJay told him 'yes' when the Trooper asked if spicy wings and sweet potato fries were okay with her, and they sipped their beers and chatted. She filled him in on her non-eventful, routine shift and then asked him about what he'd been doing.

"Not much I can talk about right now, Clare." He shrugged. "We're just getting information together about some activity that's been going on. Hoping we'll be able to move on it in a day or so. Just some…um…stuff."

She looked at him for a long time. "I need to reboot my thinking about a..." she carefully searched for the words "...a friendship with a cop."

"What's that mean?"

"Except for David, it's all been firefighters in my life. Mostly. You know, 'I go to the truck. I put the wet stuff on the hot stuff. I use the Jaws to get 'em out of the wrecked car.' It's so cut and dried. Do this; do that. Strategize, then save lives and property."

He laughed out loud. "And that's precisely why they're the heroes, Clare. Firefighters get all the accolades, and we're the bad guys because supposedly we shoot first, and ask questions later. And, we're targets. You watch the national news, right?"

"Unfortunately, Jeff, sometimes I do. And now I guess I get to see the other side. Like the secret squirrel stuff that I've never really thought about before."

"Like always sitting with your back to the wall? And carrying a gun at all times? And wondering if you're going to come home from your shift? If you're going to see your family again? You mean that kind of thing?" He stopped, then went on. "Especially these days."

She looked into his hazel eyes. *Yeah. that kind of thing, Trooper.*

He sat up. "So, what do you think about it?"

Their wings arrived then, and they tucked into them while CJay thought seriously about his question.

"Are you asking me if I would consider not seeing you because you're a cop?"

"No, but I'm…um…" he paused, "…asking if it makes a difference that I don't wear the stereotypical white hat of all the 'heroic' firefighters in your life? Or that I might get shot on the job. Or I might be gone for days at a time. I might die in an aircraft. I might have to injure or even kill someone with only split seconds to decide what's right while I'm doing my job. And then be second guessed by those who were not there – and didn't see what I saw."

I think it makes you very sexy to me, but I suppose I shouldn't say that. "Maybe you forget that my brother's Deppity Dawg?"

"No, I certainly don't. And honestly, Clare, I'm glad he *is* your brother, because maybe that makes it easier for you to grasp the difficulties he and I face. When it's your own husband or wife – that person who shares your life with your children, it's a real consideration. It's a true paradigm switch."

She smiled and shook her head. "A paradigm switch? I can see that stubborn, hard-headed streak you were talking about the other day coming out right now," CJay finally said, a serious expression now on her face. "Are you pushing me away?" She put down a sweet potato fry and looked at him, narrowing her eyes and compressing her lips.

"I don't *want* to push you away. Just the opposite. But, I also want you to be aware of the ramifications of being a trooper…um…'friend'…as you put it. It's all fun and games until someone gets their eye put out."

CJay laughed, thankful the moment appeared to be lightening up. "This is some serious conversation, Trooper.

226

Listen, I come from an emergency services family. I know ramifications. I know the plusses and the minuses. I know the joy, the fear, the pain; the ups and downs; the ins and outs. Want more clichés?"

"No. That was pretty good."

"Tell you what. You don't know me and I don't know you. I birthed your nephew after I tried to take you to bed and you refused me. We've had some laughs. We've had some tears. You've eaten my chicken parmesan…"

"And it was delicious."

"…you're not gonna get me to shut up…and I've drunk your pinot noir – and it was delicious also. Why don't we just take it one freakin' day at a time. You might find out you *hope to hell* I can't stand having a cop as a 'friend'. Or, vice versa. And, maybe it'll turn out not to be an issue at all. I'm willing to take the chance."

She stuck a fry in her mouth, chewed, and watched him. He reached up his hand and brushed her lips with his thumb. "You have fry grease on your lips."

"Sexy, huh? Also changing the subject."

"Whatevah, yo. Incredibly sexy," he continued, still on point, and looking at her lips with softness in his eyes.

"You want to kiss it away?

"Yes."

She tilted her head towards him, and he gently kissed her mouth, growling in his throat. *The last thing we need in Little John's is to have someone spotting us necking in the corner.*

God, you taste good, Trooper. She pushed her face against his and he kissed her a second time.

"Can we do this again sometime soon, Clare? Perhaps in a more private venue?"

"Your university edjimacation is coming out, Jeff. A 'more private venue?'"

"Only if you have one," he murmured, against her ear.

I just may have, Trooper. But not tonight.

Chapter Twenty-nine

The Trooper was still buzzing the next morning following his late date with Clare. The smell of her skin, her greasy fries lips, her hand on his knee. He really had wanted to take that hand and put it high on his thigh, but knew that would be seen as colossally crude and probably would end their date – and their budding relationship – right then and there. But as of now, they were good. And he would see her tomorrow for breakfast....

But he was also being honest when he said they were doing some investigative work – stuff he couldn't divulge to her.

A week ago, he'd walked into his office, and Ruby, the Admin Assistant, told him that Anchorage had called and he needed to contact Darren Cooper, the Statewide Drug Enforcement Agency Supervisor. ASAP.

Jeff punched in the Anchorage number and then Darren's extension.

"You're going to like this, Sergeant. The AITF – the Alaska Interdiction Task Force – just took down a big delivery of heroin and cocaine this morning at Ted Stevens – Anchorage International Airport. This mule flew in from Sacramento via Portland on Alaska Airlines with two large check-ons full of well packed drugs and was loading up on a bush plane to finish the trip to Fairbanks. The AITF sniffer dog caught him."

"Well, that sounds good, Supervisor." Jeff said.

"We've been tracking this guy and his shipments since we first got suspicious about his activities. The ultimate end of his delivery is in your area of the North Star Borough. From there it quietly goes out to the villages. He sang like a Golden Crowned Sparrow. This isn't a small deal. We're talking multiple hundreds of thousands of dollars' worth – and it's well organized. Our investigation indicates that it's tied up with your two troopers in Mantishka." There was a long pause. "You still there?"

Jeff could feel his heart thud. He took several slow, calming breaths. "I'm with you one hundred percent."

"The bad guy's phone LUDs show he's been in contact with three phone numbers consistently for at least six months – both sending and receiving. One is a landline in North Pole." The Sergeant wrote down the phone number as the supervisor gave it to him.

"Secure email me what else you've got, Supervisor," Jeff said. "We'll take care of this."

He hung up on Anchorage and put his head in his hands, elbows on the desk. He knew he would try to atone for what had happened to Susan and Mark. On his watch and at his bidding.

"Ruby," he yelled. "Get Clark and Greg on the horn. And, track down this phone number." He got up from his desk and walked out to hers where he handed her the slip of paper with a North Pole landline written on it.

Troopers Clark Mildenhall and Gregory Ellcott sat in the Sergeant's office while he outlined what the DEA Supervisor had shared with him. "Ruby tracked down the phone number and we know where it's located. We need surveillance on this address – figure out how we'll approach it if we do go in. Figure out if this is truly drug central before we lay waste to it." He looked at Clark. "The cheesehead that hit my sister...he still in the Correctional Center?"

"I'll check..." Clark answered. "...and get his residence at the time of the crash."

Jeff nodded. *Wouldn't it be just retribution on several counts if we could nail these A-holes?* The horrifying sorrow he'd felt at the deaths of Susan and Mark washed over him again until he could shake it off yet one more time, in order to do his job.

Chapter Thirty

The town of North Pole has only 2200 residents, but because it is located between Fort Wainwright and Eielson Air Force Base on a major south-southeast artery, this suburb of Fairbanks receives a great deal of traffic.

There used to be two oil refineries located in North Pole that provided many jobs, but both have ceased functioning as big payrolls for the area. Now one of the community's biggest draw is the Santa Claus House – a tourist attraction known internationally for the world's largest fiberglass representation of iconic Santa located outside by the parking lot. In keeping with the spirit of perpetual Noel, North Pole's fire engines are red and white, and its police cars are a festive green and white. The town's street lights have a candy cane motif.

However, elves and choo-choo trains were not on Jeff's agenda during the forty-eight hours that he and his two troopers spent surveilling what they felt was the main distribution point for Supervisor Darren Cooper's drugs in this town famous for reindeer and Christmas joy.

The one-and-a-half-acre compound, located away from town off Badger Road in trees, was surrounded by eight-foot-tall fences. It sheltered two single wide mobile homes, several shed-like outbuildings, and a number of steel shipping containers, all locked securely.

"Not the least bit suspicious," Clark scoffed. "There are six individuals living inside. Male, female, and what looks like a six-year-old male child in one trailer; two males and a second female in the other one. Front and side gate. Side always locked. Front closed, but unsecured during the day with traffic through it."

"We canvassed some of the neighbors and heard there was a tunnel that opens up outside the fence – which we located," Greg added. "Oh – and two big dogs, too."

Jeff breathed in, then out. "Okay. Write it up. I'm gonna enlist North Pole PD and Fairbank's PD's guys and Fairbanks' dog, plus you two and the other SERTs, and Craig's replacement in Nenana. I'll get Pius to do some flyovers in Helo Two and take pictures. Good job, fellas."

* * * * * *

Sgt. Jeffrey Douglas, three of his SERT troopers, Tyler Frisbee – Craig's replacement from Nenana, Pius – the AST pilot with his AST sharpshooter, Robyn, plus four officers from North Pole PD and the K-9 handler from Fairbanks PD gathered for roll call at 0300 two days after the Sergeant's late hot wings date with the Aurora flight nurse at Little John's.

"This is what we have," Jeff announced, pointing to a projected image of a fence and gate on the screen at the front of the room.

"We've got this compound outside North Pole with an eight-foot fence around it, two entrances, front and side, marked 'Private Property,' allegedly filled with drugs and more than likely high-powered weaponry. Our surveillance shows that at least six people, including two women and a child, come and go out of there regularly. There are five working vehicles, including two 4X4 pick-ups, two Suburbans, and a Subaru sedan."

A NPPD team member raised his hand. When the Sergeant acknowledged him, he asked, "You think ten of us, two dogs, and a helicopter are going to be enough?"

Jeff clicked onto the next image in his PowerPoint presentation. "Hope so. With Pius in Helo Two with Robyn for overhead surveillance and fire power, plus Trygve and Argus for both drug sniffing and subduing any miscreant who tries to get away, and two additional Fairbanks PD to back up the front and side gates – I think we're staffed."

I think, he thought.

Moving on, Jeff pointed to the image he'd just pulled up. "This is a photo taken yesterday by Pius. You can see this compound is jammed full of crap, including the two mobile homes, several disabled small vehicles, a couple of Tuff Sheds, plus these large shipping containers. There are lots of clever hiding places in case they're not in their beds, not to mention the bunker tunnel.

"Four of us Troopers and my dog will go in the front and announce ourselves," he continued. "North Pole PD – you guys will be around the compound on the outside to subdue anyone who gets out from either the side entrance, or under the fence –

and you will go in with Jeremy and Argus..." Jeff waved at the SWAT-clad Fairbanks police department K-9 handler at the back of the room, "...at the side gate."

Jeremy acknowledged Jeff's greeting with a nod. His big German Shepherd – also in SWAT gear – lay sprawled next to his handler, nonchalantly licking himself.

"The front gate is generally closed but unsecured during the day. Both front and side are secured at night. Obviously, we need to get both opened simultaneously to maintain any element of surprise. Be prepared for the bad guys to scatter or try to shoot us. Based on what we've dealt with in the past, they're more likely than not heavily armed. I don't want this to be Ruby Ridge, especially since there's a little kid in there, but I definitely don't want it to be Custer's Last Stand either. Don't want anybody hurt, including them. We want to catch them sufficiently off guard."

Jeff switched to a third image – a close-up of the two dwellings, located near the rear of the compound, not far from the side gate, taken from the air.

"We need absolute simultaneous ingresses here – front and side. And Jeremy, please address the activities you guys did earlier," Jeff requested.

The Fairbanks K-9 handler spoke up from the back of the room. "There are several homes within shooting distance of the compound. North Pole PD evacuated the nearby North Pole residents this morning around 0100. If we have to exchange fire with these folks, we want to minimize collateral damage. We don't want to shoot civilians, Santa, or any elves." The cops in the room laughed uncomfortably at the image.

"We also threw some good-sized steaks over the fence liberally laced with Ketamine – for the two junkyard dogs," he added. "If we're lucky, they'll be snoozing and we won't have to 'terminate' that particular threat."

"And, I don't need to add..." Jeff reinforced, "...that because we're coming in two entrances at once, we don't need friendly fire either. It's my hope that I'm worrying for nothing, and we'll close this place down in 10 minutes. But it could be we'll make the national news by 0700 yet not in a good way. I don't want that to happen." He paused and looked around the room.

"Questions?" Jeff asked. "You gentlemen – and Robyn – know what you're going to be doing?"

The officers nodded.

"Okay. Saddle up. North Pole – in your armored vehicle. Clark, Greg, Tyler, the dog and I are taking the Bearcat. The rest of you, get your vehicles and let's gather out in front. Pius – you and Robyn get Helo Two in the air."

It was 0430 as the heavily armed law enforcement officers, wearing NVGs for the low light environment, approached the North Pole compound on foot via the gravel road that ran in front. They fanned out to their respective places around the fenced-in property. They heard the dogs behind the fences start to bark.

Jeff waited impatiently until he heard the radio clicks in his ear that indicated that all were in position. "Pius, now!" he told the helo pilot over the secure intercom. NVG's came off the officers on the ground.

Helo Two, low on the deck to minimize the sounds of the AStar's turbine, rose over the trees and the compound, and Pius activated the ship's NightSun's 40 million candlepower light, virtually turning the darkness into day. At the same time, simultaneous explosive devices brought down the gates' security and allowed access.

"Alaska State Troopers! Come out with your hands on your heads. Alaska State Troopers! Come out with your hands on your heads!" Jeff called out as they jogged towards the mobile homes. The North Pole officers came through the side gate at the same time, also announcing their presence. Though prepared for many contingencies, Jeff knew that compliance would probably not be one of them.

In getting into position, Jeff's entry team passed vehicles up on blocks, two large dogs – Rottweilers – snoozing comfortably in the snow about fifty feet inside the front gate, several abandoned refrigerators, garbage cans, old tires, and mounds of trash. The locked storage containers were on the opposite side of the compound from the side entrance, but law enforcement was not concerned with them now. Later, after the inhabitants of this compound were no longer a threat, those containers would be opened.

Sheltering with his troopers behind the working vehicles parked in front of the two mobile homes, Jeff called out again. "Alaska State Troopers and Law Enforcement! Come out with your hands on your heads! Come out with your hands on your heads! We have you surrounded! You cannot get away!"

There was a moment of palpable silence, and then the distinctive chatter of an AK-47 and rounds thudding into the car behind which he was sheltering.

Light 'em up, he thought, and opened fire.

Chapter Thirty-one

Mary's phone call woke her at 0430. "CJay – we're on standby for a police action in North Pole. It's AST and Fairbanks and North Pole PD. Thought you'd want to know."

"Thanks, Mary," CJay croaked. "'Preciate the call." CJay stretched in her comfortable bed. Today she and the Trooper were going to have breakfast together before he went to work. Maybe. If he wasn't involved in North Pole.

If he was okay.

She made coffee, showered, fixed her hair. Dressed in a flannel shirt, jeans and boots. Sat down to read the paper until he came to get her. Maybe. If he was okay.

Eight o'clock came and went. She texted him, but there was no response. She tried calling several times, but his phone went immediately to voicemail.

She texted at 0900, but there was no response. By then, she was both worried and also feeling guilty about being miffed at not being contacted by the Trooper himself. She threw off her clean smelling clothes, put on running clothes and warm outerwear, and took off to the Chena River to blow out her frustration and extreme concern. Is this what he was talking about – gone days at a time? One thing to be able to anticipate being gone days at a

239

time; but another thing to guess at where someone is. Or what condition they're in.

Or why they're not in touch.

I've got a lot to learn, she realized.

Chapter Thirty-two

It didn't take long to finish what they started. Though the inhabitants of the two mobile homes were heavily armed, they were outgunned by the eleven law enforcement officers, two dogs, and Helo Two with Robyn and her sharp eye.

Clark was hit almost immediately by a ricochet off one of the vehicles, lacerating his neck and jaw, but carotids had been spared and despite his pain, bleeding, and the large dangling flap of skin that exposed his teeth so he looked like a creepy Halloween skull mask (though he'd temporarily pasted it back to his face with duct tape from his kit), he'd continued the fight until almost the end. There was one dead in the trailers and two bad guys injured, but no additional law enforcement injuries. All the surviving inhabitants of the compound were on the ground, handcuffed and secured. Now the tedious job of cleanup and assessment could begin.

"Dispatch," Jeff said into his radio, "Keep EMS and Aurora on standby. We've got a Trooper down and two injured suspects, but we still need to secure this entire scene. Have EMS stage at the end of the road on Badger. We'll let you know when it's safe to respond."

The exterior teams and both K-9s were inside the compound, carefully searching the debris piles for anyone hidden in the shadows. In only a few minutes, when the rest of the compound was cleared and secured, EMS rolled in, taking Clark in one rig, and one injured suspect back to NSMC in another with a North Pole officer for protection. Another individual with a superficial shoulder wound was placed in a trooper vehicle and would be transported as soon as a third ambulance arrived. Aurora was taken off standby.

Fairbanks police rounded up the two women and took them downtown to the Fairbanks Correctional Center where they'd be remanded.

When Jeff was convinced they'd done all they could do in securing the compound for the arrival of the state authorities, he radioed up to Pius in the A-Star. "Helo Two, Trooper. Thank you immensely. We'll see you in a little while. Fly safe."

"Trooper, Helo Two. Catch you on the flip flop."

The NightSun flicked off and Jeff could hear Helo Two turning away to go back to the airport. The sky was starting to lighten and although the NightSun's light was gone, there was enough natural light for them to see what they had and, aided by flashlights, to start cutting the bolts off the shipping containers to discover what this compound was hiding.

The State Drug Enforcement Agency, or the SDEA, flew in later that morning, but by then, Jeff and his group had uncovered an enormous cache of weapons, including handguns, shotguns,

242

tactical shotguns, AR-15s, AK-47s and other long guns, some broken down, but others ready to sell. Or use.

They found what was later estimated to be over $180,000 worth of heroin, $350,000 of methamphetamine, and $200,000 of illegal marijuana. There was even approximately $180,000 of cocaine, $1500 worth of Psilocybin mushrooms and uncounted 1000s of assorted commercial pharmaceuticals – packaged for quick sale. Cases of hard liquor completely filled one of the enormous shipping crates. The drug paraphernalia filled immunerable evidence garbage sacks.

There were also six fifty-five-gallon barrels of highly flammable toxic waste left over from cooking meth at the compound. The Hazardous Waste Disposal Team from North Pole Fire Department with Fort Wainwright HazMat assisting in clean-up would be called in to deal with that. In the meantime, the officers were warned to stay clear of them.

Trygve and Argus were invaluable in sniffing out drugs hidden in the cars and SUVs used as transport vehicles. Finally, the Troopers located the money the dealers had hidden under the flooring of one of the mobile homes: Over $400,000, neatly sorted and wrapped.

The most important items they found, however, were logs and accounting books with names of other dealers and dates of transactions, including the names of suppliers in the Lower 48 who had shipped hundreds of thousands of dollars' worth of illicit drugs and alcohol over the past twenty-four months into Alaska for dispersal over the entire northern state. These would be turned over to the Feds.

A search of the compound's perimeter by Argus and Jeremy found the six-year-old son of one of the women arrested hidden in the tunnel entrance. He was taken to NSMC for assessment, and would end up at Children's Services.

"What are these people thinking?" Jeremy asked when they pulled the kicking and biting child out of the hole in the ground. "What kind of evil parents subject their spawn to this kind of life?" he asked as the child flipped him off with double fingers and screamed, "Fuck YOU!" at the top of his little six-year-old lungs.

Jeff stopped at NSMC on his way back to the Trooper post to check on Clark. The gash and resultant duct taped skin flap on his neck and the side of his face was long and ragged – indeed a ricochet – and would require stitches and subsequent cosmetic surgery

"Manly scars, Clark," Jeff told him when he finally found him in the trauma room with his spouse, Guy, at his side. He man-hugged his friend. "Glad you're gonna be okay. Oh, and take the rest of the day off, will you?"

* * * * * *

He called Clare's phone, but there was no answer. He left a message, then started to follow up with a text. When he looked at his own texts, he realized he'd stood her up. *Crap. Crap. Crap. Nice way to try to start a 'friendship'. But she can't possibly be mad at me. It's not like I'm out getting drunk with the boys. I simply forgot. I forgot I had a date with you. I'm sorry, Clare. Damn it.*

He texted her.

I'm so sorry, Clare. Things came up. Can I see you tonight when I get off?

She didn't reply.

He texted her again, this time giving a rough estimate of when he'd be free and able to meet her. She still didn't reply.

Wonder if she's mad?

Chapter Thirty-three

The flight nurse's house was dark when he drove by on his way home from the Peger Road AST Post. He called, but she wasn't answering her cell phone. He pulled the Expedition into her driveway and jumped out to knock on the door, but there was no answer. Trygve woofed from his place in the dog box, but no one responded to that, either.

Wonder if she's really mad at me? Is she really this touchy? Big red flag?

He shook his head.

"Can I help you, Trooper?" he heard a voice behind him say. The Sergeant jumped. *So much for situational awareness, Trooper.*

"I'm looking for the occupant of this house," he told the wizened old man standing behind him armed with a baseball bat he was swinging casually. "You playing fungo ball tonight?" he asked the geezer.

"Nope. Thought I'd help you out if you needed backup. Why're you lookin' for CJay? She's all right, isn't she?"

"I'm sure she is." Jeff sighed. "I'll be truthful with you, pardner. I had a date with her this morning, but stood her up. Got involved in stuff…"

"...and you blew her off?" the oldster chuckled.

"Metaphorically speaking, pretty much. She'll probably never speak to me again."

"Nah. She's okay. She might make you pay for it, but she's a sweet girl. She's helped me and my wife a lot these past coupla years. Emma took a fall and CJay called the 911 for us and made sure those medic folks knew what was going on. Then she made hot dishes for us. I got kinda tired of the tuna noodle casserole, though, but at least hers is better than mine."

"She's not answering her phone."

"I saw her go for a run this morning and then leave about three hours ago with her guns. Maybe she went on her date without you? She just might be sharpenin' up her aim even as we speak." He cackled softly.

Jeff chuckled at the old guy's humor. "She just might be."

"I'd better get back in the house. Emma's a soft touch for a man in a uniform, and you're lookin' pretty spiff in that trooper SWAT stuff. I don't want her to get any ideas now." He sniffed the air. "You don't smell too good, though."

"It's SERT stuff, but thanks. I wouldn't want to get Emma too excited, especially if I 'don't smell too good.' If you see CJay, let her know the Trooper stopped by."

"Will do. Good luck," he cackled again as he turned to limp back to his house next door.

247

Chapter Thirty-four

She could see the Expedition parked in her driveway, and spotted the K-9 in the front yard, sniffing the bushes and then lifting his leg on them. She pulled up to the curb and stepped out, her gun duffle over her shoulder. Then she saw him get out of the SUV and walk towards her.

"I'm really sorry, Clare. I got involved in this thing this morning and I totally blanked that we were going to go to breakfast. I'm sorry."

She didn't say a word, but put down her duffle, walked to him, and put her arms around him, holding him close.

"God, you smell bad." She pulled away and put her hands on his face, drawing him down and kissing his cheek. "I'm glad you're okay."

"Me, too. I'm sorry." He looked down at his rumpled camouflage gear and took a deep whiff. "And your neighbor already informed me I reek and how that would be a turnoff to 'Emma.'"

"I see you've met Sergeant Kenny, then?"

The Trooper nodded. "He was going to kill me with his baseball bat, but I convinced him to not do so."

CJay chuckled. "You're very lucky, Trooper. Kenny was infantry in Korea. Medals and Purple Hearts. Still fits in his uniform. I suspect he's tired of my tuna noodle casserole, though."

"I like tuna noodle casserole. Does yours have green peas in it and potato chips crumbled on top? That's my favorite."

She stared at him. "You've got to be kidding." Then she started to laugh. "Can you come in for a bite to eat? Have you eaten?"

"I've spent the entire day doing paperwork and dealing with the SDEA from Anchorage and the hazmat teams from North Pole and Wainwright. It was a righteous operation with good results this morning, but the paperwork is a bear. You know – CYA."

"'Cover Your Ass?' I understand. But, are you hungry?"

"I'm starving. We had lunch and then some doughnuts, but I haven't real food since 1100 and then it was thin crust Hawaiian pizza of all things from the local joint. I don't smell good, though, Clare. I don't want you to have to smell me."

"I'd rather smell you than not see you, Jeff. Do you have a change of clothes with you?"

"Yes."

"Do you feel comfortable taking a shower here and putting on your clean clothes? I promise I won't accost you in the bathroom and make you do things against your will."

"Darn." He looked downcast. "Well, despite that promise, I'll come in and shower and change. Can Trygve come inside, too? I've got his food with me."

"Of course. He's already watered every dormant plant in my yard. He might as well come shed all over my floors, too."

"You're a good woman, Clare."

"Yes, I am, Trooper. Listen, I can't fix you tuna noodle casserole with green peas tonight, but I can fix you a tuna panini with a glass of chardonnay or a beer – or coffee – if you want."

"I want, Clare. Thank you."

She put her arms around him again, trying not to breathe too deeply. "I'm so glad you're okay, Jeff. I was worried." She hugged him firmly. "And, there's a brand-new toothbrush in the bathroom cabinet. Still in its wrapper. It's yours now."

Chapter Thirty-five

The Trooper brushed the filth off his teeth, then showered, and wished Clare actually would have surprised him, naked and warm, but she kept her promise and let him have his privacy.

When he was clean and dressed in fresh jeans and a sweatshirt, he found her in the kitchen mixing up tuna, diced celery, and mayonnaise. He saw thinly sliced tomatoes, avocado, red onion, pepperoncini, and sliced provolone cheese.

"Put some butter on the outside of those Focaccia slices there." She pointed to the six Italian bread slices. "Then put that Dijon mustard on the inside of the slices, Jeff." He did as she instructed.

He watched as she expertly layered onion slices, avocado, tuna salad, pepperoncini and tomatoes, then finished with a slice of provolone cheese. She put the second bread slice on top of each sandwich and placed all three inside a preheated Breville panini press and put down the lid. He knew exactly how much that Breville cost. He'd priced them. And purchased one. For Helen.

As the sandwiches toasted, she handed him the Bud Light he'd requested and placed apples slices on two plates for them.

"Looks good," he said. "I don't have a panini maker," he added.

"Aww. Poor trooper. My mother gave that to me when I bought the house."

"I have a George Foreman grill that sort of does the same thing. It cost fifteen bucks. I have a waffle iron, too."

"I don't have a waffle iron."

"Then we're a perfect match, flight nurse. Listen, I'm really sorry about today. Things just got a little hectic there for a while."

She nodded. "I know. But don't apologize this time. Mary phoned me at 0430 to let me know they were on standby for you guys in North Pole. Then I got an update from the *News-Miner* app at 1000. I was worried though, Jeff."

She turned around to him and hugged him again, this time smelling fresh soap and his clean sweatshirt – which had an American flag on it with a Belgian Malinois dog's head and the word "Loyalty" superimposed on the top of the flag.

"I like your sweatshirt." She sniffed. "Did you use my apple shampoo?"

"I washed my head with it." He bent down so she could smell his skull. She laughed and kissed his warm ear. "You smell good now, Trooper."

He put his arms around her this time. *I want to go to bed with you. The heck with tuna paninis.* He kissed the side of her head, then her cheek, then the side of her lips. She turned toward him and he kissed her mouth, pulling her close. He groaned in his throat. And heard her do the same.

"No, Trooper. No." She pulled away somewhat reluctantly, he thought, and handed him the plate with his two hot toasted sandwiches with the melting cheese and the apple slices, and they sat at the drop-leaf table in her kitchen.

"I need to apologize to you, Jeff," she said once they'd starting eating.

"What for *this* time?"

"I didn't answer your texts. I'm sorry for the 'silent treatment.' I won't do that again. How's your sandwich?"

"I appreciate that, Clare. And, this is the best tuna panini I've ever had." He was almost finished with the first, and eyeing the second one.

"Good. Now tell me about today."

So, he did. He told her about Pius, their plan, Clark's injury, what they'd found. He also told her they were pretty certain that the meth cooks they'd busted in Nenana, and Frank Bridow – the asswipe who'd killed Susan and Mark – were all part of a drug and alcohol pipeline that went from the North Star Borough all the way outside to Sacramento, in northern California.

"Clare, I don't think I can ever really atone for what happened to my two troopers, but what started with them is ended now. These vermin won't hurt any more of my people."

"My God," Clare ventured when he was through. She put her hand on his hand. "I'm glad you and your guys all okay, Jeff. And I'm glad you're here in my house."

"I'm pretty happy about it, too. Are you busy tomorrow? Maybe we can try again?"

"I'll make time for you."

253

"1400?"

"I'll see you at 2PM, trooper. Stand me up this time, and you are well and truly screwed."

"I hear your words. I'll be here." *And I would love to be 'well and truly screwed' by you, Clare.*

He stayed for another hour until he began to yawn and she insisted he take his dog home and get some sleep.

Chapter Thirty-six

They spent more than two hours the next day at the indoor range with Jeff watching her shoot, giving her pointers, but letting her know she was really good at this and he didn't feel the need to "teach" her anything. CJay told him that David had trained her when she was only in high school and when she'd moved back to Eugene after Alex's death, they'd go to the range for practice. She didn't tell him that blasting big guns and completely shredding targets gave her great pleasure. It was a purge – a cleansing. For a long time, it was a release of her rage at Alex's death.

She watched Jeff shoot his .45 – the Springfield 1911 – and found herself thinking he looked incredibly sexy with that powerful gun in his hand. The skill and ease he showed while loading, shooting, and handling the weapon was erotic. She accepted gladly when he asked if she wanted to try it. His classic 1911 was a beautiful weapon with little to no kick to it – less than her Glock 9mm.

"I want one of these," she told him before she handed it back. He nodded and filed away the information.

She also enjoyed having him put his arms around her to help direct her shots. She knew that he knew she needed no help, but his arms were warm and comforting, and once she made the mistake of leaning back into them instead of shooting. He'd kissed the back of her neck and shooting practice might have ended right there except for the fact she still had her Glock 29 in her hands and didn't want to make love to this man on the floor in the middle of spent shells, gunshot residue, and the smell of propellant...with the shooters in the other stalls watching.

After, they packed up and CJay bought more ammunition at the range store.

"If you want, we can do 'takeout' – my treat, Trooper – and clean our guns at my place. I've got the supplies."

"Coffee?"

"Of course."

"You like Thai?"

He did. CJay called Nim's House, ordering Spring Rolls, two Pad Thai take outs ("You like Thai tea?" she asked him as she was punching in the restaurant's number. "Yes.") and two Thai teas.

It was almost 5:30PM by the time they reached her house, and both were hungry. CJay ceremoniously dumped both take out boxes into two graceful blue handmade clay noodle bowls with two sets of chopsticks – wooden with abalone insets. Jeff looked at them appreciatively. Then the flight nurse unceremoniously poked straws into the plastic tops on the plastic cups of iced Thai tea and set his in front of him. She put the box with the Spring Rolls between them.

"Nice job, Clare. You prepare a fine meal." He held her chair for her while she sat at the drop leaf kitchen table, then seated himself. He picked up his chopsticks and elegantly scooped up noodles and ate them. He looked up to see her staring at him.

"Did I spill?" He looked down at his shirt. Nope. Still clean.

"You handle your chopsticks very well."

He nodded. Thank you. "The Marines taught me a lot." He made googly eyes and twiddled his chopsticks at her. "I frequently catch flies with them too."

CJay laughed out loud. "Very good, Karate Kid. How'm I doing?" She also used her chopsticks proficiently, maneuvering noodles into her mouth with no splashes.

"I think you pass the shibboleth of Asian eating utensils very well."

She put her chopsticks down on the tiny porcelain chopstick holder she'd also placed on the table next to both their placemats and tasteful matching napkins – and shook her head.

"'Shibboleth?' You're think you're pretty damn smart, don't you?"

"Smart? Or 'Smarty Pants?'"

CJay smiled. *You make me laugh, Trooper.* "And, yes...both of those."

"Clare, I'm just a dumb cop with a good memory for words. 'N stuff."

She looked at him. At his face. At his hazel eyes. His shoulders. *I could go bed with you. I want my arms around you.* She could feel herself flushing. *Must change subject now.* She twisted in her chair, feeling her desire between her legs.

She knew what would change the mood and keep her from making a fool of herself.

"Your mother mentioned Helen. Who is Helen?"

"My mother mentioned Helen?" He shook his head as if in disbelief. "My mother never fails to amaze me, Clare, and not always in good ways. I refuse to speak of Helen until I've eaten this delicious food."

They kept eating, small talking, until Jeff had cleaned his bowl. He placed his chopsticks on the porcelain holder, carried his bowl to the sink, washed it with dish soap and hot water, putting it on the little dish drainer next to the sink, then came back to the table. He saw Clare was finished with her bowl, so he took it and repeated the washing ritual, placing her bowl next to his on the dish drainer. He put the empty styrofoam Spring Rolls box into the trash under her sink.

"Like you, I also have a good memory, Trooper."

He looked at her, sitting there at the little table, and nodded his head.

"Get your gun cleaning stuff and I'll tell you about Helen while we work. But, I also want to hear about why you've never remarried. Remember? That was also going to be our next agenda discussion." She nodded at him and went to get her supplies.

Chapter Thirty-seven

How do I tell this incredible woman with 'Balls o' Steel' about another person I loved? How do I tell her without making her feel she has to somehow 'measure up?' There's no comparison. These two women are as different as the summer and winter solstice. Both sources of joy – and reasons for celebration. But one is filled with light and warmth and a potential portent of winter, and the other – Clare – well, obviously, cold, beautiful – and challenging - but with a promise of Spring. I suppose I need to begin at the proverbial 'beginning.'

This is not a short story.

Helen lived with her Mom and grandmother – not unlike Shannon and I did after Dad died. In some ways, Helen and I are alike – and maybe, just maybe, that's why I felt so close to her.

Veda, Helen's mother, came from a village in the lower southwest. She came to Fairbanks to go to school, got an AA in Human Resources, walked into the Trans-Alaska Pipeline (TAPS) offices in Fairbanks and was hired on the spot because she filled oh so many Equal Employment Opportunity check offs and was intelligent, skilled, efficient, creative, attractive, and personable.

Veda got involved with one of the pipeline engineers and Helen was the result. The tall engineer neglected to mention that he had a wife and kids in Texas and wasn't happy when Veda let him know she was pregnant – despite taking precautions. He made the mistake of telling her he wasn't going to marry an "Eskimo" not aware that this was not only not an insult, but was a point of pride with the highly capable young Aleut woman. The Texan was extremely lucky – although he didn't know it – that she didn't off him with her Ka-Bar 7" military knife, and hang, gut, and skin him afterwards. In fact, when she was 18 she'd won, handily, the Native Skills field dress demonstration (seal skinning was a talent portion of the WEIO competition) at the World Eskimo Indian Olympics – held in Fairbanks. She was not crowned Miss WEIO, but the scholarship money she earned helped her obtain her AA degree.

Ernie McClellan transferred immediately up north and Veda never saw him again. Helen's grandmother moved to Fairbanks and for eighteen years the two women raised Helen to be a fine young woman who valued education and her native heritage. She was proud to be an "Al-ee-yoot."

They also taught her to be independent as a woman and very wary of men – who could let you down with little warning and, per Veda's experience, even less concern.

When Helen turned eighteen, she went to the University of Alaska Anchorage on a basketball scholarship and got her nursing degree. After graduation, she came back up north and hired on at Fairbanks Memorial in the ICU, moving within two years to the Emergency Department.

There's no reason to tell Clare this, but it speaks reams to me about why Helen and I clicked – why I fell in love with her independent spirit, her intelligence, her frequently hilarious sense of humor, and her fire. Why she meant so much to me during that time. And why I missed her afterwards for so long.

I do tell Clare that I met Helen in the ED at Fairbanks Memorial Hospital. She is tall, cynical, bold, athletic, serious, exotic looking, smart, funny, and professional. At that time, she was involved with a Fairbanks PD detective and you don't mess with a brother's woman. We spent a lot of time flirting with one another in those days – and having coffee in the hospital cafeteria. When she and her cop broke up, she asked me out. We were inseparable after that for almost two years.

I don't want Clare to be jealous of Helen. How honest can I be?

"Did you want to marry her?" she asks, suddenly.

"Yes, Clare. I wanted to marry her." *I wanted to raise my family with her.*

"And...?"

"She wanted the world – the 'Outside.' She didn't want to stay in Alaska. I didn't want to go. I couldn't leave."

"Did she break your heart?"

I know why Clare asks these questions. She's wary. Careful. Looking for a reason to push me away. I understand.

I look her in her pretty dark blue eyes.

"Clare, she broke my heart. Does that make you feel better knowing she broke my heart?"

It was an incredibly difficult time for me finally coming to the terrible acknowledgment that Helen and I did not share the same life goals

"No, it doesn't," she says.

Clare pauses – and I know exactly what she's going to ask me next.

"Do you still love her?" she asks quietly.

Now she looks me directly in the eyes. She looks like she's daring me to give her some kind of bullshit story.

No, I tell her, and that's the truth. I tell this flight nurse that I hope Helen finds what she's looking for, but my 'broken heart' is healed. I see her mother from time to time when I'm out shopping. I got a card from Helen last Christmas.

What I don't tell Clare (because I think it sounds like a really bad pick-up line) is that I think my 'broken heart' began its healing process the day I saw her – this flight nurse – on the flightline at Fort Wainwright – before the helicopters took off in the "Missing Man" formation flyover for our lost troopers. That was absolutely a day of anguish for all of us ASTs – but she – in that well-cut navy-blue flight suit and Aurora jacket, with her long hair tied back in a ponytail low on her neck, her dark blue eyes and that soft smile on those pretty lips – was the one bright spot, a bit of hope, I guess, for me. The way she took my hand and told me she was so sorry for what we were going through.

I think I fell a little bit in love with Clare then.

"Jeff."

I look over at her.

"What are your 'life goals' now?"

To get you in the sack as soon as I possibly can and make love to you for a lifetime, but I'm definitely not going to share that with this woman before I've even had a chance to unbutton her shirt.

Chapter Thirty-eight

They'd moved into the living room when they were finished with their guns and sat on the sofa. CJay was at one end, her knees pulled up to her chest. Jeff sat on the other, facing her. He looked tired. She knew he was exhausted from the crap he'd been through today. Probably talking about Helen hadn't perked him up any. The flight nurse definitely knew it'd been hard to listen to him: Helen the Exotic. Helen the snarky, clever person. Helen the Hotshot. Helen the Heart Breaker. Hell. Maybe she and Helen had something in common after all.

"I shouldn't have made you talk about her tonight, Jeff. I'm sorry. It wasn't appropriate. I know this has been a tough day."

"Yeah. But being here with you makes it a whole heck of a lot better. Thanks, Clare, for the food – and for just being here. Thanks."

He reached over and grabbed one of her ankles, pulling it towards him, running his hand up the inside of her jeans, feeling her smooth skin underneath. CJay was grateful she'd shaved her legs that morning. She also knew that if she made the slightest move towards him at this moment – which she desperately wanted to do – her vow of celibacy would be over. She wanted to make this man feel better. She knew what had always helped Alex feel better.

The flight nurse shook her head, then pulled her foot back and got up. "You want some coffee?" He did, and followed her back into the kitchen.

"Your turn, Clare," he asked while they were standing waiting for the French press to do its job. Questioning look on her face.

"Your turn," he repeated. "Why haven't you remarried?"

She shook her head. "Not yet, Jeff. Answer my question first. What are your life goals now?"

Street lights had been on for hours. The only light in the kitchen, however, was from the little appliance light on the stove hood, illuminating her face, casting shadows on the rest of the room.

"I have a job I love – that I'm pretty good at. That was a goal. I do the crisis intervention stuff – I help other cops and firefighters deal with the trauma of their jobs. That may sound hokey, Clare, but I feel I'm giving back in a big way what I've learned – what saved me years ago – that psychological body armor we need to keep doing our jobs."

She nodded and poured a little Irish Cream into their cups, looking up at him to continue his explanation.

"Goals. Okay. Clare, I want a family. I want a relationship with a woman I love who loves me back just as much. I want someone who wants to take care of me and share my life as much as I want to care for her and make her happy she's married to me. I want kids. I want to be a presence for them. Play hockey – or eat ice cream with them. Go to their games. Kiss their

265

booboos. Love their momma. Show them what it's like to have a mother and father who can care for one another and them, too."

He took the coffee she handed him and followed her back out to the front room again.

"When my dad died, I lost the solid core of my family. Mother was gone a lot, but dad was always there. Then, my grandmother and granddad came to live with us – raising Shannon and me while Mother was doing her traveling and research. Then my granddad died when I was fourteen, and once again I was the fucking man of the house living with a crew of women around. Listen, Clare, I'm not whining. I had good friends, sports, girlfriends, great teachers, food and shelter, and even had my kid goals then. But I needed out of that house, and I know now that joining the military was a subconscious desire for an intact kind of 'family' once again – a place where I belonged. I suppose the Troopers is part of that too – family, companionship, training and structure, autonomy, excitement, camaraderie. I told you this before."

He was back on the sofa and she sat at the other end with her sock feet up against his thigh, watching him. She kneaded his leg with her toes. He put his left hand over her socks and squeezed them gently.

"You want children." It wasn't a question.

"Yes. I want a whole family. Whole as in not just part of a family. That's not negotiable. Two kids. That number *is* negotiable." His tight jaw loosened at that last, and he half smiled and patted her feet.

266

"Your turn, flight nurse. Why haven't you gotten back in the game?"

"It's simple, Trooper. No long story. You already know most of it anyhow." She took a deep breath. "I've never found anyone good enough. Anyone who could 'take his place.'"

"'Fill his boots.'"

"Yes," she answered simply.

"And your firefighter?"

"And my cop in Eugene?"

"Okay," he sighed. "Your firefighter and your cop in Eugene. What about them?"

"They weren't good enough. No one has been. I froze them out until they both finally said, 'Screw it.' And dumped my ass." *And now, Trooper, you know.* "Aiden called me 'Ice Queen.'"

There was a long pause and finally he asked, "What do you hope to achieve by telling me your story this way?"

CJay shook her head. "What do you mean?" She looked at him.

"I tell you I'm looking for a relationship with someone who will want me and love me as much as I want her and love her. And, you're telling me you deliberately freeze people out so they leave you. Are you telling me I should protect myself? I should walk away and shut the door on you? Are you deliberately pushing *me* away? You told ME not to do that to you. What's actually going on, Clare?"

There was a long, uncomfortable silence. Finally, CJay took a deep breath and held it a moment before letting it back out. Then she looked at him. "That's a good question, Trooper. For

267

four years I've always said it was because no one could fill his boots."

"That's what you said when your brother was here – Alex, your 'frikkin' hero in a uniform.'"

"And I meant that for a long time. I think it's...maybe...it's different now, though."

He sat without a word, waiting for her to continue. She could hear her big red art deco wall clock from Pier I Imports ticking on the wall in the dining area. *If this doesn't cause him to grab his keys and gallop out the door, nothing will.*

"You know when your mother did her thing at the helicopter after Baby Gus was born?"

"Who can forget it? Welcome to my family, Clare." He made a wry face.

"What if I told you I speak with Alex in my dreams?" She saw him raise an eyebrow.

"As long as you don't play strip poker with him, I'm good with it."

She laughed and shook her head. "No, I don't play strip poker with him." And that, at least, was the truth. "For a long time, he just comforted me and told me he was okay and would always watch over me."

"He sounds like a good spirit."

The clock ticked. Finally, Jeff said softly, "And now?"

"And now...?" she echoed his question. "And now he's asking me why I haven't moved on. He asking me what's holding me back."

"What have you told him?"

"Nothing yet. But I know the answer."

"And?" He paused for her answer that did not come. Then he finally spoke quietly. "Do you want to *share* that bit of information with me?"

"Because I don't want to lose him. I feel – or at least I felt like that if I 'found' someone else that Alex's death would be made less important. It wouldn't matter that he'd died because I'd gone on to find happiness without him. Like he was just a pit stop in my life. A waypoint."

"But he's not. Jesus. You know that."

"He told me he's not my 'broken road,' but he *is* my guiding star – pointing me on."

The Trooper smiled. "I think I know a song like that."

She dipped her head, then looked back up at him. "You okay with me talking about this?"

"About Alex? Absolutely. You loved him. You had a good marriage, right?"

She nodded. *We made delicious love six hours before he died.*

"If you had a good marriage, then you know it's possible to find love and joy in a relationship. I know a lot of people who say they'll never get married again because their own relationships are so full of crap. I'd say you were blessed."

CJay nodded again. "Yeah. I feel we were blessed. So, when he was killed, I was simply blown to pieces. I couldn't eat. Hell, I could hardly get out of our bed. I quit my job. Mom came up and helped me move back home to my high school bedroom. It was absolutely, unimaginably horrible. I thought I would die, too."

269

Clare moved over to sit beside the Trooper and he put his arm gently around her shoulder.

"I'd say it's a tribute to Alex that you are thinking about – how can I put this without sounding squishy – well, moving on. But not leaving Alex behind. Moving forward with his blessing. Finding joy again."

Clare leaned her head against his shoulder, and put her hand on his leg.

"There's something else, Jeff, that's made it all the more difficult. Your mother seems to know." She saw his eyes widen. "At the helicopter – she turned around to me and said, 'I'm so sorry.'"

"I remember that. Do you know what she meant?"

CJay hesitated, then nodded. "I think I do." There was a moment of silence. "I lost our baby, Jeff."

She heard him take a quick breath.

"Aw, Clare. I'm so sorry." He shook his head. "I apologize. Now I sound like my mother. Do you want to talk about it?"

"Yeah, I do. I want to tell you everything. That way you know what you're getting – I mean, if you even want it. I don't assume anything anymore."

"Then talk to me."

"I was four months pregnant when Alex was killed. She was a little girl – Alexa Clare. We'd already named her. When I was seven months, she stopped moving. I had an ultrasound and there was no heartbeat. They induced me, a gut-wrenching experience, because I knew I was giving birth to my dead daughter. Her cord was wrapped around her neck. She'd strangled. 'Fetal demise.' I thought I was going to die again."

She could feel her throat constrict, but knew she wouldn't cry. She'd cried all her tears out almost She'd cried all her tears out almost four years ago.

The only thing he said was, "Clare, I'm so very sorry."

It was a moment before she went on. "My mother said that it doesn't matter if you lose a child at 50 years or 34 weeks. It's a trauma that you never truly get over."

CJay sniffed.

"They wrapped her up in a pink blanket and put her in my arms. She had dark hair and eyes like Alex and his nose. She was perfect. They took pictures for me."

"I really don't know what to say."

"Thank you for being honest and not trying to do peer support with me."

He shrugged and pulled her close. "Listening is all I want to do with you right now."

"There's one more thing." She waited until she heard him say "I'm all ears, Clare."

"Alex tells me that Lexie is with him and they both watch over me."

"So, you have two angels?"

CJay leaned her head against his shoulder and smiled up at him. "I do, Jeff. I have two guardian angels."

"I don't think that anyone can have too many guardians, Clare." He put his other arm around her and she embraced him with her face close to his. There was nothing he could do but kiss her, and he did so with gentle warmth. He kissed her face, her neck, and started working his way lower, his right hand on her warm left breast....

* * * * *

"What now, Trooper?" he heard her say. And felt her pull away from him. "Are you ready to bolt?"

Damn. Does it look like it? "From you? Well, unless you divulge you're a serial killer with a dozen bodies buried in the tundra that I need to investigate after arresting you, you are – if you want to be – someone I want to get to know much better. I like what I see in you." *And I know your kissing and your body are driving me nuts. I could eat you right up.*

"You don't think it's weird about my dreams?"

He looked her right in the eyes. "Seriously? Just wait until you meet my grandmother if you think my mother's scary."

CJay laughed softly. "Well, perhaps down the road. Anyway, thanks for listening to me, Jeff. You're a good sport."

Good sport? "Clare, I think 'good sport' is the last thing I want to be with you. Maybe 'go-to guy?' 'President of your fan club?'"

"I like 'President of my Fan Club'."

"You can't scare me away."

"Good."

He glanced at her wall clock, still ticking softly, and said, "You know, Little John's has a new group this week." She looked at him. "It's a band that covers a lot of Rascal Flatts music." He saw her smile. "Can I take you dancing?"

272

"Awwww, Trooper. I would love that."

"Me too." *And I love you.*

Chapter Thirty-nine

Flight nurse, you free?

Yes, but not easy, Trooper.

CJay's cell phone in dispatch rang immediately and picking up she heard, "You make me laugh. How're you doing?"

"I'm good, Jeff. Um…and thank you for your understanding the other night." She paused before going on. "I've missed you."

"Same here. So, are you free to go out tonight for some food and dancing to that cover band at Little John's that I told you about? May I push you around the floor a couple of times?"

"I'd like that, Jeff. I'll text when I leave Aurora."

"See you at your place. Don't worry about fussing and getting ready. I just want to see you. Are you working tomorrow?"

"I am."

"I won't keep you out late. Like I said, just want to see you again."

"I look forward to that," she finally said to him. "Be safe, Trooper."

She texted him before she pulled out of the parking structure at NSMC and he knocked on her door minutes after she'd arrived home, pulled off her flight suit and wool underwear, cleaned up a bit, and thrown on jeans, sweater, and some leather boots. He embraced her, holding her close, smelling her hair and the perfume she'd applied.

She looked at him, dressed in jeans and sweater, big, strong, but stress lines apparent around his warm hazel eyes. He looked tired.

"Let's go, Trooper. Let's go get something to eat and listen to some music. We can both use that."

Chapter Forty

Little John welcomed them to their spot at the dark end of the bar and put two glasses of pale ale in front of them before they even asked.

"You call ahead, Trooper?" she asked him as they clinked their glasses in a toast.

"No. I think he sees it in my eyes. Okay with you?"

I think at this point in our relationship, you could order me tap water and it would be perfect.

"Pale ale is super. How was your day?"

He put his hand around the back of her neck, pulled her towards him, and kissed her beer lips. "Clare, I'm embarrassed to admit that I just keep thinking about you." He shrugged. "And my day was good. Yours?"

"Super. Never better. Love my job. Love my co-workers." *May I climb into your lap now and….* She shook her head and took another sip of ale.

"Hawaiian chicken wings double order extra spicy okay?" she heard Jeff ask her.

"Excellent choice, Trooper," she told him. *Whatever you want – at this point.*

They ate wings and licked their fingers and kissed Hawaiian spice off one another's lips until only a plate of bones was left. CJay turned on her bar stool and pulled him as close as she could and wrapped her arms around his strong shoulders. She heard the cover band begin the opening chords to *Bless the Broken Road.*

"I want to dance to this song." So, the Trooper took her hand and led her to the dance floor and held her close about a third of the way through the first verse. She closed her eyes, allowing the words being sung to flow over her. When the chorus started, Clare melted into his embrace. He pulled her closer. He felt her breath puff against his neck as she sang along to the words:

"Every long lost dream led me to where you are
Others who broke my heart they were like Northern stars
Pointing me on my way into your loving arms
This much I know is true
That God blessed the broken road
That led me straight to you."

Now I'm just rolling home into my lover's arms. "Take me home now, Trooper."

"You sure?"

God blessed my broken road. "You question the flight nurse?"

"Never. Ever."

Chapter Forty-one

"Take me home…now." He heard the emphasis on "home" and the soft "now." He left money for Little John plus a generous tip, helped the flight nurse with her coat, held her hand as they walked to his car, then held her door. Settled her in. And drove her to her house. This time, she unlocked the door and drew him inside. She took off her coat, unzipped his and took it from him. Dropped them both on the floor.

"Clare, what do you want? What do you want me to do?"

"I want to be near you. I want you in my bed. And don't you *dare* say no." She took his hand and led him to the sofa, pulling him down next to her. Then she spoke softly.

"This is not spur of the moment, Jeff. We've known one another for, what…ten days? Two weeks? Six months?" She laughed. "I have no idea. For some reason it feels like forever."

He nodded.

"Trooper, we've had this conversation before and I'm not gonna flog it again. Alex's death killed me."

He nodded again.

"I told you I couldn't let anyone in. No one was good enough to take my husband's place."

He nodded a third time.

"Then I met you and you kept pushing me and annoying me and irritating me. You even made me laugh – for the first time in a very long time. But then you stopped. Left me alone." She shook her head. "I'm not explaining this very well."

"I understand what you're saying, but what is it you want me to know?"

"I wanted you that night after the Pump House – after we danced…."

"I wanted you, too, but it wouldn't have been right, Clare."

"I know, Jeff. I've kept trying to keep you out – push you away. I can't do it anymore."

"What does that mean to you, Clare?"

"I want you in my life. Trooper, I want your strength and warmth in my life. I want that joy you talked about in my heart again. I want to make love to you. Is that too honest? Does that scare you?"

He put both of his arms around her and kissed her mouth, then whispered in her ear, "There is nothing I'd like more than to have that happen, Clare. My beautiful, sweet Clare. You can't frighten me away."

He was so aroused it hurt, but he knew he needed to take it slowly. He wanted to cherish each moment of this new layer of their relationship. He felt her hand on his leg, next to his groin and groaned.

"Does that feel good?" she asked him. *God, yes.*

He pulled her close, caressing and kissing her breasts through her shirt. "What about the vow of celibacy? How are we going to get around that?"

She turned to him and put her leg over his lap and pressed herself against his groin. "I'll lie about it."

He growled and put an available hand under her butt between her legs and squeezed. *You are killing me. So soft....* He pulled her onto his lap, unbuttoned her shirt and kissed her cleavage. Opening her shirt, he pulled down her black lace bra straps until her breasts were almost exposed. He kissed her bare flesh, pushing her breasts together and finally pulling down the cup on the left and exposing her nipple. He paused, took a breath and realize that he was almost ready to come just looking at that sweet pink nipple. He kissed it, swirled his tongue around it, and pulled it into his mouth to suck. Hard.

Clare ground her pelvis into his lap and pushed her breast into his lips. And moaned. She kissed his face. "That feels so good. Don't stop."

He could feel her rubbing her body against his groin. He wanted his jeans off immediately. Hers too.

"Show me your bedroom, Clare. I want to see where you sleep," he said against her breasts. *I want to see your sheets and your pillows and smell your skin and taste you, hold you, bring you pleasure. Feel myself inside of you.*

He picked her up with her legs still around him and she pointed him back to her bedroom. It was dark – the only light was the street light filtering through some leafless branches of birch outside her window. She closed the blinds after he'd set her down, and then she turned on the little bedside light. There was a navy and red plaid flannel duvet on the bed. She pulled it back, revealing inviting navy flannel sheets.

"I want to see you, Jeff."

Good. I want to see you also, Clare. And taste your sweetness….

He felt her fingers tug at the bottom of his sweater, so he lifted his arms and she pulled it off of him, leaving him with a shirt underneath. One by one, she unbuttoned his buttons, taking off his shirt and throwing it on the floor next to his sweater. He had a long-sleeved thermal tee shirt on under that which she removed.

"You have many layers on, Trooper."

I didn't get the memo about sex tonight, flight nurse.

"Sit down, Jeff. Lay back." He did and she started to finish unbuttoning her shirt.

"No," he said. "I want to do that." He stood up again beside her. She had the black lacy bra over her small breasts. A sweet handful, he thought, placing his right hand over her left breast and squeezing it. He took off her shirt, then bent down and kissed her breast again, maneuvering her onto the bed.

"My turn, Clare." He lay her on her back then lay next to her, kissing her forehead, cheeks, ears, the right side of her mouth, the left side of her mouth, and watched her open her mouth to his full kiss...and groaning. He wrapped his arm around her body, relishing the feel of her smooth, warm skin against his. He kissed her neck and gradually worked his way down to her breasts, biting her nipples gently through the lace, and kissing the skin outside the lace. He pulled down the strap on her left shoulder, pulling down the bra cup and visualizing her nipple, ripe and erect. He put his tongue on it, kissed around the aureole, then sucked on the nipple. She gasped and groaned. He heard her

281

breathe 'Oh God,' and felt her hand on his groin, squeezing his cock through his jeans. The Trooper straddled her partially with his right leg, pulled her up against him and carefully assessed the number of hooks on the back of her bra. He unsnapped them and bared her breasts. *Multi-tasking.*

"You are so beautiful, Clare," he said softly, exhaling. "My God, you are so beautiful." He lay her back and clasped her left breast and sucked and kissed the nipple, repeating the same thing on the right. She drew her knees up and he could see by the way she moved her hips she was enjoying the sensation between her legs. She pulled his head down onto her chest, then pressed her thigh against his groin, causing a thrill of electricity through his body.

"Flight nurse, you continue to do that, and this will end prematurely – at least for the moment."

"My turn, then, Jeff. You lay back." He did, and he felt her hands caressing him, outlining his own nipples. Then she kissed them and sucked on them. He growled and ran his hand over her nearest breast.

"Not your turn yet, Trooper."

"Do you want me?"

He could see her smile and he felt her warm tongue wash his lips and slip inside his mouth.

"Jeff," she said simply, "I want you mightily."

She kissed her way down his neck to his chest, his belly, to his belt. Then he felt her fingers gently tracing the names he had tattooed on the inside of his upper left arm.

"This must have hurt," she whispered.

"Yeah."

Then he felt her put her lips on those names and kiss them gently. Jeff put his arms around her and she melted into them. *How can I love her this soon?* He could feel Clare caressing and kissing his left shoulder where the top of his Scottish thistle tribal ink intertwined with the letters "USMC," scrolling down and around to his elbow in a half sleeve, forever surrounding and protecting those six names of his friends. His Marine family.

"This is very beautiful, Jeff. Do you have others?"

He smiled at her. "I'm a Marine, Clare. We are born with tattoos." He opened his arms so she could continue exploring. She put her hand around his right upper arm – where there were two other names, and rubbed her thumb over them.

"Susan and Mark," he said simply.

"I'm so very sorry, Jeff," she whispered, kissing those names, and then she gently kissed his cheek, his open lips, his chest and stomach again. She waited a moment and ran her fingers under his belt, under his jeans. He blew a sharp puff of air out of his mouth.

"I'm loving this, Clare," he breathed.

He felt her fingers fumbling with his belt buckle. He wanted to help her, but also wanted to prolong her exquisite first exploration.

Clare got the belt buckle undone. He felt the Levi's top snap come off, and then she pulled open the rest of the buttons on his 501s. He expelled breath through pursed lips when he felt her hand on the knit boxers over his penis. He pushed his groin into her hand.

"Does that feel good, Jeff?" She cupped his erect penis gently...and squeezed. Electricity flooded through his body once more.

"I hate it," he answered, gasping.

"How does this feel?" she asked, slipping her hands under the boxers, and touching his naked penis for the first time, gently squeezing. She moved down to his hips, pulled down his boxers a little, and kissed his naked flesh, taking the head of his engorged cock into her mouth, tasting the salty, silky fluid that had escaped.

"Can you feel me twitch?" he groaned, placing his hand gently on her head, wanting to press harder on his groin. "Flight nurse, you are still a witch. And now you have on more clothes than I do."

"'T'is a pity," he heard her say. She pulled away and rose to kneel on the floor. Boots were untied and pulled from his feet. Socks came next.

"Stand up, trooper." He stood by her and she helped him take off the 501s, then pulled his knit boxers completely off. She leaned forward and took his cock back into her mouth, her arms around his butt. He thrust gently. *You have to stop that, Clare. I want to taste you. I want to be inside of you.*

"Clare, let me undress you. I want to taste you."

Rising, she patted the bed for him to sit.

He did sit, after he bent to kiss her breasts once more, but then he pulled her to him, his mouth in the middle of her flat stomach. He kissed her belly then put his hand around the waistband of her jeans, unbuckling the belt and preparing to unzip her pants.

"I still have my boots on," she told him.

He looked down. Frowned.

"So you do."

He bent down to untie and pull off her winter boots while she placed her hand on his shoulder for balance. Lifting up her feet, she let him take them off, one by one, along with her wool socks.

"Do you think it takes this long to undress in Hawaii?" she mused.

He looked up at her and smiled, pulling her towards him once again, kissing her stomach and again fumbling with her pants, trying to remove them.

Then he laughed.

"Good God, Clare, I hope not." He could hear her laughing, too. All he could think of at this point was getting her clothes off and making love to her and it seemed to be taking a lifetime, and then taking her to Hawaii as soon as possible.

She stepped out of her jeans and stood in front of him. He put his hand behind her firm buttocks and realized she was wearing thongs. Could he be more aroused? He thought not.

"Thongs?"

"No VPLs," she said. "No visible panty lines. All flight nurses wear them. Did you see panty lines when I was crawling out of your Expedition that day?"

He kissed her left nipple and then murmured against her right one, "No, Clare, but I was looking. You've got a lovely butt."

"I knew you were watching, Trooper."

285

Closely, flight nurse.

He pulled her close again, kissing her mound, caressing her backside, slipping his fingers under the straps of her thong.

"Is this the big reveal?" she asked softly.

She had both hands on his shoulders, gently rubbing his neck, his chin, the back of his head. He pressed his head back against her hands. *Yes, it is the big reveal.* He pulled her black lacy thongs down to the floor and she stepped out of them.

He couldn't help it. He ran his hand up her leg, her thigh, and put his fingers into the soft wet warmth of her cleft, feeling her move against him, opening her legs.

"Ah, Clare, my darling Clare." Jeff inhaled her salty musk from his fingers, reveling in her smell. He pulled her into his arms and, rolling over, deposited her on the other side of the bed.

He covered her partially with the flannel sheet and duvet, joining her under the covers. He ran his hands over her body, kissing her face and her breasts again, suckling the nipples, kissing his way down to her mound, running his hand down her inner thigh. She spread her legs and he kissed her thighs, moving slowly upward. He could feel her squirm, moving with him, breathing heavily.

"Is this all right?"

"Oh yes, Jeff. Don't stop now." She ground her pelvis against his hand and face.

I won't. Ever.

Again, he put his fingers into her cleft, exploring until they were inside of her – wet and hot. As before, she moved with him, enticing him with her fragrance. He took out his fingers, then kissed her there, his warm tongue in her cleft. CJay moaned out loud.

The big man made his way up to her face again, stopping to kiss her perfect handfuls of breasts and suckle her. He kissed her neck and her open mouth, then whispered into her ear.

"Tell me what you like, Clare. I want to bring you pleasure."

"I think you are clearly on the right track, Trooper. Just keep going. We can branch out later," he heard her say huskily, moving her pelvis on his erect penis which was pressed hard against her. He kissed his way back down to her wet sex, licking and kissing her warmth and putting his fingers back inside of her. He sucked her little button as her groans and movements intensified. She had her hands on his head, pushing him down on her, until finally he felt her rhythmic spasms and heard her cry out.

"Oh, Trooper. Oh God oh God oh God." She ground herself against his fingers and his face.

"Yes?" he said, moving up to her face and kissing her again with lips smelling of her own silky perfume. She put her arms around him, returning his kisses, moving her hips against him, inviting him in for his turn.

He lowered his body on hers, and slipped inside. She gasped sharply and moaned.

"Clare, am I hurting you?" He smoothed back her hair, kissed her face.

"Exquisite pain," she breathed raggedly, looking with half closed lids into his eyes, moving her hips against him and tightening her arms around his muscular back. "You fill me up exactly the way I knew you would."

She wrapped her legs around his, and he could feel her press against him and tighten her muscles, intoxicating him with her heat and strength. He wanted to prolong his contact with her lovely breasts and smooth belly, so he slowed his movements, gently thrusting. He knew she was coordinating her own movements with his and it was all he could do to not explode inside of her.

"Oh…Clare," he whispered into her ear, moving slowly. "This is how…how it's supposed to feel." *My sweet Clare.*

He luxuriated in her heat, the taste of her flesh, the softness of her breasts, the look on her face with her hair mussed on the pillow and her arms around him, her blue eyes watching him, the *smell* of their lovemaking.

"I…am…drowning…in you," he breathed softly into her hair, thrusting deeply as waves of orgasm rolled through him, filling her up. *I am so in love with you.*

He held her tightly, then lay to one side, their legs entangled. He could tell he was still inside of her. Jeff pulled the sheet and duvet up, then put his arm over her breasts under the covers, kissing her shoulder and drawing her closer to him. Clare turned her face towards him and snuggled into his arm.

"You can't fall asleep, Trooper, even though I know you're tired," she said. He opened an eye and smiled.

"Because?"

"Because I am not through with you." She threw her leg over his, and moved her wet, warm parts against him. He felt himself begin to harden.

Jeff turned towards this angel, this flight nurse, this woman he knew he was coming to love, and thrust again, moving slowly, slickly, feeling her melt into him, until they both experienced those rhythmic pulsations, the sheer joy of orgasm that finally allowed them to fall into deep sleep, their arms still around one another.

Chapter Forty-two

He made her breakfast the next morning, but only after they'd made love yet another time. She'd gotten up during the night to pee and clean up. She could smell his body on her and, breathing deeply of his fragrance, considered waking this beautiful man at 0100 for another go at it, but decided to let him sleep. She did wake him at 0500, however, because she had to be on duty at Aurora I. She called dispatch as soon as the wind chime alarm tinkled, asking one of the crew to hold over until she got there at 0700. She didn't need to ask him twice to make love to her one more time.

After, Clare made coffee while the Trooper rummaged around in her cupboards and refrigerator looking for something to put together to eat.

"No waffle maker?" he asked.

"No, remember?"

"Of course. I don't leave toothbrushes at other people's houses. I leave waffle mix."

"Really? Well, I already gave you a toothbrush. You'd better leave it here."

He came over to her then and put his arms around her, holding her close as she attempted to push the strainer down on the French press. He kissed her neck, then her hair, then her neck again.

"I've found flour, baking powder, eggs, an old banana, oil, and milk. Also, some maple syrup and birch syrup. Which would you prefer?" He mumbled against her neck, kissing her between the words.

"I prefer you, but you can choose the syrup," she replied, turning around to look at him, dressed in his 501s and thermal tee shirt. She knew his boxers were still on the bedroom floor. She kissed him, then pushed him gently away. "I have to go to work, Chef Boyardee. Make me some breakfast."

Clare watched him as he went back to the counter to finish the pancake batter. She could see his shoulder blades underneath his tee shirt, accentuated by his muscular shoulders. She saw the faint outline of the large Viking raven he had tattooed across his back – the Viking raven that morphed into the Tlingit raven as it flew. Tlingit, Viking, and Scots. He'd had no choice but to become a warrior.

You are so fucking beautiful to me, she thought. She went back to grabbing clean cups for coffee.

"Do you have a griddle?"

"I do." She pointed out where it was in the storage drawer under the stove near the baking sheet she'd given him at their meal with David. He bent down and pulled it out, setting it on two burners to heat up.

"How was the view?" he asked her when he'd straightened up.

291

"It was extremely fine, Trooper." She smiled at the memory of that night – the anger, fear, the tears, and the confusion she'd experienced with her brother and this man.

He found the spatula in the crockery pot on her counter and started to mix up banana pancakes with a bowl he'd scrounged and a wooden spoon.

She set the drop-leaf table in her kitchen nook with plates and utensils, butter, and the birch syrup he'd selected.

She turned back to him – to simply gaze at him.

"Are you watching me?" he asked.

"Yes."

He turned around to look at her fully as he took the pancake mix over to the stove.

"Clare, you're beautiful. I want to take you right back to bed."

She smiled. Good, she thought. "I'd like that."

She reveled in what making love to this guy had done to her. She wasn't afraid of him anymore. She wasn't afraid of what giving herself to him might mean. She wanted him inside of her one more time. She felt a connection to him. She loved watching him move about the kitchen, obviously knowing what he was doing and uttering wisecracks that made her laugh. He was strong but also vulnerable. Stern but funny. She was totally smitten by him.

"How's that look?" he asked her, coming over with a steaming platter of pancakes which smelled delicious.

"Wonderful, Trooper. Did you learn that in the little trooper school?"

He grinned.

"No, our Grandmother taught both Shannon and me how to cook. We're both pretty good. Our specialties are all Tlingit Lutheran favorites"

"I'd like to meet your family – your sister – see the baby again...," Clare said.

"Good. I'll make it happen. My mother's going home to Wasilla at the end of the week. Jordan should be home before then."

Clare nodded. Okay then.

Breakfast was hurried, but good. He really could cook.

And his kiss was far sweeter than that birch syrup.

Clare jumped in the shower, dressed quickly in her long underwear and flight suit, put on the steel-toed boots and heavy jacket. Grabbed a wool cap and gloves and went out the door with damp hair.

Jeff moved his vehicle so she could get out of the garage and kissed her goodbye in front of Kenny and Emma peeking out of their kitchen window. He waved at the elderly couple, then went back into the house, made the bed and cleaned up the dishes.

* * * * * *

Mary stayed over for her from night shift and was doing pre-flight with Gus when CJay arrived on the helipad. "Post-coital glow?" the other flight nurse whispered to her, holding up a damp strand of CJay's hair, peeking out from her wool cap.

CJay reddened. Was it that obvious?

293

"Trooper, CJay?"

CJay put her finger to her lips. Shhhh.

"Your secret is safe with me. Who do you *not* want me to tell?"

They both laughed, but CJay knew that all the Aurora flight personnel and half the ED would be privy to her new sex life before this shift was over.

Hell, it'd been well worth it.

Chapter Forty-three

"My beautiful Clare."

She heard his voice in her dream and turned to see him dressed in his Coast Guard flight suit and heavy jacket.

"My handsome husband," she breathed. How she loved him.

"You didn't choke."

"No, Alex. I didn't. I did what you said."

"Was there joy?"

"Yes," she said simply. "And there was great pleasure. Are you okay with that?"

He looked at her and started to laugh. "I'm happy that you're beginning to find companionship and pleasure again. There is nothing that could make me feel better than to know you're awakening to a new life."

"But I miss you."

"Of course you do. This man will not replace me, but he will bring you joy and will be your warrior for as long as you live and your love forever."

"How do you know that?"

"I'm your guiding star, remember? Time is not linear. I know these things, Clare."

"What else do you know?"

"Talk to Grandmother."

"Grandmother? Who? Jeff's grandmother?"

"You'll find out. In the meantime, live your life. This man loves you." Alex stood up. "Gotta go, sweetheart. Duty calls. 'Semper Paratus.'"

"I love you, Alex," she said, pulling her dream around her like a goose down comforter.

Chapter Forty-four

Working this weekend, flight nurse?

Off Saturday. On Sunday.

Can I make you lunch at my place Saturday? 1100, when the sun's up?

Yes. Can I bring anything?

Your toothbrush and your guns? Want to shoot my AR-15 & the AK-47?

Quite the incentive, Trooper.

Whatever it takes. I've got ptarmigan stew, garlic bread, and pie. I'll pick you up, if it's okay.

It is, Jeff. I'll bring a salad and some wine.

See you at 1100.

CJay smiled.

Gus had looked up from the computer when he heard the opening notes of *Alaska's Flag*, the Alaska state song, chime from CJay's phone. He waited until she stopped texting to speak.

"Trooper?"

"He's inviting me to lunch on Saturday. At his place. He's making ptarmigan stew. We're going to target shoot. I'm bringing salad. He's providing the AR-15 and the AK-47."

"Ah. Big guns. The lifestyle tour of his turf. Is this good for you?"

"I think so. But we still don't know if we even like each other," she smiled.

Jeanne, their dispatcher – and even Gus – snorted at that.

"Pretty obvious you don't like him much, CJay," Jeanne commented. "I'da had him in the hay on the first date."

CJay chuckled. *Yes, Jeanne, we know.* Thinking of Jeff – of his touch and his lips and his smell and his strength – made her very aware of her own heat. *I want to be with him. Inside his arms in his warm bed.*

She smiled. *Thank you, Alex – my guiding star.*

Chapter Forty-five

CJay and Wendell flew together Friday. Wendell had taught CJay a lot about sizing up scenes and planning for various patient scenarios. He was a skilled crew partner, with a wicked sense of humor. The team generally spent much of the day laughing because Wendell's irreverent view of the world put a lot of situations into unexpectedly strange, sometimes surreal, yet hilarious perspectives. He had a way of lightening a mood, even after grim flights.

The highlight of the day was a request for Aurora I to a residence in North Pole – "Stab wound. Police at the home; scene is secure; perpetrator is in custody."

The event was bratwurst dinner with all the family including grandkids – and Canadian hockey from the Outside. The perpetrator was Grandma. The victim, still alive and cursing, was Grandpa. While weeping family members comforted each other in the hot, cramped living room smelling of German brats, yellow mustard, baked beans, potato salad, sauerkraut and sweat, Wendell and CJay loaded Grandpa onto their gurney on his side, with Grandma's big kitchen knife still sticking out of her husband's back.

Once airborne and on their way back to NSMC, with Grandpa angrily hanging onto life, Wendell keyed his mike and proclaimed to the crew, "That's the last time *he'll* ever complain

about 'them dadgum sliced black olives in the puhtatah salad.'"
Both CJay and Rick, their pilot, laughed out loud, thankful the
irate, red-faced old man couldn't hear what was being said.

"Only you, Wendell, could say that and get away with it," Rick
replied. CJay agreed, and tucked the quip away to use later.

Their shift ended on time with the arrival of the night crew
and when all the charts were finished, CJay headed home. She
was tired, but excited about seeing Jeff's place for the first time
the next day.

CJay was finishing up a quick snack and green tea when Jeff
texted:

Are you home? Can you talk?
I'm home.

Her mobile rang immediately.

"About tomorrow," Jeff started after greeting her.

"Are you begging off?" she asked. *Doggone it.*

"No, no," he said quickly. "But I'll pick you up at 1000, if that's
okay. She knew he lived a little out of town, somewhere.

"Well...all right. Just how far away is it?" CJay asked,
somewhat perplexed.

"In Ester – it's about twenty-five minutes from your house
and my post. Great commute. You'll be able to find it a second
time if I take you the first time." There was a long pause.

"Jeff, you still there?"

"Um...are you comfortable with spending the night? The K-
9'll keep you safe. If you'd rather not, I'll be happy to take you

back to your place later in the day. But, I've got a guest bedroom, too, if you want."

"I'd like to stay. But I need to get to work early on Sunday."

"Me, too, flight nurse. I'm glad you're okay to stay."

"I like being with you," she added quietly.

They talked for a few more minutes, then CJay went to bed, setting the alarm for 0600, so she could go to the Alaska Club gym and work out before Jeff came to get her. She was looking forward to seeing him – in his own environment – 'his turf,' as Gus had put it.

Chapter Forty-six

He was a few minutes early, but CJay was ready.

She had her hair in a ponytail, and wore a thick sweater with a flannel shirt underneath, jeans, snow boots, parka, a wool cap, and thick woolen gloves. She brought along two bottles of wine to go with the ptarmigan stew – depending on whether it was a tomato based (pinot noir) or a milk based stew (chardonnay), a broccoli salad, and a couple of Presto logs wrapped with a red ribbon for Jeff's fireplace – a humorous "hostess gift."

"You look like a real Alaska girl," he told her, after he'd pushed her parka hood back, and given her a kiss hello in her living room that made her want to take off the jacket, flannel shirt, sweater, and jeans and put lunch on hold.

Jeff drove west out of town, past the University of Alaska, taking the exit off the freeway into the former gold mining town of Ester.

Ester is an eclectic part of the Fairbanks area – once known for "dry homes" – homes without electricity, running water, or indoor plumbing. CJay had read about the place ("The People's Republic of Ester"), and knew that a lot of Alaskans lived "off the grid," but it'd never dawned on her that Jeff lived there – off the grid.

A number of university students live in Ester while going to school, because the cost of renting is about half of what it is to live with all the utilities and amenities in Fairbanks. The everyday year-round cost of living for Alaskans is high.

This is going to be very, very interesting she realized.

Jeff drove past the Ester Volunteer Fire Department station off Old Nenana Highway, turned left at the old camp general store that he'd mentioned, then continued up the mountain on a wide gravel road, driving approximately three-fourths of a mile, she reckoned, through birch, spruce, and alder trees, before he turned right up a steep driveway at the corner of Opal and Beryl streets and then into a clearing with a large A-frame type home in the center of it with an attached garage. CJay could not see another dwelling from this property.

He parked in front of the house, got out, and opened her door for her.

"Welcome to my home," he said.

"Wow," was all she could say. "Just wow."

He looked at her. "You okay?"

"I'm just so surprised. Your house is incredible." She shivered.

"You're cold. Come on, let me show you the inside. I think you'll like it." He hoisted her fabric carry-all bag with the salad, wine, and 'hostess gift' with one arm, and held her hand with his other hand. She followed him, her gun duffle on her other shoulder, looking around as they walked towards the front steps.

On the right of the clearing, she saw a large outbuilding with two tall roll-up doors – soundly built – another garage? Storage?

CJay saw solar panels on the south facing side of the A-frame's roof. She noted a small greenhouse sticking out from behind the main dwelling.

She looked again at the A-frame and saw it wasn't the traditional Swiss chalet, but that the roof pitched out to the home's outer walls. There were four two-story tall floor-to-ceiling windows across the front that let in light and the view. She saw a wrap-around deck on the complete front and the right side of the house. The left third of the deck where the front door was situated was closed off, serving as a screened in porch during the summer, and now, winter, had storm windows installed so it served as a front arctic entryway. The rest of the deck was open to the elements – and the view.

He unlocked the outer door and held it for her. Then, he unlocked the front door to his house and stood aside as she entered. It was as beautiful inside as it was outside. *This is awesome.*

"Holy crapola," she mumbled softly under her breath.

She was in an enormous great room with a large metal and stone fireplace in the center, reaching up through the ceiling twenty feet above. Behind the fireplace to the left she saw a full kitchen with a big refrigerator and an island. To the right front, she saw his open office, with shelves full of books, a computer, printer, and photographs on the wall and on the bookshelves.

In front of the fireplace, there was a seating area for guests with a big sofa, two comfortable looking side chairs and a rustic coffee table. She could see the end of a dining table sticking out from behind the fireplace – convenient to the kitchen. Above it all, she saw a set-back loft that was reached by stairs on the right wall, just behind a large sliding glass wall that opened out to that open deck. Under the stairs was built-in storage – and a gun safe.

As Jeff watched, Clare set down her gun duffle and walked over to the office area where pictures hung on the wall. Jeff in the Marines, in Iraq and then Afghanistan, looking haggard and worn, dirty, surrounded by six other young men – all heavily armed. Very young. He had what must be that 'thousand-yard stare' on his face she'd heard about. His dog tags were looped around the frame of the picture. She reached up and touched them, looking at his name, his DOB, his serial number, his blood type – A neg. I'm B neg, she thought. *Babies. We could have babies….* She shook her head in dismay. I can't assume anything anymore, she knew.

Clare saw his Bachelor's Degree in Criminal Justice from UAF, pictures of his mom and his Scots dad - a tall man with wavy dark red hair – in a formal kilt! There was Shannon; a big Malamute and Jeff; Shannon, Jordan(?) and Jeff skiing; and a small photo tucked away on a shelf of a tall, slender, black haired woman looking directly at the camera, dressed in an emerald green gown. Helen. She's beautiful. No wonder he fell in love with her.

Clare turned away to look further at the interior of his home.

The floors were dark wood, with thick woven carpets in what she could see of the dining space, his office area, and under the coffee table and chairs. She could smell food cooking. She saw a pie on the kitchen counter.

305

"Do you like it?" he asked.

"It's simply exquisite," she said truthfully. "This is a 'dry home?' You have no running water? No utilities? No indoor plumbing?"

"Ah, you've heard about us Esterites, huh? I used to be dry, and there are still dry homes here, but the majority of us have moved into the twenty-first century. I'm wired for power, I have the internet, and my toilets flush. It's a great convenience. But," he added, "I'm also prepared for when the grid goes down."

He took her wool cap, gloves and coat, and hung them with his own in the closet just inside the front door. She saw two jackets in there, also, that looked like animal skin. There was a pair of large moccasins on the floor of the closet, as well as two pairs of Sorels (one short and one tall), and a pair of tall Xtratuffs.

"Are you hungry?"

She was.

"I've got a quick snack – so we can shoot before lunch without being too hungry."

He went into the kitchen and pulled a platter from the refrigerator loaded with string cheese cut into bite-sized pieces, Pepper Jack cut in squares, wheat crackers, squirt cheddar cheese in a can, dried apricots, sliced apples, and a small cup filled with Dijon mustard, country style with mustard seeds. He popped the lid on a container of artichoke heart and jalapeno dip and put it on the platter, too.

"You went all out," she smiled, looking at him as he put the platter on the coffee table along with two paper plates and a

306

paper towel for each of them. She watched him go back to the kitchen and make two mugs of coffee in his K cup brewer.

"Come sit in front of the fireplace with me." They sat. "Oh, oh, oh! I forgot the most important thing! Hold on," he said as he jumped up and went out the two front doors and down the steps.

Clare got up to watch him and saw him run to his patrol vehicle and start rummaging through a box in the back. Presently, he came back in with long, thin brown strips of cardboard, one of which he proudly gave to her. "This is the best."

"And, this is…?"

"Reindeer jerky! It's terrific." He grinned.

CJay looked at the expression on his face and saw this man as the 16-year-old he used to be, sweet, funny, serious, and trying very hard to please her. "So," she said, "I suppose you made this…this…Rudolph jerky, too?"

"Hell, no. I bought it off the local guy who sells it out of his truck at the Stop-and-Rob down from the post on Peger. Authentic." He took a bite of his own and slowly masticated it until he could swallow.

"Stop and Rob?"

"The mini-mart on Peger."

CJay laughed out loud at him, and finally took a bite. Poor Rudy. He was spicy and delicious.

They clinked coffee cups and CJay sipped, bit into a piece of dried apricot with some squirt cheese and mustard on it, chewed, sipped some more. It was very quiet, except for the snapping of the logs in the fireplace.

"I'm thinking this is an incredible house." Clare finally said. "I'm really impressed." She swept her hand around, indicating the great room, windows, the furnishings.

"Are you surprised?" he sat back, still chewing on jerky, this time with mustard on it.

"A little."

"Why?"

"I see an Alaskan, a cop, a modern man. Someone comfortable with technology, then I find you live in Ester. Now I'm thinking Daniel Boone, too. I'm speechless at your home."

He smiled. "I'm a cop, an Alaskan, and I'm comfortable with technology. But my dad was 'The Attorney' and my mom 'The Professor.' 'Til Dad died, we had people like the Governor of Alaska, politicians, the police chief, all the big wheels coming through our house. Shannon and I learned how to set a table and eat without drooling on ourselves or squirting our cheese food..." he motioned toward the yellow can sitting on the coffee table, "...onto the person sitting next to us – who more than likely was the Secretary of State." He paused. "I really love squirt cheese, by the way. But after...uh...Dad – well, after that, Grandmother came and made moose tongue sandwiches and we had the aunties hanging around."

"The aunties?"

"Grandmother's sisters and all the other female parishioners and cousins she could get to come visit in big city Wasilla."

Clare laughed. "My family taught me how to make music with my hand in my armpit. David taught me how to burp righteously, play pool, and drive someone's nose through their brain without

308

breaking my hand. And shoot to protect myself. Not near as sophisticated or 'interesting' as your family."

"But, your brother's my kinda guy. I like him a great deal."

"I'm glad, Jeff. But...tell me about your house – and this land. It's all yours?"

Jeff nodded. "When dad died, he left our mom comfortable – he was a thrifty Scotsman and a shrewd investor. But, he also left Shannon and me an inheritance – to use wisely. Shannon invested hers, and I bought fifteen acres here – in Ester. I cleared this land. I have a little tractor/backhoe/snow plow combo, a snowmachine, and a Polaris four-by ATV. They're in the shed over there." He pointed towards the structure with the two roll-up doors.

"I worked with one of mom's professor friends – he's been her 'companion' for the last several years – he's an ecology expert. He helped me set up this place with the solar photovoltaic technology. I have a generator also – just in case. There's a 500-gallon propane tank for the range in the kitchen and backup for the fireplace. Also raised beds for summer vegetables, and a greenhouse."

"Did you build this place yourself?" she asked. Maybe he was Daniel Boone, Farmer Fred, a cop, *and* an Abe Lincoln log cabin builder too.

He laughed. "You've got faith in me, Clare, but it's a cedar house kit. I actually ordered it from Eagle Rock and they trucked it up. One of our AST pilots, Pius, is a contractor, so he helped put the place together along with Jordan and about a dozen other troopers. I supplied the beer and Little John even brought his smoker over one day and smoked ribs and wings. Emmett – Hunni's husband? He and his three brothers helped, too. And, they were also our DS's."

"DS's? What's that?"

"Designated Shooters. They're Mormon, so no drinking. Safe to handle guns." He could probably see the confusion on her face. "Little John's BBQ is a calculated risk out here. Bears, you know. But aside from the threat of bears, building this place was actually fun. Like a barn raising. And, it's well insulated – R60 and R95 – walls and roof."

"Impressive," Clare said.

"The fireplace there – it's got a masonry firebox with a hydronic loop that provides warmth and heats my water supply. There are stainless steel coils built into the firebox and the warm water runs through them and under the floors to pipes in the bedrooms – like radiator or steam heating. It also heats water for the bath and showers. There's a shower outside, too for summer – passive solar heat provides the warm water there. When the grid goes down, I've got everything I need to keep going."

CJay's head whirled with his information. "Show me the rest of the place." she suggested, grabbing an apple slice for the tour.

He took her into the back part of the great room and down a hallway whose ceiling formed the loft. There was an exterior door at the end and he opened it, showing her the back entrance – also with an arctic entry way/mudroom that went out onto a small back porch and down to the greenhouse. On the left side of the hallway was a small guest bedroom with a double bed covered with a crimson duvet, pillows, and a blanket folded over the foot.

There was a closet, a bedside table, cedar chest, highboy dresser, and a small desk and chair. The big window had a picturesque view of the trees outside.

On the other side of the hallway was the Sergeant's bedroom. When he opened the door, she saw the king-size bed with a heavy comforter. Big pillows. Trygve's dog bed was in the corner. And another big window with a view of the trees. She was surprised at how 'embarrassed' – was that the word? – she was to see this very personal space of his. There was a bedside table with books on it. A good-sized closet. A highboy dresser with some coins and money on top. His big shoes at the end of the bed. *I want to make love to you on that bed. I wanted your naked flesh next to mine. Your mouth on my body.* Without thinking, she put her arm around him. She heard him rumble under his breath and felt him hug her shoulder with his own strong arm.

"So, do you have an en suite, also?" she asked, changing the direction this situation could possibly go. After all, she still had powerful weaponry to shoot and lunch to eat.

"Of course. It's the master bedroom. And, I'm the master." He put both his arms around her and pulled her to him. "May I be honest?"

"Oh, please be."

"I want to make love to you in that bed today. Um...I mean, if you don't mind." His cheeks flushed and Clare had to laugh.

"Let me shoot your AK-47 first, Trooper. Then, feed me." *And then make love to me on that bed.*

There was a bathroom off the hallway with double sinks, a tub/shower, and a toilet. And a window looking out onto the trees outside. Clare envisioned long soaks. By candlelight.

"What's on the loft?" she asked.

"Still working on that. Thought about putting my office up there, but it's so darn handy down here. But, it could be a third bedroom, or a guest area if I want to do something different with this guest room here. The view's spectacular, and it's always warm – heat rises."

A baby's room in the guest room, she thought. No, jumping way too far ahead of myself, she knew. "Septic system?" she asked, redirecting her thoughts.

Yes, he told her. "And, one more thing…"

She looked at him.

"This particular home plan has a design option built in. I can add one or two more bedrooms in the future without compromising the structure." He shrugged. "Just sayin'…."

"Flexibility is nice," she offered, suppressing a smile, thinking of the Australian Bower Bird she'd seen on the Discovery Channel, decorating his nest to woo a female. She glanced surreptitiously around the hallway floor for a pile of artistically arranged colored seeds or attractively placed bright blue bottle caps.

"Show me your other building," she finally requested.

He nodded, "And we can take the Polaris back to the range after that."

So, they got their cold weather gear back on, and he took her around to the large outbuilding. He unlocked the padlock on the personnel door set beside one of the roll-up vehicle doors, and turned on a light. She saw his tractor, 4X4 ATV, a small snow blower, and a snowmachine. She saw a workshop with hand and power tools, and shelving with packaged food items. There was another large gun safe and she noted two crossbows and two precision compound bows with arrows mounted on the wall. CJay pointed to those.

"Very *Walking Dead* and *Hunger Games* there with the bows and arrows, Jeff. Do you use those?"

"I do, Clare. I hunt with bows. Any problem with that?"

"Not at all. My brothers and dad hunt. I've cleaned and plucked a lot of ducks and geese." The trooper nodded.

He went on. "I also have rifles and shotguns. I kill moose, elk (when I can, though they're not local) and birds. I fish for salmon and halibut. I'm an Alaskan." He shrugged. "My grandmother's a Tlingit. It's a cultural thing. Except for seals. I won't eat seal. It does *not* taste good to me."

"You eat what you kill, I assume?"

"Of course. I won't shoot anything that I can't or won't eat. I share what I take with Shannon, Mother, and Grandmother, too. I use the skins for jackets, hats, gloves, and shoes."

"You make your own clothes with the skins?"

The trooper laughed. Clare felt embarrassed. "I draw the line at Martha Stewart or Chingachgook. No, I have a local lady who makes stuff for me."

He put his arm around her. "This is who I am. I'm a cop, a hunter, and I live in as much style as I can. I have enough food to

313

last for six months in this barn. I have bows, guns, shotguns, and long guns. Anything else you want to know, Clare?"

"Are you a 'survivalist'?"

He hesitated. He breathed out through his nose.

"Would that make a difference to you, Clare? Am I a 'Prepper?'" He looked at her closely. "In a way, I am – in that I can survive in Alaska with my skills. But more than a 'survivalist' or a 'Prepper,'' I'm a 'realist.' I believe deeply we should all be prepared to take care of ourselves and the people we love in this unstable world we've inherited. I want to be ready when the grid goes down. When it goes down for good, Clare."

"Wow." She looked over at him.

"Are you concerned I'm going to make you catch and dry salmon for our dog team?" He laughed, straddled the Polaris ATV and fired it up. "Climb on and let's go back and get our guns."

Clare got on behind him, and they drove over to the house where she picked up her gun duffel while Jeff unlocked the gun safe under the stairs and retrieved his 1911, another .45, a Benelli M4 tactical shotgun, an AR-15A3 and an AK-47. He also filled a backpack with the leftover cheese, jerky, apple slices, crackers, squirt cheese, and a thermos ("Hot cocoa," he told her.). His shooting area was located several hundred yards behind his house and the road took them into a heavily wooded area – weak sunlight casting shadows through the bare branches of the trees as they drove. She hugged him tightly.

"After you've finished drying the salmon for the dogs," he mentioned casually as he handed her the AR-15 at his range's firing line, "I'll teach you how to do reloads so we can man the barricades when the zombies come."

"Are you going to grow a sourdough beard?"

"Of course. And, you can quit shaving the hair under your arms, too."

She'd set down her two guns pointing forward with the slides open and placed the loaded magazines next to them on the table in front. Surprised at her initial flash of anger at his comment, she turned to face him, but kept the AR-15 pointed down range.

"Now you're just making fun of me, Jeff," she told him sharply.

He shook his head. "I do not make fun of a woman who is holding a fully loaded AR-15. That would be imprudent of me."

"You think I'm a 'Cheechako.'" She was still a bit embarrassed and miffed at him.

"You *are* a newcomer, Clare. But, I'm not making fun of you at all. Look at you – standing here with your own weapons, ready to shoot mine. And, you ride in helicopters and jump out of them to save people. You rappel down cliffs to reach hikers. You saved my sister's life and brought that baby into the world in one piece. You climb into wrecked cars upside down and risk your own life to help others. Every time I hear that ship go over, I think of you being in there. Saving people. You're fearless."

He shrugged, then went on."I can teach you how to survive in the wilderness, but I think you can probably teach me a thing or two, City Girl. I've never been able to make music with my armpit, though I have been told I have a very charming and quite melodious belch. And I *never* break wind around women."

She looked at him in wide-eyed astonishment. *Oh, my God.* "This is as bad as being with David. Except for that breaking wind thing. He has *no* issues with that."

"Your brother? Dave?"

"Yes."

"Well...," he replied, leaning back casually against a tree and looking at her with hooded eyes, "...if you mean we're similar because we both like shooting big guns, hunting and dressing a five-hundred-pound moose, driving powerful, fast vehicles with lights and sirens, taking charge and just being a true, manly, bad-assed hero...why, yes, little lady, I s'pose you're right. He and I are a lot alike."

Then, the trooper stood tall. "But if you mean taking off all those heavy clothes you're wearing and laying you down on my bed and making sweet love to you all night long? Nah. Dave and I are night and day."

Her face pinked up, but then she spoke. "Those moose you hunt...?

"Yeah?"

"The moose. What do you dress them in?"

She watched him as he considered his response.

"Pinafores," he finally answered, seriously. "Polka dot pinafores. Moose are surprisingly style conscious animals."

She looked at him: All six feet and two inches of this man with the warm hazel eyes with glints of green, now partially shaded by his watch cap; his sweet lips with the sly smile; his unassuming, dry sense of humor; his big shoulders and warm,

316

strong arms; his brave heart and sense of honor, duty, and justice.

She hadn't felt this way since she became aware of just what a "good guy" her brother's best friend was. And, just as she had been then, she was blindsided by this startling revelation. She knew she was no longer in cold control of her deepest emotions. At this moment, she realized she was crazy about this guy and the way he looked at the world. And, she knew she was terrified.

All she could do was laugh – deep paroxysms of laughter. It took her five minutes to compose herself and dry her tears after she sat down on the stump that served as a chair by the firing line.

* * * * * *

And this was when the Trooper knew he was head over heels in love with this woman who was almost collapsed with laughter on the stump he'd cut for a seat. He couldn't begin to describe his emotions, except that he hoped one day she would feel towards him the same way he felt about her.

* * * * * *

They spent ninety minutes outside at his firing range, alternating between shooting, drinking hot chocolate, and simply talking. He showed her how to fire the AR-15 with its gas impingement system. She learned to load the magazines, insert them, eject them, check to make sure the gun was empty. Her shooting was precise and accurate.

"I thought it'd have a kick, but it doesn't. I really like shooting it."

"And you're good at it, Clare. You make it look easy."

She watched him with the AK-47 and the Benelli, then tried the two powerful weapons herself. Again, her shooting was precise and accurate.

"I think you've been holding back on me, flight nurse. When the zombies come, I'll definitely want you at my side, fending them off."

They went inside after that, shedding their outdoor gear. Jeff made fresh coffee with his Keurig and poured them pinot noir from the bottle Clare'd brought. He pulled the ptarmigan stew with tomatoes, potatoes, carrots and onions out of the propane gas range – it smelled superb. Clare watched while he finished preparing the sauce. I could get used to this, she thought.

After the meal, they sat by the fire and ate dessert. Clare was glad she'd gone to the gym that morning.

She looked at him, sitting beside her, her bare feet in his lap. He was massaging them with his strong, veined hands with the short, cleanly clipped nails. She looked at his mouth. He smiled, and she was embarrassed again, just like when he caught her looking at his mouth the first time many months ago. Again, she was aware she loved what she knew of him.

"What are you thinking" she asked.

"You are aware that men hate being asked that question, right? It's right up there with 'Penny for your thoughts.' The guy's

318

usually thinking about the clanking sound his Harley is making, and can the shop have it ready in time for the rally in Sturgis?"

Clare laughed. "And the female is thinking 'Why isn't he talking? Is he mad at me? Oh my God! What have I done wrong!'"

"So, does that mean you don't want to know what I'm thinking?"

"Well," she answered. "I know what's on my mind, Trooper. And I have an idea I know what you're thinking. Would you like to put the dirty dishes in the dishwasher first?" She pulled her bare feet out of his lap, stood and took the pie plates and flatware back into the kitchen, and rinsed them off.

He followed her and put the last dishes into the dishwasher.

"Make 'sweet love' to me, Trooper," she told him, putting her wet hands around his neck and moving in close.

319

Chapter Forty-seven

They cleaned up the kitchen quickly. Jeff generally washed up as he cooked, hating stacks of dirty pots and pans. Clare grabbed her backpack and brushed her teeth after the dishwasher was started. The Trooper stayed in the kitchen to wipe down the counters.

Jeff seldom ruminated about things like "Does she like me?" But this time he knew he needed to do a lot of thinking about Clare.

The Trooper thoroughly enjoyed sex and he'd enjoyed it a great deal for a long time with good looking women. And, in fact, when he was younger, the pretty girls came to him. He'd had quite a reputation for a while when he was a new law enforcement officer. But as he'd gotten older, his focus had narrowed. His goals had changed. He wanted stability now. He wanted a family. He didn't want to go too fast with Clare. But he also knew that when he found what he wanted, he went after it. Why fiddle around?

Not always a shrewd move.

He'd done the same with Helen, once she broke up with her homicide detective, who was actually a pretty nice guy. He realized later that he hadn't even bothered to ask why they'd split.

All he knew was that his dream woman, Helen, was free and Jeff wanted her in his life. He found out that "why" almost two years later, when Helen'd stood in front of him, angry and shouting, "All you men want is to get us tied up with a bow and pregnant. It's not gonna happen, Jeffrey. My plans do not include kids and kitchens. Why the hell didn't you talk about this just a little bit sooner?" She turned her back on him and moved to Seattle.

He was stunned. And sick. But he'd learned a valuable lesson. Talk about shit early. Find out what *her* plans might be, before assuming your goals are going to be the same.

So, with Clare? Her family were first responders. Her brother was a cop. She liked guns. She'd wanted that baby, despite the death of her husband. And then, she'd endured the death of her daughter. She had an intact family of origin – mom and dad, brothers. She moved to Fairbanks of her own volition. *She's the rock star of the air.*

Well, all of those flight people are. The sergeant had been sincere when he told Gus that day that the Troopers knew when they heard the helicopter in the distance that the cavalry was coming. Granted, lights and sirens are fun, but the whop whop whop of the blades is dynamic. The flight crews were pre-hospital Rock Stars in their flight suits. And, they knew it, too; but so did the rest of the first responder community.

I love everything about Clare. I love her sense of humor, her intelligence, her lips, tongue, her smell and taste, her breasts and her body. I love the feel of her skin against mine. Being inside of her is ecstasy. I know she doesn't walk on water. She's got

321

memories of love and pain that she carries – and I'm going to have to accept that. I've got baggage too….

Jeff wasn't stupid. He knew it was total infatuation, the predictable first few weeks of learning to care about someone. That's what kept men coming back – those first flushes of dopamine and happy hormones – until the women lured them to the altar, and things started to settle down.

He knew one more thing. He would lay down his own life to protect her. He could happily – and easily – kill anyone who wanted to hurt her.

He wanted this beautiful woman to want him – the real man, someone beyond the uniform, someone with "issues" inside. Someone who got angry, could be quite violent. Someone who'd killed a lot of people in the line of duty at the behest of his government, and, occasionally, had enjoyed doing that, too.

Someone who'd sent two of his troopers to their deaths in Mantishka. He grimaced again at that painful memory.

She came up behind him then as he was wiping down the kitchen sink, looking out at the darkness. CJay put her arms around his chest from behind.

"Deep in thought, once again. What is up?"

"You, Clare. I won't deny it. Thinking about what time you need to be back at your house so you can get ready for work." *Thinking about getting you naked….*

While she was preparing for bed, Jeff stoked up the fireplace, then took Trygve for a perimeter check. They both visited the Sitka spruce that night, then walked back to the dark A-frame with his flashlight guiding their way on the ice.

322

Clare was already bundled down in his bed when he returned. He liked seeing her pretty head on his pillows for the first time with the duvet pulled up around her neck.

He brushed his teeth, then took off his own clothes while she watched him, crawling naked under the covers into her warm arms. *I am so in love with you. I want you so much. Be with me always.*

The flight nurse wrapped her long legs around him and opened her mouth for his kiss.

I'm in heaven with you, Clare.

Trygve lay on the rug in front of the great room fireplace listening for sounds from both inside and outside the sturdy log home. Then he closed his eyes, knowing that his human was happy again.

Chapter Forty-eight

"Clare?"

Clare heard the voice behind her left shoulder and turned around from the tomatillos she was inspecting at Fred Meyers to see Jeff's sister with a similar grocery cart, but hers was three-fourths filled with disposable diapers and there was a car seat turned backwards in the little front pocket. A smile lit up the flight nurse's face.

"Shannon – and Gus? What a delight to see you!"

"None other," Shannon laughed. "Come check him out."

Clare scooted around until she could look the baby in the face. He was still small – six weeks early – but his eyes were bright. He waved his arms. And legs.

"He's sweet, Shannon. You did good. How old is he now?"

"Six weeks. And he weighs eight and a half pounds. It took him a bit to catch up, and he spent several days under the bililights at the hospital because of his bilirubin levels, but he's doing well now." She turned to face Clare and put her arms around her. "I never had a chance to really thank you, but I pray for your safety and the safety of your friends in that helicopter every single day. You saved our lives."

Clare embraced the younger woman and immediately thought about how Gus's birth had brought Jeff and her together. *Maybe Gus is a miracle in more ways than one.*

"Can you have dinner with us sometime soon, Clare? I know you have a crazy schedule – like Jeff's – but I'd love to have you come see us on post. We owe everything to you."

"Shannon, you did the real work, so don't give me all the credit. You were the hero."

"That's sweet, but we'll argue about it some other time. Can you come to dinner? I'll ask Jeff, too – you can come together and see our house, meet Jordan – and catch up with Reese. She asks about you all the time." Shannon leaned in close. "She's a lot like my Grandmother and mother, if ya know what I mean - except more uninhibited. Sometimes it's a little weird."

I'm not going there, Clare decided. *Your mother's unnerving enough. I can't even begin to imagine a child like that.*

"I'd love to come visit, Shannon. I would."

* * * * * *

Jeff stopped by after his shift that night and ate dinner with Clare – enjoying the chili verde pork with the fresh tomatillos that had been purchased earlier in the day.

"So you saw Gus and Shannon? She called me as soon as she got home and unpacked all those diapers."

"Are you comfortable taking me to dinner with them?"

He put his fork down and looked at her. "I've never been more comfortable. But you asked the question. Are YOU comfortable?"

"What's not to be comfortable with? I had my arm halfway up her birth canal." *With her butt in my face.* "I can say I know her

325

intimately." She winked and smiled. "I'd liked to see your sister and meet baby daddy and talk to Reese." Clare paused, "And hold Gus."

"I haven't seen him for a couple weeks, but I like holding him too. I can't look at him without thinking of you."

Trygve, laying in front of the stove in the living room lifted his head and woofed.

"Trygve likes to visit, too. He and Reese play Barbies."

Clare laughed. They cleaned up the dishes and the Trooper made love to her before he packed up some leftovers for lunch the next day, and went home to Ester.

I pretty sure I love you, Trooper, she thought as she sent him on his way, remembering his touch and his kisses. *But I'm afraid to admit it to myself.*

* * * * * *

Jeff picked Clare up in the Forester Monday night with Trygve in a large crate in the back. The dog gave a sharp hello bark, then stuck his nose through the wires to kiss CJay's fingers.

"I love your dog, Trooper" she said as she wiped her fingers on Jeff's jeans.

He laughed. "I'm pretty sure the feeling's mutual, flight nurse."

Clare and Jeff showed their photo IDs to the young soldier at the Fort Wainwright guard gate requesting it, who gave Officer Trygve and his badge a double take. "Love K-9s, Sir. Have a good evening."

326

"Thank you, soldier," Jeff said and they drove on through.

Jordan and Shannon lived in recently constructed post housing – a medium sized, clean looking townhome with an attractive front porch entryway, across from Arctic Light Elementary School. Clare saw a "Welcome Home" banner in the window, acknowledging not only Shannon's husband's return to the post after the birth of Augustus, but the return of his entire Stryker Brigade two months later. This was a joyous time for Wainwright spouses, their families and the inhabitants of Fairbanks. The city was proud of the post and its soldiers.

The front door opened as soon as they pulled into the townhome's driveway. Shannon came towards the car as carefully as she could since there was ice on the sidewalk, followed by six-year-old Reese. A good-looking man in military uniform stood back in the doorway, holding a baby wrapped in blankets.

"Uncle Jeff! Uncle Jeff!" the girl squealed and hugged Jeff's waist. He lifted her up in the air and held her tightly before setting her back down in front of him and tousling her hair.

"Reese, you've grown at least another inch since I saw you last," he told her. The little girl beamed at his praise.

Shannon had a smile on her face as she approached them, still standing by the car. "I'm so glad you both could come for dinner." She put her arms around the woman who'd delivered their son. "Welcome to our home."

"Thank you, Nurse Clare," Reese said, formally. "I love my baby brother. Thank you for giving him to us." She put her arms around CJay's waist and hugged her too, like she'd hugged Jeff.

CJay bent over and put her arms around the child, drawing her close.

"You're welcome, Reese. Did you know that you and I have the same first name?"

Reese's eyes got wide.

"Are you named Clarice, too?" she asked.

"I am, indeed. Do you know that our name means *'bright and shining?'*" Clare bent down closer to Reese's ear. "It also means *'famous.'*"

Reese jumped back with her hands on her cheeks and her eyes round with surprise.

"Famous? Will I be famous? Are you famous?"

CJay smiled broadly at the expression on the child's face.

"I'm not famous, but you might be one day because we have a special name."

"My great-grandmother's name is Clarice, too," the little girl told CJay.

"I know. Maybe I can meet her one day, also."

"She's 'tuitive," Reese added.

"She means 'intuitive,'" Shannon interpreted. "And Reese is right. Grandmother Clarice is very intuitive. She told me when I got pregnant with Augustus that he would be 'born inside the northern lights and placed in my arms by an angel.'"

CJay saw tears in the young mother's eyes and felt adrenaline course through her own body. She shivered. *Holy crapola.*

"We did our best, Shannon." That's all she could say. She turned towards Jeff and he put his strong arm around her shoulders.

"Let's get you two back inside," he said to his sister and niece. "It's cold out here."

"My Grandmother...," Jeff whispered into her ear, "...can be unnerving sometimes." Together they followed his sister back into the house where Jordan and the baby waited for them.

Jordan handed the infant to Jeff to hold and embraced CJay as soon as the front door closed behind them in the comfortably warm townhouse living room. A fire blazed on the hearth, and CJay could smell familiar Italian spices coming from the kitchen nearby.

"It is an absolute pleasure to finally meet you, Clare," he said after the hug. "Jeff's told us some pretty amazing things about you."

"I'm humbled, Jordan. But thank you."

"Jeff told me about Gus' birth when he got hold of me at the FOB. You changed the course of this family's story."

"We were doing what we train for, Jordan." *Actually, dad, we pretty much were flying by the seat of our pants. Thank God for that NALS instructor so many years ago....* One day, she would tell them the inside story about Baby Gus's birth. Maybe.

"Would you like to hold Gus?" Shannon asked Clare, taking Gus from Jeff.

The flight nurse handed her coat to Jeff and held out her arms. "I'd love to hold him."

Shannon guided her to a comfortable chair by the fire and placed the six-week-old old, dressed in a camouflage onesie and flannel blanket, in her arms. At that moment, Augustus opened his eyes, saw Clare, reached for her face with his hand and smiled. For a single moment, Clare expected him to say, "Hi again, Clare." She held his warm body close and breathed deeply of his baby fragrance.

"He knows who you are, Clare," Jeff said seriously. "He knows you're the 'angel from the northern lights' – the angel from Aurora."

Wonder if he recognizes me without the helmet and the terrified look? Clare looked up at Jeff, smiled, and snugged the infant closer. She and Gus had definitely witnessed a miracle.

* * * * * *

When Shannon finally took Gus from Clare's arms, the flight nurse followed her into the kitchen to help if she could, and to talk. Jordan and Jeff stayed in the living room, drinking beer and watching the Seattle Seahawks while Reese sat on the floor playing Barbies with Trygve, who appeared quite interested in the activity, sniffing and licking each doll. When the baby started to fuss, Shannon sat and nursed him at the kitchen table.

Clare found it easy to spend a little time with Shannon. The younger woman's cheerful conversation naturally centered around the new baby, Reese, life on the army post, and some news about their mother, Hannah, and their grandmother.

"I met your mother after Gus was born. Jeff brought her to the hospital so she could look at the helicopter."

"I remember her talking about that. In a way, she's like Gramma, though not as detailed."

Shannon must have seen the questioning look on the flight nurse's face because she went on to explain, "Sometimes Mother 'sees' things. Colors mainly...uh...emotions, stuff like that. Not like Grandmother who has 'visions'. Now that can be kinda weird."

Clare laughed. "Your brother used the term 'unnerving.'"

"Seriously, no kidding."

Reese came into the kitchen at that point, followed by Trygve, looking for a cookie. Shannon handed her an apple slice from a tray on the counter.

"Can Trygve have one, too?" Shannon nodded and Clare handed an apple slice to the K-9 who took it gently from her hand, chewed twice then swallowed it.

Reese stood there staring at Clare until the flight nurse felt slightly uncomfortable.

"What is it, Reese?"

"I like you a lot better than her."

"Her who?"

"That other nurse lady Uncle Jeff had for a friend. She was okay, but she wasn't *really* 'friendly.'" Reese then turned around abruptly and headed back to the living room. Trygve followed her.

Shannon looked embarrassed, but Clare shrugged. "I saw Helen's picture at Jeff's place. Jeff's told me a bit about her. I actually remember her from a mandatory recertification class I helped teach at Memorial. She seemed like she knew what she

331

was doing and performed well during the hands-on clinical applications." She shrugged. "We all have memories and baggage, Shannon. Tell me about your dad," attempting to redirect the conversation away from Helen.

Jeff's sister touched on what life had been like after the death of Cameron Fraser Douglas when she was four. She didn't remember much about him except the sadness in the house that followed for a long time. Their grandparents had come to live with them, and then their grandfather had died when she was six. That she did remember, because she missed having him read to her at night.

"My Mother was gone a lot with her teaching and research and writing, and Gramma ran the place. Jeff was the big brother and it drove him crazy having to watch me and then be put in the position of 'Man of the House.'" She made finger quotes with the hand that wasn't holding Gus.

"He was always so much older and I guess I kinda looked up at him like a dad, too, in many ways. When we were both grown, I found out how hard it was on him. I know he joined the Marines to get away. Then I really *did* miss him." She made a wry face. "You can't imagine how glad I am that we've finally ended up near each other, as adults."

"He said that your grandmother and mom taught you two to cook."

Now Shannon laughed. "They did. We've both gotten good at some Tlingit traditional foods – like salmon and game – and Lutheran 'potluck foods.' I'm especially good at green Jell-O salad with canned pineapple and cottage cheese, and my potato

332

salad is the bomb! I whip up a pretty good mac 'n cheese, too. But Gramma is the whiz at wild meat and fish. Did Jeff mention the moose tongue sandwiches?"

"Um...yes, he did."

"The absolute best!" She closed her eyes with a dreamy expression. "What a treat for us as kids in Wasilla."

"Sounds yummy." Clare felt her stomach churn.

"You'll have to get Jeff to make you moose tongue after he goes hunting next Fall. Mmmmmm."

I can hardly wait. Clare smiled wanly.

Shannon snuggled the sleeping baby into his baby basket on the counter and turned back to the stove. "Are you aware that Jeffrey loves you?" she asked Clare suddenly.

Shannon's casual comment caught her off guard. Clare considered her words carefully. "He says he thinks about me all the time."

"Do you love him?"

Gee whiz, Shannon. "I've only known him for a short time, Shannon." *I'm taking my time. I know I love his warmth in my bed, and I haven't been able to say that for a long time. I know I love the concept of him. And...my dead husband approves....* She laughed to herself. *I'll see your grandmother's "tuitiveness" and raise her my dreams.*

"My brother and I talked about your husband's death," Shannon went on without waiting for Clare to say anything else. "Jeff said he was taking a class in Sitka when the accident happened in Oregon. He knew the Coasties at the Sitka air station. I know I worry myself sick when Jordan deploys."

"Yes, it's difficult." Clare paused. *Let's redirect, Shannon. Dear God. Please.* "Tell me about Jeff, why don't you? What was he like as your brother?"

"He's been a good brother, Clare. He was dealing with a lot of crap when he came back home after the Marines. He had six buddies killed at one time – an awful big loss. It really took a long time for him to process that, I think. He was bulked up, pretty mean looking, and very, very angry. So, you can *imagine* the impact he had on any boys I brought home while I was in college. He stopped short of telling them he'd still be sitting on the front porch cleaning his bazookas when they brought me home – but not by much. He was extremely protective until I had to beg him to back off."

"Did he scare Jordan?"

This time she giggled. "Jordan and I hooked up at a dance when he was stationed at Fort Richardson in Anchorage. I fell for him big time." She had the same dreamy look on her face that she'd had when discussing moose tongue sandwiches. Then she got back on track. "They stood eye to eye, flexed their testosterone, and threw down their deployments at each other until Jeff finally relaxed and shook his hand. I think Jordan's one of his closest friends now."

She chattered on. "I've wanted him to find someone he deserves. Not someone like Monica – they were waaaay too young when they got married – or some of the girls he's introduced me to since. All they can think about is that he's a cop. And cute. I guess he had lotsa girlfriends in high school. Hell, he's monumentally good looking. Who wouldn't want to go out

334

with him? He did have that long-term relationship with Helen...," Shannon stopped talking.

There was a very long pause.

"Helen keeps popping up in this conversation," Clare finally said. "Is there something you think I need to know, Shannon?"

"No, of course not. She and Jeff just dated for a couple years...."

"I know that, Shannon. Like I said, we *all* have history and baggage."

Shannon gave a sheepish shrug. "She hurt my brother when she turned him down. But I only know what he told me at the time."

"So she didn't want to marry Jeff?"

"She did want to marry Jeff."

Clare, trying to keep her expression blank, looked at Jeff's sister. *Oh, for Heaven's sakes, Shannon, cut to the chase.*

"But, Jeff wants a family, Clare. Helen wanted a career. Supposedly she would have been perfectly happy with Jeff and a career. But not kids. Not ever, evidently, per Jeff. She broke it off, moved to Seattle, got a job with some helicopter medevac program down there." Shannon motioned with her hand at Clare. "Like you," she said.

"She's a flight nurse?" Clare asked. *Did not* fucking *see that one coming.* She managed not to laugh out loud at this astonishing new information offered by Jeff's surprisingly oblivious younger sister.

"Yes."

"Well, she seemed to be a capable ED nurse at Memorial, so I'm sure she's a capable flight nurse, too." Clare smiled graciously, but it did not extend beyond the tip her nose.

Do I feel threatened? She took calming breaths. *What's wrong with me? For four years I haven't given a single flying rip about a boyfriend's past. And now I do?* God! I'm jealous! *I'm feeling pretty freakin' possessive of this guy right now.* She started to laugh again at this sudden, new revelation, but stifled it. She could hear footsteps coming their way from the living room.

"We're hungry, ladies," Jordan said as he came through the door. "Can we help? Let me get my man Gus out of the way, Shann." He gently picked up the baby basket.

"Send my brother out here to make the garlic bread while you put Gus in bed. Then, we'll eat."

"Shannon," Clare said, "It's been nice talking to you."

The younger woman nodded, put dried spaghetti into a pot of salted, boiling water and set the timer.

Eight minutes later, Clare drained the pasta, put it in Shannon's Italian pasta bowl, tossing it with the marinara sauce. Meatballs and spicy Italian sausage were served in a separate matching bowl. Salad, parmesan cheese and a grater waited on the table. Jeff filled wine glasses with Chianti, then took the perfectly toasted garlic bread out of the oven. They all sat down.

"This smells terrific," Clare said. "Thank you for inviting me."

Reese, who'd insisted on sitting next to her, leaned over and whispered, "I'm glad you're finally here. So, when are you going to marry my Uncle Jeff?"

Clare was speechless. Shannon intervened.

"Reese, that's not our business. Why don't you say the blessing?"

"But, mommy," the little girl pouted, "I saw it in my head."

"The blessing, Clarice Hannah." The little girl bowed her head and prayed;

> "Come Lord Jesus be our Guest;
> And let these gifts to us be blest.
> And may there be a goodly share
> On every table everywhere."

"Thank you, Reese," her mom said.

"Dig in, guys," Jordan added.

CJay met Jeff's eyes. She saw humor. And for the first time, she knew she *was* jealous of Helen. She was jealous of Jeff's memories and history. The one thing she didn't know was if she should be glad or terrified – one more time – of this new emotion.

Chapter Forty-nine

There was laughter at dinner, but also serious conversation as Jordan shared some of the things he'd experienced in Afghanistan. Shannon told Reese to go run and find a book for Jeff to read to her later, so the adults could talk privately over coffee now.

CJay felt comfortable with these people. Jordan was a cop – Military Police. Shannon was Jeff's sister – raised in essentially the same slightly unusual matriarchal family environment in Wasilla. She couldn't detect any obvious mental pathology. They laughed frequently but could also be serious – and capable of listening before commenting. She sensed love here for one another.

I've been alone emotionally for so long.... I think I'm afraid of losing this moment – this man – this sense of family. I'm afraid of wanting this so much - and maybe losing it again – like I lost Alex. And my baby.

Shannon offered chocolate peanut butter ice cream ("Jeff's favorite," she whispered to Clare) with their coffee, and Jeff helped his sister clear the table and put the dishes in the dishwasher. He encouraged Clare to sit in the living room with Jordan while he and his sister got dessert ready. Reese sat by Trygve. The K-9 licked her face while Reese giggled.

"Good for her immune system," Clare offered when Jordan told his daughter to not let the dog lick her face. "Kids who live with dogs are healthier than kids who don't. Dog germs are generally dog specific and don't hurt children. Dirt's good too. Did you know that kids who pick their noses and eat their boogers have stronger immune systems and are sick less often than kids who don't?"

Jordan looked appalled.

"Seriously. They are. And kids who chew their nails are healthier, too. Dirt under the fingernails – good for you."

"Who knew?" Jordan said, laughing. "How 'bout mud pies?"

"Nature's probiotic," CJay replied with a straight face. They were both laughing when Jeff and Shannon came back with ice cream.

Jeff read to Reese before she went to bed. He tucked her in and kissed her.

"I really like your friend, Clare," Reese whispered to him.

"I do too," Jeff confided.

"So, when are you going to marry her?" the little girl asked. "I saw you marry her. She was wearing a long ecru dress."

"'Ecru?'" He laughed. "You saw it? Were there flowers too? Or a hat?"

Reese looked offended at his remark, but that didn't stop her from continuing after frowning at him. "Blue and pink and purple flowers with one white rose and one pink rose – like a bouquet with lots of ribbons. And flowers and ribbons around her head, too. But Momma wouldn't let me talk about it." She stuck out her lower lip. "Little John was there, too, with his food. Not the smoker, though, 'cuz he didn't want the bears to come, too."

Her uncle smiled, then became thoughtful with the little girl. "Well, that sounds like quite a fun party, Reese, but it's really up to Clare – if we get married, I mean. Maybe sometime. But do me a really big favor – don't be saying things like that out loud."

"Nobody gets mad when Great-Gramma does it."

Jeff conceded that fact and realized Reese was wise beyond her years. "But she's old, sweetheart, and we've gotten used to it. Sometimes you have to earn the right to know about stuff ahead of time."

"Seriously?" She rolled her eyes. "Okay. Well, just between you and me then, Uncle Jeff, can I be flower girl?"

"You might be all grown up by that time."

A look of skepticism passed over the child's face. She sighed, slightly exasperated with her uncle. "Well, then can I be a bride's maid?"

Jeff laughed. "Up to Clare, isn't it? Who knows? I love you, Reese."

"I love you, too, Uncle Jeff. And I like Auntie Clare much better than that other one." She paused, choosing her words carefully. "But, to be charitable, I think Helen may have had some deep-seated issues about relationships that kept her from making wise choices."

Jeff stared at her. *Holy Toledo. Great-Gramma, what have you wrought?*

Chapter Fifty

The adults sat and chatted by the fire for another hour. Jeff saw Clare sneak a glance at her watch and caught her eye. He knew she had to go on shift at 0630 the next morning.

"Clare, what say we tear ourselves away from these people and let them go to bed?"

The flight nurse nodded. "I've had a very enjoyable evening," she told them. "Thank you for inviting me tonight."

Shannon went to CJay as soon as the flight nurse stood and held her close. "You've no idea how much I've enjoyed meeting you again in a more relaxed and much less terrifying setting. My ears still ring from having Gus shout at me."

They said their good-byes at the door, and Jeff walked with CJay to the car, his arm around her shoulders. He opened her door for her, then went around to the driver's side.

"Okay. How did it go for you?" he asked her as they pulled out of the driveway.

"I'm honest when I said this was an enjoyable evening. I like your sister and Jordan. Reese's a smart kid, too."

Jeff smiled. "Yeah, Reese is pretty smart – and a whole hell of a lot older than her tender years. I sense she's got some of my grandmother's gifts. I'm glad you liked my family." Jeff paused, took a deep breath, then said, "We've talked a little about this, but do you still want children, Clare?"

She looked at him – at his strong profile in the darkness of the car, with the lights of Fairbanks coming and going through the windows. *I wanted my baby very much.*

"Yes." Her voice lowered and when she spoke again, he had to concentrate to hear what she was saying. "I was over the moon when we found out I was pregnant. I told you that."

He nodded. "I'm so sorry, Clare. I know Alex and your baby can't be replaced in your heart. I can't replace Alex. No one can."

"And that's why I gave you such a hard time – not wanting to go out with you."

He nodded. "I saw you holding Augustus and wondered if it was something…I don't know. Maybe something I could envision for us one day."

"Maybe, but it's too soon, Jeff. We don't even know if we're compatible beyond eating, shooting guns, and having fairly phenomenal sex." She saw him smile. "I've buried my yearnings very deep for a very long time and you don't really know me yet, Jeff. I won't lie to you. At the moment, the thought of having you in my life..." She let the thought trail off before she continued. "But you'll find I have feet of clay, like everyone does. I might find the same about you – that you're difficult to live with or have a nasty temper or need to have your own way all the time. 'Bull-headed,' remember?"

342

She turned to look more squarely at him. "I haven't seen those qualities yet, but we've *both* been on our best behavior with one another. Maybe you fight dirty during arguments. Hell, for all *you* know at this point, I become a shrieking fishwife if I disagree with you."

Clare paused, then went on, her voice carrying a new raw edge of tension. "You know jack diddly freakin' squat about me. I love my job. You told me you were in awe of me – of what I did as a flight nurse. I still want to do that. I still want to fly." She stopped. Took a deep breath and blew it out loudly. "And just how long are you willing to wait before you have kids?"

Jeff pulled into Clare's driveway. Coming to a stop, he shut off the engine and turned towards her, speaking quietly and very formally with measured words.

"Your concerns are valid, Clare. I've got time left to be a parent. So do you. You and I both love our jobs. I don't see any reason that we can't get to know one another over the course of the next few months and think about what this means for us going forward at that time."

He took her hand. "I didn't mean to come across as 'It's my way or the highway.' Life can be tragically short, bloody, and brutish – and awfully unfair besides." Susan and Mark's smiling faces when he gave them orders to fly to Mantishka and 'figure out what's going on with those two villagers and their doggone kitchen furniture' passed yet one more time before his eyes.

"Clare, I've been frittering my time away. You guys have biological clocks – at least that's what I've read. Maybe I do too.

343

For me, it's past time to settle down. To find a woman I love to spend my life with. To have children of my own. With her."

He stopped, glancing at the increasingly appalled expression on her face and realized he needed to be more specific.

"With you, Clare."

CJay chuffed softly and took her hand out of his.

"I glad you didn't want to come across as 'My way or the highway,' Trooper, because you came pretty damn close. I have a question for you."

He sat back and waited, watching her.

"Helen came up tonight at least three times, and one of them was particularly odd." She raised her eyebrows at him. "Do I need to worry about her?"

"Make that four times, Clare," he said, remembering his own 'odd' conversation with Reese.

He rubbed his eyes and sighed. "I know you saw that picture of her on the bookshelf. I apologize. I should've put that away. Shoulda burned it. Shoulda shredded it."

"Or put it face down in your sock drawer. Listen, I told Shannon tonight that we all have history and baggage." She stopped, forming her thoughts. "I have no room to talk. I still display that wedding picture of Alex and me and I'm *not* ashamed of it. I loved him and you know it. You loved Helen – and I respect that. But I'm...hell, I don't know what I am."

"I want you," he interjected. "Not Helen. Not anyone else. That should be enough."

She chuckled, but it wasn't a humorous sound. "I appreciate that, Jeff. I really do. But I think I'm trying to sort out my own emotional responses here."

"Well, uh, you sound sorta angry."

She grunted. "I am 'uh, sorta angry,'" she mimicked, then paused. "No. I'm not angry." Took a long breath. "Nah, I am. I *am* really PO'd, Trooper."

"Well, per my crisis management training, anger is a secondary emotion. It almost always covers up a primary emotion."

"So, 'What you hear me saying is'...?" He heard her chuckle again to herself.

"'So, what I hear you saying,' Clare.... Do you want me to guess?"

"Why not, Jeff? Why don't you just go right ahead and guess. You're smart."

"You wonder if I'm over her. You're feeling vulnerable right now. Afraid. Maybe even jealous. But – trust me on this – you have no reason to be jealous of anyone or anything. Still, you're wondering if I'm so intent on having a family and a sense of stability that I'm zeroing in on you because Helen turned me down. You're afraid you're the understudy in this drama of my life."

CJay stared at him. She knew, once again, that her mouth was hanging open. She clapped it shut. "Wow. Yeah, Jeff. Pretty much that. I'm scared. I don't want to be the default winner in your...um...effing 'drama.'"

"Well, I'm glad you're telling me this now and not shutting me out. I think the only way I can convince you is to make my actions fit my words. I loved Helen. I'm won't try to deny that to you. But in hindsight, because of our differences about what 'family' means, it would have been a very short, miserable marriage for both her and me."

He laughed out loud, but like her chuckle, it wasn't a cheerful sound. "Despite that, it took me awhile to get over what I perceived as a great loss when she left Fairbanks. But I got over it. And, kinda like when Monica got pregnant and married her Wasilla auto mechanic – who's bought her a freakin' mansion AND several expensive cars – I realized, in hindsight, just what sort of an enormous .50 caliber bullet I'd dodged.

"Hmmph."

"That photo of Helen on my bookshelf? You know why I kept it there?" He shrugged. "To be honest, Clare, I'd actually forgotten about it until I saw you looking at it."

"So why was the picture still there?"

"A reminder, I guess. Be smarter next time. Or I simply stopped seeing it." He shrugged.

"Do you feel you're 'being smarter' this time?" She looked over at him, the light from her front porch casting shadows over those beautiful cheekbones and straight nose that had so caught her eye at Moose Man.

He reached over and pulled her as close as he could with the console between their two seats. "If you'll let me, Clare, I'd like to prove to you I'm being a whole hell of a lot smarter this time. I...I...really, really...um...like you."

She smiled and held him close. "One day at a time, bull-headed Trooper," she said. "We need to take our time."

"Do you want to know when I started to get over Helen?"

"Tell me," she mumbled against his neck.

"I started to get over Helen that day on the flightline at Wainwright – before the Missing Man flyover. I looked into your eyes and I saw my future. I've never wanted anyone else."

Chapter Fifty-one

Jeff pulled the Trooper Expedition into the parking space in front of the Safeway store and got out after letting Trygve know he'd be right back after he got coffee for the pot in his office. He heard someone say, "Oh darn!" and looked around in time to see a native woman struggling to get bags out of her shopping cart and into the back of a weather beaten red 1991 Dodge Ram pickup truck with an equally weather beaten camper shell attached to it.

"Veda, let me help you with those," he called out to Helen's mother. He slammed the door to his vehicle and took the heaviest bag out of Veda's arms and placed it in the pickup bed.

"Jeffrey! You're a sight for sore eyes. Give this woman a hug." She flung her arms around him and he bent down to embrace her. Standing back up, he told her she looked good.

"And I feel good, too, Jeffrey. I'm retiring in a few months and thinking about maybe moving down to Seattle – to be near...um...Helen. Did you know she's getting married?"

Jeff stood there. "No, I did not know that. Well, good for her. When's the big day?"

"January. Some kind of 'destination wedding.' She's buying my ticket for me, since Hawaii is a little steep, even if Alaska

Airlines does fly there now. They're getting married on Maui. On the beach. Seems to be the thing to do these days." She shook her head "Kind of limits the guest list, though."

"Well, good for her," he repeated. "Who's the lucky fella?"

"He's a Washington State Patrol pilot. Flies for them. He's retired military – been with the state for close to five years."

"So, she's staying with LEOs, despite...?" He didn't finish his sentence. Didn't want to sound too sarcastic, but Veda caught it and nodded.

"That was a nasty business, Jeffrey. I felt really bad when she up and left..." Veda didn't add 'left *you,*' which the trooper appreciated.

"Well, obviously she's landed on her feet, and that's what's important."

"How about you, Jeffrey. Are you doing well? Are you seeing anyone?"

Jeff hesitated. He didn't mind telling Veda he was seeing someone, but he didn't feel it was Helen's business. Ah, hell. Why shouldn't Helen know that even *she's* disposable and he'd mourned her loss for at least a week? Or was it eight months?

"Yeah, Veda, I *am* seeing someone – one of Aurora's flight nurses. Met her on the job."

Veda laughed. "So, you're staying within the fold, too? A nurse? I love you, Jeffrey, and I wish you every happiness because you deserve it. You're a good man. You would've made a formidable husband for that daughter of mine."

Jeff shrugged, loaded the rest of Veda's bags, then bent to hug the Aleut woman again. "Veda, fly safe to Hawaii in January.

And I hope that retirement in Seattle is everything you want it to be. And you'll be a good mother-in-law to that cop."

He turned away with a wave and strode on into the grocery store to pick up the coffee he wanted. *So, Helen's getting married? To a pilot? Bet he's got grown kids and probably doesn't want any more. Funny how things turn out....*

* * * * * *

"Sergeant," Ruby said when Jeff picked up the phone, "When I hang up there's a call for you."

She hung up and Jeff said into the phone, "Sergeant Douglas."

"Sergeant," he heard in his left ear. "You've blocked me from your cell phone so I can't call you directly."

"Really? Who knew." He shut his eyes and shook his head. *Helen.*

"Yes, who knew. I didn't block you from mine."

"Right now, I can't think of an appropriate smart-ass answer, but since I haven't tried to call you since you blew town, it really doesn't matter. What is your business?"

"'What is my business.' You're very official today. My business is that CareLift is going to pick up a patient at North Star tomorrow and I'm on the flight. I'd like to see you – maybe have a cup of coffee with you and just say 'Hi.'"

"I think not, Helen." *Geez.* "But fly safe." He started to put the phone back in the cradle but heard her voice.

350

"Please don't hang up, Jeffrey. I'm not coming on to you. I just want to have a cup of coffee – like we used to do. Just a cup of coffee. Just friends."

"I think not," he repeated.

"I thought you'd be over me by now. Sounds like you're still hurting."

He almost laughed out loud at her audacious – nah, snarky *and* mean-spirited – presumption. *I was over you several months ago, Helen. And please note I'm not the one calling you for a coffee klatch.*

"Surprisingly, perhaps, to you, Helen, I'm doing quite well. Busy here – lotsa trooper stuff, working on the house, looking forward to the new year. It's great. Never better. Rainbows and unicorns."

"Are you afraid that seeing me will turn everything upside down? Is that why you don't want to have coffee with me?"

"I don't want to have coffee with you because I don't *need* to have coffee with you. I can't think of a single reason why I would *ever* need to have coffee with you."

"Mom's moving down to Seattle in the Spring to live near me."

"Great." Jeff didn't mention that he'd met Veda earlier at the Safeway. *Coincidence? I think not.* Neither Jeff nor Leroy Jethro Gibbs believed in coincidences – Rule 39.

There was a long silence before she finally said, "We're going to be arriving at FAI around 1300 tomorrow. We'll be back in the air by 1700. I'd like to see you. Just to say hello." Her voice lowered and softened. "And...um...I miss you."

Oh, Helen. That ship has sailed. "I think not, Helen. Fly safe."

This time he did hang up. An image of Clare's naked breasts flitted across his mind and he felt his cock respond. *So very much sailed, that ship has.*

"Good for you, Sergeant," he heard Ruby say from her desk around the corner.

* * * * * *

"Hi, Jeff. How are you?" It was good to hear his voice, even if only on the phone.

"Can I bring Mexican takeout over to you after you get off shift, Clare?"

The flight nurse sat in the corner of dispatch with her back to Gus and Big Mike. There was a stack of charts in front of her that she was auditing. Gus was speaking with Norma and monitoring the local EMS and AST frequencies, while Big Mike monitored frequencies and multitasked with data entry.

"I'd like that a lot. Can you stay the night – you and Trygve?"

"If it's all right with you."

She smiled. *I love sleeping with you.* "No pressure. Well, maybe just a little, in all the right places."

She heard him laugh quietly. "Give me a text when you're done and I'll stop by the joint near the Post. See you tonight, flight nurse."

"'Til tonight, Trooper."

* * * * * *

352

He was there within twenty-five minutes after she texted, carrying two large sacks of Mexican takeout with extra sour cream, salsa, and cilantro. Clare supplied the Bud Light Lime. The two unloaded the foam boxes filled with chicken and cheese enchiladas, carne asada, fish tacos, refried beans and rice, and an enormous chile verde chimichanga onto the dining room table and toasted one another with their ice-cold bottles.

"Mmmmmm," Clare moaned, biting into a fish taco.

"I think I'm getting jealous over here."

She laughed. "Don't be, Trooper. You are much tastier, even without salsa or sour cream...or cilantro." She pushed guacamole back into her mouth with a finger.

"Thank you, flight nurse. You're better than any chimichanga could ever hope to be."

"High praise, indeed, Jeff. What's the occasion?" She pointed to the veritable cornucopia of spicy, hot Mexican food on the table.

He chewed, took a cleansing swallow of Bud Light Lime, and put down his fork. "I saw Veda today in the Safeway parking lot."

Clare looked at him uncomprehendingly, then he saw her eyes narrow as she remembered who he was referring to. "And?"

"It's the first time I've seen her in a year. She was having trouble with her groceries, so I helped her load them into the truck."

"You are such a nice trooper. What a boy scout." Her eyes were still narrowed. "Let me repeat myself. And...?"

"She said that Helen is getting married."

Her face brightened. "Are you going to the festivities? Am I your Plus One? Where's the wedding going to be? Will there be a flyover of medevacs?" She shut her eyes and shook her head slightly. "I'm sorry. That was not nice. I'm delighted for her. I hope she's found someone who doesn't want kids and doesn't mind following in her wake as she…. I'm sorry. There I go again. I'll shut up."

"It's in Hawaii and I'm not invited, Clare."

"Bummer."

She put down her fork and leaned forward, elbows on the table, her hands steepled in front of her chin, a serious expression on her pretty face. "And how does that make you feel?" she asked in a concerned voice, her eyebrows lowered in a thoughtful way.

Jeff burst out laughing. "Have you thought about joining the crisis management team, Clare? You'd be a shoo-in."

Clare smiled. "'If you can fake sincerity, you've got it made.' Seriously, my favorite trooper, why are you telling me all this?"

"Then, I got a phone call. From Seattle."

She sat up straight and took a deep breath. "And...?"

"She's coming up with CareLift to transport a patient from Med Center back to Seattle. She wants to have a cup of coffee at the hospital with me tomorrow."

"I'm on duty tomorrow, Jeff, so Wendell and I will be meeting them when they arrive. Are you aware of that?"

"Yes. You'll get to greet her."

"Does she know you and I are an item?"

354

"I told Veda was I seeing a flight nurse. I said I was very happy, too," he added quickly.

"I asked if *she* knows about *me*."

"I didn't tell Veda your name. I also told Helen I didn't want to or *need* to see her."

"Jeff, if you want to see her tomorrow for a cup of coffee, go ahead. If I can't trust you...well, maybe I can't trust anyone."

"I don't need to see her."

"Of course, you don't *need* to see her. But I'm not going to tell you that you can't. We're not married. We're not engaged. Hell, we're not even 'going steady' for heaven's sakes." Her voice amped up, then she quieted. "Have coffee with her. Sort this out. I'm a big girl. We're adults here. Get this out of *her* system."

"Damn it, Clare. Look at me."

She picked up her knife and fork and began to attack the carne asada in its foam box, slashing off several strips of steak and folding them into a flour tortilla with the refried beans, salsa, sour cream, and extra cilantro torn on top. She bit off a large portion, leaving sour cream on her chin, washing it down with the last of her beer. She wiped her face.

"Clare. I'm *not* going to have a cup of coffee, tea, or even warm piss with her. Do you understand that?"

"¿Quiere uno más cerveza?" she asked, standing up to get another one for herself. "You driving tonight?"

"Beer, but only if I'm not driving...."

"You're not driving. Another beer for the trooper." She came back from the refrigerator with two more Bud Light Limes. "Sort it out, trooper. It's only a cuppa coffee." She smiled at him, a toothy grin that did not extend to her pretty blue eyes.

There was still some cilantro on her cheek.

Chapter fifty-two

She ditched him when he told her he wanted a family and kids, kicking him to the curb and blowing the state, leaving him to pick up whatever pieces of his ego he had left.

And for four years, I've been dealing with Alex's and Lexie's deaths – and when I finally find someone I think I can maybe, just maybe, have a new start with – a new chance at happiness – back into the picture she steams. A fucking 'cup of coffee.' Fat fucking chance that's all she wants.

And she's getting married? And angling for a little get-together with my man? Just a little one last romp in the hay? Not much they can do in the short period of time they have between packaging the patient and hot-footing it back to the aircraft, but if she could, I bet she would.

Just one last time? Just for old time's sake? I'd bet a month's pay she told him, "I've really missed you."

The flight nurse swore in the crude street Spanish she'd learned from her husband.

* * * * * *

357

After dinner, he had his clothes off before her, and was snuggled in the flannel sheets before she'd finished brushing her teeth and, naked, joined him. She crawled under the sheets and sat on top of his hips, rubbing against him as he lay on his back. Then, she moved to the side and took his engorged cock into her mouth.

He groaned and pushed against her mouth and tongue as she sucked on him. He could feel her hand cupping him gently as she tasted his fluids. The trooper maintained contact with his hands on her shoulders, pressing himself against her.

She stopped after a bit. But he could be disappointed, she drew back the covers and straddled his knees.

"My turn, Trooper." She bent down so he could see her take his cock into her mouth for another moment. Then she sat up, licked her fingers, moistened her own cleft and gently lowered her body onto his, slowly, in and out, in and out, in and out, slippery, fiery, dripping wet. She saw him close his eyes, probably because if he didn't, this moment would end.

Quickly and involuntarily, he moved with her, thrusting inside of her.

"Easy, Big Fellow," she said, putting her hand on his smooth chest.

"Are you the Lone Ranger?" he asked, grunting, as she moved on him.

"I am *your* Lone Rangerette, Trooper."

She saw him watching where her hips straddled his and knew he could see his cock coming and going from sight as she

358

moved on him. She concentrated on finding just that spot that felt so good to her. She saw him look up to her face. *Does that feel good, Jeff?*

She continued her movements, then lowered her body onto his, resting on her elbows.

* * * * * *

Jeff closed his eyes, cleared his mind. He didn't want to come so quickly. He opened them again when she lay on him, resting on her elbows. He could feel the moisture on her belly and see the silky sheen of sweat on her breasts. He felt her muscles clasping and releasing him, deep inside of her. All he could think was *God.* He cupped her left breast, caressing it, squeezing the nipple – his other arm around her back. He heard her gasp and felt her pelvis move and her muscles tighten around him. *I'm your toy and I love it, Clare. Use me. Find your pleasure with me.*

She continued to move on him, her breasts so tantalizingly close to his mouth that he could reach them, and he did, suckling her as she growled in her throat and ground her pelvis on him. Suddenly, he saw her closed eyes tighten and felt his cock become extremely hot.

"Oh...oh...oh...oh...Trooper, oh...Jeff," she panted with her mouth open. He felt the rolling spasms of her orgasm against him and forced himself not to come at the same time she was.

"Was that good?" he asked her, after she lay against him, spent.

359

He felt her smile and she lifted her head to look at him.

"Ah, my handsome stallion. We must always make love." She moved her still sensitive sex on him, extending her pleasure. And his.

Finally, she put her hands under his shoulders and rolled to the left with her legs around him. He followed her lead and ended up on top still engorged and inside of her. Thrust gently, felt the silken heat. He relished the ripeness of being inside this woman. He moved more, lifting himself up on his elbows and then he reached down, embraced her and pulled her up to his chest, still inside of her, sitting back on his knees. She wrapped her arms around his neck and tightened her long legs around his butt as he continued to thrust into her.

His breath quickened as his strokes increased. Then he slowed, but increased his strength, deeper, deeper. Intentionally deep and forceful. He groaned, thrusting, and his orgasm burst inside of her. He laid his moist cheek against hers and heard her whisper, "Hi-ho Silver," in his ear. He tightened his arms around her, pressing her close to him for a long moment, smiling.

* * * * * *

"Hi-ho Silver," she whispered in his ear. She could feel his smile against her cheek.

Thank you, Trooper. Thank you for the pleasure you give to my body. Thank you for making my heart grateful I am alive tonight.

Clare held him firmly as he lay her gently back down on the bed. Jeff, still breathing heavily, pulled the covers up over the two of them, lying side by side now, on their backs, his arm under her shoulder.

"Clare...," he said, softly.

She turned to look at him. "Jeff...?"

"You know I think about you all the time...."

And I think about you, Trooper. She kissed his shoulder.

"Your brother likes me."

She nodded. *Yes, he does.*

"I don't want anyone else."

"I know. Go have coffee with her tomorrow. I trust you." She kissed him. "Sleep well, Big Fellow." Clare turned on her side and he spooned himself against her back, his arm around her breasts, his breath on her shoulder. She could feel him chuckling.

* * * * * *

But I sure as hell do not *trust her. Remember what we did tonight, Jeff, when you're drinking coffee with her tomorrow. Remember how it felt when I took you in my mouth. When you saw your purple veined cock moving in and out of my hot wet flesh. When you were kissing my breasts. When you heard our sounds and you smelled our sex. Remember how it felt when you came inside of me. Think about that tomorrow when you're with her. When you're with that one who is going to ask you for 'just one last time, for old time's sake.'*

Witch.

Well, at least it rhymed with 'Witch.'

Chapter Fifty-three

Helen Tall's King Air arrived at Fairbanks International Airport's General Aviation Terminal at 1300. When the stairs went down, she hoped beyond hope that Jeffrey's Expedition would be waiting for her alongside the Fairbanks Fire Department ambulance rig that had been dispatched to take them and their equipment to North Star Medical Center so they could pick up the skier with the broken pelvis and transport him back to Tacoma to his family.

She was disappointed. He and that dog weren't there.

But the good news was that their aircraft had a warning light display flicker about seventeen minutes before they landed that required them to shut down and investigate what was going on with the plane's mechanical system before they could depart again.

Well, doggone it. That'll take a while. She smiled.

"We're here for the night, ladies," their pilots finally told them. "CareLift's gotten us rooms at The Suites and if things go well, we'll be lifting off at 0900 tomorrow. Get some rest and don't party too hard here in Fairbanks."

The two pilots looked at each other, then laughed.

Helen turned to her crewmate and told her, "I'm staying at my mother's tonight, Lauren. You've got the room to yourself. Have fun. Fairbanks is a nice town."

Then she called her mother to come pick her up at the hospital in an hour.

* * * * * *

Clare and Wendell greeted the CareLift crew on their arrival to the ambulance bay in the fire department rig. They exchanged pleasantries, discussing weather, the aircraft they'd flown up in, items of interest nationally to the industry. The Aurora crew learned the fixed wing aircraft had an 'issue' that needed to be checked out mechanically before they were safe to fly again.

Then, the two Aurora crewmembers escorted the two Washington flight nurses to the ICU where they would be assessing the skier for the trip back to Tacoma in the morning.

"You look familiar," Wendell said to Helen as they rode the elevator to the 4th floor.

"I'm from here. I worked at Fairbanks Memorial before I went down to Seattle."

"I thought so," Wendell replied. "I think we've taken ACLS and PALS together at some point.

"Very possibly," the tall, exotic looking beauty said, smiling. "I was at Memorial for over eight years."

"Helen Tall," Clare commented.

"Yes. Have we taken classes together too?" The CareLift nurse looked carefully at her, her face, her flight suit, her embroidered name *('Valenzuela'),* her ID badge *(CJay Valenzuela),* her boots – and back up again.

A serious once over, Clare thought. "I don't think so," she lied. The last thing she needed was for Helen to figure out who she was – that she'd helped teach those certification classes – if she didn't already know. "What are you two nurses going to be doing tonight?"

"I'm going out to dinner with the pilots and then to bed," the nurse with 'Lauren Borden' embroidered on her uniform replied. "I'm exhausted."

"And you, Helen?" Clare asked. "What do you have planned?"

"Can you keep a secret?"

"My lips are sealed," Clare replied with a small smile. She glanced at Wendell and shook her head slightly. Wendell kept a straight face.

"I plan on surprising an old friend at his house."

"Oh? How lovely. And who is this friend who will be surprised?" Wendell asked.

"Just an old trooper friend." She paused and with a hint of a smile added, "I'm bringing dessert." Then, she winked.

"Very thoughtful," Wendell said. "Well, you have a wonderful time, and I'm sure we'll see you tomorrow morning."

"I may be tired." She yawned, patted her mouth dramatically and then smiled again as they stepped out of the elevator.

"Oh, my. That sounds naughty! Scratching an old itch?" Clare offered with her own conspiratorial wink. *I'll give you a little 'scratch.' Mano a mano, puta.* Clare wanted to punch her in the nose, but knew that would be imprudent, here in the ICU hallway, with others as witnesses – including patient family members who were watching the four elite flight crewmembers closely.

"And well scratched, perhaps." Helen looked as if she had suddenly gone far away before they came back to the present company. "He *is* tireless." She rolled her eyes, smirking lasciviously.

Clare had not physically moved, but she felt Wendell's hand on her arm nonetheless. *Looking out for me, Wendell? Thanks, bud.* Puta, she repeated to herself, an outwardly pleasant expression on her face.

She visualized blood spurting from Helen's smashed nose.

Chapter Fifty-four

I haven't been back to Fairbanks in over a year. Mom's been down to Olympia a couple times, and that's the only reason I've seen her at all. It feels strange being here even though nothing's changed. It looked so familiar flying in – it smells the same. Crap weather, as usual. But I've missed it. A lot.

She shook her head as if that would make the memories retreat. It didn't work.

I wonder if that CJay person is the one he's screwing now. He goes for the type – tall as me. But she's not native. Maybe his kilt-wearing Norwegian Lutheran is taking a walk on the white side now.

She visualized him in a kilt – like that TV series – 'Outlander.' He'd look good.

I loved him. It broke my heart to tell him I wouldn't marry him – because I wanted to. So handsome and strong and warm and sweet and brave and fucking horny. God, I loved having sex with him….

She trembled slightly and moved her pelvis provocatively in the Fred Meyers outdoors section, her hand around a spray bottle of mosquito repellent, as she visualized his naked body on top of her, thrusting slowly, bringing her to climax.

Why why why did he have to make it contingent on kids? He has his dreams. I do too. What about MY dreams? Don't they matter? What the hell am I? Chopped liver?

My mother was so right. She and Gran always told me that a man's agenda seldom coincides with ours. We have to be able to take care of ourselves because it's so easy to be screwed by someone else's promises.

She took her time going up and down the aisles, checking out the specials, wandering in the home furnishings and kitchen departments, fingering the dishware and linens and admiring the pots and pans. She'd changed into civilian clothes and suddenly felt she fit right back in. She bought a couple of shirts in the ladies' clothing section. It was almost as if she'd never left.

Randolph offers me what I need. Financial security, stability, and no threat of kids. Somebody who thinks I'm special the way I am. Patient with my need to go back to school for my PhD. Proud of me.

She smiled as she pictured Randolph in his Washington State Patrol flightsuit. He was also tall, strong, sexy, brave. And widowed. And fairly accomplished in the bedroom. He had kids, but they were over 18 and out of the house. Like she liked it. And they tolerated her.

I'm sorry, Jeffrey. I'd take it back if I could, but it was your fault. It was all your fault I had to leave....

Chapter Fifty-five

Jeff realized there was an issue when Trygve alerted to a noise on the road and started barking. The trooper had just sat down to a square of Stouffer's previously frozen leftover lasagna reheated in the microwave and a small bowl of kale and Brussels sprouts salad (good for colon health), pine nuts and dried cranberries, and some sort of organic raspberry vinaigrette, when he heard a vehicle pull into his driveway and crunch to a stop.

What the heck?

He turned out the floor lamp which cast the room into darkness, grabbed his Remington 870 tactical shotgun and racked a shell into it. Looking out the side of the window with the shotgun in one hand, he saw Veda Tall's weather beaten red 1991 Dodge Ram truck with the equally weather beaten camper shell park in front. When the truck door opened, Helen stepped out.

I don't fucking *believe this.* As he walked onto the deck still holding the shotgun, he saw her take a small grocery sack out of the bed of the truck and start up the stairs.

"Jesus, Helen. What the hell do you think you're doing?"

"Just a visit, Jeffrey. Just a visit. You wouldn't come to me, and our plane has an issue, so I'm coming to you. And, I brought dessert." She held up the bag. She pointed at his tactical shotgun. "You can put that away, too. I come in peace, white man."

He stood at the top of the stairs barring her forward progress. She stopped in front of him and waited. Finally, she asked, "Aren't you going to invite me in? I have chocolate peanut butter ice cream. Your favorite. Remember?"

"What the flaming flying fuck do you think you're doing here?" he asked quietly, somewhat repeating himself.

"Language, Jeffrey. I already told you. I'm bringing the proverbial mountain to Mohammed – me and ice cream for you. Do you have coffee? I still want that cup I asked for." She smiled at him. Still that quirky sideways smile, he saw. And those beautiful, exotic, deep, dark brown eyes.

He could hear Clare's voice echoing in his ear: *"If I can't trust you, who can I trust?"*

Well, obviously not Helen. He also flashed back to that horrifying 1987 Michael Douglas movie he'd just watched on television – what was it? *Fatal Attraction?*

The stench of boiled rabbit filled his nostrils.

"You need to leave, Helen. I don't care if your plane has an issue. You can't be here. Go back to Veda's." Trygve stood next to him, his lip back, teeth showing. Jeff could feel the dog rumbling against his leg.

"Your dog still doesn't like me, does he?"

"He's turning out to be an excellent judge of character."

"Tell you what. Call off your hellhound and give me a cup of coffee and I'll leave. I just want to see you for a minute. No hidden agenda, Jeffrey. No strings. Just a hello. I'll even leave the ice cream." There was a very long pause and the trooper did not move from his position blocking the top of the stairs to the deck.

"Please," she finally implored. "Just a cup of coffee."

No way this can go wrong, he thought as he stepped somewhat hesitantly to the side to allow her to pass. Trygve, still rumbling, backed away but did not take his eyes from her face.

"Your house is still beautiful, Jeffrey," Helen told him as soon as he closed the door behind them and switched on a few lights. He saw her gaze go over to his office space.

Looking for your picture?

"Have you done anything with the loft yet?"

"Nope." He was already in the kitchen, grabbing randomly for a K Cup out of a variety pack and inserting a chocolate-strawberry flavored selection into his single cup coffee brewer on the counter. *Good choice. She hates flavored coffee.*

Placing a mug that proudly displayed the faded logo of "Skinny Dick's Halfway Inn" under the spout, he activated the brewing process. Moments later, he handed Helen the cup, then went and sat back down to eat his now congealed lasagna. She sat across from him at the table.

"Mmmmmm. Tastes good. Chocolatey-strawberry. You pulled out all the stops. Any milk or sugar?

"Milk in the fridge. Sugar in the cupboard with the spices." *Just like it's always been. I am a man of tradition.*

371

"I feel like I've gone back in time," she said, smiling and getting up to find the additives.

Trygve rumbled at her as she passed.

She grabbed a spoon from the silverware drawer and brought the milk and sugar back to the table, adding, stirring, tasting, adding more, stirring, tasting again. "It's hard to kill the flavor," she noted, straight-faced.

Jeff looked up at her and, against his will, smiled. *I'd forgotten how funny you are.* "I generally add Jägermeister to it so I can drink it."

She made a face then smiled back at him. "Thank you for letting me come indoors, Jeffrey."

"What do you want, Helen?"

"Just to see you. See how you're doing. My mother told me you were going out with an Aurora flight nurse."

"I am."

"I always knew you had good taste."

"I do. Your mother told *me* that you're getting married in January."

"I am."

"He's a Patrol pilot." It wasn't a question.

"He is. Military. Flew scouts in Desert Storm and gunships in Iraq and Afghanistan. Now he flies for the state patrol. I met him during a state law enforcement conference. I was presenting the full-day workshop he attended," she added, nonchalantly, shrugging. The pride was evident in her expression. "We hit it off."

She pulled out her smartphone and scrolled through the picture gallery until she found what she wanted, then turned the phone around and showed him. Jeff saw a tall, good-looking older man in a navy-blue flight suit standing next to a Cessna 206.

"He also flies their new helo - an AStar."

"'Service with Humility'. Nice, Helen."

"He's a widower. His wife died of breast cancer six years ago."

"Sorry to hear that. But, convenient."

"Has kids."

Jeff's eyebrows went up.

"They're over 18 and out of the house. Two are married with families living out of state. The youngest is at UDub – the University of Washington, studying to be a marine biologist. She seldom comes home – too busy."

"Also convenient. You like them?"

"Sure. They're nice. They just want their dad to be happy, and they tolerate me. I don't ask for more than that."

"Wise. I assume he doesn't want any more kids?" Only a little bit of snark showed.

"No. He's got his full complement of progeny. But, Jeffrey, I didn't come here to fight with you."

"I can't figure out why you came here in the first place." He pushed the lasagna and salad aside and went to get a glass of Gentleman Jack. Neat. "Want some?" He held up the bottle."

"Sure, just put it in this mug o' crap." She held up her hand. "No, I wouldn't do that to Jack. Yes. A glass, please."

He got her one, also neat, and sat back down at the table. Helen sipped and closed her eyes.

"Mmmm." She put the glass down on the table and wrapped her fingers around it, appearing to study the dark golden liquid as it shimmered in front of her. There was a long silence. She cleared her throat.

"I've missed you." Jeff knew beyond the shadow of a doubt that's what was going to come out of her mouth next.

"Randolph is a nice guy. We both live in Olympia and he flies out of the patrol base there, so we see each other almost every day. He's got a beautiful home on the peninsula with a view of Budd Inlet. Lots of trees and wildlife."

"Nice. You live with him?"

"Not yet. I've got an apartment in Olympia, but spend nights at his place when I can. When we're both off. Crazy schedules, of course."

"Oh, of course."

"I've gone back to school."

"Nice. Masters?"

"Actually, an accelerated PhD in Healthcare Administration." He saw a second slight, poorly concealed smile of pride when she said that.

"Challenging."

"But Randolph is very supportive. I've got another eighteen months, and then he's taking me to the South Pacific. He's renting a cat down there and we're going to sail for a bit to celebrate."

"A 'cat?'"

"I'm sorry," she chuckled and ducked her head. "Sailor talk. Bluewater catamaran. Ocean going. He grew up in Washington and has sailed all his life. We, I mean, *he* has a 50-foot sailboat that we take out from Olympia. And a summer place in the San Juan Islands that we sail to. We're also sailing around the Hawaiian Islands after the wedding for ten days. Not in *his* boat, although he's sailed *to* the Islands before. He's done the Transpac twice. I sorry, I mean the Transpacific Yacht Race from San Pedro to Honolulu. Next time – in three or four years – we'll be doing that race together."

Jeff looked at her, lifted his Gentleman Jack to his lips, took a long sip – and smiled. *And I'm a state trooper who used to live in a mold infested studio apartment in King Salmon.* He smiled. *All my exes live in luxury. I see a trend. Sorry, Clare – no big boats for us. But I can hunt a moose for you and serve you the tongue.*

"I'm happy for you. Sounds like you're doing well and having a good time too." *Perhaps she did just want to catch up.* He raised his glass of Jack to her in a symbolic toast.

"Yes, a good time." She cleared her throat again. Took a sip of her drink and put it down slowly. "But I've never been able to put 'closed' to our relationship. I miss who you are."

Doggone. Spoke too soon.

The trooper sat up straight in his chair. "Helen, damn it," he said quietly. "You walked out on me. Don't be comin' here with the 'I've missed you' song and dance and try to...I don't know what you're trying to do. You're engaged for God's sake. You miss me. I missed you, too, for a time. But that ship has sailed for both of us." He laughed at his own pathetic 'ship' pun, then shook his head. "Don't even go there with me."

She stood, then came around to his side of the table, pulled out the chair next to him, and sat in it, facing him. She put both her hands around his left upper arm and leaned her forehead against the side of his shoulder.

"I made a mistake, Jeff. I shouldn't have left. I miss you and I still want you. Can't we get back together again? If only for one last ti…"

He stood up, knocking his chair away, and tried to jerk his arm away from her hands, but she hung on tight and he dragged her to a standing position beside him. Trygve scrabbled away backwards on the hardwood floor and barked loudly at the ruckus.

"Stop it, Helen. I won't let you embarrass yourself by finishing that sentence." He saw genuine tears in her eyes. And pain. "Stop it, Helen. Just stop." He relaxed his arm and she dropped her hands, putting her arms around his body instead, moving in and holding him close.

Involuntarily, his own arms went around her. He felt her smooth skin on his face and smelled the lotion she'd applied. He remembered the soft curved paths beneath his heated fingers and the silken flesh he'd tasted with his mouth for almost two years. The Trooper wrapped his hand around the shiny black braid that fell down her back and pulled her closer. *How very familiar you feel. How I loved you.*

"Make love to me, Jeffrey," he heard close to his ear. "I dream about you still." He felt her lips on his cheek. Then he felt her lips on the side of his mouth. He felt his body responding as it had for two years to her smell and her warmth. He opened his mouth and kissed her.

"Make love to me," she repeated after a bit, against his lips, pressing herself into his groin. "You want me, I can tell."

Oh my, yes I do. I loved you for so long. He pulled her closer and cupped her butt, enjoying the feel of her hard muscles in his hand and the softness of her belly and breasts against him. *Jeffrey Cameron. What the hell do you think you're doing?*

"I'm a guy," he said somewhat reluctantly, pulling away from her and releasing her from his arms. "Of course I want to have sex. But 'No' has to mean no, Helen. We need to stop this now." *No, I need to stop this now.*

He reached around behind his back to try to loosen Helen's grasp on him. *I've also forgotten how strong you are.* "Let go of me, Helen." He grappled with her hands until he finally got them free. Bringing them forward, he crossed her arms in front of her and gave her a push back.

"I'm not going to aid and abet your cheating on a guy you're engaged to. And, I'm not about to do what I know is wrong for me." *My body may want to get you naked on a soft surface, but I still have choices I can make. I won't betray Clare's trust. I'm a Lutheran! I have Free Will.*

Helen's beseeching expression became one of bewilderment, then sorrow, then embarrassment, then red-faced anger. He watched her eyes narrow and her jaw tighten. She whirled away from him and walked over to the office area and, with her finger, roughly tapped Clare's newspaper photo clipping he'd taped to one of the shelves, ripping it.

"Since when have *you* – *you* of *all* people! – become Sergeant Goody Two Guns? This one. I know her. This your flight nurse? Dramatic. CPR on a gurney. In the *News-Miner*. Wahoo! Real cowgirl, isn't she. CJay? Is she the one? Is that her name? She and some guy named Dwindell or Wynton or something met us at Med Center when we drove in. Took us up to the ICU. Podunk Air Ambulance, at your service." She saluted, rather smartly as it were.

Jeff willed himself to be calm. She was angry – and angry, vulnerable people say mean shit. He knew that, but still wanted to slap her. He wondered where his beautiful Helen had gone in the past couple of years. He was embarrassed and – yes – ashamed that he'd kissed her. And other things.

The Trooper took a deep slow breath in, then let it out. "I think our chat's over now, Helen. Yes, that's CJay – Clare." *I'm in love with her, though I haven't told her so yet. Yes, I want to marry her at some point. I want kids and she wants kids. Also at some point. And I think she feels the same way about me.* "Let me get your jacket, Helen."

"Is she as good in bed as I am?"

He stared at her, incredulous, then said very quietly. "None of your fucking business, Helen. And, pardon my second bad pun."

She shrugged on her coat when he handed it to her, then zipped it up. Standing in the now open doorway, she turned to him. Trygve was at his left side, rumbling quietly.

378

"I wanted you when I was going with Gary."

Your Fairbanks PD homicide detective.

"I broke up with him because I wanted you. You don't know how much I looked forward to drinking coffee with you in the 'caf.' I waited for you every day, hoping you'd come into the ED."

And then you asked me out and I fell completely in love with you.

"I've always wanted only you."

Jeff waited.

"It's your fault."

Jeff waited.

"Say something."

He sighed, shrugged, and shook his head. "Helen, I loved you, too. I bade my time waiting for you to split from Gary because I didn't want to betray the brotherhood. And, I actually respect you for not betraying him."

"I've missed you so much. I loved you so much."

"And, you left me because you didn't want a family. And now, you want to betray a good man who is trying to find happiness after the death of his wife? You want to betray a man who thinks he has an opportunity to spend the rest of his life with the perfect woman? Class act, Helen." *And, class act on my part, too, Helen. You're not the only fool standing here in this room right now. We both have a few things to atone for.*

"I just want one more time with you. No harm, no foul."

"No, Helen. I still care about you in the sense that I want you to find happiness and fulfillment. You've found it with this Randolph. He's support, security, and a lover. I don't want you to even think about making that dirty with me." *Straight up, Helen – I love Clare, even if I haven't told her. I want to make her happy and I'm won't break that unspoken promise I've made to her.*

"I want you."

"And I can't...no, that's wrong. I *won't* give you what you want. What you *need* is Randolph. Go back to him and pursue your career and sail the seven seas in his fifty-foot ocean-going pleasure palace. You and I both made mistakes. But you know something?" He smiled.

"What?"

He laughed and shook his head. "I've learned one thing in the past few months."

"What?"

"God has blessed my journey. You're a guiding star, Helen." *You've guided me to the woman I will love for the rest of my life.* "And for that, I'm grateful to you. Now, go be an answer to prayer for a guy who really deserves it. I wish you both great happiness."

She looked at him blankly, and he could see tears forming once more in her eyes. He was sorry for whatever loss she was feeling, but was not sorry for the joy he felt in his heart. *I hope Clare loves me, because I know I sure as hell love her.*

"I'm sorry, Helen."

He closed the door behind her, listened to her faltering steps going down the deck stairs, heard the truck door slam, the engine start, and the 1991 weather beaten red Dodge Ram pickup with the equally weather beaten camper shell on it drive off into the night. Trygve relaxed and laid down on his dog bed by the fire.

Picking up his glass of Gentleman Jack, he drained it. Then he picked hers up and drained it, too. He rinsed out her coffee cup and put all three in the dishwasher. He knew that every time he looked at that Skinny Dick's mug in the future he would be grateful for the events of this evening.

He took the chocolate peanut butter ice cream carton and put it in the freezer. He'd serve it to Clare when she was here the next time. She didn't need to know where it'd come from. All she needed to know was that it was his favorite flavor.

And he loved her.

Chapter Fifty-six

It took all her strength to not call in and leave Aurora in the lurch for flight personnel. The last thing she wanted to do was face the CareLift crew at 0700 when they came back to the hospital to package the Tacoma skier. She'd be with Gus today though, and that made her calmer.

Wendell had embraced her at the end of the shift, called her "Sweetie," and told her she had nothing to worry about with the Trooper and 'Seattle Slew,' as he termed her. "Jeez, CJay. You know he's a decent guy."

She knew, but also sensed that Helen generally got what she wanted. Except for Jeff.

Seattle'd chosen to opt out of his life. It was a pretty safe bet she was regretting parts of that decision. But Clare was concerned that perhaps she was regretting the entire decision – and wanted a do-over. She trusted the Trooper, but was also aware of the sexual power of an 'ex' – the familiarity, the history, the warm paths traced by desirous hands for almost two years....

A wave of pain and fear swept through her gut.

She'd wanted to call him at 0500 when her wind chime alarm woke her, but didn't want to…*Don't want to what? I don't want to wake him when he still has the smell of her sex on him. Don't want to hear her call out, 'Who is it?' in the background. Don't want to hear him hem and haw and stumble around trying to sound normal.*

"Fuck it," she said to the image in the bathroom mirror. "It is what it is. I've lived through a whole hell of a lot worse than this. I can survive this, too. Fucking piece of cake." The flight nurse pulled on her parka, zipped it up and stood tall. She visualized strength, courage, and inner fire. She was powerful.

Now, go to work and prove it, girlie.

* * * * * *

Helen's mother dropped her off at North Star's ambulance bay entrance at 0630 and the CareLift flight nurse found her crewmate already in the ICU nurses' station talking with the nurse caring for the skier. Lauren saw her and waved; pointed to the patient.

Helen fetched the crew's gurney from the ICU employees' lounge where they'd left it the afternoon before, and wheeled it to the patient's bedside. This should be a 'margarita flight,' she figured, but also knew that no crewmember *ever* says that out loud because, sure as hell, it's a jinx. Everything that can go wrong *will* go wrong, including having a perfectly stable patient code and the nurses end up doing CPR for two hours. Or, 'calling' the code and flying for three hours with a dead person next to you. She'd done both, but didn't care to do either today.

Especially after last night.

Helen knew she wasn't comfortable with introspection, and thinking about last night roused angry emotions. She couldn't fault Jeff for having a relationship with this CJay person. He was a healthy male and enjoyed sex. *They'd* enjoyed sex. But quite honestly, 'what's another slice off a loaf that's already been cut?' Neither Randolph nor that...*that CJay person* needed to know if he'd pulled off her shirt and kissed her breasts like he used to, or traced the line of her inner thigh until she was crazed with desire for him. *Omigod.* She trembled remembering how just looking at him naked made her hot and wet. And his mouth. And how he'd explored every inch of her, kissing, caressing...she closed her eyes and leaned over the gurney next to the skier and...moaned slightly.

"You okay, nurse?" the man asked her.

Helen jerked. *Did I moan out loud?* She felt her mocha skin pink up.

"I'm fine, sir. Just an old war injury. I'll be packaging you up on our gurney and we'll probably be out of here within forty-five minutes. My name is Helen and my crewmate is Lauren. How are you feeling, Mr...um..." She glanced at the paperwork. "...Kimball?"

"Good. Ready to blow this pop stand and go home. Some extreme skiing adventure this has been. Haha," he said to her, without mirth.

"Well, we'll give you a safe, uneventful flight home and before you know it, you'll be with your family again."

She assessed the patient as they talked. Pelvis stabilized, IVs (two) clean, dry, and intact. Skin pink, warm, and dry. A&OX4. Obeys commands. Moves all 4 extremities. Pain 4 on a 10 scale – tolerable at this time. No complaints.

Lauren came into the room and sidled up to her partner. "How'd it go last night? Are you walking funny today?" She snorted back a laugh.

Helen smiled slyly. "Even better than I could ever have imagined," she lied to her friend.

"The Aurora crew was busy pre-flighting their little helicopter when the pilots and I got here. I think they're going to be coming up pretty quick..." She looked at her watch. "...to make sure we get safely out of their territory. That CJay nurse was looking a tad peakèd after our convo yesterday. Wonder how she is today?"

"She's Jeffrey's girlfriend. Jeffrey. My trooper."

"You're kiddin' me." Lauren's eyes went wide and her mouth dropped open.

"I didn't realize it until I got there. He has her picture up."

"You know these Alaskans are all armed, right? More guns than bears and moose put together. You might want to watch what you say around her, Helen." Lauren searched Helen's face. "Are you okay? You looked exhausted."

"A good roll in the hay is incredibly therapeutic, Lauren."

Lauren laughed. "I'm definitely into alternative therapies. But be careful around her. These Alaska people are...um...different from us."

"Uh, Lauren…" Helen made a 'V" sign with two fingers and waved them around her own café au lait face. "…I'm an Alaskan Aleut, remember? I think I can handle the…the…sourdough-wannabee."

Helen flexed her ankle and felt the Ka-Bar BK9 Becker Combat Bowie strapped there and felt well prepared to take care of this CJay person if she came armed (which more than likely she was) to the party. As angry, sad, and humiliated as she might be, Helen did smile slightly at the thought of the two of them knifing it out. Ka-Bars at ten paces – right here at the ICU nurses' station. She envisioned international headlines – and blood splatter.

They heard the ICU doors open and bootsteps coming down the hall towards them. Lauren gave Helen a meaningful glance and the two busied themselves as Clare and Gus walked into the patient's room.

There was no trace of friendliness on Jeffrey's girlfriend's face, but neither was there open hostility. She was all business. Helen knew that eventually the Aurora flight nurse would learn the truth – would learn that Jeffrey had turned her down. But there was enough humiliation and anger and – yes, she knew, even though it was wrong – enough pain and spite left that Helen simply could not resist screwing with her, if only for a few more minutes.

Gus introduced himself and offered to help them get paperwork together if they needed that. Lauren told him that they'd already taken care of the transfer packet, but it would be really nice if the two Aurora crew would help when it came time to move Mr. Kimball over to the flight gurney. He was big, you know, and that pelvis fracture – well, they needed to be extra careful, you know, not to hurt him, you know.

Gus nodded. "Of course." He didn't add, "You know."

"You look tired, Helen. Rough night?"

Helen glanced up to see the nurse, CJay, staring at her from across the patient bed.

"As a matter of fact, not rough at all. Smooooth as silk." She emphasized the 'smooth,' pursing her lips, and gave Clare a sly wink. She saw the other woman's lips tighten. Helen flexed her ankle again. The Ka-Bar was still there.

"'Smooooth as silk?'" the Aurora flight nurse mimicked.

"Oh, yes. Quite." Helen looked at the other woman. "I...I guess I need to apologize to you, um..." She glanced at Clare's employee ID badge to show her that remembering the Aurora nurse's name was just this side of inconsequential. "...CJay, right? I shouldn't have said anything yesterday. That was definitely thoughtless of me...but I didn't know you two, were...you know...until after...." She smiled shyly.

"After dessert? How was it?" Helen detected only a small amount of snark in the question.

"Lovely. Went well with the cup of coffee in the Skinny Dick's Halfway Inn mug...and the Gentleman Jack after that...later." Her face brightened. "And it was good to see Trygve again. I've always loved that big dog. But Jeffrey still hasn't done anything with the loft. It's been over four years." She paused, allowing a sheepish look to pass over her face. "I'm sorry about your picture."

"My picture?"

"You know – the CPR pic from the *News-Miner*? He crumpled it up when he saw me looking at it." She hung her head, convincingly, she hoped. "I really am sorry. I didn't know." She shrugged. "All's fair, though, right?"

"Fair?"

"Didn't Shakespeare say 'All's fair in love and war' in one of those plays of his?"

The other woman lifted the corner of her right lip. It really did look like a sneer. "No, actually. It was Cervantes. *Don Quixote*. And perhaps there are times when that's true. But in this particular case, I'd be more inclined to describe what you did last night in a far more biblical way."

"I don't even know what you're talking about." She waved her hand in dismissal at Clare.

"David and Bathsheba. Uriah the Hittite. Nathan the prophet."

"I'm lost."

"It's an old story, and, yes, you're absolutely right. You *are* lost. You see, you've got your man. Helen, but you can't keep your hands off of mine. I don't envy you. I think you're a despicable…"

Helen saw the other woman's lips clamp shut, cutting off whatever nasty name she was about to be called in the nurses' station. They'd been speaking very quietly, but had gradually moved out into the hallway for more 'privacy.' Helen knew Lauren and that Gus guy were watching them with their mouths open. Not to mention all the day and night shift nurses doing pass-over

388

reports in the unit. There was a full house witnessing the interchange between the two of them.

Hospital gossip: The staff of life.

"I'm sorry you feel that way. But, no harm no foul. What's done is done." She gave a nonchalant shrug. *Nothing to see here. Move along. Knife fight in ten….*

Then Helen saw Clare move close to her. Before she could do more than jerk to protect herself, Clare put her arms around her in a warm embrace. Helen felt the other woman's hot breath on her ear. "Go back to Seattle, Helen," she heard the Aurora flight nurse whisper coarsely. "Get married and live your own life. If I were not a nice person – and I'm truly struggling with that right now – I would tell you that I hope you get fucking sucked out of your aircraft at fifteen-fucking-thousand feet AGL. But…I'm a *decent* person and I won't wish that for you."

The Aurora flight nurse pulled away and winked pleasantly at her.

Helen followed Clare back into the patient room to assist with the transfer to the gurney. Between the four of them, it went quickly and without discomfort to the patient. When the Aurora crew received a heads up that Med Center's critical care ambulance was waiting for them in the ED ambulance bay to transport the CareLift nurses to FAI, Gus volunteered to take them down to the ED while Clare went back to dispatch.

Before she left, Helen watched Clare turn to her and say sincerely, "Fly safe, Helen. And best wishes on your upcoming nuptials. May you and your husband have many blissful years together."

Chapter Fifty-seven

Clare watched Gus guide Helen and Lauren to the ambulance bay where they'd load up for the trip to the airport. She tried to quiet her mind as she turned back and punched in the code to dispatch and pushed through the door. Big Mike was behind the console today and greeted her with a wave of the hand.

"Welcome, CJay. We've got some weather coming in, but we're flyable for the next coupla hours. After that, you'll be helping in the ED, I think."

Clare blew a miniature raspberry. "I don't care, Big Mike. I'd want to be really really *really* busy today."

"You okay?"

"I think so. Maybe. I...no, I don't know. Listen, I have to make a phone call. I've got my radio and I'm going down to the chapel to call...call Jeff."

"Okay. You sure you're okay?"

"Not at all, Big Mike. I'll be back in a little bit."

Clare went back out and down the hall to the chapel. It was empty and she tucked herself into a corner and punched Jeff's cell number into her phone. It rang and went to voicemail. *Coward. You can't even talk to me. You can't even face me.* She bowed her head and let the tears come. Finally, she leaned back against the wall and simply looked at the little pulpit; the faux stained glass backlit backdrop; the flowers that the Ladies Auxiliary kept fresh on the altar. This chapel serves for non-denominational church services on Sunday and frequently as a quiet place where families pray for their loved ones, and others grieve. She let out a long sigh and knew she needed to go back to dispatch. After she washed her face.

"CJay, Dispatch. Visitor coming your way."

She heard Trygve's dog tags as he turned the corner into the chapel and ran up to her, standing tall to kiss her face. Jeff followed, but didn't kiss her face. He didn't even try to touch her. He did sit down beside her.

"We need to talk," he told her.

"I'm don't think we do. I know you 'had dessert,' gave her coffee in your Skinny Dick's mug and also had Gentleman Jack. And my little newspaper clipping got trashed somehow. I have to say one thing for her, mercifully she didn't go into detail about the sex. I appreciate that. Not sure I would have handled it well." Clare stood up. "I have to go back to work."

She walked off and Jeff went after her. "She was lying to you. She was yanking your chain. Nothing happened between us. Thinking about that makes me sick to my stomach. And to be honest, Clare, thinking you may *think* that happened destroys me. Nothing happened – because I wouldn't allow it." He reached out and grabbed her arm to stop her.

391

She shook his hand loose. "*You* wouldn't allow it?" She turned back to him, but was interrupted by her handheld radio. Big Mike was talking to Charlie about weather and an incoming front.

"I have to go."

"When can we talk?"

"Talk?" She shook her head. "I don't know."

"Clare, nothing happened. I sent her on her unconsummated way. Half the time I had my shotgun in my hand."

She closed her eyes. She couldn't look at him right now because he looked scared. "'*Jeffrey,*'" she mimicked uncannily in Helen's voice. "just go away and leave me alone for a while. I have to go to work."

She punched in the code, passed through the door and shut it behind her before he could push his way in, leaving him standing alone in the doorway alcove.

Please God. A nice juicy scene call is exactly what I need right now, she thought.

* * * * * *

Within fifteen minutes they heard radio traffic from the Fairbanks Alaska State Trooper dispatch about a snowmachine accident near Mount Aurora Lodge – off a ridge and down into trees. Gus, CJay, and Big Mike perked up their ears.

"Pilot, Dispatch," Big Mike said, calling Charlie on the handheld radio.

"Dispatch, Pilot. What's up?"

392

"We haven't received a request, but AST dispatch is talking to a trooper near Mount Aurora Lodge concerning a snowmachine off a ridge, into trees. Evidently a group of tourists on a scheduled ride. Fairbanks AST states their ship is on a two-hour delay for maintenance."

"Okay," Charlie responded. "Any coordinates yet?"

"No – just Mount Aurora Lodge and Cleary Summit."

"'Kay. I'll look it up and check weather."

Big Mike notified AST dispatch on the landline that Aurora Flight had heard their traffic and Aurora 1 would be glad to help if they needed helo transport back to NSMC. Their dispatch thanked him and immediately they heard the AST dispatcher telling the trooper at Mount Aurora Lodge that Aurora Flight was available if the snowmachine rider needed transport to Med Center in Fairbanks.

"Good job, Big Mike," Gus said.

"And *that's* why I get paid the big bucks, Gus."

Within fifteen minutes, the AST at Mount Aurora had snowmachined to the site of the accident off Fairbanks Creek Road and requested Aurora Flight. Charlie was already in the right seat ready to enter latitude and longitude when Gus and CJay arrived, unplugged the electric heater and stored it in the maintenance shed.

"Pilot, Dispatch," Big Mike called, giving coordinates for the AST trooper up the hill, then telling them, "Trooper states there's a meadow there with hard packed snow, suitable for an LZ. The location of the victim is approximately a half mile away and 30 feet over the side of the ridge in trees. The tour guides will be at the LZ to bring your crew to the ridge. They've got a sled and our crew can put the snowmachiner on our gurney on the sled to bring him back to the ship."

"Roger that, Dispatch. Give me the trooper's frequency so I can contact him when we get closer."

When Big Mike did, Charlie pulled pitch and the helicopter rose off the deck.

"Aurora 1 to Dispatch. Lifting off to Cleary Summit and Mt. Aurora Lodge. Three hours of fuel remaining. Three souls on board. Twenty-minute ETA."

Charlie contacted Flight Control at Fairbanks International Airport to let them know the helo was outbound, giving them the destination. Then, he entered the frequency for the state trooper and contacted him. Radio reception can be spotty in many areas of Alaska, but Charlie had clear communication with the trooper. The pilot informed him of arrival time and the possible need for vectoring the ship to the site.

Once again, Gus and CJay went over possible scenarios. Thirty feet over the side of the ridge in trees – could mean they'd need to rappel down to him if the ridge is steep. Might need additional assistance with the snowmachine – stabilizing it. Gus was lead crew for this trip.

"Pilot, medic."

"Go ahead."

"Ask the trooper if he knows the patient's condition."

"Roger that."

Charlie contacted the AST and asked the questions. Per the trooper, patient was not trapped, but was against a tree. The snowmachine had continued down the slope and was 200 feet below at the bottom of the ravine. One of the tour guides had gone to assess the patient. Positive loss of consciousness. Serious facial trauma, suspected broken jaw. Guide had positioned him so the victim could breathe, but it was evident he needed immediate transport to NSMC and his condition was worsening. Also, the guide was staying with the patient.

Flight crew wouldn't need to rappel, but would need ropes for descent to the patient, and for pulling the Stokes rescue litter back up the slope. The second guide was coming to get them on his snowmachine with the sled. The crew would ride in the sled. Both guides would help with getting the patient back to the ship.

CJay and Gus looked at each other and shrugged. Just another day in the tundra. They practiced for this kind of rescue. Barring unforeseen problems, the call should go well.

Chapter Fifty-eight

It's easy to spot the LZ from the air. Big Mike's coordinates are good and the state trooper stands out in his orange parka in the meadow. I can see the snowmachine with the sled, and as soon as Charlie sits us down on the snow and ice, we pull the gurney with our trauma and airway bags, O2 cylinder, heap o' warm blankets (which are going to be cold within 9.2 seconds) and Propaq EKG monitor strapped to it off the ship and trudge to the tour guide and trooper who are planted well beyond the disc of the powerful blades. When we get to them, the guide helps us secure the gurney on his sled, then indicates that I get to ride behind him, and Gus gets to ride on the sled, yeehaw cowboy-style. I grin at Gus' expression and point to myself then the gurney, telling him I'll ride back there next time.

Then I think of cowboy CPR on Rachel and wonder when I'll be able to forget. Then I think of the picture that Jeff tore up when Helen saw it…. I redirect my attention back to the present. I have to. I am a professional pre-hospital caregiver. Mr. Snowmachiner depends on me not to be distracted by my love life while I save his life. Then I think, "Bull shit."

It takes six teeth-jolting minutes to reach the location off Fairbanks Creek Road. We see five warmly clad individuals huddled together at the edge of the ridge, talking with one another. According to the guide, they're Icelanders, but the patient speaks English – well, at least he was speaking English at one point. A distraught looking female runs toward us as we get there, imploring us to help her husband – in clear English.

"At least they speak the language and are familiar with cold weather," Gus mutters to me.

The Stokes rescue litter is waiting for us. The state trooper has pulled it behind him from Mount Aurora Lodge when he was dispatched to the site – just in case. We need to tell the AST post – Jeff's post – dammit – about his quick thinking when we get back to base.

Gus informs me that the two guides have secured ropes down to the victim in order to get the litter and equipment down to him – and to bring the litter back up safely. We wear the two trauma bags like backpacks (I have the airway bag because I'm airway this time), and we've got everything else, including our gurney, strapped onto the Stokes.

Fuck!

I slip on tricky footing on the way down this forty-five-degree slope, but manage not to kill myself by going down into the trees below – or over the ledge beyond to my death at the bottom next to the snowmachine. I can feel the hair on the back of my neck stand up straight from the raw rush of adrenaline. I'm thankful for the rope handholds.

The second guide ("Moose," he introduces himself) tells us that the Icelander has gotten worse. He was conscious until about a minute before our arrival at his side, but then 'passed out again' and is unarousable. He's got a pulse, I ascertain, but it's thready. Moose has removed his helmet ("Just like I learned in First Responder class," he tells us proudly.), but beyond that he lets us know we're the bosses. Just tell him what to do.

Good job, Moose, I praise him. Keep maintaining that airway.

Our patient's face is smashed, his jaw hanging askew. Trees'll do that to you. Moose's gloved hands are bloody.

Gus hooks the patient up to the Propaq monitor and pulls out the now rapidly cooling Lactated Ringers fluid and an IV start kit and IV tubing from his trauma bag backpack.

While Gus is doing this, I pull off my identical airway bag backpack and open it next to the patient. It's obvious to Gus and me that airway is going to the key issue with this guy. Smashed face and broken, twisted jaw. No nasal or oral intubation is going to be easy. Even Rapid Sequence Induction (RSI) is a no-go because of his unstable face and jaw. And, besides, he's already unconscious. This leaves a cric as our clean and comparatively effective option. Whoo, I think. Let's do this.

Cric, Gus, I say. He nods.

Moose, I say to the large tour guide, who totally fits his name – except for the lack of antlers – tell your buddy up top to get down here now. We're gonna need him in a moment. While he's radioing his friend, I pull the cricothyrotomy kit with the scalpel, spreaders, tracheostomy tube, twill tie, Betadine antiseptic swabs and 20cc syringe out of my backpack.

Gus unzips our Icelander's jacket as far down as he can, then cuts the man's expensive Polartec turtleneck with trauma shears, offering a clear view of his throat. Thanks, Gus, I say. I pull off my wool gloves and put on the sterile gloves from the kit,

398

knowing that my hands will freeze in mere moments if this isn't fast. I take my gloved fingers and follow the man's neck down to his larynx and then to the cricothyroid membrane below that on his neck. I swab the area with Betadine. Moose is back to C-spine, but moves his fingers so I don't paint him, too. Gus hands me the #11 scalpel, and I carefully slit the skin on the man's throat, then the cric membrane underneath.

I smile. I can hear Moose starting to vomit. Keep it to the downhill side, buddy, I tell him, and keep maintaining that C-spine....

Gus hands me the spreaders. He has the trach tube ready to place, with twill tie attached for securing. I use the spreaders to widen the membrane's horizontal slit from top to bottom, making the hole rounder and, taking the tube from Gus, insert it into the hole. Gus secures the trach tube around the man's neck with the twill tie and I inflate the tube's bulb in the bronchus with the 20cc syringe through the bulb's external port. The inflated bulb will allow air to flow into his lungs, ventilating him, but prevent blood, vomit, or other fluids from slipping from his facial injuries back into his lungs, risking possible pulmonary aspiration and later pulmonary issues – like pneumonia – in the hospital.

Gus places the end-tidal CO_2 detector on the trach tube's end, and begins ventilating our North Atlantic guest with the ambu bag and oxygen from the little cylinder. The end-tidal CO_2 indicator turns that pleasant shade of yellowy tan we all love, showing proper placement. I listen for bilateral breath sounds. Yes. Goody. Wahoo. I do the tiny happy dance in my head.

Most excellent, Gus says. Moose, he tells our tundra guide, I'm going to place this cervical collar now, and then we will get "Bjorn" onto the stokes with your help. He nods at me. I'll continue to ventilate "Bjorn" until we get to the helicopter.

Moose and Gus maneuver the Stokes next to the patient, and between the three of us, we tip it and the Icelander up and log-roll him onto our backboard and the litter. We secure him firmly with all available nylon webbed straps so he won't roll out and back down the mountain to join his snowmachine when he's going up the hill.

That looks tacky and generates a ton of paperwork.

Jake scrambles conveniently to our side at that moment from up above, and the four of us pull the litter up the slope, easing it over the top onto the level ground. I do not slip again, because I saw just how far it was to the bottom of that ravine to my death. 'Bjorn's' wife (Vilborg, we later learn) is at her husband's side immediately, becoming faint when she sees his bloodied face, broken jaw, and the Shiley trach sticking out of his neck. I don't blame her. It looks pretty damned gnarly to the uninitiated.

Gus tells Moose to take care of the wife, thanks him, then informs Jake that it's his turn to shine. He needs to get us back to the ship in one piece.

Working together, we load our new best friend, 'Bjorn,' and his Stokes onto our gurney, and then load the gurney onto the sled. I straddle the patient's torso and continue to ventilate. Gus mounts up behind me and, working between my legs, pushes up the man's sleeve and starts a 14-gauge IV in the large vein in his right wrist. Later, when we're in the helo, he'll slice up the sleeve

400

on Bjorn's incredibly expensive and good looking Icewear snow jacket and start another 14-gauge higher up.

It takes Jake nine minutes to go the half mile back to Aurora 1 because he doesn't want to buck the two of us out into the ice and snow. Charlie spooled up the blades when we radioed we were coming, and with the help of the trooper on scene we load 'Bjorn,' as Gus continues to call him, into the ship and lock him in securely. Gus politely thanks the trooper and we're in the air within thirty seconds.

* * * * * *

"Aurora Dispatch, Aurora 1 lifting off from Cleary Summit, four souls on board. Two and a half hours fuel. ETA twenty minutes."

"Aurora 1, Dispatch. Four souls on board. ETA twenty minutes. Two and a half hours fuel. Stay in touch. See you soon," Big Mike answered.

Chapter Fifty-nine

The trauma team was waiting for them when the crew pushed the gurney into the main resuscitation room. Gus had prepared them with his report to the MICN for the snowmachine rider's injuries and the patient was in the operating suite within twelve minutes. The two crew members suspected obvious traumatic brain injury (perhaps coup contra coup -- similar to shaken baby syndrome) subsequent to his Mr. Toad's Wild Ride down the side of the mountain and extensive facial trauma from the crash into the tree. But they also were gratified that the cric and oxygen had allowed him to wake up somewhat, with stable vital signs continuing during the flight. They ran warm fluids into him on the helo and managed to keep his temperature up, despite the below zero air outside.

Gus and Clare cleaned up the helo and helped push it back into the maintenance shed, and start the little electric heater once again. The clouds had gotten lower, darker, and threatened snow. They knew that if this accident had happened just one hour later, 'Bjorn' would still either be coming down the hill in an ambulance, or would be DRT (Dead Right There) on the mountain.

"Gus," Clare said, once they got into dispatch and her crewmate booted up the computer so he could write the chart.

"CJay," Gus answered.

"All I can say is that we rock."

"Yes, you are right. We do rock. Once again we are rock stars. I do not lie."

They laughed out loud.

"And, we're lucky. I'm glad you're my partner," Clare added.

"As I am glad that you are my partner."

The phone rang – the private line, not the emergency line.

"Gus, for you," Big Mike said, handing the phone to him.

Gus listened, then said, "I will be there in ten minutes. Do not worry. They are still far enough apart. Wait for me. I love you, Norma. It will be fine."

He looked at Clare.

"I have to go now."

"Does this mean I have to write the chart?" she asked, innocently, standing to embrace her friend.

Gus stared at her blankly, then focused.

"It does. But, you were there. You will do fine. I have to go now," he repeated, sounding anxious and pre-occupied. He peeled the 2" silk tapes covered with their scene times off his flight suit leg and stuck them, dangling, on Clare's sleeve.

"You go, Gus. Tell Norma we love her. We'll see you guys in a little bit. Please drive safely. Take care."

Big Mike and CJay waved at him as he ran out the door, then looked at each other. The dispatcher crossed his fingers for 'good luck.' CJay thought a prayer.

* * * * * *

403

Norma and Gus were back within twenty-five minutes and the obstetric team had her upstairs, laboring immediately. The first twin, a girl, was born an hour later. Her brother followed within ten minutes. They were a healthy four and a half pounds each.

The Inuit couple named both their daughter and son Inuit names that mean "companion" in Inuit. Together they had grown inside Norma's body, and they would forever remain companions in life.

CJay thought that was beautiful and took out her phone to text Jeff. Jeff. She laughed. Like Schrodinger's cat: He may have gone to bed with Helen. Or he may not have gone to bed with Helen. Right now, she simply didn't know and she was afraid to open the box. And see the stained sheets. She stepped into the dispatch toilet, closed the door, and vomited.

Kelly said she'd be glad to finish Gus's shift when Big Mike called her at home.

Chapter Sixty

Kelly came in to take the rest of Gus's shift, and within minutes of her arrival Aurora was requested again, this time to the Angel Rocks – at the 48.9-mile marker on the Chena Hot Springs road – for a fallen hiker on Angel Rocks trail.

"The patient's friends and EMS will meet the helicopter at the trail head. Looks like an approximately 10-foot fall, positive LOC, broken right ankle, complaint of pelvis pain, vital signs stable at this time per EMS," Big Mike relayed to them as Charlie spooled up the blades on the AStar once again.

"Fire will have an LZ on the road." Kelly was busy taking notes on the 2" wide strips of silk tape on her flight suit leg as Big Mike spoke over their headsets.

"Kinda rough time of year to take the Angel Rocks trail," Kelly mentioned to dispatch.

"Tourists," Big Mike explained. "Staying at the Springs. 'Nuf said."

The crew remained silent as Charlie pulled pitch, told dispatch that Aurora was off the deck headed to Angel Rocks, with three souls on board, three hours of fuel, fourteen-minute ETA. The A-Star turned to head northeast up the Chena River.

"Formidable," Clare breathed, keying the mike when it was all right to talk again. "The clouds…"

"Incredible," Kelly agreed. "Sorry about the hiker with the broken ankle, but can you believe they pay us to do this job?"

Charlie chuckled over the intercom. "By the way, we can't fly back to Cleary Summit now, but in case you're wondering, we won't have an issue with weather on this short flight."

The two flight nurses planned briefly for care, but knew that unless anything untoward happened, they'd use the monitor, an air splint, start two lines, and get back to the hospital in under an hour. Then, Clare could have lunch. She relaxed back against her seat, enjoying the clouds and scenery and feeling the comforting rumble of the turbine and helicopter rotors through the airframe.

BAM!

Silence.

"Aurora Dispatch. Mayday! Mayday! Mayday! We've had a bird strike. We're going down." Kelly and Clare looked at one another. They could hear Charlie calmly giving Big Mike clear coordinates in the deafening quiet. Then he spoke to the crew.

"Buckle up, ladies, and assume the position. It could be a hard landing. And get the fuck out as soon as we're on the ground and run like hell."

Clare knew they were at 1000 feet, the turbine was gone, and Charlie was autorotating to the ground, hoping to land someplace with as few obstructions as possible. Below them, all the two flight nurses saw were Sitka Spruce and very few convenient clearings.

Adrenaline slammed her. Time stopped. Silence rang in her ears. She heard blood pulsate through the carotids in her throat and felt her heart pound. Her vision narrowed and she saw Kelly's freckles. *I never noticed Kelly had freckles before.* The hair on her arms and the back of her neck stood up.

Both women pulled their restraints snug, cinched their helmets tighter, lowered the visors to protect their faces, and prepared to hug their arms under their legs so the ship's impact would not compress their spines and break their backs but would be dissipated out by the muscles on their thighs – so they could get out fast. It was almost guaranteed that the AStar would go up in flames on impact. They'd all seen the pictures. They'd all been through the safety briefings. Here's how you fucking save yourself and your buddies. Maybe.

Why's it taking so long? I remember that short story we read in high school English – "The Occurrence at Owl Creek Bridge?" *How long was it between the fall and the snap of the neck? Two-three days? Why is this taking so long? Jeff... Alex....*

Let's get this over with. Knees together; feet together back behind your knees. Hugging your legs is what you do while you're waiting to die. She chanced a peek and saw that Kelly was doing the same. Their eyes met through the clear visors and electric fear sparked between them.

"It'll be okay, Kelly," she said out loud to her friend, and realized that the other flight nurse could clearly hear her through the silence. Kelly nodded.

"Aurora Dispatch," Clare heard Charlie say calmly, "Coming in on flare in the campground. Down in ten. Contact you then. Girls, Brace! Brace! Brace!"

This is how my story ends. I know the statistics. I know the odds – slim to none.

Clare was amazed at how calm she was. She saw faint shadows through her closed eyelids and knew they were in the trees. *Thank you, Mom and Dad. I'll be waiting for you. I forgive you, Steve and Jack, for being such rude double douche bag know-it-all big brothers. Don't forget me, David. Alex, watch over me. I...I love you, Jeff. I'm so sorry.*

She took a deep breath and then blew it out so she wouldn't have a chestful of air that could blow her lungs apart on impact. She felt Aurora flare. She felt warmth...like someone's arms around her...and peace.

So, this is how it feels to die. Lord, I'm in your hands.

The AStar hit the icy snow and slid.

Chapter Sixty-one

Jeff left North Star Medical Center and drove immediately to Wainwright. *I need to talk to somebody about this. I need a disinterested, objective, third party: Jordan.*

Shannon gave him coffee and made him a potato scramble with cranberries, onions, peppers, tomatoes, and cheese. Jordan sat across from the Trooper with his cup of coffee. Trygve entertained Reese in the living room.

Between bites, Jeff outlined the previous evening for them: Helen showing up; Helen pleading for that damn cup of coffee; Helen talking about her fiancé; Helen up front propositioning him for one last romp in the hay – betraying her state patrol future husband. He didn't mention his arousal and the macro-seconds of temptation because, frankly, he was ashamed of his body's evidently quite efficient autonomic response to Helen's touch and her smell.

Finally, he told them he'd seen Clare at North Star and she wasn't happy because Helen had lied to her about...having sex. Clare didn't feel she could believe him. Told him to just leave her alone for a while.

Reese looked up at him from the living room. "Why'd you let that lady in, Uncle Jeff?"

The trooper sighed deeply, realizing too late that his little niece had heard the entire conversation even though he'd been speaking quietly. "Because your Uncle Jeff is a nincompoop, Reese. That pretty much sums it up."

"I don't think you're a nincompoop. But I think Clare must be sad. I like Clare."

"I do too, Reese. A lot."

Jeff heard the distinctive sound of Aurora flying over the house right then and wondered where the ship was going. *Fly safe, Clare.*

* * * * * *

The AStar hit the icy snow and slid.

Clare felt the impact of the fuselage and the instant jolt in her hips and legs. She knew Charlie was struggling to stay upright on Aurora's snow skids. She clung to her legs, her head down, dazed and in pain, maintaining a grip on consciousness because that's the only way any of them were gonna get out of this alive. *Stay awake stay awake stay awake.*

There go the blades. She could hear Aurora's rotors striking the Sitka spruce and then continuing on their way into the air, ricocheting in multiple directions. *Still alive….*

Freezing air assaulted her face and she knew the ship was falling apart. The helo came to a crooked stop then tipped over. She was hanging down from her seat. Kelly was on her back looking up at her, dazed. "Help me, CJay." The peace Clare had just experienced was instantly replaced with a sense of *Out, out, out! We're still alive!*

On my way, Kelly. Soon as I get out of this fucking seatbelt. She kept her helmet on – *just until I don't need it.* She loosened her restraints and, clinging to them for security, dropped on her feet next to Kelly. A spasm of pain almost brought her to her knees.

"You okay?" she asked her friend.

"My back, CJay...." Kelly opened her restraints and reached for Clare. Clare wrapped her arms around the other nurse's torso and, tightening her abdominal muscles, disregarded the pain in her own legs and spine. She lifted the second woman up and dragged her screaming through the twisted hole where the back end of the fuselage used to be. *How handy is that,* she thought.

She pulled her paramedic as far as she could away from immediate danger from the helo, then limped back, flinging her helmet away. *Dammit. Owww, dammit.* Charlie was on the downturned starboard side of the ship, still strapped in. *Can't get him out that door. Can't get him out the port door that's now on top, either. Fuck fuck fuck fuck fuck....*

She saw smoke starting to curl from underneath and knew that curling smoke was not going to be an issue. A fucking explosion would bring all of this to an end real fast. *God please help me.* As she pulled at the partially disengaged windscreen on the pilot's side of the twisted fuselage, it came loose enough for her to get inside knowing that at any moment she and Charlie could die horrifying deaths in an explosion of avgas. She undid his four-point restraint and realized that the cyclic was going to be

411

a fucking issue right there between his legs. She couldn't get him over that. *God god god god god god….*

"Just pull me over the cyclic, CJay. I don't need my nuts anymore anyhow," she heard Charlie mumble.

"Nuts'r important. Won't lose 'em for ya. Can you move at all?"

"Can't breathe. Just leave me. Get away from her 'cuz she's gonna blow up. Get away, CJay. Just leave me." He coughed and reached for her.

"That's better. Hold onto me, bud. Let's see if we c'n slither you sideways past the cyclic." She pushed her back against the windscreen, opening it wider. Then, she wrapped her left arm around his torso like she had Kelly's and pulled Charlie onto his right side with her right hand, attempting to get him past the cyclic. She could see his right femur was broken. And his right arm was twisted funny. *Aw, buddy. I'm so sorry.*

"This is gonna hurt, Charlie." She tilted him from side to side and levered his good left leg over the cyclic and then his absurdly bent right leg around the cyclic. He was bleeding from the open femur fracture. He screamed and clung to Clare with his left arm, trying to help her move him with the one leg that worked.

Out of her peripheral vision she saw flames starting to burn on her side of the upturned bottom fuselage. Only the snow prevented complete ignition and a death sentence by fire.

"Really have to get outta here, Charlie. Hang on." She held him with both arms now and stumbled backwards around the windscreen as quickly as she could. Kelly appeared at her side accompanied by loud grunts of pain that competed with Charlie's screams.

"Goddammit, Kell! I left you back there where you'd be safe!"

"I'm not letting you get *(groan)* all the glory *(grunt)* for this heroic rescue, *(unnh)* Ninja Flygirl."

"Then don't just stand there. Lend a hand."

Between the two of them they dragged and then sheltered Charlie and themselves forty feet away behind several big rocks arranged on the edge of the clearing near the campground's *Welcome* sign. Charlie was unconscious, and for an eerie moment there was silence again except for Kelly's labored breathing and soft moans. Then, Aurora One exploded.

"Ah, poor girl." Clare choked back a sob. "Poor baby."

"There's good news, though, CJay," Kelly said. She rolled on her side and crying out with spasms of pain, dragged the Segar splint over to them from where it had been ejected during the crash. "At least we can get Tommy's leg fixed." She winced and cried out. "My fucking back is fucking killing me. Where's a fucking ambulance when you fucking need one?"

* * * * * *

"Aurora Dispatch – Chena Fire! Your helicopter crashed! I saw it go down," the firefighter screamed into his radio. "We need two more ambulances and another chopper up here right now!"

"Chena Fire – Aurora Dispatch." Big Mike's voice shook. "Do you see them? Can you get to them? Do you have coordinates?"

"Oh God Oh God Oh God," the firefighter yelled. "We're taking the engine and getting as near as we can. They're in the trees at the campground I think. I don't see any smoke. It's about a half mile away. Oh God Oh Fuck!"

Big Mike switched frequencies to the Trooper radio. "Trooper Dispatch – Aurora Dispatch. Aurora One has gone down on the way to Chena Hot Springs. Can you get your bird in the air now?" He gave coordinates to the Alaska State Trooper dispatch on Pegar Road. Big Mike could hear their transmission to Helo Two at the airport.

"Aurora Dispatch – Trooper dispatch – we'll be in the air in three minutes. How many souls on board?"

"Three." Big Mike choked out. "Three souls on board, Troopers." *My guys. My three guys.*

"We're on our way, Aurora. Saying prayers." Big Mike could hear the strain in the voice of the dispatcher at the AST center.

"Fuck fuck fuck fuck," Big Mike mumbled over the open frequency and hailed Aurora. "Aurora One – Dispatch. Do you copy? Aurora One – do you copy? Charlie – do you copy?" He repeated the hail several times until he was interrupted by Chena Fire.

"Aurora – Chena Fire. We see smoke now. They're on fire. Oh Jesus Jesus," Big Mike heard the firefighter breathe. "We got 1500 gallons on the engine – they're off the campground area – we're almost there. We're taking the engine through the fence. We'll take care of them. Oh fuck me. Hang on guys."

Big Mike heard a crash and knew the fire guys had run their brand new fire engine – the pride of their fleet – through the wooden fence at the campground. "Please God, please God, let them be alive," he prayed.

* * * * * *

Fifteen minutes later, the Sergeant heard Helo Two flying over in the same direction Aurora had taken. *Wonder where they're going?* Jeff stepped out into the freezing back yard to track Helo Two's path and called AST dispatch. He saw Reese standing expressionless in the slider doorway of the kitchen watching him. He nodded at her absently.

"Hey, Frankie," he said when the non-emergency line picked up. He heard radio traffic in the background, some urgent shouting, and the unusually loud voices of the other dispatchers. "This is Sergeant Douglas. Where's Helo Two going?"

"Hold one, Sergeant." Jeff knew she was talking to another responder and waited. "Chena Fire, we've got Helo Two in the air and they should be by you in eight. Do you have an LZ for them?" The dispatcher rogered Chena Fire's response, then gave them Helo Two's contact frequency before she got back to Jeff. "We've got an incident up towards Angel Rocks."

"Okay, thanks. Just wondered where Helo Two was going, because it seemed to be following Aurora."

There was a pause. "Um, yeah, Sergeant. Aurora went down on its way to a call at Angel Rocks. Sorry, gotta go. We're up to our ass in alligators at the moment." Frankie disconnected.

"Thanks, Frankie," Jeff said to the empty air. He stood motionless in the freezing backyard. He felt a hand slip into his

415

and looked down to see Reese. She opened her mouth and Jeff's grandmother's words came from her lips.

"She is a powerful woman, Uncle Jeffrey," was all his niece said. He looked at her, stunned.

"What's up, Jeff?" his sister called from the open kitchen slider.

"Aurora crashed. They went down," *I can't believe this. Well, I'm sure as hell not gonna sit here and* wait *for someone to bring me the fucking bad news.*

He heard his sister scream and start to cry.

"Jordan, you got any helicopters available?" he yelled out to his brother-in-law as he sprinted back into the kitchen. Reese followed him.

* * * * * *

The volunteers of the Chena Fire Department drove Code 3 – lights and sirens – to the site of the crash.

Through their fog of pain, Kelly and Clare heard them responding and then heard the crash of splintering wood when the Driver took his engine through the spruce fence surrounding the campground. The rig rumbled past them as the firefighters jumped out, pulled hose, and began attempting to put out the helicopter's avgas-fueled flames.

"Hey! The crew's over here!" they heard someone shout and soon two firefighters appeared at their sides followed by an ambulance bumping over the remains of the fence and stopping in the clearing not far from their rocks.

"I'm feelin' kinda whipped," Clare whispered to Kelly. "You guys take care of the pilot," she told the EMS crew. We got the Segar on him…I'm so freakin' tired." She lay down with her face in the snow and closed her eyes.

That feels good. Nice and cool. 'What the fuck, over,' she mumbled before darkness enveloped her.

* * * * * *

"Jeff! Get your jacket. Chena Fire requested a Medevac. There's survivors! They're holding the ship for us! Come on!"

Jordan backed out of the driveway in his F250 4X4 within thirty-five seconds and burned rubber down Neely, drifting the left turn onto Santiago. He braked to a cop stop in front of Fire Station #1, next to the flightline where a Black Hawk dust-off was waiting, powerful rotors turning. A medic impatiently waved for the Trooper to hurry it up. He handed Jeff a helmet and pointed to a seat. The Trooper was still buckling his harness as they lifted into the air and turned towards Angel Rocks.

"We're praying for them," Jordan yelled. "Be safe."

* * * * * *

Clare roused as she was being secured onto the uncomfortable EMS backboard with that miserable No-Neck C-collar around her neck, a 100% O2 non-rebreather mask on her mouth and nose, and that dumbass plastic Deluxe Orange Emergency Head Immobilizer strapped over her forehead and chin. "I don't need this immobilizer," she told the volunteer medic. "I won't move my head, I promise."

"Sorry, Ma'am. You have to wear it."

She knew that nurses made the worst patients, and still attempted to turn her head to see where Kelly was. *And, Charlie. God, Charlie.* "How's our pilot? Is he still alive?"'

"He's still alive. We're taking care of him, Ma'am. Please keep your head still."

"How's Kelly?" She attempted to turn her head again.

"Please don't turn your head, Ma'am. you might make yourself a quad."

"I'm not gonna make myself a fucking quad, dammit. Tell me how Kelly's doing or I'll get up off this backboard and go find her," she barked as fiercely as she could. It sounded feeble even to her. She also knew that, despite her threatening bluster, there was no way she could 'get up off this backboard' without at least four people helping her.

"I'm fine, CJay," she heard Kelly moan weakly from next to her. "My back fucking hurts like hell, but at least I'm not dead."

Clare relaxed. *That's all I want to know. That we're all alive. Poor Aurora. Dammit. But we're all alive.* She heard another AStar landing somewhere nearby – the ASTs maybe. *Jeff.*

Moments later, she heard a second familiar sound – the whop whop whop of a Blackhawk. Dammit. *The fucking Army's here.* She closed her eyes and felt the tears start to come. *It's gonna be okay. The Army's taking us* home.

She felt the medic cut the sleeves on her Aurora-issued parka and start a 14 gauge IV in her right antecubital space, and

418

then another one in her left. "Do you really have to start such a large line," she moaned. He started to answer, but she interrupted. "I know – protocol, but those fuckers hurt."

"Yes, Ma'am." Then, as if relieved, he added, "...and the Army's here to take you back to Med Center. All of you."

"How's the pilot?" she asked again.

"They're loading him now, Ma'am. Intubated, bad leg and arm, but the Seger helped and we air splinted his arm. They're coming for your paramedic now."

Thank God. Thank you, Lord.

She felt someone else kneel next to her and without opening her eyes, croaked, "Do NOT start another fucking IV on me."

Her eyes flew open when she heard a familiar voice say, "I promise I won't start 'another fucking IV' on you." She tried to find him without moving her head.

"Jeff. I didn't think I'd ever see you again." Her voice cracked as she tried to reach her hand towards him, but the backboard restraints and the IVs in her antecubitals kept her from bending her arms. "I was afraid." *And then I was calm….*

"I know. It's gonna be okay. They say you helped get your crew out of the helicopter before it burned. You're a hero, Clare."

"No, I'm not. I just didn't break my back when we crashed. And Kelly helped me get Charlie away from Aurora before she blew up. Poor Aurora," she rambled on. "It wasn't her fault. It was that damned bird. Aurora tried so hard to keep us alive as long as she could." She tried to see him but the head immobilizer kept her head firmly in place. "Jeff, I've never heard silence so loud. I don't think I'll ever forget it – the complete utter quiet when I knew

419

we were going down. It was just so scary...and so final." She attempted to reach his hand, but couldn't, so he took her hand instead and held it. "Can you fly back with us? Jeff, please? "

"If they say I can, I will."

"...and call my mom. I want my mom."

"Whatever you need, Clare."

The flight medics loaded Clare into the Blackhawk and when she was secured along with Kelly and Charlie, Jeff strapped himself in near her and the powerful helicopter lifted off from the Chena Hot Springs Road and turned back toward Fairbanks. Clare closed her eyes, her hand in Jeff's. She wasn't afraid.

Chapter Sixty-two

The off-duty flight crews gathered at dispatch, spilling out into the hallway and down to the chapel. Those who'd monitored the crash over emergency frequencies and lived close by were at the helipad when the Wainwright dust-off landed and accompanied the three survivors into the ED trauma rooms until finally they had to be ordered out so that on-duty emergency staff could care for the injured team.

A minor skirmish broke out in the emergency department ambulance bay between news photographers and three of the flight personnel who didn't want them taking pictures of their injured, bloodied colleagues. North Star security quelled the disturbance.

Hospital social workers arrived to talk with those staff who wanted to talk, but at the moment the only thing most of them wanted was to know was that their crewmates were alive – and what had caused the crash. Later, the AST crisis management team would schedule a Crisis Management Briefing meeting for the crews and their family members to give reliable information about the crash, provide coping skills for the next few days, and answer as many questions as possible before the National

Transportation Safety Board started their investigation and shut down the communication of information.

One-on-one peer support from the Trooper crisis team would be available for the duration of the incident.

Clare groaned and attempted to shift her position on the backboard to get off her butt and take the pressure off her legs. Her head and neck ached. *Helmets are wonderful inventions, but it's like having an anvil strapped to your head when you fly into the ground.*

But they were all alive. *Thank you, Lord.*

Poor Aurora. *I'm so sorry, baby.*

* * * * * *

Charlie was in the OR within ten minutes of arriving at North Star. Femur stabilization was crucial, as was work on his broken right arm. Clare's ED friends kept tabs for her, updating her on Kelly's and the pilot's situations.

"They're saying that it's a good probability that Charlie'll be flown down to the university hospital in Seattle by CareLift once he's stabilized, CJay," Hunni was finally able to tell her.

"Tell them not to send that Helen Tall this time," Clare mumbled, still in a fog.

"Helen Tall?"

"Never mind. Where's Jeff?"

"Talking to your mother on the phone."

Clare nodded. *Good.*

Charlie had lost a lot of blood from the femur fracture and was on a respiratory ventilator. He'd also taken Aurora's cyclic control – which was located in the helicopter between his legs – to the chest, badly contusing his lungs. There were rib fractures on his right side along with that broken right arm.

"How's his nuts?" she asked Hunni, sleepily.

Hunni turned red. "Uh, I...I don't know, CJay. His 'nuts?'"

"You know I love you, right, Hunni?" Clare groaned. *God, I hurt and it ain't gettin' any fuckin' better.* "Sorry. Didn't mean to say that," before remembering that only Jeff's mother could read her thoughts. *Sorry to say fuck in front of you, but I thought I was going to have to drag his nuts over the cyclic. Never mind, it's a flight nurse thing.* She groaned again, her head spinning.

"Kelly's in CT – they're still scanning her. Looks like some spinal compression issues. They're gonna to do an MRI, too. The neuro ortho guy is with her. Got some numbness and tingling in her legs. You're going next."

"She helped me get Charlie outta the ship. I don't know how she could even walk. Hunni..." Clare tried to turn to her friend, but her neck hurt too much. "We're so lucky. At the end, before we hit, I felt okay. I mean, I knew it would be okay. No bright light or anything like that, but I felt peace. I prayed." *Alex had his arms around me....*

Hunni knelt beside Clare's gurney in the resusc room with tears in her eyes. "I prayed too, when I heard you'd crashed and were coming to us. I prayed God would take care of you all." She wiped her eyes. "What a crappy job we have sometimes."

Clare smiled. "Never thought I'd hear the word 'crap' come from your lips."

"God will forgive me," she answered.

Yes, He will.

Gus had been at the helipad when the three came in, checking Clare and apologizing to Kelly and asking for her forgiveness. "It should have been me," he told the other flight paramedic with tears in his eyes as they rolled down the hallway to the resusc room. "I should have been on board when she went down. I'm so sorry, Kelly."

Kelly patted his hand and mumbled softly, "It's okay, Gus. You need to take care of Norma and your babies now. It's okay. It's good."

I love my friends, Clare thought, as she drifted off to sleep.

* * * * * *

The next twelve hours were crucial for Charlie. Like Rachel, his orthopedic injuries caused a great deal of tissue and circulatory damage. And, also like Rachel, he suffered his own pulmonary contusions from taking the cyclic control to the chest and from the roll of the ship to starboard.

The cyclic controls the disk – the rotors. Push the cyclic forward, the disk tilts forward, pulling the helicopter behind it. Left or right, the disk tilts that direction – changing the "angle of attack." When Charlie flared Aurora prior to impacting the ground, he pulled back on the collective – flaring like a goose flares before landing in the water. It slows the aircraft and offers control.

However, since the cyclic's situated between the pilot's legs, when he or she pitches forward and down on hard impact, the chest is forced into the cyclic at tremendous speed and with immense pressure. It's far worse than being hit in the chest with a baseball line drive.

It's like being shot with a cannonball.

CareLift was scheduled to transport Charlie down to Seattle twenty-four hours after the crash.

Kelly remained in neuro ICU, and the ortho guys were considering surgery, but wanted to put if off if possible. First steroid drugs, then rehab. It was very conceivably the end of the flight paramedic's medevac career.

Clare had pelvic trauma, but no broken bones. She had deep tissue bruising on her legs and butt, and muscle strain to her back and neck. But of the three crewmembers, she had the fewest apparent permanent injuries.

She woke when they took her to the CT scanner, and again when they loaded her into the MRI. She spent most of the day and that night in a medically induced fog because of pain meds. She didn't see Jeff, or didn't remember seeing Jeff, or didn't care at this point. She was in no condition to deal with Helen. Clare just wanted to be in tolerable comfort (3-4 on a 10-scale) and to know the others were safe.

Chapter Sixty-three

She was floating on water.

She heard gentle murmuring and an occasional metallic clink of a travel mug on a hard surface. She tried to turn her head toward the sound but stopped because it hurt too much. *Why does my neck hurt? Where am I?* It didn't smell like her house. It smelled like…. Suddenly, she saw flames, smelled avgas, felt crushing spasms of pain in her back and legs, and felt Charlie's sticky blood on her hands. She cried out and opened her eyes, seeing only shafts of light coming through the blinds on the windows in her room in the hospital's Step Down Unit – the SDU.

"Clare," she heard someone say. Then her mother's concerned face appeared over her and smiled. "You're safe, sweetheart. How're you feeling?" She felt Patty's hand squeeze hers gently.

"Like warmed over dog poop, Mom, but I'm glad to be alive," she said groggily, trying to piece together the last twenty-four hours. "Thank you for being here with me. How're Kelly and Charlie? Did they take him down to Seattle yet?"

"Your pilot just left for the University Hospital. Gus came by earlier. He and Norma are taking the twins home today. There've been at least eight of your friends stop by, too. Kelly's just in the next room."

"Where's Jeff?"

She heard a masculine clearing of the throat and then he said, "I'm here, Clare." He moved so she could see him, but did not try to touch her. He was in uniform.

"You look tired, Jeff." *You look good.* She could feel her heart constrict along with her tear ducts. *I will not cry.*

He shrugged. "I just wanted to make sure you were okay."

"Thank you. Uh...Jeff?"

"Yes?"

"Thank you for being there at the crash. I was glad to see your face."

"Jeff said he saw your helicopter go over on its way to the Hot Springs."

"You did?"

"I was at Jordan's talking to him."

"Oh?"

"Yeah. Just needed to talk to somebody." He shut his mouth and shrugged a second time. He looked as if he were putting some thoughts together – debating internally about speaking again.

"That...Helen...thing," Clare said, interrupting him before he could say anything else.

"Yeah."

She shifted her position a little, wincing as she did so, in order to see him more squarely. "Did you...um...come to any...uh...amazing conclusions?" It was hard for her to string words together. Must be the drugs, she thought.

Jeff hesitated. "I'm not sure this is the time for a discussion, Clare. You just woke up and you're on high levels of pain killers. Maybe you should just rest and we can talk later, when you feel better."

"Clare," her mother asked. "Do you need anything? Are you in pain? Are you hungry?"

"Something to eat?" The flight nurse snorted gently in disbelief. Her mother was a nurse, but first of all she was a mom who wanted to make sure her child didn't need a ham sandwich or perhaps a taco and a cold soda.

"No, Mom, I'm not hungry." The flight nurse glanced up at the IV pump next to her, slowly dripping 5% Dextrose and Normal Saline into her right wrist vein. "And apparently I'm not thirsty, either. Maybe later. What day is it?"

"Friday noon," Patty told her. "Your crash was Wednesday afternoon." She picked up her jacket and turned towards the door. "I'm going to the cafeteria to get something to drink. Give you two some time to talk."

Clare shut her eyes. "Do we have anything...to talk about...Trooper?" she asked when her mother had left the room.

"That depends completely on you. Are you up for any talking?"

"Schrodinger's Cat."

428

"Cat?" He smiled. "Oh, the thought experiment. How'd you come up with that in your heavily medicated, unconscious state?"

Clare ignored him and persisted. "The paradox: Is the cat dead or... alive?"

"Did I sleep with Helen or didn't I?"

"Exactly, Trooper." She shifted uncomfortably again, then rubbed her eyes. "I'm out of it, Jeff. I'm sorry."

He nodded. "Clare – sweetheart, there's no reason we need to discuss this until you're feeling clearer." He waited a beat, then smiled at her and shrugged. "But, seriously, if you want, I can get our crime scene investigative team out to Ester to scrounge for fiber and fluids in my bed or the rug in front of the fireplace. I haven't changed the sheets since you and I slept in them. Haven't vacuumed. They could dust for prints on the headboard, the kitchen table, or on those empty whisky bottles that got left under the sofa. Check for hair in the shower."

"You're disgusting." She managed successfully not to smile at his words.

He shrugged yet another time. "This is a 'He said; She said' situation. I can maintain my innocence until the caribou deplete all the lichen and migrate home, and it wouldn't make one bit of difference. I could still be lying to you. There is no way I can prove I didn't have sex with her. But, Clare, I didn't. I *wouldn't*."

His voice was sharp with that last sentence.

"You're right, Trooper. I'm not in any shape to talk about this. I'm doped up, I hurt, I'm mixed up. I'm sick to my stomach. I can't believe what she did – the mess she made." The flight nurse glared as sternly as she could at Jeff. "Did you *really* destroy my picture when you saw her looking at it?" Her head swam.

"Did she tell you that?"

"She said...you...crumpled it up." She thought she just might throw up.

"She stuck her finger through it and ripped it."

"Jeff, you probably need to go away until I can get myself straight." She shook her head as if to clear away cobwebs, then stopped abruptly. "Owwww," she moaned out loud and started to retch. "Get me that basin there." She waved her arm in the general direction of her bedside dresser and Jeff looked around frantically for what she wanted. Finally, he simply grabbed her water pitcher and, ripping off the lid, held the pitcher under her face while she vomited bile onto the ice. He held back her hair so she wouldn't puke on it, too.

"Geez, Clare. Poor sweetheart." He smoothed back her hair and helped her lie down again. Then, he wiped her mouth with a hospital tissue.

"I'm sorry. You shouldn't have to do that."

"Yes, I should." He held the plastic glass of water with a straw to her lips and she drank, rinsing the bile from her mouth. "I want to take care of you, Clare."

"No," she said softly, starting to cry. "Yes. No. I'm so mixed up. I feel so betrayed. I don't want this. I can't deal with it. Just go, Jeff. Just go." She kept her eyes shut so she wouldn't have to look at him.

"But seriously, just how far away do you really want me to go, Clare? And for how long? I don't want to leave you."

"I guess...until I guess I don't feel betrayed...anymore."

"Well, dammit, good luck with that. I can't clear my name because the only witness was Trygve who kept growling at her until she left under duress."

"She said...she loved...Trygve."

Jeff barked a laugh. "She never really liked the K-9. I told her Tryg was an excellent judge of character." He stopped for a moment. "Your picture didn't get crumpled up, Clare. She ripped it. I taped it back together until I can get another one, because I like to look at you being awesome. Would you like me to bring the clipping to prove that? I can get CSI to dust *it* for prints, too."

She stared numbly at him. "Just go away, Trooper." She shook her head then gasped. "Ooowwww. Let me get better. Get my brains back together."

"I'd rather be here helping you do that."

"No. Yes...no. I don't know! Just go to work and serve with *Loyalty, Integrity and...Nice-ity,* or whatever the hell it is...you guys do."

"Courage. And Nice-ity. That's what we state troopers do." He put his hand on her shoulder and squeezed gently. "I'm glad you're alive. It would've killed me to have lost you. Especially under these circumstances, Clare."

He bent down and gently brushed his lips across her forehead and then her lips. He gave her his nonchalant Hawkeye Pierce salute. Finally, the big man turned and walked out of the room without a backwards glance, followed by Trygve.

* * * * * *

431

Clare tried to make herself comfortable again, realigning her hips, poking awkwardly at the pillow behind her shoulders and head. She touched her lips where the moisture of his kiss still lingered, then put her open hand over her forehead and massaged it, feeling the cool.

This is my fault. I let it happen. I knew she was going to Ester. She said it out loud. And I let it happen. I didn't call him to warn him. And I didn't go out there to be the one who opened the door to her.

I told Jeff she made this mess. Oh, God. I made this mess. I'm totally to blame.

She started to cry again. *My brain isn't running on all eight cylinders. I'm not the brightest bulb on the tree. My lunch plate is missing a taco...and definitely salsa and sour cream. And the cilantro's a wilted, slimy mess. Just like me.*

Jeff, I'm so sorry. I'm the one who betrayed you. This is all my fault.

* * * * * *

"They had fresh baked chocolate chip cookies in the cafeteria," her mother told her when she returned. "I bought us some." She looked around. "Where's Jeff?"

"He left to go to work."

Patty offered her daughter a cookie, but Clare waved away the food with her hand, mumbling something about "I'm NPO, mom."

432

. Her mother sat down, then said quietly, "I don't know all the dynamics, Clare. Just what went on that's causing all this turmoil with you two?"

"What'd he...tell...you?"

"Only that an old girlfriend flew into town and led you to believe that he and she'd played some slap and tickle the night before the crash."

"Slap...and tickle? Is that what he...said?"

"No. He was much cruder. But is that accurate?"

"Only if slap and tickle means...they had sex, yes, that is exactly...what that bit-...the woman...led me to believe."

"If he's telling you the truth, Clare, what she did is evil."

"And if she's telling the truth? What does that make her now? Or him?"

"How long have you two been seeing one another?"

She stopped and tried to think – which was pretty tricky work at the moment. It seemed like months to her. So much had happened...had changed...since Moose Man. "I think a couple of months – the middle of October when...David was up here. We...all had dinner together."

"Hmmmm." Patty's eyes searched the ceiling as if looking for answers in the acoustic tiles. "Are you engaged to him?"

"Of course not!"

"Going 'steady?'"

No.

"Have you told him you love him? Has he told you?"

Clare shook her head. "No." *Ouch. Don't do that again, flight nurse.*

"And you have no proof whatsoever that he either took her to bed or kicked her out."

"No. He says he kicked her out. And the dog growled at her the whole time."

"What do you want to happen, Clarice Joan?"

Clare looked up sharply at the use of her full given name. *Ouch.* "What's up with...the 'Clarice Joan,' Mom?"

"Dammit, Clare. You guys hardly know one another. I'm not envious of your situation, but you don't have much to go on here. Is he a good guy or not?"

"Schrodinger's Cat."

"There's also another way to look at this."

"What's that, Mom? Oh, enlighten me for fuck's sake."

"Language, Clare! You talk just like your brothers!"

Clare shrugged abruptly. *Ouch.* Her mother was beginning to annoy her a great deal and she'd only been awake a few minutes.

"I can understand your pain and indecision. But on the other hand, if you guys haven't even told each other you love one another, haven't made promises, haven't taken vows.... Well, seriously, Clare, at what point does a one-night stand with someone he had a serious relational history with – when does it become 'betrayal?'" She used finger quotes to illustrate her point.

"That is just semantics, Mom!" Clare spoke, her voice rising. "Semantics!" she repeated as forcefully as she could, hoping her mother realized just how angry she felt – especially at *her* for taking *his* side.

"No, Clare," Patty answered quietly. "It's reality. But on the plus side, this gives you the opportunity to take your relationship with him slow. Pay attention to his actions – and his words. If you decide to 'forgive' him for a transgression you don't even know happened, words and actions will prove whether he's the decent good guy you want him to be – or he's the incredibly attractive, opportunistic, philandering scumbag you're afraid he might be."

"Mom?"

Her mother glanced up.

When Clare spoke again, her voice was very soft and Patty struggled to hear her words.

"This is all *my* fault, Mom. She told Wendell and me...when we met them at the hospital...exactly what she was going to do that night. Everything, including getting him into bed. I knew about this...and I did nothing to stop it." A tear bloomed once more at the corner of her left eye and slid down the side of her face into her ear.

Her mother stared at her, then wiped away the trail of the tear. Finally, she spoke. "Well, that wasn't very loving, Clare. Were you testing him? What the dickens kind of a Pop Quiz is that?" Patty narrowed her eyes and was silent for a long moment. "That was wicked, Clare. Just not right." She paused again, then spoke. "I think you need to tell this man what you just told me."

The flight nurse closed her eyes. "I know. I have to...own up to it."

"Yes. You shoulder a great deal of the responsibility for this messed up situation because of your own actions. Or rather, Clare, your *inactions*."

Clare thought she heard her mother mutter, "I taught you better than that," but she chose not to respond to it. She felt sick enough – and angry enough at herself – already.

And she wasn't very happy with her mother, either.

Chapter Sixty-four

"Get up, Trygve, and hit the head. We've got places to be this morning."

The dog got up off his dog bed in the great room and trotted to the backdoor, waiting patiently as the Trooper stepped naked out of his bedroom, then opened the back doors so the K-9 could go outside to relieve himself. The trooper fixed a cup of coffee before taking a quick shower to help wake up further. It was a little after 0600, and he wanted to get to the hospital early before the docs and Clare's mother arrived. He needed a chance to speak with the flight nurse privately, quietly, without angry tears on her part – or his.

The dog was fed and in the Expedition by 0630, and they arrived at NSMC, pulling into a "Law Enforcement Only" parking space in the ambulance bay by 0700. "You're coming with me, Tryg. I'm gonna need all the backup I can get."

Jeff knew the docs started rounds at 0800. Clare's mom usually arrived earlier so she could be present during rounds. NSMC had loosened many restrictions about personal visitors for the flight crew, simply because this was such an extraordinary time – and these were *their* flight personnel. The crash – and the subsequent incredible rescue on the part of the two female crew members – was national news.

Trygve was always welcome, especially in the ED, and they were stopped multiple times by the trauma staff so the K-9 could say "hello" to the day shift employees. Hunni hugged the dog and told Jeff to "Tell CJay I'll be up to see her during my break this morning."

"I will, Hunni," he promised. *Of course, I may have to write it on a Post-it and stick it to her door if she doesn't let me in.*

There was a flowering plant in fairly good condition sitting at the vacant Information Desk in the main lobby of the facility. Jeff grabbed it on the way past before he pressed the elevator button for the SDU's level. Trygve sat down beside him, sniffing the air for miscreants.

After identifying himself, the Sergeant was buzzed through the doors of the SDU with Trygve at his side, the K-9's dog tags jingling down the hallway and echoing throughout the unit. Her door was open.

* * * * * *

CJay put down her cup of weak, lukewarm hospital coffee and covered the partially eaten waffle and egg with the scratched, cheaply made plastic plate cover with the hole in the middle for your finger. *I hear the dog.* She willed herself to be calm. This could not possibly be any worse than autorotating into a sixty-foot clearing in the middle of a campground knowing you

438

were facing death, she told herself. *I will not die from having to talk to him.*

She'd been awake since 0500. She cleaned up as well as she could, given the circumstances, and combed her hair, pulling it back with a scrunchy. She maneuvered herself into an *Aurora Crew* sweatshirt over her tee shirt from home. Lipstick. Lotion on her face. Teeth brushed. She took a swig of water from the carafe cup on her tray, swished it around, and swallowed. Felt in her teeth with her tongue to see if there was any lingering waffle wedged there that would most definitely take away from any feeling of strength and fire and righteous indignation she wanted to project.

The dog rushed in and jumped on the bed, knocking the bed table askew and spilling her water. He licked her face. "Auf," she commanded, and Trygve laid down next to her. She petted his head and pulled gently on his big ears.

With her peripheral vision, she saw a shadow enter the door. When she looked up, there was the Trooper, in uniform, with his trooper ball cap in one hand and the potted plant from the Information Desk in the other. She shook her head. She pressed the fingers of her left hand against her forehead and massaged, as if rubbing away a headache.

"Ya know, Trooper, I distinctly remember telling you last night that I need to be alone for a while. And yet here you are with your damn dog and the flowers from the hospital lobby to try and…. I don't know what you're trying to do."

She rumpled Trygve's ears again, then rang her call light.

"I don't want to lose you," he told her quietly.

439

She harrumphed, then repeated more slowly, as if to a special needs trooper, or perhaps one who spoke a different language. "I distinctly remember telling you last night to leave me alone for a while."

The day shift nurse came into the room – the new Grad – a sweet young thing. She smiled at the trooper and gave him an 'elevator look' – eyeing him up and down – definitely a sexual-harassment-in-the-workplace issue in most settings. Clare smiled despite herself. The man did look mighty fine in the uniform. But she quickly turned the corners of her lips down.

"Yes, Ms. Valenzuela. Can I take your breakfast tray away? What do you need? Oh, look! You have the police dog with you. Oh please, may I pet him?"

"Ask the trooper. But hurry. He was just leaving." The pretty young nurse looked up at Jeff.

"Yes, you may pet the 'police dog,'" he sighed.

Clare put her hand over her mouth to hide her smile.

While the young nurse was petting Trygve – who licked her face, Clare looked away from the Trooper. Finally, tired of Trygve's betrayal too, she said, "That's enough. The dog isn't a family pet." The K-9 stood up on the bed to get closer to the girl's hand. "Auf," Clare commanded, petulantly. He laid down again.

"Wow! He obeys you. Cool!" It was obvious that the flight nurse's status, which was already high in the eyes of the star struck young woman, had just risen even more.

"Well, Trooper, thanks for stopping by. And thanks for the... uh...lovely potted plant. Flowers are always a gracious touch. Did you steal some candy for me, too?"

440

"The gift shop wasn't open yet."

She tried not to smile. "Well, too bad. Stay safe." Clare noticed her nurse still observing their conversation. "Larissa," she said, "I'm good here. Thank you."

"Just ring the call bell if you needed anything, then," she said before checking out the trooper one more time and going back out into the hallway.

"Clare, don't…"

"Don't what?"

"Don't put an end to us." There was sadness in his eyes.

"Bye, Trooper." Then she reached out and took Trygve's ears in her hands and ruffled them. Her voice caught, changed, became softer. "Good-bye, good dog. Be safe."

"Trygve, come." The dog looked at Clare, then reluctantly jumped off the bed and went to Jeff's side.

She looked at this beautiful man she loved and as she watched, he lifted his chin and tightened his jaw. A look of resolve and grim determination came over his face. It frightened her. She made up her mind.

"Don't go, Jeff," she said quickly. "I need to talk. I…I…have to tell you something."

He lifted his eyebrows. "Should I sit down?"

"Yeah. I think so. And take off your coat. Please."

Chapter Sixty-five

So, I take off my coat and sit down in the little chair by her bed and look at this woman I love who just barely avoided being burned alive in a flaming helicopter crash, and saved Kelly and along with Kelly saved Charlie, and is now lying on this bed with her messy hair in a scrunchy and wearing an "Aurora Crew" sweatshirt with a piece of breakfast waffle on her chest.

She can't even look at me.

Tryg noses my hand, trying to get me to pet him. I scratch his ears and turn my attention back to Clare.

She continues to avoid my eyes, and proceeds to tell me that she knew what Helen was going to do, because Helen told them all about it beforehand. About 'dessert,' about – well, about having sex with me.

Clare knew?

Stop, I finally tell her, raising my hand like a sixth-grade crossing guard. Just. Stop. You knew about this and didn't call me? You know I would have insisted that you get out to my place. At the very least, I would have had some warning and could have dealt with it outside on the deck, still holding my shotgun, with Trygve rumbling at my side.

Seriously, I'm pissed, and I guess my expression shows it.

I stand. Clare mumbles an apology. She's 'so sorry.'

I ask her if this was some kind of a perverted test? Will the Sergeant give in to his carnal nature and screw the Ex? Or will he be brave and noble and turn her away, forever proving his fealty to the maiden queen?

I simply can't avoid the snark, considering what her silence has led to. I have to admit I'm truly pissed. Yeah, I know. "Anger (or being 'pissed') is a 'secondary emotion'" – in this case for having been blindsided and left incredibly vulnerable, twisting in the wind (by Clare, of all people!), and having to deal with…well, with what I had to handle with Helen. And, I admit, I'm scared shitless at the thought of losing Clare because of this total, unwinnable idiocy.

She finally looks at me. She looks terrible. She tells me that after giving it a lot of thought, she thinks subconsciously – yeah, it was a test. Does he care about her? Will he keep it in his pants for her? Can she trust him? Can she finally put her sense of past loss in its proper place and move forward with this man? With me?

I shake my head in disbelief. Why did you do that, I ask her. Why would you gamble like that? I laugh at her. You keep talking about Schrödinger's fucking cat, I say. How about the famous marshmallow test?

I can see she's forgotten that experiment from Psych F101X.

443

Give each kid a marshmallow, I explain. Then tell them if he or she doesn't eat that marshmallow for fifteen minutes, they'll get another one (Cool!) so they'll have two treats to eat, thereby proving that willingness to delay pleasure as opposed to instant gratification can lead to greater rewards. And is a big predictor for how well someone will do in the future, handling stress and dealing with the vagaries of life.

I did pretty well in Psych F101X, as it turns out.

I can see her trying to figure out how the hell that applies to Helen. Maybe it's best she doesn't figure it out. I know how it applies to Helen. Helen was that first big, delicious, succulent marshmallow, put right in front of my face that night. And, dammit, I resisted it. It took a minute, but I didn't succumb to the temptation.

I would wait six months or six years for that fucking second marshmallow, I inform this woman who is looking appropriately wretched at the moment, if it means that I get you for the reward.

I hesitate, because dammit, I haven't told her yet.

You see, Clare, I finally verbalize, I'm in love with you. I adore who you are. I admire and respect you. Fucking hell, I'm in total awe of you. There's nothing Helen could have said or done that would make me risk losing what I think I might have right now with you.

What I don't add is that I really do not want to have to regret turning Helen down for that one last romp in the sack. I want my refusal to eat that fluffy sugar treat to truly have been worthwhile – and actually mean something.

Then, before I can say anything more stupid – or incriminating, I turn around and walk out with Trygve clattering behind me. Yeah. I do love her. What the fuck.

Let her chew on that….

Chapter Sixty-six

Patty Herndon arrived a few minutes before the trauma team showed up for their morning rounds. Clare spoke to her briefly about the Trooper's visit. "I apologized to him, Mom. He asked if it was a 'test.'"

"And...?"

"I know it *was*. I think I knew it when Helen was talking about going out to Jeff's place. I'm thinking if he takes her bait, then he's not for me. If he doesn't – he's a 'winner, winner, chicken dinner.' I'm worse than a thirteen-year-old playing puppy love games with her boyfriend."

"Gideon and the fleece," Patty said, smiling. "If the wool is wet and the ground is dry, the people will be victorious over their foes."

Clare nodded and smiled wanly. "I guess."

"Gideon did the test twice. You gonna risk a second test? Push your luck?" Before Clare could interpret that, her mother went on. "So, what'd *he* say?"

"He said he'd wait six years for 'that fucking marshmallow' if it meant he got me as the reward. Mom, he told me he loved me." The flight nurse coughed painfully. "Then he walked out."

"Good for him," Patty said. "'Winner winner, chicken dinner,'" she whispered softly, with a smile.

"Mom, I want out of here." Clare said, abruptly changing tacks. "How long can you stay in Fairbanks?"

"What are you planning *now,* dear daughter?" Clare saw her mother lower her face into her hand, covering her eyes.

"Are you doing that so I won't see your eyebrows fly off the top of your head?" She saw her mother's head nod, but she went on anyway. "I need to go home, Mom. If you can stay for a couple more weeks, I'll be able to drive and shop then, even if I have to use a walker for a while. I'll be able to go to rehab appointments, defrost frozen dinners to eat. I need to get back in control. I need to be outta here."

"That's pretty dramatic, Clare."

"Mom, you're a nurse. You just have to make sure I don't fall and can't get up. That's all you have to do. I'll pay for the groceries, the gas. It'll be fun..." She coughed painfully.

The trauma team came in at that moment, interrupting her new action plan.

The team spent ten minutes discussing her as if she weren't there, then debating about the course of treatment over the next week. Finally, they included her in the conversation.

"Do you have any questions, CJay?"

She looked at her mother who was determinedly counting the acoustic ceiling tiles.

"I want out. I want to go home today. My mother is a nurse practitioner and can take care of me there."

"Well, young lady, that is simply not possible," the attending surgeon told her.

Clare flared at his condescension. "Then, I'll sign out AMA." She rang her call bell for the nurse. "Just bring me the paperwork and I'll get started on it."

"That's truly unwise, CJay," the surgeon advised, perhaps realizing belatedly that she was serious.

"Okay, then how can we compromise so I can get out of here and go home today without jeopardizing my recovery?"

The team turned away from her and again discussed her case as if she'd suddenly been struck deaf and blind. At last, they turned back around.

"This is what we can do. How long can your mother stay?"

"Two weeks," Patty said from the other side of the bed.

There was silence as the surgeon thought.

"I suggest...," he began slowly, "...that we assess you today and tomorrow – chest film, CT scan, perhaps another MRI, to see how your pelvis and back are healing." He ticked the tests off the fingers of his right hand as he spoke. "You still have tissue injury that must be assessed, but that appears to be progressing. Your urine is no longer bloody. There's no sign of infection or rhabdomyolysis. Let's draw STAT labs again tomorrow AM, do another urinalysis and check the results. If everything looks like you're trending upwards, then I'll consider allowing you to go home day after tomorrow – but no sooner without signing out AMA, which would be an incredible mistake at this point..."

"When can I start rehab?" Clare interrupted.

"Are you implying you want to get back on the helicopter?"

"Absolutely. I can do light duty in dispatch. No heavy lifting."

"But not until you're *cleared* for light duty."

"Agreed."

"Rehab can start this week. Your mother can bring you?"

Patty answered this. "Her goal's to drive as soon as possible, Doctor, so she can be independent ASAP. But until then, I'm available. After I leave, she has friends who can give help as needed."

"Understood. All right, CJay. Let's see what we can do for you. But if there're any setbacks, you're coming back to the hospital, or at least to a skilled nursing facility – a SNF – until you can function on your own."

Clare smiled and looked at her mother. *A SNF. No, thank you.* But out loud she said, "Thank you. I'll be the most compliant patient you've ever seen if you let me out of this place day after tomorrow."

Chapter Sixty-seven

"Do you need some help crossing the street, Miss?"

Clare smiled. She was on her fourth lap around the nurses' station on her aluminum walker with the tennis balls, and knew she was closing in on a forty-five-minute mile. She was pretty proud of herself. She'd stopped by Kelly's room several times to talk.

"Can I walk with you?" The voice came around her shoulder and she looked up into Chad's face.

She chuckled. "Do you think you can even walk this slow?"

"I can try. Do you want to take it down to the cafeteria for a cup of coffee?"

"That's my next goal, pal, but for today, it's gotta be a wheelchair for road trips."

"Let me find one, CJay. Let's get something to drink."

Larissa, the young grad, gave him the same elevator look she'd given the Trooper, but got him a wheelchair to use for their excursion. Clare knew she'd have to speak with the pretty nurse before she left the hospital to tell her that if she wanted to meet eligible, drool-worthy males, she'd have to get out of the SDU and into the Emergency Department.

Chad whisked her out of the unit and down the hallway to the elevator that would take them to the basement cafeteria. He made motor sounds with his mouth and squealed to a stop in the elevator alcove. CJay laughed at him.

"Why are you laughing? Didn't you know I'm a Driver now? I get to drive the engine! I get to make mouth sounds." His loud air horn impersonation followed by a 'whoop whoop' had her trying to turn around to look at his expression, then wincing. He came around from behind and knelt down in front of her.

"It's good to see you laugh, CJay. I'm just so glad you weren't…" He stopped talking.

"Killed?" She finished his sentence. She couldn't bring herself to even say the words 'burned alive.'

"Yeah. Killed. Among other things."

The elevator doors opened and he pushed the chair into the empty car and pressed 'B',

"Me too, Chad. I'm going home day after tomorrow. I told the doc I was gonna sign out AMA if he didn't get me out of here."

"Your mom staying with you?"

"For two weeks. I've promised myself I'll be able to fend for myself in two weeks, if only to drive to Fred's and fix meals."

"Geez, CJay, I can drive you, too. There're plenty of people who'd help you out. Don't do anything stupid that's gonna slow down your recovery." He looked at her with a question in his eyes. "Are…are you trying to get back on Aurora?"

"I am. I need to. I won't be too stupid, but I need my control back. I need to be able to take care of myself by myself since..." She abruptly stopped talking.

"Since what?"

She compressed her lips tightly and gingerly shook her head.

The elevator bumped to a stop and the doors slowly opened into the basement corridor that led to the brightly lit cafeteria. It was lunchtime and the dining area was filled with hospital personnel and visiting family members. The food smelled good to her.

"You hungry?"

Clare flashed back to the waffle and dry scrambled egg she'd not finished for breakfast before the Sergeant stopped by, and suddenly realized she was. "I'm famished, Chad."

"You need food to maintain your strength so you can go home day after tomorrow. Let me buy you a delicious hospital burger and perhaps some red jello for dessert." He smacked his lips appreciatively.

"I'll say yes to the burger. Please. And...thank you, Chad."

He parked her wheelchair at a corner table and joined the line at the grill. She could see the entire dining area, and waved at Kelly's dad and mom who were visiting their daughter from Oakland, California, sitting four tables away. Kelly was doing better, but would be staying in the hospital another week before going to an outside rehab facility for further care.

Then, Clare watched Chad. He was like Jeff. Easy on the eyes. Lean and muscular. He was aware of his good looks, and sometimes came across as somewhat smitten with himself, but underneath it all, he was a solid guy and a good firefighter-medic and now a Driver. He'd cared for her, and she'd essentially shat on him. He deserved better.

I need to ask about the South African girl he was dating.

When he brought the steaming hamburger platter back to the table, she lowered her face to it and breathed deeply, inhaling the meat, pickles, ketchup, onions and lettuce, and greasy fries fragrance. "Mmmmm, Chad. Real health food. This is simply wonderful. Thank you so very much."

She sipped at the dark coffee he'd also purchased for her and watched him take a firefighter-sized bite of his own Philly Cheesesteak sandwich. Juice dribbled down his chin and instinctively she reached out to wipe it away with her fingers.

"Was I leaking?"

"I'm sorry. I should have just let you drool unawares onto your shirt."

He shook his head. "I don't mind. That's what friends and chimps do – take care of each other. Now, eat your burger or I'll have to." CJay took a grateful bite. She was pleased her appetite was returning.

She asked about the job, and he told her he'd been a Driver for four months now, and was planning on going back to UAF to complete his Bachelor's in Emergency Medical Management and then start studying for the Captain's exam the following year or two.

"You know what else?" He looked excited. "I'm buying a house. Moving out of my parents' garage. I'm looking in North Pole at a house with a storage structure for the ATV and the snowmachine. Trees. It's pretty sweet. Easy commute to work." He looked at her closely. "I'm growing up, CJay."

They'd been talking for a while when he suddenly reached over and put his warm strong hands over hers on the little table between them. "I've missed you a whole hell of a lot, CJay. Is there any chance…," he paused, self-consciously, "…we could see if we could…maybe…try again?"

She squeezed his fingers, shook her head sadly, withdrew her hands from his, blew out a breath, and then looked at her watch. "No, Chad. Um…listen, I'm having a chest film done in twenty-five minutes. I need to get up to my room so the tech can bring me back downstairs again."

"Can I stop back by after dinner? 1900 – 7PM?"

She hesitated, knowing this was not going to be one of her better decisions. "If you want. Mom will be here then."

Good, he told her. He liked her mom. And he'd bring ice cream.

* * * * * *

The Trooper's flowers arrived at 3:30PM as the flight nurse was finishing up her seventh consecutive lap around the nurses' station hallway. They were a lovely combination of lilac roses with the usual baby's breath, ferns, and curly sticks in a clear cylinder.

"Lilac?" Clare asked.

"They're beautiful," her mother said. "Read the note, please."

Still standing, Clare tore open the envelope and pulled out the small card, written in Jeff's hand with black ink.

Flight nurse – Thinking of you. Trooper

"What's the significance of the color, Mom?"

Patty took the card and laid it on the bedside table, then pulled out her smartphone and Googled *'Significance of lilac roses.'* "'Mystical with symbolism tied to enchantment, desire, and even proceeding cautiously. Terrific flower for Valentine's Day,'" she relayed to her daughter. "And," her mother continued, looking over at the card, "It seems he actually went *into* the florist shop to order them. He didn't just phone it in."

Frowning, Clare sat, then carefully lifted her legs onto the bed and using her arms scooted back against the raised head, adjusting her butt until she was comfortable. It was a slow process.

"Mom, I really screwed up."

Her mother nodded and sighed. There was silence until Patty finally said, "Since Alex was killed, I've watched you go through at least two failed relationships. Jeff comes across as someone who means more to you than those others did." She shrugged. "And I have no advice to give you."

"That's it? Even bad TV moms give better advice than that."

"David likes him and he's an excellent judge of character."

"I should talk to David about this."

"Well, you may have the opportunity. Your brother wants to come up next week for two or three days to make sure his little sister's okay. But, *you* have to decide what you're going to do about Jeff on your own."

455

She could hear the jingle of Trygve's dog tags and the clicking of his nails coming down the hallway to her room.

"Sooner rather than later, Mother. He's coming through the main door right now."

* * * * *

We might as well have a brass band announcing our arrival, Tryg, with those damn tags of yours. At least she can't hide under the bed – she's not fast enough.

By the time he stood in the doorway, his K-9 was on her bed, licking her cheek. Clare had her arms around his neck and was laughing. Patty, sitting in the visitor's recliner chair, had a smile on her face. He saw the lilac flowers on the bedside table. The card lay next to them.

"Jeff," Patty said. "It's good to see you again." She stood and gave him a pat and a gentle squeeze on the arm. She turned back around to Clare. "I'm going down downstairs for the new *People* magazine and a cup of coffee. Do either of you want something from the cafeteria?"

"Mom! You're leaving again? Why are you always disappearing"" Clare asked, looking slightly...nervous?

"Just down to the gift shop and the basement. I'll be back in a bit." She smiled at her daughter, winked at Jeff, and walked out.

Finally, the Trooper spoke. "I see you got the flowers. Did you see the note?"

"I did. It's in the trash."

"Did you read it before you threw it in the trash?"

456

Clare closed her eyes and sighed. "I did. It was reminiscent of some of Elizabeth Barrett Browning's finest work."

"'How do I love thee? Let me count the ways?' That Elizabeth?"

"Exactly."

"Shannon's concerned she might have to give back Baby Gus if something happens to us."

"She doesn't have to worry about...about giving him back."

They sat in silence with Clare idly petting Trygve and Jeff examining his cuticles. Finally, he stood and told the K-9 to "Come." The dog jumped off the hospital bed.

"Clare, it's been good talking to you."

"I'm going home day after tomorrow."

He nodded. "Good. Your mother staying with you?"

"For two weeks. David's coming up to visit for a couple days, too."

"Tell him hello from me."

She nodded. "I will. Maybe we can all...um...have dinner together?" Clare waited a heartbeat. "Trooper?"

He stopped. "Yes, flight nurse?"

"Do you really love me?"

He turned around to her. "'Let me count the ways.'"

"I see."

He nodded and walked out the door without looking back, followed by his dog.

* * * * * *

Clare went for several slow sojourns around the nurses' station, feeling stronger each time. She still hurt a lot, but knew she was improving. Her mother helped her clean up in the walk-in shower in her room's tiny toilet area and she put on clean flannel pants and a tee shirt. Then Patty blew dry her daughter's long hair.

I'm cutting my hair when I get home. It'll grow back. It'll be a while before I wear a helmet again.

Dinner arrived and Clare picked at hers while Patty ate a salad from the extensive salad bar downstairs.

"Mom?"

"Hmmmm?" Patty looked up her

"Chad's stopping by tonight around 7PM."

Her mother looked sharply at her. "Why?"

"Just to be friendly. He's bringing ice cream.'

"Sniffing around the still warm corpse of your relationship with Jeff?"

"God, Mom. Stop it. He's just being nice."

"I think your drugs are addling your brains." Patty stared at her daughter. "Don't do this. It's wrong."

"Wrong to have ice cream?"

"I can pick up ice cream for you, Clare. Don't give that firefighter hope after you've just shit canned the Trooper. It's not fair to either man."

"Language, Mom! You sound just like my brothers. And, I just want ice cream. That's all," Clare replied, frowning, her lips tight.

"And what does Chad want?"

He wants me again. And you're right. I'm no better than Helen. Clare shook her head – *Ouch* – and glared angrily at her judgmental mother.

* * * * * *

Chad arrived promptly at 1900 – 7PM – bearing mint chocolate chip ice cream sandwiches ("Won't melt as fast.") for Clare and her mother. Patty was gracious to him, but made sure her daughter knew the older woman was not happy with this situation. She made her excuses to go back to Clare's place, putting on her coat and giving Chad a brief embrace. She'd met Clare's former boyfriend three times on visits to Fairbanks to see her daughter. She'd always liked him – and cared about him.

Patty bent over to hug her daughter before she left, too. "Don't you dare…," she whispered sternly into her ear before standing up. "Good to see you again, Chad. Clare, get some rest tonight. Big day tomorrow." She waved at them, then left to go back to the house.

The two ate their ice cream until Chad broke the silence. "Can I be nosy?"

"What?" She wiped her mouth with the back of her hand.

"Are you still seeing the Sergeant, CJay?"

She pulled a wry face and made a waggling gesture with the hand not holding the ice cream sandwich that indicated 'Maybe yes, maybe no.' "Just an issue, Chad. And, to be honest, it's totally my fault. I have to own it."

459

He grunted, then said softly, "Do you know I tried to fight him at Little John's?"

"I heard, but not from him. That was awhile back."

"Yeah. After you and he...you know...you and he were dancing at the Pump House. I was just so angry to see him at Little John's with some other trooper dude. They were in civvies, not on duty."

"Mano a mano?" Clare thought back to Helen. "Did you take it out to the parking lot?"

Chad nodded glumly. "'Mano a mano.' I tried to. I was drunk. Angry that he was..." He sighed. "...moving in on what I felt was my territory. He never even laid a hand on me, but I slipped and fell on my face. Broke my nose. Acted like a real douche. I'm surprised he didn't tell you."

"No, he didn't."

"Did you hear that Jean broke up with me?"

"I did, Chad, and I'm really sorry. She told me herself."

Chad looked at her, surprised. She shrugged.

"Small world, Fairbanks EMS, Chad. I taught PALS at FMH a while back. She was in the class and talked with me privately during lunch. She told me she liked you – thought the two of you might have a future together. You really hurt her."

Chad stood up and walked around the room a couple of turns, then came back to sit on the edge of Clare's bed, next to her knees. She moved over to give herself more personal space.

"Do you know why I broke up with you, CJay?"

"Chad, that was a long time ago. You don't have to explain anything now. Seriously."

"Do you know what it's like to love someone so much it hurts and you know you can't ever have them?"

She stared at him without expression. *Duh.*

"I was so angry. I wanted to hurt you as much as I was hurting."

"I understand, Chad." *I do* understand, *Chad.*

She saw his lips tighten and saw some of the old Chad fire behind his eyes.

"I guess that's why I felt so helpless." He stopped.

"Is that when you met Jean?"

"Yeah. She flirted with me – made me feel important. She's cute, has that accent. Clever, smart. Likes to have fun. She can drink me under the table." He laughed. "We used to take turns being the designated driver when we went out."

Clare nodded. "She really liked you, you know."

"I know." He was silent for a moment. "I think when I found out that you were starting to go out with the Trooper...I think that's when I started finding it hard to get along with Jean. I'd hear about what you were doing or some of my guys would work with you and let me know they'd seen you. Of course, Kevin'd talk about Kelly and you'd get mentioned. It's not like we can escape the gossip in Fairbanks."

"What's your point, Chad?"

"She broke up with me because she got tired of being on the outside. I had some pictures of you and me at my place and she'd see them – and ask me to put them away. I was just being hard-nosed."

"Why were you punishing her?"

461

"Darned if I know, CJay. Anyhow, she got tired of it. She's got quite a mouth on her, and is fluent with a lot of Afrikaans cuss words I've never heard before, plus the American ones she's picked up. She swears like an ice road trucker. She finally told me off. Said she was 'too proud to compete with a memory.'" His imitation of her accent was eerily precise.

"Turnaround?" Clare really did understand.

He laughed ruefully. "Not proud of that. And the thing is, CJay, I miss her. She was a big support. A good listener. Lots of common sense. Pretty, fun to be around. She made me laugh. But I can't slink back now. I've made a mess of it."

Clare looked into the face of this young man she'd spent so much time with. "I'm really sorry, Chad. But it sounds like you've got some good plans ahead of you."

"Now, yeah. But I went off the rails after Jean broke up with me. I didn't expect that at all. I've spent so many years being able to act like a kid – I guess when reality and the shit hit the fan...I couldn't handle it."

CJay studied his face. He looked well, but also seemed tired. Like some of his bluster had worn away. Some of the cockiness. The arrogance. There were actually a few lines around his eyes. "What do you mean you 'went off the rails?'"

"I got in my truck and went down to Anchorage. I camped, stayed in some crap ass hotel once I got there. Spent a lot of time drinking and feeling sorry for myself. Got clobbered good in a fist fight at the Hotel Captain Cook bar with some businessman from Puyallup, Washington. Got thrown in jail, CJay. I spent forty-eight hours in the clink. But, it gave me time to sober up and start

462

thinking about what I had to do now. I knew I needed to get out of the funk. My Battalion Chief flew down to bail me out. Lemme tell ya, CJay, that drive back to Fairbanks with the Chief in my truck was long and very quiet. I knew I needed to finally fucking grow up. I needed to stop thinking about Jean, my stupidity, my attitude. And...well...about you."

She nodded. "And now?"

"I'm okay. I screwed up so badly, I thought I'd never get over it. But it taught me a lesson."

"A lesson?"

"Grow up, Chad, me boy. Be a man."

Clare smiled slightly, then took a deep breath. "I told you that I had to own up to being responsible for the 'maybe' status of my relationship with the Sergeant?" waggling her hand again. "I deliberately chose to do nothing about a situation and it came back to bite me big time. I've apologized, but things are still kinda...iffy." She put her hand over his. "I need to apologize to you too, Chad. I need to clear the air."

"What're you talking about?"

"You became my friend at a time when I needed it. I grieved over my husband and you were there for me. But I didn't do you any favors."

"I fell in love with you, CJay," he told her quietly.

"I know. I shouldn't have let it happen. I cared about you too, but it definitely wasn't fair on my part. I used you to soothe my soul. And, Chad," she smiled up at him, "quite honestly, you were very, very good at it. But, I blew it and...I'm so sorry."

"You were the Ice Queen to me." He squeezed her fingers.

She nodded. He was right. "Just what you did to Jean, Mr. Ice King."

He laughed a little. "Yeah. We're a pair, CJay. We should sharpen our skates and choreograph a routine." He squeezed her fingers, then did a graceful pirouette motion with the hand she wasn't holding.

Clare smiled at him. "If you still care about Jean, go tell her what you've just told me. Make amends, Chad. Fix this if you want her back."

"What about you, CJay? What are *you* going to do? You know how I still feel about you."

She shook her head. "I'm going to follow my own advice. I'm going to try to make amends with the Sergeant."

"Do you love him?"

"I pretty certain I do."

He sighed. "Well, I'm glad, I guess, CJay. I'm happy for you" He leaned forward, lifted her chin with the hand that did a pirouette, said "You deserve happiness," and then gently kissed her lips once, then twice, a little longer the second time.

Clare heard a childish giggle and watched as Shannon, Reese, Jordan, and Baby Gus peeked around the corner and knocked on the door.

"Hi, Clare! Are you..." Shannon stopped just as Chad pulled away from his kiss. He released the flight nurse's hand and stood.

"Hi, Shannon." Attempting to keep her composure, the flight nurse greeted Jeff's sister. "Please come on in. Chad, this is Jeff's sister, Shannon; her husband, Jordan; Reese, his niece;

464

and this is Augustus, the little guy that was born with Gus and me. It's good to see you all. This is Chad...he's an...old friend of mine."

"I'm a Driver with Fairbanks Fire," he broke in. "I'm here with my Captain who's married to Kelly who was in the crash with CJay. I just thought I'd stop in to say hello to CJay. We were chatting about my...um...girlfriend. CJay knows her from Memorial. It's great meeting you all, but..." He looked at his watch. "...look at the time! I gotta go now. On shift tomorrow. See you sometime, CJay." He grabbed his jacket, waved at her and hurriedly left the room.

"He didn't have to leave so quickly, Clare," Jordan said, one eyebrow raised. He and Shannon looked at each other briefly as Reese ran over to Clare with a bag of Dove chocolates and attempted to climb on the bed, pulling on the woman as she scrambled up. Pain shot through the flight nurse's legs and her back spasmed. She groaned sharply and grabbed for the bed rail.

"Are you okay?" the little girl asked. Clare breathed through her mouth slowly, trying not to move until the spasms passed.

"I'm sorry," Reese said. "I didn't mean to hurt you."

"It's okay, sweetie." Clare ruffled her hair with the hand not white-knuckling the bed rail. The flight nurse was embarrassed that the adults had seen Chad kissing her. She knew her face was flaming red. She knew they would tell Jeff.

"Clare, should we get the nurse?" Shannon asked quietly.

Clare caught her breath and said, "No, no. I'm better now. I still hurt, but it's getting better day by day." She pressed her call light. "But, it *is* time for better living through chemistry."

"We won't keep you long. Jeff said you're going home day after tomorrow and we just wanted to stop by again. Reese wanted you to have the chocolates."

After the evening nurse brought Clare some oral pain medication, Reese talked about school. Shannon shared about Gus' growth charts and how he well was doing. Clare was glad to hear their good news. The family stayed for fifteen minutes before saying they needed to get the kids in bed.

Chapter Sixty-eight

Da Dum.

Her brother's familiar ring tone woke Clare up the next morning. 0400. Obviously, David was on graves, calling at 0500 his time.

"What the hell's going on?" she heard when she finally out-fumbled the phone and hit the "Accept" icon.

"Hi, David," she croaked. "How are you?"

"Thought I'd call when you're at your groggiest on high doses of Demerol."

"Mmmmm. Demerol. My favorite. But they've me on oral meds now and I'm weaning myself off them and onto acetaminophen and ibuprofen."

"Mom says you're going home tomorrow."

His sister confirmed that. On the home front, David reported, he was presenting again about crisis management and the peer support team to his bosses this coming week and he and Jeff talked yesterday...

"You talked to Jeff?" she interrupted. "Did *he* call *you*?"

"Hey, you interrupted me, Clare. I called *him* for suggestions on the presentation. He linked me to a good video and some information from an experienced PsyD out of Austin, Texas, who's done a boatload of stuff with law enforcement, flight programs, commercial airlines, the military, *and* the impact of parental trauma on children."

"Did *he* say anything?"

There was a long moment of silence. "*He* indicated there'd been a glitch."

A 'glitch?' "A 'glitch?'"

"It's not my beeswax, Clare. Anything is between you and Jeff. Unless you want to talk about it." He waited.

She began with Helen's arrival and segued into the Seattle nurse's smug demeanor the following morning. Continued on with Schrödinger's Cat – did or didn't he? Her anger, her tears, his denials.

"You screwed the pooch, little sister," he finally remarked when she wound down. "Why the hell didn't you pick up the phone and warn him about what was going down? You left him clueless and vulnerable to baseless accusation. What was this? A test of fidelity to you, Missy Precious Princess?"

She chuffed angrily over the phone. *I wish people would quit asking me that question.* "Listen, David. I'm already bruised from slapping myself upside the head for the past week."

"Do you want him?"

"Yes."

468

"Then freakin' use your effing common sense and work it out. Now, get better. I'm coming up in six days, so you need to be well enough to go out and party with me." He hung up on her.

The phlebotomist came in at that moment to do the morning lab draws on Clare. The results would help determine whether the docs sent her home or she signed out AMA.

Use my 'effing' common sense and 'work it out.' Easy for you to say, David Dumbhead.

* * * * * *

Patty arrived at 0730 with good dark coffee to share and sat with her while she ate breakfast. Clare mentioned that David had called. But he'd only said he was coming up in six days, she told her mother.

The trauma team made rounds at 0815, and the flight nurse re-emphasized her desire to get home as quickly as possible. At 0930, hospital transport came with a wheelchair to take her to CT for a scan.

At 1030, flowers arrived from Chad. Coral-hued roses. "Desire," her mother informed her, after checking Google. *"I liked talking to you last night. Thank you,"* read the note, written in Chad's own precise hand.

At 1130, flowers arrived from the Trooper. Red roses. Jeff had handwritten the note. *"May you feel better day by day. I miss you."*

The room was beginning to smell like a funeral parlor.

She went for an MRI at 1530 – 3:30PM.

469

By 1800, the flight nurse had circumnavigated the SDU hallways thirty times and visited Kelly five times.

At 1845 – 6:45PM, she heard Trygve's dog tags coming down the hallway. She took a deep breath and brushed some tendrils of hair away from her face. Patty looked at her and Clare said firmly, "Don't you even *think* about leaving."

The K-9 came through the door first and immediately jumped on the bed to greet her. The Trooper appeared next, in uniform, bearing an enormous gold foil box of very expensive, imported chocolates.

"I stole them from Walgreen's," he told her, and handed the candy to Patty, who grinned, thanked him, and said it was good to see him again.

Clare watched him look at the flowers – including the plant from the Information Desk, several from workmates, the Icelandic snowmachiner's wife, and the Aurora program lined up on the window sill – and nod appreciatively.

"I'm going down to the cafeteria to get some mint tea to go with these wonderful chocolates. Either of you want anything?" Patty asked, standing and indicating that Jeff could have the chair.

"Mom!"

Her mother turned to her and repeated, "I'm going to go get some mint tea. Would you two like something?"

Clare shook her head resignedly. "No. I'm good."

"I'm good, too. But thank you for offering," Jeff said. Patty turned and left the room.

He remained standing. "May I sit down, Clare?"

She gave a sharp nod. He sat in Patty's chair.

They sat quietly for several minutes until the Trooper finally broke the silence.

He turned to count out aloud the flowers lined up on the window sill. "So far, I'm winning."

Clare looked at him.

He shrugged and pointed to the multiple floral bouquets and the one purloined plant. "I have three in the race, and everyone else has only one." He pulled out his smart phone and typed in several words. "*Desire*, huh? The coral roses must be from Chad," he finally said.

She refused to return his gaze.

"Yup. From the fireman." He blew out a breath. "Clare..."

She grunted, but didn't speak.

"Clare, you and I are both strong willed people who're good at our jobs. I've respected and admired you for a long time. And, you apologized for leaving me twisting in the wind with Helen. Now, I actually *need* to know where we're going. Do you care about me at all? Are you willing to risk it when I say the last thing in the world I wanted to do was screw her? Can you believe me when I say I'm in love with you and I don't want anyone else?"

She kept very still.

"Or, perhaps you'd rather have Chad come kiss you and hold your hand?"

"I'm sorry they saw that." Her cheeks flushed again at the memory, and she took an active interest in her drink of water from the hospital's baby-poo-colored plastic cup.

"But are you sorry it happened?" He stood and put his coat back on.

"You told me you loved me." Putting down her glass, she hid her eyes with her hand. "I can't imagine not being with you in your bed or not having your arms around me holding me tight and keeping me safe. Is that the same thing?"

"I'll take it, Clare." He pulled the little visitor's chair next to her bed and sat in it, still in his heavy jacket. He took her hand and kissed her palm, then laid his forehead against it.

"I love you, Trooper," he thought he heard her mumble, but he wasn't willing to risk having her repeat herself.

Clare pulled his hand towards her, so he stood and then sat on the bed when she made room for him. Her other arm reached out for him.

"I love you, flight nurse," the big man whispered as he bent forward to kiss her mouth. She put her hand behind his neck to pull him closer and parted her lips. They both groaned in their throats and kissed again.

And that is what Patty saw when she came back to Clare's hospital room. She leaned against the doorjamb and smiled. Trygve licked Clare's hand, then woofed at Patty.

Chapter Sixty-nine

The trauma team arrived before 0900 the next morning and after discussing the results of the lab tests, the chest XRay, the CT scan, and the MRI, determined that rather than have the flight nurse sign out AMA, it was permissible for Clare to go home in the care of her mother, provided she return immediately if there were complications; she keep up with her physical therapy; and follow up with both her primary care doctor and the surgeon on a weekly basis. By 2PM, the discharge paperwork was signed and a transport tech was pushing Clare down to the patient loading zone where the Subaru with her mother driving was waiting.

"There was a moment there when I thought I'd never see this place again," Clare admitted as they rounded the corner and her mother put on the blinker and slowed in order to pull into the driveway. Then the flight nurse noticed a wheelchair ramp leading up to her porch allowing easy access to the front door. Patty came to a stop, turned off the engine, and opened the driver's side door. A rush of frigid air blew in.

"Mom! Where'd that ramp come from? Who built that?"

"Who do you think, Clare? Jeff and some of his trooper friends put it together as soon as he heard you were coming home. He didn't want you to have to struggle up and down those stairs. It's only temporary – until you get back on your feet. He cares about you," was all she said as she went around to the back hatch to pull out the wheelchair they'd rented from the medical supply store. A state-of-the-art walker with a seat and a cup holder was folded up alongside it.

Patty would come back in a bit to bring in Jeff's flowers. The rest went either to the nurses' station or, along with the purloined potted plant, back downstairs to the Information Desk.

Clare did have to stand and step up in order to go from the porch into the house, but she had the new walker to steady her, and the warmth emanating from the front door along with the fragrance of her mother's chicken casserole heating in the crock pot in the kitchen brought joy to her heart. *I'm home. I'll survive.*

"Thanks, Mom. I wouldn't have been able to do this without you. Thank you so much." She gave her mother a careful embrace, then pulled a chair from her little drop leaf table and sat down to watch her mother stir the crock pot.

"You're going to get through this and back on the helicopter if that's what you need to do. I'll do everything I can to help you make it."

Clare's doorbell rang, and Emma and Kenny from next door stood there with a homemade, ready to bake tuna-noodle casserole with green peas for them and a bouquet of bright flowers from Fred Meyers.

"Turnabout," Kenny said. "We're glad you're home."

"Would you like to ask Jeff to stop by for dinner tonight when his shift is over, Clare? We've got enough chicken for six people."

"Mom, let's make it tomorrow night. We can heat up the tuna-noodle casserole. He loves it, especially with green peas."

"You're kidding? Okay. Ask him. I know you're tired. Tomorrow would be good."

Clare texted the trooper and he called back in an hour, apologizing for the delay. It's okay, she told him. She knew his schedule was always dependent on current events. And, yes, he said, accepting the invitation, he'd loved to come for tuna-noodle casserole. Thank you. Could he bring ice cream for dessert? Of course. Excellent, because he had a half gallon of chocolate peanut butter ice cream in his freezer he wanted to share with her and Patty.

* * * * * *

"Delicious," Jeff told Clare and her mother after tasting the neighbors' tuna-noodle casserole. "Thanks for inviting me over."

Clare and Jeff relaxed with chocolate peanut butter ice cream as Patty cleaned up.

"The casserole's not as good as mine, but it was sweet of Emma and Kenny to fix it."

"Kenny admitted yours was better."

"When?"

"About a million years ago when I missed our shooting date."

She laughed. "Yes, Jeff. It was a million years ago, wasn't it?" So much had happened since then.

They were sitting on the sofa, and she shyly reached her hand over to touch his arm. "I love you," she whispered.

"I love you, too." He paused. "Do you want to see how far we can take this relationship?"

"I do."

"Me, too. How are you feeling?" He leaned in to kiss her.

"Do you mean can we go into my bedroom and take off our clothes and make love while my mother does the dishes?"

"Pretty much."

Clare laughed out loud, but lowered her voice. "I still hurt like a mother fucker – oops! Sorry. But as soon as possible…."

"I have ways to bring you pleasure that do not involve a lot of wrestling."

"I've missed your pleasure, Jeff." *And I think I know of some things I can do to you that won't land me back in the emergency department….*

"Back atcha, flight nurse."

"More ice cream, kids?" her mother called from the kitchen. "And there's still some more coffee."

"We're good, Mom." *Seriously. We're good.*

"Yes, we are," he whispered to her. He put his arm around her and kissed her. She put his hand on her breast and squeezed it tight.

I've missed you so much. I'm so glad you're here, Trooper. Welcome home.

* * * * * *

Three days later, Clare talked Patty into driving her back over to North Star and wheeling her to see Kelly who was preparing to go to a rehabilitation facility for at least four weeks in the next few days. Her little girl was in the room with her, playing games on her mom's phone.

"They're saying I've got some permanent deficits. I may still need surgery. I guess at this point I'm done on Aurora. Maybe a miracle…." Her voice trailed off

"I'm really sorry, Kell." Clare paused, then went on. "But, you know something, maybe all three of us have already had our miracle?"

Her friend nodded. "CJay…" The other flight nurse dipped her head. "…when Charlie told Big Mike he was coming in on flare…right before we hit the ground…."

"What, Kell?"

"I felt someone's arms around me. I wasn't scared anymore."

Clare smiled. "That was Alex, Kelly. He held me, too. I knew we were going to die, but it was okay." She felt the tears coming, but didn't try to stop them. Her loving husband had come to give her and her friend peace at the end.

"Do you still dream about him?"

"I haven't for a while." Clare wiped her nose on a napkin from Kelly's bedside table.

"Next time, tell him 'Thank you' from me. It meant a lot not to be afraid." The tears glistened in her eyes, too. "He must have been a good man."

"One of the very best, Kelly."

"You crying, momma?" her daughter asked.

"Tears of gratitude, sweetie." She pulled her child close. "I've given a thought or two to being a stay at home mom, CJay. I think *this* is my time."

The two dried their tears and Clare learned that Charlie was stable in Seattle, and off life support. His femur and humerus fractures were healing. Pulmonary contusions were still an issue, but prognosis was good for him. His wife was at his side. She'd already spoken with their pilot safety officer, Tommy, and informed him Charlie'd decided to hang up the flight suit, even if he recovered fully. His wife seemed to want him around for a few more years.

Patty took Clare down to dispatch after the two women embraced and promised to be the President of each other's fan clubs in the coming months.

Gus and Jacque were on duty, set for any fixed wing flights, but mainly working in the ED. She learned that a new helicopter was in the pipeline, but it would probably be another four months. In the meantime, they were leasing an AStar which was due in Fairbanks in a week from a major national vendor. At the present time, down a nurse, pilot, and paramedic, the program was back to 'hostage situation' status. Flight nurses and paramedics were now working 24-hour and 48-hour shifts, dependent on pilot status and flyable hours.

"Come back to work, CJay," Jeanne told her. "Quit slacking!" They laughed, but knew it was a tenuous time for the Aurora program. A job search was on for a permanent replacement for Kelly and at least a temporary replacement for Clare. And, a new, full time pilot.

But Clare knew her status wasn't guaranteed. Her career could also be at an end.

'Bjorn' (their Icelandic snowmachiner) – whose name was actually Sigurður – had the crich closed and a tracheal tube placed. His jaw was wired and he had plates and screws in his head. But, he was alive and mentating appropriately. Prognosis was excellent. Clare was able to tell Gus that Sigurður's wife, Vilborg, had come to visit Kelly and her in the SDU and brought flowers and her profound thanks to the two of them, and her sincere wishes for recovery. Yes, she'd stopped by dispatch that next day, Gus said. She'd been shaken to hear of the crash of the helicopter that had carried her own husband to the hospital just three hours before, and very grateful for the crew's survival.

The twins were good, and Norma was feeling well. Her mom had traveled to Fairbanks to help out for several weeks. Gus pulled out his phone and showed her multiple pictures of the two infants. Norma's mom looked just like her – older and more serious, but with the same big brown eyes that smiled on the babies.

"'Moose Man' went home!" Gus informed her. "His wife made him promise he'd always fasten his seatbelt anytime he's in their new truck from now on."

Then he wanted to know about 'The Sergeant.'

479

"It's good, Gus. It was my fault this Helen thing all happened. I should have told him what she'd planned. I can't blame anyone else but..." She pointed her finger at her own self. "I let him down. I set him up for her. I was terribly wrong. I betrayed him."

"You did not mean to. But you are still together?"

"Yes. I apologized with great shame. I admitted my mistake." She bent close to him and whispered, "He told me he loves me."

"And what did you say, CJay?"

"'Back atcha, Trooper.'"

Gus's nod and smile said it all. "That is good news. I have wanted you to find happiness. I am glad for both of you."

* * * * * *

David flew in two days later. Clare was napping on her bed when Patty and her brother arrived at the house, but David had no problem bursting into her bedroom and then giving her a careful hug after he saw the expression of terror on her face when he lunged at her.

"You scared the crap outta me, David!" she told him, hugging him back. "But I'm glad to see you."

"Glad to see you too, Punk. How are you?"

"Help me sit up and I'll race you to the living room. Hand me the walker."

He handed her the walker and she started to stand, then sat down again. "I'm fine, David – considering. My back hurts like crap, and my legs hurt from the tissue bruising. And my neck hurts. But, they're all getting better and better, day by day."

480

"You gonna be okay?" He sat down next to her on the bed.

"If okay means I've survived, then yes." She turned to him. "Do you know the stats for survival after a crash – especially in an AStar?"

He shook his head.

"Statistically slim to none of getting out of it unscathed. Lotsa burns, and if you survive, lotsa rehab. And that's on a good day. And, seriously, ours *was* a good day. We all survived. Aurora did her best to keep us alive as long as she could." Clare took a deep breath and felt like she was going to cough. Instead, a huge sob burst out of her. "Oh, God, David. I knew we were going to die. But I made my peace...." She gasped as the tears came.

David held her as closely as he could without hurting her. "I love you, Clare. It would've been awful to lose you 'cuz then I'd have no one to pester."

This made her laugh. "You want to do peer support again?" She wiped her eyes on his jacket.

"If you want. I'm serious. Talking makes it easier."

"Yeah. Maybe later." She paused, then spoke in a soft voice. She could tell he was bending his head to hear her. "I've only shared this with Kelly, Mom, and Jeff. David, at the end, before we hit the ground, I felt peace. I told God I was in his hands. I wasn't afraid." She looked away from him, her throat tightening.

"'Tonic immobility,'" she heard him say. "That's the body's way of bringing you solace at the very end when you know you're going to die. It's a wave of endorphins that sweeps over you, taking away the terror. It's called 'peaceful death.'"

481

She looked at him. "I believe it was Alex holding me. Kelly said the same thing. Alex held both of us before we crashed."

Now, it was David's turn to look away. "That, too, Clare." He hesitated. "I dream about him sometimes. Please don't think I'm bonkers."

"I already know you're bonkers."

"He says he watches over me." He turned to look at his sister. "I believe it's him speaking to me."

She nodded. "He's a busy guardian angel, because he tells me the same thing. And I'm not bonkers. Yet."

David followed Clare out to the living room. She knew he was watching how she walked, attempting to assess her status, but she didn't question him. If the situation had been reversed, she'd have been doing the same thing. His presence comforted her.

Their mom made Lasagna Bolognese with Fontina Béchamel – lasagna with white sauce – for dinner, her signature dish and one of the favorites of both kids. They lingered over the meal, catching up on home news.

Finally, David looked at Clare and asked, "Can we get Jeff over here? And, I'd like to meet his sister and her husband, too. He's military police, right?"

Clare nodded and looked at her mom. "Is that all right? It'll put a big burden on you."

"Not if we make it a potluck. Let's do it as soon as possible. Tomorrow for Jeff? The next day for his family?"

Clare called Jeff after dinner and he volunteered to make his famous moose ribs with homemade BBQ sauce for them the following night. He'd bring them over at noon and slow cook them in her oven until he was off shift.

Shannon and Jordan were thrilled to be invited with their children for potluck the night after that. Patty planned to reheat the leftover lasagna and ribs (if there were any left), David would be in charge of grilling steaks, Shannon volunteered salad and cobbler. Jeff would make garlic bread. Reese would entertain the K-9. Clare would direct traffic.

She felt good about their dinner plans. She was beginning to feel the sense of a new normal – like there really *was* a light at the end of this long, very dark tunnel. And, she would see Jeff at noon when he brought the ribs over to cook.

And, she could see her future in his eyes....

* * * * * *

Clare savored the interaction between her brother and the man she knew she loved at the moose rib dinner. Their humor meshed and the laughter wrapped her in warmth and comfort. Even Patty sat back and basked in the rich flush of testosterone at the dining table.

Chocolate peanut butter ice cream was a hit for dessert with coffee. Jeff invited David to do a ridealong with him the next day in the K-9 Expedition, delighting her brother with the prospect.

"Just be back in time to help with our potluck dinner," Patty admonished the two of them. "Clare and I can't do it all."

"Yes, *Mother,*" David said, rolling his eyes. The Sergeant politely stifled a laugh.

And, the ridealong the next day was memorable: Working with the Fort Wainwright military police, Jeff, Trygve, and Ridealong Dave helped apprehend a Wainwright soldier who'd brandished a weapon at a university apartment complex, threatening a former girlfriend. After Trygve rousted him out of hiding in a nearby Fairbanks neighborhood, the soldier was remanded to the MPs' custody, specifically, Jordan's custody.

It made for another lively conversation that night at the potluck.

"So, come do a ridealong with *me*, Dave," Jordan suggested. "See how the Army does it."

"Different than anybody else?"

"Way different, Deputy. We don't have a Bearcat like the SERTs, but we have Blackhawks. Whop whop whop."

Clare laughed, but sobered quickly and spoke quietly. "That was the best sound I'd ever heard, Jordan – when that Blackhawk came to get us. I will never forget the feeling of knowing we were *all* going home." She looked at Jeff. "And seeing you there for me. It...it meant everything, Trooper."

"Even if you were angry at me?"

"Despite being...'angry.' You gave me strength." She reached over, took his hand, and for the first time in front of others, she told him, "I love you, Jeff."

There was a chorus of 'Awwws' from the family gathered at the table. Jeff brought her hand to his lips and kissed it. "Back atcha, fly girl," he said. "You had my heart on the Wainwright flightline last March." He smiled. "Blackhawks brought us together."

"And, Baby Gus – don't forget," Shannon added, holding the bright-eyed infant in her lap.

"And, sweet Baby Gus with his little foot stickin' out," Clare acknowledged, nodding her head.

It was late when the evening concluded. The men cleaned up while Clare, Shannon, and Patty lingered in the living room. When only Patty and her two children were left, Patty drew Clare aside.

"It sounds like you and your Trooper are straightening things out?"

Her daughter nodded. "I think so."

"Take your time, Clare. You've got a lot on your plate right now, what with rehab and getting back to the regular activities of daily living. I'm glad you've got Jeff to support you, but…dammit. Take your time. Really get to know one another. At least a year before you start to make wedding plans."

Clare shook her head. "No, Mom. The crash changed everything. Everything seems emergent now. 'Life is short' used to be just a clichéd phrase to me, but I got to experience what it's like to almost die and I don't want to miss anything now. I want what Alex and I had – again. And, I want it with Jeff."

"He seems to be a good man."

"He is. But, you're not wrong. One day at a time. I'm not going to rush into anything." She paused. "Nah. I am."

"Are you thinking about moving in together?"

"No. I want to be married before we live together. But I also want him to feel that he's welcome here, just as I'm welcome at his place. Truthfully, once *you* leave, it'll be scary to be on my own, even if I was pretty pushy with that surgeon. It would be nice to have Jeff as a support. And to even have him here with me…when he can be."

"Hmm," her mother commented. "I can understand."

"Can you and Dad come up together pretty quick?"

"Of course. He needs to meet Jeff and put in his two cents, too. But," she added, "I know he'll like your trooper."

Her mother put her arms around her only daughter, her last child, her baby. "I was devastated when Alex died, Clare. I thought I'd hardly survive my granddaughter's death. I am so thankful you have become such a beautiful, strong – and strong-willed – woman. I'm so proud of you and what you do. From everything I can tell of Jeff, he's a good man. David definitely thinks so. I'd like to meet his family – get to know them, but I think you've found a keeper in this one. One day at a time. You're very smart, sweetheart. No, you're very wise." Patty pulled Clare close, gently. "I love you."

"I love you too, Mom. Thank you." Clare replied quietly.

Chapter Seventy

"Clare, how are you doing?"

"Big Mike, I'm doing amazingly well," she told the dispatcher on her phone, honestly.

They exchanged pleasantries for a few minutes. Clare learned that a new, full-time flight paramedic had been added to take Kelly's place ("Although no one will be able to take her place," Big Mike told her. Clare agreed.). A flight nurse position was also posted both locally and nationally for Clare's job, although her position was being held open. Aurora was the only flight program in the region and needed to expand, anyway. Once the new paramedic was integrated into the flight schedule, a second position would be posted for another paramedic, as well. There was even some talk of adding a third aircraft to the program.

"There's a letter here for you, Clare. That's why I'm calling. Can you come pick it up or shall I have Gus bring it out to you? He's volunteered to do it after work today."

"Have Gus bring it, Big Mike. I'm definitely up for company. Thanks." Then she asked, "A letter? Who's it from?"

"Hmmmmm. Postmark is Olympia WA. Address is Olympia, too, but no name. Just a return address."

"I don't think I know anyone in Olympia," she told him. *I don't think I know anyone in Olympia….*

It was four weeks since Clare'd come home from the hospital, and ten days since her mother had flown back to Eugene. It wasn't as easy as the flight nurse had hoped it would be to take care of herself, but before Patty had left she'd made up two weeks' worth of frozen meals, and stockpiled her daughter's larder with easily prepared packaged food, including gut-clutchers like mac 'n cheese and ramen noodles, and canned favorites like soup.

Patty knew Jeff would also bring take-out and make food for her daughter. Several of Clare's flight crew colleagues volunteered to both shop for her and take her shopping. The girl wouldn't starve to death. And, she'd make all of her doctor's appointments and rehab appointments, too, with friends helping.

In the past two days, Clare took her Subaru to the gas station and picked up ibuprofen and acetaminophen at the drugstore. Of all of the things she'd done since the accident, perhaps those two tasks had brought her the greatest sense of normalcy and efficacy.

But now Gus was bringing her a letter from an unknown person, sent to dispatch. He'd also be bringing pictures of the twins, and a casserole from Norma – both welcome diversions. But the letter…?

* * * * * *

Ms. Valenzuela:

I couldn't believe it when we got back to Seattle and I found out that Aurora crashed and you and your crew almost died. The TV coverage said your survival was a miracle. We were very glad to hear that down here, because our program has experienced the grief of losing flight colleagues.

I want to clarify what happened when I was in Fairbanks.

My mother told me Jeffrey was dating a flight nurse, but I didn't know it was you until I went out to Ester and saw your picture on his desk. I went there just to talk to him. We meant a lot to each other when we were going together. I have missed him, but I have also moved on.

You see, I am getting a PhD in Healthcare Management. I am getting married in Hawaii in January to a terrific man I met when I was teaching an eight-hour law enforcement seminar. He's a Washington State Patrol pilot, Randolph. I have everything I need.

What I implied that next morning to you was inaccurate. Jeffrey told me he cared for you, and despite any history the two of us had, he was not willing to compromise this current relationship.

I don't know if you are still dating, because I haven't heard anything from him since that night. I hope you are still together, because Jeffrey is a good man.

Fly safe, Helen Tall.

PS: Thank you for not punching me in the nose in the nursing unit. You sure looked like you wanted to.

* * * * * *

Actually, Helen, I'd gotten beyond wanting to punch you in the nose. By that next morning, I wanted to shiv you with the M-Tech MX8054 Extreme Tactical Fighting Knife that was strapped to my ankle. But, I knew that would be counterproductive and would probably put the kibosh on my career for a while.

As if being hurled from the sky hasn't already done that….

Clare smiled and folded up the neatly typed letter with the precise signature and tucked it back into the envelope. She didn't need to read it again, nor did she need to show it to 'Jeffrey.' *I'm glad she wrote, but I can just smell the smugness between the lines as she brags about her accomplishments and her new man, and then gives me permission to be with her cast-off. 'Current relationship,' my freakin' foot. And I also know she's lying her freakin' teeth off if she thinks I believe a single word about going*

490

out to Ester *'just to talk.'* What I do choose to believe is that Jeff *didn't compromise himself* or our *'current' relationship.*

She laughed quietly. Though she still felt extremely proprietary about Jeff; though it made her furious to think that this woman felt she could snap her fingers and Jeff would do her bidding; though she realized she really *was* jealous about what Helen Tall had meant to the man she now loved – she *also* knew that Jeff loved her and, face it, was an admirable, honest, loyal, loving, true blue hero to her.

And we all have memories, sorrows, and baggage. I hope Helen is happy, but if I never see her again, I will not shed one tear. She needs to stay in Olympia. Forever. Jeff said her husband was taking her sailing in the South Pacific after her PhD. I hope her boat sinks.

And, if I had punched her, her jaw would still be wired shut.

Clare chuckled and stood up from the little drop leaf kitchen table where she'd poured a cup of coffee before she tore open the envelope. As soon as Gus handed it to her, she'd known who it was from. But, she put it aside and spent thirty-five minutes with her crewmate catching up before he indicated he needed to get home to Norma and "the twins." They embraced, and he assured Clare he'd give Norma her greetings and they'd have her and Jeff out to dinner sometime soon. He missed her! He hoped she'd come back to Aurora quickly – the permanent Aurora helo was scheduled to arrive in two and a half months. It would be fun to work together again.

Yes, it will be, Gus.

491

Supporting herself with the walking stick to which she'd graduated in the past week, she made her way into the living room and over to the bookshelf where her wedding picture with Alex rested. Jeff had never said anything about the picture being there, but she knew it was time for it to come down. Not go away. Not be destroyed. Simply be put away as part of who she had been. She would always be Alex's wife. But now, perhaps, she would also be Jeff's wife – and she felt Alex approved.

She picked up the photo and kissed it, remembering how happy she'd been that day. She knew that being married to Alex had made her who she was now – and that the love she'd found with Jeff had come directly from the relationship she'd had with Alex. Without Alex's role in her life, she'd never have found the Trooper. Alex was *her* north star.

Clare opened up the back of the frame holding the picture of the two of them, taken so many years ago, and pulled out a second picture from behind their wedding photo. Turning the photo over, she looked again at the face of her daughter, Alexa Clare, so tiny, so sweet, so looking like her daddy – being held in Clare's own arms after her birth, swaddled in a pink blanket. *My little Lexie. I love you so much.*

She tucked both pictures back into the frame and secured the back.

Clare took a sheet of tissue paper from the drawer under the bookshelf and gently wrapped her wedding picture in it, folding it carefully and taping the tissue. She placed the wrapped picture in a large manila envelope, then sealed the envelope and put it back in the drawer. There was a photo of Jeff on the bookcase taken when he was leaning against his patrol vehicle with his arms crossed casually against his chest with Trygve sitting on the ground beside him, his pink tongue lolling happily to one side. She placed it in the same spot where her wedding picture had sat for almost three years.

She took the letter from Helen over to the Franklin stove, opened the door, and slipped it into the fire. She watched as the flames consumed the other woman's words.

And now the next part of my life begins. Thank you, Alex. I love you, Jeff.

Chapter Seventy-one

"Hello, my beautiful wife."

She opened her eyes in her dream to see Alex, dressed in jeans and a T-shirt sitting casually on the side of her bed.

"Oh, my handsome husband," she said to him. "It's been a while. How are you?"

"Been busy watching over you and Kelly. And, David. And, now – your Trooper."

"Thank you, Alex. David said he felt your presence. I love you, Coastie."

"I know, sweetheart. And I love you." He took her hand, kissed it, then turned around to look behind him. "See who I brought with me."

Clare saw brightness out of the corner of her eye, and as she watched, the brightness came to stand next to Alex. A young girl emerged from the light – slender, her face still luminescent, with brown eyes and shiny brown hair. "Lexie," Clare gasped. "How beautiful you are." She reached out her hand and the girl took it in her own warm hand. Clare pulled the little girl into her arms and held her closely. She felt Lexie's thin arms go around her neck in a tight embrace.

"My daughter. My baby. I love you so much." Even in her sleep, tears filled her eyes, spilling to the pillow. "I don't know what to say, Alex. But thank you for letting me meet her again."

He nodded and put his arms around his wife and child. The three of them held one another for a long while. "We did good, Clare. You and I."

His wife nodded in her dream.

"Are you healing well?" he asked, when he finally released Clare and Alexa and sat back.

She shrugged. "I think so. I want to go back to work in Aurora dispatch when the new helicopter arrives. I feel good, Alex. But, you know that." She paused, then spoke again. "Thank you for being with me and Kelly when we went down. Thank you for the peace you gave us."

"The endorphins and I gave you peace. I didn't want either of you to be afraid. Charlie was preoccupied with landing the AStar, so I let him stay focused." Clare smiled at him.

Lexie stepped away from her mom and sat cross legged on the floor at her feet. Alex took Clare's hand then. "Are you afraid now?"

She smiled again. "Afraid?"

"Of what lays ahead for you."

"I've already faced death. I don't fear it anymore. But what else is there for me? You told me time is not linear."

"It isn't. I also told you to talk to Grandmother, but that can come soon enough."

"Grandmother? Jeff's grandmother?"

He nodded. "She's a font of knowledge and advice and wisdom and patience and moose tongue sandwiches. And, she texts, too."

"Oh, great," Clare chuckled. "And, I heard about those moose tongue sandwiches." Even in sleep her stomach churned with the thought.

"They're about as delicious as you think they might be, depending on the preparation and the spices. And how you feel about the texture."

Clare laughed out loud in her dream. "Please tell me more, Alex."

He waited and looked as if he were pondering whether or not to tell her more. "About moose tongue? Well…"

"You're still a tease!"

"Always, Clare. But…," he continued slowly, "…you will give Lexie a sister and a brother. The boy shall grow into a tall, strong young man who will bring you great delight with his humor, his honor, his wisdom, and his father's sense of duty."

"My daughter?"

"She will drive you crazy with bull-headed obstinacy and a strong-willed nature. You'll see her father in her hazel eyes. You and she will butt heads for a lifetime. But, you'll be proud of her, her insights, and her accomplishments, despite the fact that there are moments when you'll want to throttle her."

"So, she'll be like her father and me?"

He nodded solemnly. "But she will love you with every fiber of her being even as she is arguing with you. You'll need to get used to that, and learn patience."

Clare laughed. "I can hardly wait. But what about Jeffrey...?" she finally asked.

"He's a fine man, Clare. You've chosen well once again. He'll love you forever, as I do. He'll always protect you and care for you and your children."

"And me? What about me?"

"Your decision, Clare. What about you? It's up to you. Get well first, then enjoy what the future holds. You'll have pain and sorrow. You'll have hills to climb and vistas where you can see the world. You'll have delight. You'll have intense love. But the most important thing, Clare, is that you'll have profound joy in your life; profound contentment in your soul. And you will have peace."

The flight nurse wept now, openly, in her dream, saturating her pillow in reality. "You're leaving me, aren't you?"

"Only for now, Clare. But we'll meet again. Remember that you shall be strength and joy for Jeffrey, just as he shall be your strength and your lover. You'll be the core of your family and he shall be the protector.

"Don't leave me, Alex."

"I'm not. But there's just one more thing..."

"What's that," she interrupted.

He shook his head at her. "I tell you I watch over you and Jeffrey? I'm not *watching* you two. I mean...you know...uh...when you and he...um...are...uh...ahem...."

Even in her dream state, Clare felt hot and knew her face was crimson. He squeezed her hand and chuckled.

"You've chosen wisely. You've found what you sought since I died, and I'm glad. Don't ever feel guilty or worry that Jeff is replacing me. It's never been a matter of him or me. It's always been Jeff *and* me. You've always been blessed. And I will always love you."

Alex stood up from the bed and took Lexie's hand as she rose from the floor. Clare watched as they morphed into light and then disappeared. She pulled the dream around her, and when she awoke later, remembered the sweetness of seeing Lexie – and Alex's promise that there would be joy in her life with Jeffrey.

And that one day she and Jeff would have an honorable son and an obstinate daughter…with her daddy's hazel eyes.

Chapter Seventy-two

Jeff, on duty, went 10-7 with takeout at Clare's house for lunch later that day. She greeted him with a strong hug and kiss when she opened the door.

"Where's your walking stick?" he asked her, when she pulled away, taking his hand and leading him into the kitchen where she had fresh coffee brewed.

"I'm high on ibuprofen and I'm feeling good, Trooper. I think I could even go dancing, if there weren't a whole lot of two-steppin' going on."

His smile brought her delight. The glow that she'd felt when she woke that morning after her visit with Alex and Lexie remained. Her heart was full of this man in front of her.

He opened his arms to her in the kitchen and she walked into them, conforming her body to his, just like she had that very first night they danced together at the Pump House. He held her close.

She lifted her face to his and he kissed her, running his hand down her back and gently cupping her butt and pulling her closer. She moaned softly. *I can't live without you, Trooper.*

"Are you hungry?" he asked.

"I will be in about twenty minutes."

"What happens in the meantime?"

"You're going to take me to bed and make love to me."

"Are you okay? I don't want to hurt you."

"I'm okay. I want you to make love to me. Like a nice slow dance...."

He released her and pulled off his gunbelt with one hand while leading her down the hallway with the other. He helped her with her sweater (no bra!) and jeans (she wore no shoes either, this time), and her panties. Then, she watched him from her bed as he undressed. First his Kevlar, then his uniform shirt, then his winter tee, then his boots and socks, his trousers and long underwear, and finally, those knit boxers.

She was so full of him – full of his vulnerability right now as he stood over her, naked and aroused.

"God, I love you," she said, when he lay down on top of her, careful not to hurt her, and spread her legs with his hand. She rose to meet him as he entered, slowly, warmly, thrusting gently. She groaned with the pleasure of it, her arms wrapped tightly around his shoulders.

She was surprised at how fast she came – just the anticipation of his touch had inflamed her. The fullness of him sent her to the top, and his gentleness and strength pushed her over the cliff with powerful pulsations.

"Oh my God. Oh my God," she panted into the side of his face, carefully thrusting her pelvis into him.

She looked him directly in the eyes, those wonderful hazel eyes with the laugh lines around them, and remembered Moose Man and those eyes and those cheekbones and that straight nose and those lips and those wonderful shoulders.

He came then, filling her up with his fluids. "I'm drowning in you, Clare. I love you so much." He kissed her forehead and cheeks.

She could smell their sex and feel their sweat. They kissed again and she tasted his saltiness. She loved the way he smelled – his skin, his mouth; loved the texture of his rough hands. She pulled the duvet up over the two of them and they lay there for several minutes, caressing one another and enjoying the intimacy.

"Are you hungry now?" he asked, finally.

"I will always be hungry for you, Trooper. And...about your takeout menu – it's *quite* spectacular."

He laughed and pulled her close.

"Marry me," he said abruptly, then muttered, "God...um...let me rephrase that, flight nurse. Will you marry me...at...um...some point...in the foreseeable future? Maybe?"

She hesitated, perhaps long enough that he felt he'd stepped out of bounds.

"I'm sorry," he started again. "I know we haven't been seeing one another that long. I take it back. I spoke out of turn. Forget I said anything."

She heard him whisper "God," again and saw him put his hand on his forehead, shaking his head.

"Yes," she said.

"I know. I spoke out of turn. Forget I said it."

"No, I won't. 'Yes,' I said."

He looked at her. "Uh...'yes' what?"

"I'll marry you." The memory of her dream, plus the afterglow of having had sex made her reckless with her love of him. "I'd like that. I want to marry you."

"When?"

"Soon. But there's a condition. We have to go visit your grandmother first." She could see the question in his eyes. "We need to talk to your grandmother first. Then, we can make plans." *I have it on good authority that we need to see your grandmother.*

"Okay. I want you to be happy."

"I want *you* to be happy, too. I want to make you happy."

"I want to make you happier."

She laughed out loud at him and got out from under the duvet and stood to gently stretch out her back beside the bed. With her arms over her head, her breasts tightened and rose up provocatively.

"God, you're beautiful. I can't watch you do that or I won't be able to get my pants back on."

"May you always be under my spell." She looked at him with hooded eyelids.

"Under your spell always shall I be, Clare."

"Back atcha, Trooper Yoda."

Their cold Taco Tuesday Takeout fish tacos with melted ice in the sodas and tepid coffee were the best that either of them had ever had.

Chapter Seventy-three

Clare wasn't the type of person who'd dreamed from childhood of her wedding day to a magical Prince Charming – even when she married Alex. She was a practical woman who strove for simplicity and efficiency.

I'd like an ecru or ivory dress. Flowing and drapey. And flowers – the color of Springtime in Alaska. I want flowers and ribbons and lace around my head and red and purple and yellow flowers in the bouquet. With one white rose and one pink rose…for Alex and Lexie.

And Jeff can wear his Class As, his dress uniform, if he wants. And good food (Get Little John and his crew out there at Jeff's house for the reception) and good wine and champagne (and beer) and music and laughter and lots of dancing…and joy. And Hunni's husband and his brothers just in case the bears decide stop by.

And Reese can be flower girl.

Joy for all of us. That's what I want. Very simple.

I want life. I want peace.

I know that I've finally found the love I sought.

Thank you, Alex.

Epilogue

"I need to talk to you, Clare. I need to bare my soul here," he told her. He'd brought her a cup of coffee and sat next to her on his sofa in the Ester house in front of the fire. Trygve was on the dog bed near the hearth, luxuriating in the warmth, his soft snores adding to the peaceful moment.

She looked at him, a little puzzled. "What's up?"

"You made a difference for me at the Missing Man flyover – remember? I told you?"

She nodded. Gestured. Go *on.*

"I sent Susan and Mark on that flight to Mantishka. I'm the reason they went there. I'm the reason they died."

"You didn't know. It wasn't your fault, Jeff."

He held up his hand to stop her. "In my mind I know that, but let me finish. I need to tell you some stuff that's pretty important to me – that's made a difference in my life – changed me; the reason why I do this crisis management stuff and lead the Peer Support Team. I want you to know why and how important this is to me."

* * * * * *

505

I take a deep breath, look at Clare, and tell her the story that I always tell the students on the first day of the class when I teach the peer support and crisis management training course. I tell this story because it brings it home right away as to what a so-called "critical incident" is, and why we need to have "psychological body armor" when we do the jobs we do to "protect and serve" – whether we're cops, firefighters, nurses, flight folk – or military. This is a drum I beat regularly, because I believe in the concept. I also feel the story gives me a little initial street cred, too.

I tell her about sitting up on a roof overlooking my squad. I tell her about shooting the girl and male. I tell her about the dog – and how the combination of a young female and a skinny brown dog with a black nose and black ears and a nest of puppies became my personal 'collateral damage' that day.

Clare puts her hand on my leg and squeezes my thigh gently – bringing me back to the present from that dark time. I take a sip of coffee and tell her I thank God that my Gunny made me go to the military chaplain. "Crisis talk?" Yes. Just like Dave and I did with you that night.

The Padre explained about how the brain is working at high speed making decisions during the crisis moment, so these images are literally "burned" into the frontal cortex. In addition to that, the fact that the entire thing was out of the ordinary, unexpected, and highly emotional personally (the girl – my sister's age, and that poor mama dog) – all flowed together to make this my particular critical incident. Someone else might have had no issues with it.

But, I did.

The Padre explained about how the rush of adrenaline, the stress-induced elevated heart rate, the pinpointing of focus – is nature's way of keeping us alive during life and death scenarios. But, it sucks afterwards, because the brain remains in "go" mode, still trying to protect you with DVD recaps, heightened awareness, increased startle response, inability to sleep or always dreaming about the event, and constantly doing both mental and real "perimeter checks" – all while trying to deny that anything happened.

I think the information that made the difference with me, I tell Clare, was knowing how this kind of trauma affects the body and the mind in so many different facets – and how it is an absolutely normal response of a normal person (well, as normal as any of us are over there) to a horrifyingly abnormal event. And sometimes it takes a while to process the event and its aftermath.

"That's what you and David told me about Rachel."

Yes. Absolutely.

I pause. When my guys died…. I have to stop. I talk about this scenario only in the crisis class. Yeah, it tells the students that I've been around the block a time or two, but I think it also makes them aware of what they can expect to experience if they're going into law enforcement, firefighting, or pre-hospital work of any kind. This is the kind of "pre-incident education" they need to have. Here's what you may one day also face. Be ready. Steel yourself. Strap this on at the start of each shift. You may lose friends.

I grab Clare's hand and kiss it. You may lose someone you love very much doing the jobs we do.

Hell, you may be the one to die or be critically injured doing the jobs we do.

You may be the one who has to talk a colleague off the ledge when he or she has seen one horror too many.

I sip coffee, take a breath.

When my guys died, I begin again, I was almost destroyed by the physical, emotional and psychological responses I experienced. I'd escaped death by being puking sick and unable to go on patrol with them. Why me sick? Why not one of them? If I'd gone, maybe things would have been different. Or, more than likely, we'd all be dead.

I was overwhelmed with what I now know is 'survivor's guilt' – the guilt of not being there with them and for them. But I was also grappling with the realization that I was grateful I hadn't been there and feeling the guilt of that. I've seen vehicles hit by IEDs, and I've seen the bodies of personnel brought into the CASH for treatment. I simply couldn't reconcile my emotions and the deaths of my guys.

I was pretty fucking angry at God, too, for allowing this to happen to young men who were only trying to survive in a wretched sixth century country where everybody hates them.

I can hear Clare breathing raggedly next to me, but she doesn't say anything. She just keeps holding my hand.

I went to the Padre we had at that time. He'd been through the crisis training, too, like the first one. I knew that because I'd sent some of my guys to talk to him before. This time I went and

508

spilled my guts. He walked me through my event, frame by
frame, just let me talk. Asked a few questions – the same ones
David and I had you answer.

What was the worst part?

Yes.

They went out on a "routine patrol," never suspecting it would
be their last. Their deaths came as a surprise, even to them.
They died brutally, leaving unfinished business.

I take another sip of coffee – rapidly cooling. I need to drink
my coffee from an insulated cup, even at home. My private had
just finished skyping with his girlfriend. He told her he was going
out, but they'd talk later that night. My Master Sergeant – he'd
only been with us two months – had just learned his wife was
pregnant. One of the other kids was his mother's only child. We
always gave him grief about being a "momma's boy." She sent
him wonderful care packages, jammed with all kinds of delicious
stuff he shared with us. I think that hit me the hardest, because
his family's line ended that day with his death.

All those broken hearts. All those broken promises. All that
pain. God. It almost killed me. And I was sick and puking my guts
out in my room in the CHU while they were getting blown up and
slaughtered like animals. I was spared because I wasn't with
them.

But, once again, I knew what I was experiencing was the
normal response of a supposedly 'normal' person to the worst
thing that could ever happen to us. It also helped me come to a
decision. I needed to get out of there before I went crazy and

became the nutcase who loses control and randomly murders the local population.

"'Cuz, Clare, that's what I wanted to do. I wanted vengeance. Retribution. I wanted to kill those people."

"Shannon said you were angry when you came back home."

I laugh, but even to me it's not a pleasant sound.

Angry, Clare? Insane is more like it. But I wasn't stupid, thank God. I came back to another Padre here and joined a group of like-minded vets who saved me. I knew I wasn't alone and wasn't crazy. Knew what I was experiencing wasn't uncommon. It was as "normal" as anything could ever be over there.

I spent some time with a trauma trained mental health provider and went through Cognitive Behavioral Therapy – CBT. This helped me to identify my own unhealthy responses to stimuli and deal with them on a controlled and rational basis rather than blindly lashing out at the people who loved me – or the driver who cut me off in the street.

I also did some EMDR – Eye Movement Desensitization and Reprocessing – to soften some of the more devastating images I still carried with me. I don't tell this to Clare this right now, because – quite honestly – it's an involved rabbit trail I'll explore later with her.

She asks me if this is why I got involved in crisis management and peer support and "that kind of stuff."

Yes. Because I see what it can do to protect people – to provide the psychological body armor to OUR people: The

Troopers, fire, PD, EMS, you guys in air medical, nurses. Everyone.

"Mantishka," she whispered.

Yeah. I was directly responsible for sending them there. I wasn't responsible for their deaths, but I couldn't change the outcome. All I could do was to make sure our people received the kind of emotional and psychological support they needed to get through the terrible trauma of having your friends die in the line of duty, doing the same job you do.

And, I needed help to forgive myself and to deal with their deaths – just like everyone else.

"Clare, when I say *our* people, I don't mean just the troopers and our other employees. I mean their families, too. Their spouses and their children. Their moms and dads. Brothers and sisters. All of them need support, because trauma has this terrible ripple effect that can go out to the other family members and then on for generations. The same goes for family members of our other emergency services personnel, too. It's for *all* of us."

The other thing I could do, which was a bit more pragmatic, was to help find the ass clown who killed Susan and Mark, and bring him and the rest of his pipeline to justice. Which is what we did. Our crisis team's Clinical Director set up interventions for the Troopers and their families after Mark and Susan's deaths and after the memorial service, and then the Troopers worked to stop the inflow of alcohol and drugs. For the moment.

I have no grand ideas that the job is now over. But, we've written "finished" on these bad guys for now. For this moment.

Jeff turned to look at Clare and then pulled her close. "There's another item I want to talk to you about. Well, two items. Maybe three."

"Should I be worried?"

"No. When I told you my story, I mentioned the impact of trauma on family members?"

The flight nurse nodded.

"If we get married, you'll be my family – my spouse. You can talk to other law enforcement spouses and their families. You know personally how much crisis management has helped you – with Rachel, and after Aurora crashed. Our clinical director said she was told by Aurora the interventions we did with your crews were very helpful. I want you to consider seriously taking the crisis training and coming on our team as a spouse. Because of your experience, what you say can be invaluable."

"That's one item. I'll consider your request."

"Item two: The ASTs are adding another K-9 handler. Trygve will be spending one more year with me, and then he'll be 'retired.' He'll be our home dog after that. And I'll be handing over the leash to this new guy from Florida we've hired."

Trygve raised his head when he heard his name mentioned. Clare reached over to fluff his ears. "It'll be you and me, good dog. Can you handle it?" She sat back to look at the Trooper. "I'm a little afraid to ask what Item Three is, Jeff. Please don't tell me you're being relocated."

He smiled. "No. Item Three: Headquarters wants me to take over the Peer Support and Crisis Management Team on a statewide, full-time basis. I'll still be here, but will be dealing with events and trainings that occur all over the state. It will entail a bit of travel, teaching, providing interventions, and doing pre-incident education with a *big* push at the Academy."

"How do you feel about that?" This time, she wasn't being facetious.

"I'm freakin' tickled pink. Seriously. I can hardly wait."

"I'm proud of you that admin thinks so highly of your training and experience. But...um...when does this new job start?"

"With the next fiscal year. That will give us time to work on our own relationship – to figure things out. I think this will be a good thing for all of us. Listen, sweetheart," he said, abruptly changing the subject. "Let me fix you some dinner. I bake a tasty Stouffer's frozen lasagna."

She laughed. "You *do* go all out. "Can I take you to bed after that?" She turned to him, and putting her leg over his, sat to face him on his lap. She closed her arms around his shoulder which put her breasts fully in his face. The Trooper kissed her soft sweater. Then he pulled down the V neck and kissed the warmth of her cleavage. She pushed into his face and growled. "I want to make you feel good, Jeff."

"Then, you can take me to bed now, sweet Clare. The lasagna takes seventy-five minutes to bake in the oven."

"Plenty of time," she smiled. "I love you, Trooper."

"And I will love you until the day..."

"Stop." She put her hand over his mouth. "Don't say that. Tell me you'll love me forever."

"I will love you forever, Clare Herndon Valenzuela."

"And I will love you forever, Jeffrey Cameron Douglas. And you shall protect me and our two children and I shall be the core of our family."

"Two children? How do you know…" He didn't finish the sentence, just shook his head. She'd tell him, eventually.

"Don't even ask. Just remember we need to go see your Grandmother soon. And, if I'm going to be on your crisis management spouse team, I need to marry you pretty quick – after break-up – after the river ice breaks up. As soon as it's 'warm.'" She chuckled at that concept.

He smiled at her then stood up, putting her back down on the sofa. "I would love that, Clare. I'll put the lasagna in the oven in a minute, but, dammit, this is as good a time as any." He reached into his sweatpants pocket and took out a small velvet box from a high-end jewelry store in Fairbanks. He knelt down, then opened it and showed her the contents.

"Officially, Clare, will you marry me and make me the happiest trooper ever born?" He took out the one carat bezel-set diamond solitaire on a thick gold band, and put it on the ring finger of her left hand that she held out to him.

"Officially, Jeff, I'm speechless. It's incredible," she breathed. "Oh, Jeff, it's absolutely gorgeous." She leaned forward and wrapped her arms around his shoulders and kissed his lips, his cheeks, his forehead, then his lips again. "Yes, Jeff, I will marry you. With joy."

He stood so he could sit beside her again, holding her left hand and turning it slightly to let the warm light from the fire glint off the stone.

"I chose the bezel set so you can wear it now and not worry about getting it caught on anything or in the way at work. It means the world to me that you want us to be together, Clare. You're everything to me. You're my life. When you're ready, we'll go back to the store and you can pick out any other setting you want to put this stone in."

"Jeff," she took him in her arms again. "You're everything I need. You're everything I want. Thank you for loving me."

He returned her embrace and they sat holding one another for a very long moment. He nuzzled her neck before he reluctantly broke away. "Lasagna. Oven. Bake."

"Excellent idea, Trooper. And bring a couple of glasses of wine with you when you come back to the bedroom. I want to take my time with the man I love – my 'fiancé.'" She got up slowly, looking at her hand and the powerfully beautiful ring he'd given her, and then watching his perfect shoulder-to-hips-ratio walk into the kitchen to start the lasagna. *I love you, Trooper. And I will love you forever.*

Her heart full, she headed towards his bedroom and the king-size bed with the soft comforter and picturesque view of trees.

* * * * *

515

Trygve lifted his head, watching them go their separate ways, but he sensed they'd be together soon. The dog stood up, turned four times, and laid back down again on his comfortable bed by the hearth. He closed his eyes. Content. He knew he liked the woman a lot because she petted him, fluffed his ears, let him lick her plate when the trooper wasn't watching, and made his trooper happy. And that made the canine feel good.

No, seriously, Trygve thought, it brought him...a feeling of peace. He laid his head on his paws, and if one could see him at just the right angle before he closed his eyes again, well, it looked like he was smiling.

Appendix

I would like to thank the International Critical Incident Stress Foundation located at 3290 Pine Orchard Lane, Suite 106, Ellicott City, MD 21042 for the general information about Critical Incident Stress Management and posttraumatic stress.

In addition, I would like to thank Tania Glenn, PsyD, LCSW, CCTP, of Tania Glenn and Associates, 1001 Cypress Creek Rd. Suites 403/404 in Cedar Park, TX, for the information about Posttraumatic Stress Disorder, PTSD Treatment, and the valuable adjunct therapy Eye Movement Desensitization and Reprocessing.

Dr. Glenn has worked for over twenty-six years with law enforcement, the fire service, commercial airlines, air medical providers, Austin/Travis County STARFlight, the Customs and Border Protection Office of Air and Marine, the United States Border Patrol Special Operations Group, Army and Air National Guard, and the USMC 4th Marine Division and 4th Aircraft Wing. She is the Clinical Director of several Critical Incident Response Teams.

The motto of Tania's team of Associates is: *"Pain is inevitable; Suffering is optional"*

Two highly recommended books written by Tania and published in 2017:

First Responder Resilience: Caring for Public Servants. Tania Glenn, PsyD, LCSW, CCTP. Progressive Rising Phoenix Press, LLC.

Protected But Scared. Tania Glenn, PsyD, LCSW, CCTP. Progressive Rising Phoenix Press, LLC.

This book is designed for families of law enforcement personnel and their children, ages five and older.

* * * * * *

What is a Critical Incident?

A Critical Incident is *any* incident that has the impact to overwhelm the normally very good coping mechanisms of emergency first responders, including law enforcement, firefighters, front line hospital personnel, and individuals in the military. These are some examples of a defined Critical Incident:

1. Line of duty death
2. Suicide of a colleague
3. Serious work-related injury
4. Multi-casualty, disaster, or terrorism incident
5. Events with a high degree of threat to the personnel involved
6. Significant events involving children
7. Events in which the victim is known to personnel
8. Events with excessive media interest
9. Prolonged events which end with a negative outcome

10. Any significantly powerful, overwhelming, distressing event for personnel involved

11. Any incident where individuals perceive or realize they have made a mistake

12. Administrative abandonment

The aftermath of a critical incident can change the way an individual (or a group who has experienced the same incident) thinks, behaves, or looks at the world in five different areas:

1. **Cognitive:** Confusion; Hypervigilance; Intrusive images, thoughts, or dreams; Poor problem solving; Inability to make decisions; Poor concentration; Memory problems.

2. **Emotional:** Anxiety; Guilt; Grief; Denial; Anger; Panic; Fear; Loss of emotional control; Depression; Feeling overwhelmed; Agitation

3. **Physical:** Fatigue; Nausea and/or vomiting; Elevated heart rate and/or blood pressure; Hyperventilation; Grinding of teeth (TMJ); Headaches; Dizziness; Profuse sweating; Faintness

4. **Behavioral:** Withdrawal from family and friends; Emotional outbursts; Increased suspiciousness or paranoia; Loss or increase in appetite; Increased self-medication (alcohol or drugs); Hyperstartle response; Increased retail therapy

5. **Spiritual:** Loss of faith; withdrawal from faith community; or, Increase in personal faith

Alleviating the symptoms of posttraumatic stress following a perceived critical Incident

The Critical Incident Stress Management model provides both proactive and reactive protocols for dealing with the stress that may follow in the aftermath a "critical incident."

"Proactive" elements include Pre-incident education concerning crisis stress, the types of events that might occur during a tour of duty, and resources available. There is an emphasis on resilience training – teaching individuals to adapt and recover quickly after stressful events, trauma, or tragedy.

"Reactive" interventions following a critical incident include Peer Support (one-on-one responses); small group discussion and education (the Defusing – a discussion and educational group meeting for up to twenty people held within eight to twelve hours following an incident); and large group discussions and education (the Critical Incident Stress Debriefing – discussion and education for up to twenty participants; and the large Crisis Management Briefing for dispensing information – often to an entire community or agency. This last can be done in a single room or using media – CCT, television, or live on the internet, for example).

Other responses include Family Support – discussions held with family members of those involved in the original event,

Spiritual Support through the use of crisis-trained chaplains or ordained ministers as requested by a participant, and Follow-up services. The latter service, which is mandatory, entails checking back with the individuals and groups offered interventions, and assessing and triaging how they are doing at the current time.

* * * * * *

What is Posttraumatic Stress Disorder?

Posttraumatic Stress Disorder (PTSD) is a potentially debilitating anxiety disorder that is the result of exposure to a psychological trauma beyond a person's coping capacity. It is important to recognize each person has a threshold for stress and an individual's coping capacity is defined by their prior experience and interpretation of an event. Everyone has a threshold for stress; and, the type of event that causes PTSD will be beyond a person's individual coping capacity.

Potential events that can cause PTSD include real or perceived incidents, actions, or issues; actual death or the threat of death of an individual; or any event that compromises the physical, sexual, or psychological integrity of an individual.

The elements of PTSD include intrusion, arousal, and avoidance. The intrusive element involves intense re-experiencing of the event, nightmares, flashbacks and overwhelming responses to stimuli that a person associates with the trauma. Arousal includes the intense anxiety, anger, hypervigilance, and difficulty falling or staying asleep due to the arousal. The avoidance element involves actively avoiding any stimuli associated with the event in order to feel safe.

The diagnostic requirement for PTSD is that the symptoms are present for at least thirty days. Prior to the thirty-day mark, the symptoms of intense anxiety and re-experiencing of the event are called Posttraumatic Stress Syndrome or acute stress response. The acute stress response is frequently a very normal response of a normal person with good coping skills following a serious event. However, PTSD is neither a normal, nor desired, response.

Are there solutions for PTSD?

It is extremely important that individuals with either Posttraumatic Stress Syndrome or PTSD seek help. There are a variety of techniques that can assist individuals in overcoming trauma and moving forward with life. PTSD treatment is designed to help the brain process information and trauma in a way that helps the brain overcome the intensity of the stimuli. One of the most effective techniques in treating PTSD is Eye Movement Desensitization and Reprocessing (EMDR).

What is Eye Movement Desensitization and Reprocessing (EMDR)?

EMDR is one progressive method of treatment for PTSD. EMDR is a type of therapy during which the patient recalls a traumatic event while simultaneously undergoing bilateral stimulation that can consist of moving the eyes from side to side, vibrations or tapping movements on different sides of the body, or tones delivered through one ear, then the other, via headphones. The success rate in treating PTSD through the use of EMDR has been extremely positive.

Other techniques widely used to help individuals overcome PTSD include **Cognitive Behavioral Therapy** and **Progressive Desensitization.**

Author Biography

M. Dixie Watson, RN, MN, retired from a Level I trauma center located in Northern California, after twenty-four years of service – twelve of them as a flight nurse for the hospital's helicopter program.

Urged to write about her experiences by her daughter, she hesitated to pen a memoir because she was but one of thirty-plus flight nurses who all put their lives and their skills on the line every time they strapped themselves into their medevac helicopter. So, the author opted to fictionalize her experiences, throwing in a dedicated state trooper, a K-9, heartbreak, trauma and tragedy, birth, joy, hope, a magnificent backdrop of mountains and snow, freezing cold, true friends – and romance.

Ms. Watson has been involved in Critical Incident Stress Management since 1989. She is an active trainer for the International Critical Incident Stress Foundation, and has been provided crisis interventions for Law Enforcement, the fire service, hospitals, air medical programs, schools, and the military for over twenty-eight years.

She lives in Northern California, and continues to work as a PACU RN while penning her second book about the staff of North

Star Medical Center, the crewmembers of Aurora Flight, and the brave personnel of the Alaska State Troopers.

She has two adult children and four grandchildren who bring her great joy, while always encouraging her to spend their inheritance.

Made in the USA
San Bernardino, CA
15 December 2017